Praise for Nicolle Wallace and *EIGHTEEN ACRES*

"One of the best novels I've read about life in the White House. . . . Delicious. . . . Entertaining, sometimes moving."

—*The Washingon Post*

"Nicolle Wallace actually knows what she's talking about. . . . [Her] firsthand experience comes through."

—*USA Today*

"A game-changer late in the campaign gives the plot a nice boost, revealing the strength of the female bonds."

—*Publishers Weekly*

"This inside-the-beltway thriller about the first woman president has an authentic ring."

—*Entertainment Weekly*

"Wallace . . . infus[es] the story with the richness of her professional experiences. . . . A must for political junkies and fans of political fiction."

—*Library Journal*

"When I finished reading *Eighteen Acres*, I missed its characters and wanted them back—which is novel feeling for me about a bunch of Republicans! It's very funny, very reflective of some certain someones we all know, and it's peppered throughout with true, smart insight into the fraught interdependence of top-tier politics and media in D.C. A great read."

—Rachel Maddow

"An enjoyably gossipy dishing of inside-the-beltway residents of all persuasions."

—Kirkus Reviews

"Realistic characters and unusual insight into the West Wing. . . . There's a certain irresistible quality to *Eighteen Acres*. The book is genuinely hard to put down, a testament to its well-drawn characters."

—Associated Press

"Nicolle Wallace neatly melds the political and personal facets of public life to produce an absorbing suggestion of future possibilities in the American presidency in this absorbing novel."

—*BookPage*

"*Eighteen Acres* is not a dirty politics exposé, if anything, it's about teamwork, imperfect people trying to do the right thing, and an acknowledgment that working on the White House 18-acre ground is a privilege of a lifetime."

—*The Weekly Standard*

"This hybrid model of commercial writing paired with a sharper regard for female characters is a rare find."

—Bookslut

This title is also available as an ebook.

EIGHTEEN ACRES

A Novel

Nicolle Wallace

WASHINGTON SQUARE PRESS
New York London Toronto Sydney

WASHINGTON SQUARE PRESS
A Division of Simon & Schuster, Inc.
1230 Avenue of the Americas
New York, NY 10020

Copyright © 2010 by Nicolle Wallace

First Washington Square Press trade paperback edition July 2011

WASHINGTON SQUARE PRESS and colophon are registered trademarks of Simon & Schuster, Inc.

For information about special discounts for bulk purchases, please contact Simon & Schuster Special Sales at 1-866-506-1949 or business@simonandschuster.com

The Simon & Schuster Speakers Bureau can bring authors to your live event. For more information or to book an event, contact the Simon & Schuster Speakers Bureau at 1-866-248-3049 or visit our website at www.simonspeakers.com.

Designed by Kyoko Watanabe

Manufactured in the United States of America

10 9 8 7 6 5 4 3 2 1

The Library of Congress has cataloged the hardcover edition as follows:

Wallace, Nicolle.
  Eighteen acres : a novel / by Nicolle Wallace. — 1st Atria Books
hardcover ed.
    p. cm.
1. Women presidents—United States—Fiction. 2. United States—Politics and government—Fiction. I. Title.
  PS3623.A4437E54 2010
  813'.6—dc22   2010030072

ISBN 978-1-4391-9482-9
ISBN 978-1-4391-9593-2 (pbk)
ISBN 978-1-4391-9496-6 (ebook)

For my husband, Mark

CHAPTER ONE

Melanie

Melanie pushed the tissue paper aside and gazed adoringly at the Dior bag she had splurged on for her thirty-seventh birthday. It was a ridiculous extravagance. The second most expensive bag in her closet was a Marc Jacobs she'd purchased on sale years before. The elegance of the two-thousand-dollar Dior purse would be lost on most of Melanie's colleagues, but its perfection brought her a surprising amount of happiness.

As Melanie pulled the purse out of its protective cloth and removed the paper stuffed inside, she suddenly felt worried that all of her electronics wouldn't fit into it properly. She looked at the three BlackBerrys—one for the classified e-mail system, one for the normal White House e-mail system, and one for her personal Yahoo account. She considered leaving one of them behind but thought better of it. Gently, she stacked the BlackBerrys, two phones, her ID for the West Wing, an ID and key for the underground command center she'd be evacuated to in case of a terrorist attack, her passes to the Pentagon and the State Department, an ID for the Camp David guard station, a West Wing parking pass, and her wallet and keys inside and closed it.

She stopped in front of the hallway mirror to attach her hard pin to the lapel of her black Armani pantsuit. The small, round pin bearing the presidential seal signaled to the United States Secret Service that she was to be granted full access to the president. Only a dozen White House staffers were given hard pins. She glanced at her reflection and nodded approvingly. Five years on a strict no-carbohydrate diet had banished her full cheeks, and the miracle of chemical straightening had finally tamed her red curls. Melanie's hair hung in a stylish strawberry-blond bob. She scrunched her nose and leaned in to examine the creases and dark circles that rimmed her eyes. "Those look like the eyes of an old woman," she said to herself before turning out the lights in her Georgetown condo and walking out.

"Morning guys," she said to her agents as she hopped into the SUV that would take her less than two miles to the White House. She'd resisted full-time Secret Service protection at first, but on mornings like this, she was glad she'd relented. Snow had been falling since late the night before, and at five-thirty A.M., they would make fresh tracks.

"Happy birthday, Ms. Kingston," Sherry said. Sherry was one of her regular agents. She turned around, smiled at Melanie, and handed her an envelope. "Open it—it's from both of us," she said, gesturing at Walter, Melanie's other agent.

"Thanks, Sherry, but my birthday is a classified national security event. I didn't even remind Char—er, President Kramer that it was today."

"Mmm-hmm," Walter said, glancing at Melanie in the rearview mirror as he navigated M Street in the snow. "And it's not like she has the CIA or the FBI to turn to if she wants to find out for herself when her chief of staff's birthday is, so you should be fine, Melanie." He smirked. "Your secret is safe with us."

"Shut up, Walter. Just keep your eyes on the road," Melanie said.

"Yes, ma'am," Walter said, still smiling.

A minute later, he pulled the car as close as possible to the entrance of the West Wing and jumped out to open the door for her.

Melanie stepped out of the SUV, holding her Dior bag protectively under her suit jacket so the fresh snow wouldn't touch the leather. She wished she'd worn a coat, but she'd stopped dressing for the seasons years ago. It could be ninety-seven degrees outside, or minus seven, and the climate was always a cool sixty-six degrees inside the West Wing, where she'd be for the next sixteen hours.

Melanie climbed the single flight of stairs to her office and walked inside. Her assistant, Annie McKay, was already there.

"Happy birthday," she whispered, even though no one else would have heard her if she'd yelled at the top of her lungs. Melanie always arrived before anyone else on the senior staff.

"Thanks, Annie," Melanie said.

"Let me see it," Annie said.

"What?" Melanie replied innocently, opening her suit jacket.

"Oh, my God, it is amazing—totally worth the splurge. It has *elegant* and *expensive* and *woman of substance* written all over it," Annie exclaimed, standing to get a better look at the bag.

Melanie smiled. She settled in at her desk, casting an admiring glance at the fire that had already been lit in the fireplace. *Cozy*, Melanie thought. *Maybe today won't be so bad.*

She looked around her spacious office on the main floor of the West Wing and wondered if it was her elevation to this most lonely job on the White House staff or growing fatigue from so many years in the political trenches that had made her reflective to the point of distraction.

Every room in the White House brought back a memory of a time when she had felt fortunate to be there. These days, she usually found herself standing in these rooms, asking—sometimes begging—the walls to talk to her. Sometimes the history that she and Charlotte were making struck her as embarrassingly overdue—many other countries had been ruled by women. And at other time, it was exhilarating to think that a new generation of women would grow up knowing that the glass ceiling had been shattered once and for all. But the vast majority of the time, Melanie's life was exhausting, her assignments unseemly, and the rewards nonexistent.

She read the intelligence reports from the overnight, a memo from the national security advisor about troop reductions that would go to the president that morning, and the jobs report number that would be kept secret until eight-thirty A.M. She finished the front sections of the *Wall Street Journal*, the *Washington Post*, the *New York Times*, and Washington's first official tabloid, the *Washington Journal*.

When she noticed that the sun had come up and brightened her office with an orange glow, she glanced up at one of her five televisions. She unmuted one of the stations just as it was teasing its lead story: "Coming up at seven A.M.: Is President Kramer AWOL on the economy? We'll have some surprising reactions from our viewers to that very question."

"The president is on her way to the Oval," Annie said, appearing in Melanie's door. "You should probably walk over. She'll want to see you about the speech, I'm sure."

"I'll head over in a couple minutes," Melanie said.

Melanie had been given a desktop device that told her where the president was at all times. "Wayfarer" was the president's Secret Service code name, and whenever the president moved anywhere—other than the bathroom—an automated voice would announce her whereabouts: "Wayfarer departing residence. Wayfarer arriving Oval Office. Wayfarer departing Oval Office. Wayfarer arriving Cabinet Room." The voice had driven Melanie crazy, so she'd moved the box to Annie's desk, and it fell to Annie to inform her of the president's movements.

Annie reappeared one minute later. "Sam just called. The president wants to see you," she said. Samantha Cohen was the president's assistant.

"Tell her I'm coming," Melanie said. She stood up and walked the twenty-five feet to the Oval Office, stopping briefly at Sam's desk.

"Morning, Samantha. Is anyone else in there?" Melanie asked, even though she knew no one would be.

"Nope, she's waiting for you," Sam said.

Melanie walked into the Oval Office and stood a few feet away from the president's desk.

"Good morning, Madam President," Melanie said.

"Good morning, Melanie," the president said.

"How are we doing today?" Melanie asked.

"Crappy. Did you see the jobs number?" the president asked.

"Yes. One hundred thousand is better than they predicted. The markets might hold up," Melanie said.

"I don't think so. We're going to get killed today. The story writes itself: 'President Proves She Is Tone-deaf on Economy.' I don't know why I'm giving this speech in Detroit. Why couldn't we go to Silicon Valley or New York or somewhere with an economy that isn't in the toilet?" the president asked as she took her black Sharpie to the speech text and started slashing huge sections—a tactic she employed to show her displeasure and make staffers nervous.

Melanie's head started to throb.

"Sam, get the boys from speechwriting down here," Charlotte ordered. "This speech was either written by an idiot or someone got drunk last night and wrote it as a joke. The press will kill me if I say the economy has turned a corner. Tell that to the unemployed mother of four. Who writes this garbage, Melanie?"

Melanie sighed. She had told Ralph Giacamo, the White House political director and Melanie's nemesis, that the president wouldn't like the spin. He'd launched into a tirade about how he was in charge of getting her reelected and needed to have his voice heard on message matters. Melanie didn't have the energy to fight with him, so his language remained in the draft that went to the president.

"Earth to Melanie? Did you even look at this?" the president snapped, tapping her perfect bone-colored high heel—a Manolo Blahnik, for sure—on the floor under her desk. The president always dressed in the same color from head to toe. Today she was in a crème skirt and matching belted jacket. She wore a silk camisole underneath and a single strand of tiny pearls. Her thick blond hair was pulled back in a ponytail, and she didn't have any makeup on yet. Her hair and makeup team came in at seven forty-five. From a distance, she could easily pass for someone fifteen years younger than her forty-seven years.

"Of course I did, Madam President, and I'm sorry it isn't to your liking, Madam President. We'll write you a new speech, my lady," Melanie said, bowing her head down toward the president in an exaggerated act of deference. She stayed in that position until the president spoke.

"Oh, shut up, and stop with the bowing," the president said, stifling a smile. She rose from her desk and walked over to one of the sofas. A fire burned in her fireplace. "This fire is a little much, don't you think?" she said.

"It's a little more robust than the one they lit in my fireplace," Melanie said.

"Looks like a goddamn bonfire," the president said, gesturing toward the sofa across from her for Melanie to sit.

Melanie laughed and sat down, relieved that Charlotte's dark mood had passed. The president needed to be "on" for the trip to Detroit. Half a dozen small-business owners and a handful of members of Congress were flying on Air Force One with her for the speech, and if Charlotte were brooding the whole time, the trip would be a waste.

"Sam—will you please bring Melanie's present in here?" Charlotte yelled. "And two cups of coffee with cream." She turned to Melanie and broke into a full smile for the first time that morning. "Happy birthday, smart-ass," Charlotte said.

"Oh, God, no presents, please. I'm trying to go to a happy place in my mind—a place where I'm not thirty-seven years old, single, childless, and working steps away from the office where I sat when I was twenty-three years old," Melanie said, sinking into the couch and looking up at the ceiling.

"Oh, your life is so awful. You're just the White House chief of staff, that's all. What an underachiever you are. Open your present," Charlotte said, smirking and pushing the gift toward Melanie. She let the speech scatter on the carpet beneath them.

Melanie picked up the carefully wrapped box. As she slowly untied the bow and removed the tape from the wrapping paper, Charlotte grew impatient.

"Hurry up, the speechwriters will be here soon," the president said, grabbing the box from Melanie and removing the wrapping paper herself.

Melanie stared at the black Bulgari box and said softly, "Charlotte, what did you do?"

"You've been so depressed lately, I thought you needed to be cheered up," Charlotte said. "Open it, already. This Hallmark moment has gone on too long."

Melanie stood up to give her a hug.

"Open it first," Charlotte squawked, pushing Melanie aside. "I have to go to Detroit in this damned blizzard to console the inconsolable about the crappy economy in a few minutes."

Inside was a thin white-gold chain dotted with diamonds—the most tasteful and beautiful thing Melanie had ever seen and, by a factor of one million, the most elegant piece of jewelry she owned.

"Thank you so much. I love it," Melanie said, sliding it over her head and admiring the way the long chain sparked against her black silk blouse.

She knew she was lucky to work for Charlotte, and it almost hadn't happened. She had been planning to move back to Colorado with Charlotte's predecessor, President Martin, to head up his presidential library. But then she'd agreed to meet with Charlotte two weeks after she'd won the election.

When she'd walked into the room for their first meeting, she'd been struck by how small Charlotte was. She was a natural blonde, but her hair looked like straw. It was her one feature that actually looked better on television than in person. The toll of the long, nasty campaign was apparent on Charlotte's face. Her blue eyes looked gray, and the lines around her mouth that usually disappeared behind her campaign smile were deep. She was so thin that the black slacks and jacket she wore looked as if they belonged to someone else several sizes larger. She wore low heels that almost passed as sensible, but when she crossed her legs, Melanie noticed the red soles that gave away both the price tag and Charlotte's commitment to fashion.

Melanie hadn't wanted to like her enough to be tempted to say yes. She really hadn't wanted to like her at all. There was a cushy job waiting for her in Colorado with "nine to five" and "private jet" written all over it if she agreed to take President Martin up on his offer. There was nothing tying her to D.C. She could have easily flipped her condo to someone in the new administration—even in a down economy, people would be looking for places to live close to the White House. But something had nagged at her. She felt a sense of obligation at least to go through the motions and meet with the president-elect during the transition.

Melanie had been told that President-elect Kramer had made a special trip to Washington to meet with her.

"Please call me Charlotte," she'd said. "It took me two years to get used to 'governor,' and now all this 'president-elect,' and then 'Madam President,' who can keep track of it? Call me Charlotte—I insist," she'd said.

She was smart and funny and self-deprecating. She'd seemed to have been handed a briefing paper so detailed about Melanie's career that Melanie wondered if the FBI had been involved. After some small talk about the current unusually cold temperatures for Washington, Charlotte had told Melanie that she'd seen her on the *Today* show years earlier and that she had admired and tried to emulate her cheerful toughness in her own television appearances. She'd praised Melanie's decision to have the president do weekly press conferences in media markets around the country instead of from the White House. She'd said she agreed with the outgoing president's decision not to campaign on her behalf because of the ongoing wars in Iraq and Afghanistan, which she must have known had been Melanie's advice to the president.

Melanie's defenses had been down. She was feeling more and more flattered by the minute. And the idea of being the highest-ranking staff person for the first female president in America's history did capture her imagination. Despite the fact that in the recesses of her mind, she understood that it was all part of an elaborate scheme to entice her, she'd said yes on the spot to serving as chief of staff to the nation's forty-fifth president.

That was three years ago. Melanie fingered the smooth gold chain around her neck and stared at the reflection that the diamonds made on the wall of the Oval Office.

"If you're still in there, Melanie, you're welcome," the president said, waving her hand in front of Melanie's face. "I'll see you tonight. We need to talk about the campaign. I'm sorry I'm missing your party, but at least I'm taking Ralph off your hands."

"Party? What party?" Melanie groaned.

"I told them you'd hate it, but as usual, nobody listened to me. Act surprised. Sam and Annie have been working on it for weeks." The president turned back to her desk. "Sam, please tell the speechwriters to get on the helicopter. We have to write a new speech."

Melanie turned to leave and smiled sympathetically at the speech-writers who were huddled in front of Samantha's desk.

"Good luck, guys," Melanie said. "I'll throw Ralph under the bus later. She's just being melodramatic. Roll with it."

Melanie endured the senior staff singing "Happy Birthday" to her at their seven-thirty meeting. She took calls from most of the Cabinet members, wishing her a happy birthday and from many of the reporters she'd known from her eight years as press secretary for the previous president. Her parents sent a dozen white roses mixed with white tulips, her favorite flowers. But nothing could have prepared her for her own reaction to the slide show that the White House staff assembled to pay tribute to her fifteen years of service.

Thank God the lights were dimmed and the music blaring. Against a soundtrack of depressing spinster ballads from Natalie Merchant and Tori Amos, the images flooded the room. There she was at twenty-three—in the group photo of all the White House interns—smiling and oblivious to the three chins she'd had in those days. President Phil Harlow was the first president Melanie had worked for. She'd lied about being a student to get the internship, since the White House intern program was only available to college students earning credit for their free labor. When a spot opened up for a junior press aide, she'd confessed about graduating the year before, and they'd given her the job. She spent nearly three years in the same cramped fourth-floor office in the Old Executive Office Building, across the driveway from the West Wing.

The next images were from her days as a campaign aide to President Harlow's nephew, Christopher Martin. He'd surprised everyone when he announced a run for the presidential nomination during President Harlow's last year in office. Melanie had signed on as his campaign press secretary. Everyone was shocked when he won the nomination and, eventually, the presidency. President Martin made Melanie his first press secretary, and at twenty-six, she'd been the youngest White House press secretary in history. The pictures of Melanie as President Martin's press secretary made her cringe. Fortunately, her clothes, hair, and figure improved with age. There were pictures of her sleeping with her mouth wide open on Air Force

One, plenty of shots of her fielding questions from the podium in the White House briefing room, and images she recognized as having been Photoshopped to remove all evidence of Matthew, her husband for a brief period during the Martin administration.

Photos of Melanie as Charlotte's chief of staff made up the last and longest part of the slide show. She'd been around the photographers so long that she didn't notice them anymore, but there she was: speaking to Charlotte as they walked across the South Lawn to board Marine One, being summoned by Charlotte as she stepped off Air Force One, whispering in her ear in meetings with foreign leaders, hiking with her at Camp David with the dogs, and laughing with her in the Oval Office over one of their many inside jokes.

Melanie stood and applauded when the slide show finally came to an end.

"Thank you so much. It has been the privilege of a lifetime to serve this president alongside all of you. Thank you for this great surprise. I don't know what to say, other than thank you, from the bottom of my heart."

She stayed and thanked everyone for coming and asked the stewards to bring the leftover cake to the residence. She and Charlotte would eat it for dessert.

Fifteen years, three presidents, and seven executive assistants later, Melanie thought to herself as she walked back to her office. "And all I've done is move forty feet."

Around eight P.M., Melanie heard the sound of Marine One as it neared the South Lawn. She loaded her BlackBerrys and phones into her purse and walked down the hall toward the residence where she and Charlotte would have dinner. Charlotte had been bugging her for an answer about running her reelection campaign for weeks.

As the chopper came closer, her mind flashed back to her first ride on Marine One. It fell on her twenty-sixth birthday, and she had been nervous and excited about joining the elite group of top staffers who rode on the presidential helicopter instead of driving the short distance to Andrews Air Force Base. They'd been traveling to Detroit that day to talk about the economy, and President Martin's poll numbers were almost as battered as Charlotte's. More than a decade later,

Melanie still remembered how her stomach had churned and the sweat from her underarms had soaked her blouse that day. She had heard the sound of the helicopter as it neared the South Lawn, and she'd raced down the hall to the Oval Office. President Martin had looked at her, clearly enjoying her anticipation.

"You ready?" he'd asked.

"I'm ready," she'd said with a grin.

He'd flung his arm around her and walked out to the South Lawn, where the helicopter was parked. He'd waved to the cameras and the crowds and mouthed "Thank you" to the friends and staffers who had gathered to see him off. Melanie had walked on her toes to keep her heels from getting stuck in the muddy grass, but it wasn't enough. She lost one of her Stuart Weitzman pumps in the mud and was too afraid to stop and pick it up with the cameras rolling. She'd boarded Marine One and taken a seat across from the president.

"You sit here—you won't bump into me the way these thugs would," President Martin had ordered, referring to the male staffers who would bump into his knees if they sat in the seat across from him.

"Yes, sir," Melanie had agreed as she sat across from the president and peered out the window of the helicopter. Melanie had no idea what to do about her shoe. She hoped that no one would notice. She'd send someone to buy her a new pair in Detroit. Ernie Upshaw, President Martin's deputy chief of staff, noticed her bare muddy foot first.

"Where is your shoe, Melanie?" he'd asked.

"Uh, it fell off."

"Where?" the president had asked.

"Somewhere between the Oval Office and the helicopter," she'd admitted, her cheeks and neck turning hot.

The president had howled with laughter and sent Buckey, his personal aide, out to find her missing shoe. The shoe was wedged so deep in the mud that it took Buckey about five minutes to find it. The helicopter pilots had eventually powered down Marine One, and all three of the cable news networks had carried the shoe hunt live.

Melanie's BlackBerry had filled with new messages.

Her assistant: "They aren't looking for *your* shoe, are they?"

Her mother: "All the news stations are calling you Cinderella. Why didn't you wear flats?"

The White House chief of staff: "Way to go—the president will be late, but you will have your shoes."

He is such a jerk, Melanie had thought.

Buckey had finally returned to Marine One with Melanie's muddy black pump in his hand. The president thought the whole episode was hilarious. As they lifted off from the South Lawn of the White House and flew over the Washington Mall, Melanie had felt as if she'd been transported to a different world. The Tidal Basin glistened in the morning sun, and the Washington Monument jutted out of the ground. The flags that surrounded it flapped in the wind below her window, and the tops of the buildings on the mall looked like doll houses.

"It's pretty spectacular, isn't it?" the president had said.

"Amazing," Melanie had replied, not moving her eyes from the sights below.

"How could that have been eleven years ago?" Melanie thought, not realizing she'd muttered to herself until one of Charlotte's agents spoke to her.

"Ms. Kingston, is everything all right?"

"I'm sorry; I'm fine. Losing it, perhaps, but fine. Is she upstairs yet?"

"Yes. She said to tell you to come on in."

Melanie walked past the table that had been set for two with fancy china and flatware and out to the Truman balcony. Charlotte had installed heaters so they could sit out there year-round. Melanie sat in her usual spot and pulled a blanket over her lap. She took in the view and tried to work herself into a positive frame of mind for Charlotte's benefit. The Washington Monument was directly in front of her, lit to perfection by carefully placed spotlights and brightened by the full moon reflecting off a blanket of fresh snow. The Lincoln Memorial could be seen off to her right, and if she leaned forward, she could make out the top of the Capitol to her left.

One of the president's dogs put her two front paws in Melanie's lap and started kissing her face. She leaned back and let the dog lick her.

Melanie had never planned to spend her entire adult life working for the president. When people gazed at the wall of presidential commissions that hung in her West Wing office, she used to feel proud. Now, they embarrassed her.

With the thirty-five-pound dog now sitting in her lap, Melanie practiced what she would say to Charlotte that night: "Charlotte, I can't run your reelection campaign, because you can't run for reelection."

CHAPTER TWO

Dale

D ale finished her live shot at six thirty-three P.M. She grabbed her overstuffed bag, flung her white cashmere coat over her arm, and raced toward the car waiting for her outside the northwest gate of the White House. She dialed Peter's personal cell phone as soon as she shut the car door behind her.

"Hey. If the seven o'clock shuttle is running late, I might make it. Otherwise, I'll be on the eight o'clock," she said.

"Hey, yourself. Didn't I just see you on live television?" Peter asked.

When she heard his voice, Dale relaxed for the first time that day—the first time that week, for that matter. She missed him so much during the week. All she could think about was seeing him.

"Yes, that was me, but I'm working on finding a clone, so I can get the hell out of this place earlier on Fridays and see more of you," she replied.

"That would be nice. Do you have any candidates?"

"A few. Do you want to audition them? See if they are as good at keeping secrets as I am?"

"That's not all they'd have to be good at. Harry has a basketball game at one, and Penelope is studying for a French test, so I can get a late start tomorrow," he said.

"That sounds good. I'll call you and let you know which shuttle I'm on. We're at the Mandarin, right?" Dale asked.

"Yep. Forty-fifth floor. Did you remember your hard pin this time?"

"Got it," she said, reaching into her coat pocket to finger the lapel pin that would allow her full access behind the Secret Service security perimeter set up to protect the husband of the president of the United States.

"OK. See you soon. I love you."

"I love you, too," she replied.

As the car sped around the snow-covered monuments on the Mall, she dialed her weekend producer and left a voice-mail saying she'd be in around noon. Much to the jealous dismay of her colleagues at the network, she'd been given the weekend anchor job. Like everything else in her life these days, her promotion could be traced back to her relationship with Peter.

Dale didn't permit herself to dwell on the risks they were taking. With Peter, she didn't feel she had a choice. She loved him with every fiber of her being, and in some ways, it had made her success at work possible. It was as if her instincts took over when her mind became consumed with keeping her relationship with Peter a secret.

She was also always available to work when others were not. She had volunteered to work on Thanksgiving Day during the first year of her romance with Peter. Her parents had been disappointed that she wouldn't be coming home for the holiday, but she'd wanted to be in New York in case Peter could find an excuse for a quick trip to the city. Billy Moore, the news director and her boss, had picked Dale to anchor that night over more experienced reporters who were dying for the unofficial audition.

On Thanksgiving Day, around five P.M., a wire story had crossed her desk that made her palms sweat: "First family evacuated from Camp David after terror plot deemed credible." Terror threats were quite common, but it had been years since a president had been evacuated because of one.

Her first instinct had been to call Peter, but she knew better. The Secret Service would be on high alert. They would be monitoring all communications, and she was certain that Peter would call when he could. Of course, her job was to confirm that the president was safe and to report, on behalf of the network, on the president's actions, but once Peter was in the picture, that was always an afterthought. Her colleagues had been suspicious of her scoops in the early months of the Kramer administration, and she was careful about never implicating Peter as a source. But that Friday, their relationship had come close to creating a national security incident.

As the start of the newscast had neared, Dale was working her sources to try to determine the nature of the threat against the first family at Camp David. She had calls in to Melanie Kingston, the defense secretary, the national security advisor, and every single press officer from the Secret Service to the Department of Homeland Security and the State Department. They'd all been tight-lipped, telling her nothing that would allow her to advance the story. Then her cell phone had rung, and she'd reached for it frantically, hoping it was Peter.

"Hi, it's me," he'd said.

"Hi, you," she'd said softly. "Are you OK?"

"Yeah, we're all fine. I can't talk, but we're going back to the White House tonight. I'm going to bring the kids back up to school in Connecticut in the morning. I can meet you in New York tomorrow night before I fly home to San Francisco, if you want."

"Yes, yes, of course, I want to see you. Call me when you get here." Dale had hung up and gone back to her calls.

She'd never intended to reveal what Peter had told her, but when she finally got the national security advisor on the phone, she'd said, "When was the decision made to bring the first family back to the White House?"

The line had gone quiet. Dale had thought he'd hung up.

"Are you still there?" Dale had asked.

"Dale, who told you that a decision had been made to bring the first family back?" the national security advisor had asked.

"Uh, no one. I just assumed that they would get back to the White House, you know, to be in the Situation Room, in case, you know, in case there's something g-going on," Dale had stuttered.

The national security advisor wasn't buying it. "Dale, I need to know right now if someone told you that the first family is returning to the White House. It's a matter of national security," he'd said.

"No, but I'm going to take your reaction to my questions as confirmation that the president is indeed returning to the White House," Dale had responded.

"Don't do that," the national security advisor had warned. "Don't do that, Dale, or you'll regret it."

"The country has a right to know where the president is at all times, sir, and with all due respect, I had a hunch that she'd return to the White House, and you've just confirmed it, so I'm going with it in ten minutes unless you tell me it isn't true."

Fuming, the national security advisor had told Dale she'd regret her brazen abuse of the First Amendment and that he'd make her source pay.

Dale had led the news that night with her exclusive report about the first family returning to Washington. The higher-ups at the network had been thrilled, and she'd been given the weekend anchor post.

Since she'd been anchoring weekends, ratings were up twenty percent, and her contract had been renewed for four years at a salary she wasn't sure she deserved. The best thing about the weekend job was that she got to spend Friday and Saturday nights with Peter.

"Thanks, AJ," Dale said to her driver now as he pulled up to the US Airways gate at Reagan National Airport at exactly six-fifty P.M. Dale went flying through the airport, stopping at the kiosk and ramming her American Express card into it to retrieve her boarding pass. Friday nights were always busy at Reagan, and with the snow falling outside, Dale was praying for a delay that would hold the seven P.M. shuttle until she could reach the gate. The kiosk spit out a boarding pass, and Dale ran toward security. The TSA agents recognized her and helped her unpack her laptop from its case.

"Thanks, guys—I'm trying to get on the seven," she said.

"Slow down, pretty lady," one of the regular TSA agents said. "Everything is backed up. You'll be fine."

"Oh, good. That's good news. Thanks." She yanked off her wet high-heeled boots and threw them on top of her coat and purse.

"Slow down and get yourself another bin. You're gonna get mud all over your fancy jacket," the TSA agent said.

"It doesn't matter—I just need to get to the gate," Dale said.

Once through security, she pulled her boots back on, grabbed her coat and bag, and ran toward gate 41. Her flight was delayed. She called Peter again.

"Hey, so, the seven is delayed about forty minutes, but I bought a ticket on the eight, too, so I will get on whichever one takes off first," she said.

"Halibut or salmon?" Peter asked.

"Are you ordering from Asiate?"

"Yeah. As soon as you land, I'll put in our order," he said.

"I want a steak."

"You got it. I'm not going anywhere. Relax. You'll get here when you get here."

"I know. I just hate to waste any of our time together traveling," she said.

"Me, too, but it's awful out there. Listen, Steve is at his daughter's prom, so Danny will be outside my door. He knows you're coming . . ." Peter trailed off.

All of Peter's regular Secret Service agents knew her by now, but Steve had been there since the beginning. The Secret Service had a narrow and all-consuming mission: to protect the president and her family from harm. While they could not participate in arranging a rendezvous, a protectee's wandering eye was not the responsibility of the Secret Service.

"OK. I hate the stupid shuttle. I should have taken the train," Dale moaned.

"You hate the train, too. Relax, honey. I'll see you soon," he said.

As Dale sat waiting for the delayed seven P.M. shuttle to La Guardia, she remembered the very first time she'd met Peter.

She had flown out to California to do the first interview with the country's first-ever "first man." At twenty-nine, she was one of the youngest network reporters on the White House beat, and the interview was a major get.

She had thought he'd seem emasculated by his wife's success. Nothing could have been further from the reality she encountered that day. He was the center of the family, and their teenage twins clearly worshipped him. He also had a full workload and a staff of deputies, nannies, and personal assistants swirling around him that rivaled the size of his wife's entourage.

He'd been pursued by NFL teams after two seasons as UCLA's starting quarterback, but he'd passed on the NFL and finished college. After that, he'd gone to law school and turned to the business side of sports, where he was known as one of the last honest brokers in the sports agency world. Athletes knew him as someone who would die for them. He'd built one of the most successful shops in the industry, and when his wife became governor of California, he'd thrown himself into his own business with even greater fervor.

When Dale had started the interview, she'd made good use of the extensive research she'd done on the first man, asking him about one of the professional football players he represented who'd gone straight to the NFL after one year at Miami and probing him for his views about the debate over the college football ranking system. Dale's father was an orthopedic surgeon who worked on dozens of famous athletes, and as an only child, Dale had no choice but to absorb his passion and encyclopedic knowledge of sports. Dale and Peter had talked for more than an hour before she turned on the cameras.

Although he was humble and funny when the cameras were rolling and spent the interview praising his wife's record and vision, she'd seen glimpses that day of a sharper, more sarcastic side to his personality that she found surprising. She'd left Sacramento with new respect for the president-elect and more than a twinge of jealousy that Charlotte Kramer had found time for a career and a relationship—a balancing act Dale hadn't quite mastered.

Dale smiled now at the memory. She had a recurring nightmare that she and Peter would be discovered and that he would deny knowing her. She knew it was ridiculous, but they'd been so careful not to leave any trace of their relationship that she worried she would be easy to erase if that ever became necessary. That was why Dale replayed every conversation, every kiss, every moment together, over and over, so that there would be a record somewhere of their shared history, if only in her mind.

They had seen each other again at Charlotte's inauguration, when Dale had conducted a short interview with the first couple that was to air the night of the inaugural address. He'd been friendly, but Dale had assumed he was turning on the charm with the new White House press corps to curry favorable coverage for his wife's administration.

As Reagan National filled with other delayed travelers, Dale played back one of her favorite memories: their first kiss.

Peter had traveled with Charlotte on her first European tour. It was his first and last overseas trip with the president. Dale traveled to cover the president's first meetings with European leaders, and she had been promised an exclusive interview with President Kramer. She'd been sitting in her assigned seat on Air Force One listening to her iPod and skimming the *Wall Street Journal* when a clean-cut White House aide touched her arm and asked her to come to the president's cabin.

She had smoothed her hair and popped a mint into her mouth before she stepped over the sleeping correspondent in the seat next to her and into the aisle. As she'd traveled the long distance from the press cabin to the president's private quarters, Dale had felt the eyes of curious White House staffers on her. She'd smiled at a couple of junior press officers she recognized in the staff cabin and glanced quickly into the senior staff cabin, where she caught a glimpse of a snoring secretary of state.

The aide had smiled. "They handed out Ambien before we took off," he'd said.

Dale had smiled back. "I'll take any leftovers."

The aide had knocked softly on the door to the president's cabin. A cheerful Air Force One steward had answered right away.

"I have Miss Smith for the president," the White House aide had said.

"Right this way," the steward had replied.

Dale had stepped into the president's cabin and crossed her arms in front of her body. She felt frumpy in her black leggings and long sweater.

"Hi, Dale," the president had said coldly. She was wearing jeans and a crisp white blouse.

"Hello, Madam President, how are you doing?" Dale had asked.

"Just fine. Now, tell me what you know about Maureen's work for 'thugs,' as your network put it tonight."

Maureen was the president's nominee for attorney general, and her confirmation was in serious trouble. Making matters worse, Dale had an exclusive source with mountains of dirt on her. Dale's network had devoted eight minutes—an eternity in network news—to a long report about her work for corrupt politicians.

Dale had swallowed and steadied herself against the wall while the president glared at her. She felt unprotected without the hovering White House staff or any of her crew around. She'd looked around the cabin and noticed a stack of *Sports Illustrated* magazines and the John Adams HBO special on DVDs.

"Madam President, I spoke to Melanie about this earlier. Our reporting on your nominee is backed by rock-solid sources who thought you'd never pick her because of her record of defending white-collar criminals and former elected officials who are now sitting in jail."

Dale was trying to hold her ground, but she'd known she was mounting a futile defense. She'd felt herself sliding toward the door so she could return to the safety of the press cabin as quickly as possible.

Charlotte had said nothing but continued to glare at Dale.

"Honey, how do you turn on the DVD player?" Peter had shouted from the next room. "The kids want to watch a movie."

The president, looking slightly irritated, had shouted back, "I'll be right there." She'd looked at Dale and said, "I hope you didn't travel for the interview, because the interview is off."

Dale's stomach had sunk, and she'd turned to leave as soon as the president left the room. She was halfway back to the press cabin when the same aide who had retrieved her grabbed her arm again.

"Can you come into the conference room for a minute, please?" he'd asked.

Oh, God, what now? Dale had thought. She'd sat on the couch in the empty conference room, assuming that Melanie was on her way in to threaten to cut off all access to administration officials. Melanie and the president were already known for their one-two punches with reporters who crossed them. To Dale's surprise, Peter Kramer had walked in, wearing faded jeans and a sheepish smile and holding a plate of chicken wings and two beers in outstretched hands as though they were peace offerings.

"Hey, I'm sorry about that. That wasn't about you in there," he'd said.

"Really? Because it sure felt like it had a lot to do with me."

"No, she had a lot of pressure to appoint Maureen. They go way back, and she's been lobbying for the attorney general job since before the primaries were over as a reward for supporting Charlotte," he'd said.

"This will be a very long four years if your wife refuses to do any interviews with me," Dale had said.

"She doesn't stay mad," he'd promised.

They were both quiet for a minute, and then Peter had launched into a playful probe of press corps gossip. He wanted to know who was married, who was dating, who was cheating, and whom Dale liked and disliked. They'd finished the plate of wings and their beers.

Dale had put her head in her hands and sighed. "Thanks for the snack."

Peter had looked at her for a long moment. "Why does it bother you so much that she's mad?" he'd asked.

"Because I was just assigned to cover her for the next four years, and if she hates me, I won't be able to do my job."

"The next four years, huh?" he'd said, with a smile that started in the corners of his eyes and worked its way down his face.

Dale had smiled back. "Easy for you to say."

"Listen, she scares the shit out of me sometimes, too. But she is trying to do right by everyone, so just, you know, don't take it personally," he'd said.

Then he'd checked his watch and stood up and stretched his arms above his head, revealing a very flat, tanned stomach that Dale couldn't peel her eyes away from. When she'd returned her gaze to his face, he was smiling at her again.

"I'm glad you're on the beat, Dale," he'd said, and it was clear that the visit was over.

Dale had gone back to the press cabin and thought about how to tell her boss that her exclusive interview had been pulled. They'd sent an extra crew over to shoot the interview, and now it was off. And to spite her, and the network, the White House would probably do an interview with one of her competitors. *Great start,* Dale had thought.

The interview was never rescheduled during the overseas trip, but every time Dale had looked up from a live shot or during a press conference, Peter Kramer was looking in her direction. Sometimes he would smile at her or wave at her and the other reporters. Other times, he'd pause just long enough to catch her eye and mouth a quick "Hi." Dale had found herself thinking about their chat in the conference room more often than she knew she should.

After midnight in Budapest, where they had made their final stop of the five-day trip, Dale had finished taping a stand-up for a morning show package and walked back into the hotel where they were staying. The bar area was empty; the rest of the reporters must have hit the town on their expense accounts.

"Still working?" a voice had asked from a booth near the back of the bar.

She'd turned around and noticed the Secret Service agents first, and then she'd seen Peter Kramer sitting at a table with his wife's deputy national security advisor and chief of staff. There were two others at the table whom Dale didn't recognize.

"Just finished," she'd said.

"Care to join us?" he'd asked.

"Sure, that would be great."

Melanie had watched her suspiciously, but the others were nice enough. Dale had told them about the raunchy conditions on the press charter. The press charter was a leased commercial plane that followed Air Force One around the world carrying the press corps. On the flight from London to Budapest, a couple (both of them married, not to each other) had engaged in noisy sexual activity that had every one of the reporters angling for one of the twelve press seats on Air Force One.

Three bottles of wine and two hours later, she and Peter had outlasted the others and sat in the booth talking about college football, the sorry state of skiing in the Northeast, and the downfall of the Tour de France from steroid abuse.

"You are wasting your time covering the White House. You should be covering sports. No one cares about politics. Everyone loves sports," he'd said, winking at the Secret Service agent standing a few feet away.

If the agent had noticed Peter's gesture, he didn't let on. He'd stared directly ahead and seemed to try to fade into the wall.

"But if I didn't cover the White House, you wouldn't get to buy me drinks at strange dark bars in foreign countries that you have to follow your wife to," Dale had said. As soon as the words were out of her mouth, she would have killed to pull them back.

"So the truth comes out," he'd said.

"No, no, that's not what I meant."

"It's what everyone thinks, and no one says it out loud. I'm actually glad you did say it out loud. Especially if it's what you've been thinking since our first meeting in Sacramento," he'd said.

"No, no, I swear to God, it is not what I think."

"No? I think it myself. I am a pathetic husband following the leader of the free world around while I visit museums with the wives."

"No, I swear, that is not what I think," Dale had insisted again.

"Then what is it, Dale, that you really think?" Peter had asked, staring directly into her eyes.

She'd looked away and tried to pull her thoughts together before she spoke again. "What I really think is that you are amazing," Dale had said quietly, without looking him in the eye. She'd glanced nervously at the Secret Service agent. He didn't appear to be listening to their conversation, but Dale had lowered her voice anyway and leaned closer to Peter. She was close enough to notice a small scar under his chin and the lines around his eyes and mouth.

She'd taken a breath and noticed that he had moved closer to her. Their legs touched under the table. The wine had emboldened her, and she placed her hand on top of his. He'd looked down at her hand and seemed to stop breathing for a second. She'd continued without making eye contact.

"What I really think is that your wife seems to have no idea how utterly amazing you are, and I've decided that if I ever have what she has, I would never take it for granted, and what I really think . . ." Dale was still talking when his mouth met hers. His free hand had moved to her shoulder, turning her body to face his. She'd moved her hand from the table to the back of his head and pulled him closer. For the first time, she'd noticed that a horribly remastered version of U2's "Beautiful Day" was playing. As they'd kissed there in the dark, near-empty bar in Budapest, with a Secret Service agent staring straight ahead as though nothing out of the ordinary were happening, Dale was aware of how badly she'd wanted this to happen since she'd first met Peter Kramer. When they'd stopped kissing, they sat with their foreheads touching. His fingers were still tangled in her hair and they were both breathing deeply. He'd kissed her closed eyelids and the top of her nose. She'd sat perfectly still.

"I guess it was only a matter of time before that happened," Peter had said.

She'd smiled as he pulled her hands into his and held them. "What does your agent think when you do things like this?" she'd asked, glancing at the Secret Service agent assigned to protect Peter.

"When I do things like this?" he'd asked, kissing her again.

She'd smiled and pulled away.

"For the record, I don't do things like this," he'd said. "But I would assume that unless you get very angry at me, which I hope you never do, and come at me with a dagger, he won't do anything at all," Peter had said. "Think about the things JFK's agents saw. This is nothing."

"So, we're safe from the United States Secret Service. That's one less thing to worry about," Dale had said.

"Yes. I guarantee you they have seen much worse. Do you have any ideas about what to do about everyone else?" he'd asked.

"I'm thinking."

"OK, well, let me know if you come up with anything."

"How would I do that?"

He'd reached over, picked up her cell phone, and entered his personal cell-phone number into it under the name "Budapest." He'd placed her phone back on the table and took her hand again. "This is a very bad idea," he'd said.

"I know," she'd agreed.

"And as much as I would like it to—and believe me when I say that I would like it to—this probably shouldn't happen again."

"I know," she'd said, smiling.

"I should probably get upstairs," he'd said.

"I know."

"Are you going to say anything other than 'I know' to me before I pull myself away from you?" he'd asked, kissing her hands again.

"Sweet dreams," she'd said.

"Thanks," he'd said, laughing.

He'd kissed her on the lips one last time and then rose and walked out of the bar. The agent had followed him without looking back at her. After fifteen minutes, she'd gone upstairs to her room, one floor below his, to catch a couple of hours of sleep.

In the morning, she'd reached for her BlackBerry before her eyes were completely open. She was sure that someone must have been down there at four A.M. and seen them. She was sure that someone had phoned her news director and told him to fire her for kissing the president's husband.

But no one had e-mailed.

No one had called.

She couldn't look at him when they had boarded the plane for the return trip to Washington, but she was thrilled when he'd smiled at her after they landed at Andrews nine hours later.

She and Peter had immediately struck up a friendship. It started with short text messages. Because he'd maintained his sports agency, he was allowed to keep a private cell phone and an e-mail account that was secure but not part of the official White House system. He would e-mail her from his work account about a college football game he'd seen, and she'd send him funny stories from the sports section or snow conditions from the ski resorts in Tahoe and Colorado. Eventually, their e-mails turned to near-daily phone calls, and sometimes she'd come up to his East Wing office, where they'd chat about everything from the news of the day to the personal lives of the White House staff. Dale had told him about her frustrations at the network, and Peter had sought her advice about how to handle the public relations predicaments some of his young athletes faced.

They'd never talked about the night in Budapest, and it didn't happen again for a long time.

Dale now snapped out of her reverie and looked at her watch: seven forty-five. She stood up and approached the gate agents. "Any updates on the seven P.M. shuttle?" she asked.

"We made an announcement about ten minutes ago. The seven was canceled, but the eight o'clock shuttle will leave around eight-thirty," the agent said.

Dale knew it wasn't their fault, but she couldn't help glaring at them.

"Ms. Smith, we've got you in first class on the eight o'clock. We'll board in a few more minutes," the agent said.

"Thanks," Dale said, returning to her seat. She didn't want to start their weekend off with a meltdown, so she e-mailed Peter with her update: "7 pm shuttle is dead. I'm on the 8, which leaves at 8:30. See you when I see you."

He wrote back right away: "Stop stressing. I'm not going anywhere."

Dale hated how clingy she felt. It was as if she couldn't get enough of him. They'd spend Friday nights together, and then he'd get up on Saturdays and drive the two hours to the Connecticut countryside, where his kids were at boarding school. She'd work all day Saturday and then get into the car after the newscast and spend Saturday nights with him at the house he rented in Washington, Connecticut, to be near the kids.

On Sunday mornings, they'd stay in bed as long as possible. Dale would say, "I'm getting in the shower in five minutes," over and over again, until she was so late she'd leave his house with wet hair and no makeup. Then she would return to the city to prepare for the Sunday evening newscast, and Peter would return to Kent to have lunch with the twins before he headed back to D.C. Sometimes he'd stay Sunday nights, too, and about once a month, Dale flew to California to meet Peter on her days off. Her weekend schedule meant that Monday and Tuesday were her Saturday and Sunday, so she'd get on a late flight out of JFK on Sunday night and meet him in San Francisco or Los Angeles, where he kept offices and homes.

Dale saw the gate agents reach for the PA system and prayed for news that her flight was boarding. "Boarding all first-class passengers for the eight P.M. US Airways shuttle to La Guardia," he said, smiling at Dale as he said it.

She settled into her seat and stared out the window. She sent Peter a text: "on my way see you soon xo." He wrote back instantly: "safe flight."

They were seventh in line for takeoff.

Dale sighed and sipped the glass of wine that the flight attendant had brought her without asking. She closed her eyes and thought about all the little things she wanted to share with Peter—the every-day things that made her laugh or struck her as curious. They never had enough time to talk. But that had always been the case with them, Dale thought as her plane sat waiting to take off for the twenty-five-minute flight.

More than two and a half years had passed since they'd first slept together. Dale looked out the window of the plane as it took off from Washington a few moments later, the White House and the Capitol shining beneath them. She wondered what her life would be like if she hadn't fallen in love with the president's husband.

CHAPTER THREE

Charlotte

Charlotte spent the weekend much the way she'd spent most of her weekends as president. On Friday night, she and Melanie finished a bottle of wine and half a pack of cigarettes and talked into the night about what their lives would be like when they left the White House. Melanie had said something about needing to talk to her about the campaign, but then the twins called to ask where their ski stuff was stored up at boarding school, and Melanie never raised it again.

On Saturday, Charlotte traveled to Camp David with Melanie and the dogs, where she'd conducted a meeting with her military commanders and national security team by video conference. They'd woken up Sunday to six more inches of fresh snow and taken a long hike in snow shoes around Camp David with the dogs. They'd returned to the White House at noon, and now Charlotte was in the Oval Office catching up on paperwork.

"Down, get down. Get down right now!" Charlotte shouted at her three vizslas, who were trying to make mouth-to-mouth contact with her new Secret Service agents.

"Get off the nice men. Sit down. Kennel!" She tried every command that the trainers had taught her, but while she commanded the United States military, she could not get her three dogs to stop jumping off the floor to try to kiss the agents on the mouth.

"It's OK, Madam President, really. I have two dogs at home, and they like to kiss humans on the mouth to see if they know them. It's all in a book I read when I got my first problem dog. Not that your dogs are problems, they are not, of course, but, you know. I'm sorry . . ." He trailed off, embarrassed.

"No, of course, they are problem dogs," Charlotte said, "Look at them."

The smallest of the three dogs was peeing on the rug of the Oval Office, a habit she didn't seem able to break despite Charlotte's efforts to have her trained by the best dog trainers in the country. The last trainer had quit when the puppy bit her.

"Melanie!" Charlotte yelled from the Oval Office. Charlotte's assistant, Samantha, ran into the Oval Office just as the middle dog was squatting to pee on top of the wet spot created by the puppy.

"Sam, please ask Melanie to get the trainer over here to deal with the dogs. Tell her Mika is still peeing on the rug in the Oval Office."

"Ma'am, I can call the trainer myself. Why don't I take the dogs to the park for you? Have they been for a run yet today?" Sam asked.

"Yes, we hiked for more than an hour this morning. They just don't tire out. I don't know what to do. Mika peed all over Camp David. And Emma followed suit, but just to outdo her. The only one who is still behaving like a good girl is my sweet Cammie. Come here, peanut." Charlotte summoned Cammie, her seven-year-old vizsla. Cammie jumped into her lap and curled into a small ball of cinnamon-colored fur and licked Charlotte's face—eyes, nose, mouth, and chin.

"That's my good girl. That's my best girl. Why aren't your sisters good girls like you?" Cammie looked at the other two dogs with disdain as she settled in for what she obviously hoped would be an afternoon nap on her mistress's lap.

Charlotte never thought she'd be the type to collect pets, but Cammie was such a special dog that when the breeder had called three years later with a puppy from his final litter, she couldn't say no. That was how Emma had joined her family. The youngest, Mika, was a gift from the Hungarian ambassador, who was thrilled to learn that the American president was a fan of the Hungarian vizsla. Charlotte took the dogs everywhere. The best thing about being president these days,

Charlotte thought, was being able to travel with the dogs. She knew people suspected she was becoming eccentric, but the dogs provided more companionship than anyone could imagine.

Melanie helped create the image of a working mom with photo ops of Charlotte and Peter at official White House functions with the kids or traveling together to Camp David over the holidays, but the presidency had a way of isolating even the most well-rounded individuals. Charlotte stroked Cammie's soft fur as Cammie let out a loud sigh and shut her eyes. Charlotte glanced at her briefing papers and started in on a lengthy report from her director of management and budget about the size of the deficit.

Everyone always has an explanation for why they can't do what I want done, Charlotte said to herself. *Everyone except Roger.*

Roger Taylor was the defense secretary. She was having dinner with him and his wife at their home in Wesley Heights that evening.

I'll bring the dogs, she decided, feeling better instantly at the thought of her three vizslas running around with their two standard poodles. Roger was just as nuts about his dogs as she was about hers.

Roger and his wife, Stephanie, were rarities in Washington. They were happily married, liked by everyone—Democrats and Republicans—and seemingly oblivious to their status as power brokers. Roger drove the secretary of state and the national security advisor crazy, but Melanie had a way with him. The rest of the national security team called Melanie the Roger Whisperer and counted on her to mediate interagency power struggles. Melanie had worked closely with Roger when he'd served as deputy secretary of state for President Martin and she was press secretary. During the transition, when Charlotte was interviewing candidates for defense secretary, Melanie had suggested Roger for the job. After a brief phone conversation, Charlotte had offered him the position without a single face-to-face meeting. He'd roared with laughter when she'd made the offer.

"So, Melanie's got your ear, I presume from this phone call. That's a good thing. A very good thing," Roger had said.

He was smarter than the others, and he wasn't intimidated by Charlotte's strength or lack of female charm. He was never disappointed by her, as all the others seemed to be, because he never expected more than her focus on his issues and her complete loyalty, and he had both in abundance.

Together, they'd done what the two men who had come before Charlotte hadn't managed to do: they'd won a war.

Roger and Charlotte had traveled to Iraq three days after Charlotte's inauguration. He'd shown her where all the insurgent strongholds had been and where the most deadly fighting had taken place following the original invasion. They'd driven the roads that had been lined with deadly IEDs for the first six years of America's occupation. He'd shown her where the "Sunni awakening"—the turning point in the war—first took hold. Iraq was still in tatters, but the worst was over, and American troops were on their way home with a victory under their belts.

They'd traveled from Iraq to Afghanistan on that first trip, and for all the progress that had been made in Iraq, it seemed that the situation in Afghanistan had deteriorated. It was not for lack of effort or for lack of popular support—the war in Afghanistan had always maintained higher levels of popular support in America than the Iraq war. It seemed to lack a strategy, but what strategy could be crafted to get young boys out of caves where they studied bomb making and adhered to the radical teachings of the madrassas so they could grow up and fly airplanes into buildings? Charlotte and Roger had been back to Iraq and Afghanistan more than a dozen times to meet with local leaders, diplomats, commanders, and U.S. troops. Iraq, while ghastly and heartbreaking, at least seemed to have a pulse. Afghanistan felt as if it had been flatlined since the Dark Ages.

Charlotte couldn't help thinking about her son when she traveled to the war zones. In every speech she gave, she praised the men and women of America's military and their families. Yet in order to get through every speech without showing emotion that could be interpreted around the world as weakness, she forced herself never to contemplate sending her own son off to either of those godforsaken places. She knew herself well enough to know that she could never send her child to fight against faceless enemies on hostile terrain. She was deeply ashamed of her thoughts, and she'd even started going to church with Roger and Stephanie to ask forgiveness and to offer extra prayers for the mothers who did have the courage—and most likely did not have the choice—to send their baby boys and girls into battle. She let herself cry for the mothers when she was alone at night. The dogs were the only witnesses to the tears she shed when she wrote the letters.

Each night, she brought with her to the residence the names and details of the lives and deaths of every U.S. soldier killed on her watch. She spent hours crafting handwritten notes to mothers, fathers, husbands, wives, sons, and daughters. Sometimes she went through several drafts. No two letters were the same. This was the least she felt she could do. The letters to the mothers were the hardest for her to write, so she separated them and worked on them last. She stayed up all night sometimes, until just the right words formed on her personal stationery in her messy cursive. She always finished the letters emotionally drained and aching for her own children.

Charlotte revisited the decision to send the twins to boarding school every morning when she woke up to an empty house.

"This is the last year at Kent," she'd often said to Peter and the twins. The problem was that the kids were thriving at Kent. They were growing into clever, kind, and daring young people who cared not at all for material items (other than their iPhones) and very much about the world around them—just what every parent of teenagers prays for. Peter traveled to Kent every weekend to watch their soccer games in the fall, hockey in the winter, and water polo in the spring and summer. Sometimes he brought his players with him, and the kids loved introducing the famous athletes to their friends. Charlotte wished she could pop in on them and surprise them for a weekend, but she made such a commotion with the motorcade and security. It was best to have Peter visit and allow the kids to pretend that they were just like the rest of the students.

When this is all over, the kids and I will travel around the world, Charlotte thought while stroking Cammie's belly.

She finished her briefing papers, having made notes and written questions all over them that she knew would leave her economic team peeling themselves off the ceiling when they got in the next morning. She gathered some reading on intelligence reform for later that evening and walked the dogs across the South Lawn back toward the residence.

It was quiet on Sundays. A large crowd always gathered to greet her and the dogs upon their return from Camp David, but now all the staffers were home with their families or out with friends, and all the tourists had made their way back to the train stations or airports or bus stations where they'd arrived days earlier.

Charlotte was claustrophobic; she never took the elevator. She loved to look at the art, so she and the three dogs made their way toward the grand staircase. She glanced into the room where the portraits of the former first ladies hung. She often wondered if they'd been happy here, if they'd seen much of their husbands, or if the weight of the office had come between them.

Not that the presidency was what had come between Charlotte and Peter. They'd begun to drift apart years before, but the formality of life in the White House had made their distance official. His living quarters were separate from hers. She didn't even know when he was in the residence. And since he was the first-ever first man, he was afforded more latitude to maintain dual roles as first husband and working spouse. No one expected him to host teas for visiting spouses of the leaders Charlotte met with. She had hoped that the move to Washington would be a new start for them, that they could laugh together and re-create the chemistry that had drawn them to each other nearly twenty years earlier. He'd always been keenly aware of the roles that spouses played in the success of politicians such as Ronald Reagan, Margaret Thatcher, and Charlotte's predecessors, Presidents Martin and Harlow. But instead of bringing them together, the move to Washington and the new and inflexible demands on Charlotte's time extinguished any hope for the recovery of her marriage.

She passed the East Room, where all major White House events and ceremonies were held, stopping briefly to scoot Mika along. She greeted everyone on her personal staff with a smile and a wave and entered her suite of rooms. She had an hour to kill before the motorcade would take her to Roger and Stephanie's.

She turned on the television and flipped around looking for *Dog Whisperer*. Sometimes she heard something helpful, and the dogs always stared intently at the television when it was on. She looked at her elliptical machine and contemplated a quick workout but decided against it and called the twins instead. She tried Harry's cell phone first. When he didn't pick up, she tried Penelope.

"Hi, Mom," Penelope said on the first ring.

"Hi, honey. Are you with Dad?" Charlotte asked.

"No, he left after lunch for a meeting in New York tomorrow," Penelope said.

"Oh," Charlotte said.

"There's another storm coming in, and he didn't want to drive in the snow, which is smart, because there were a lot of accidents last week because of black ice," Penelope said.

She always worried about her father. Charlotte didn't realize that Peter was spending Monday in New York, but he didn't tell her much of anything these days.

"Did you have a good time with Dad?" Charlotte asked.

"Yes, we went skiing yesterday afternoon and out to dinner. I brought Rebecca, and Harry brought Jason. We went to fondue."

"That sounds great, sweetie. Where's your brother?"

"He's at study hall, but he's probably just listening to his iPod," Penelope said.

"Tell him to call me before bed," Charlotte said. "I love you."

"Love you, too, Mom."

Charlotte thought about calling Peter, but she didn't want to bother him. She'd check in on Monday to ask him about the kids. Then, thinking she was being ridiculous, she changed her mind and decided to call. He was still her husband. Surely, she could call him without worrying about bothering him. She dialed his cell phone. After five rings, he picked up.

"Hello?"

"Hi, Peter, it's me."

He paused.

"Charlotte," she said.

"Of course, I know. Is everything OK?" he asked.

"Yes. I'm sorry. I just wanted to see how the kids are doing. Penelope says you went skiing and then to fondue," Charlotte said.

"Yeah, they are getting really good, and if they learn to ski out here on the sheets of ice that pass as ski runs, they'll be incredible when they get out to Tahoe later this season."

"I'm so glad they still enjoy skiing. I was afraid they'd lose interest when we pulled them out of ski team."

"Me, too."

There was an awkward silence, and then they both spoke at once.

"Go ahead," Peter said.

"I was just going to say that I'll, uh, see you when I see you, and, um, I hope you have a good week. Penelope said you have a meeting in New York tomorrow . . ." Charlotte drifted off, not sure what else to say to the man she'd been married to for nineteen years.

"Yeah, I will be in New York tomorrow, and then I give a speech Wednesday in Chicago with two players from the Bears about the importance of staying in school, and then I'm in the San Francisco office for the rest of the week," Peter said.

"That's great. Anyone I would have heard of?" Charlotte asked.

"Two rookies—I'm sure you haven't heard of them. I signed them last year while you were crazed with the midterms."

"Oh, yeah. I've tried to block out that period in my life completely," she said. Her party had lost twenty-four seats in the House and two Senate seats in the midterm elections the year before.

"A president's party always loses seats in the midterm," he said.

"I know, I know—the old 'history was against you' excuse. I've got that one down," she said.

Peter laughed. "I will be at the state dinner next week," he offered.

"Fantastic," Charlotte said, a little too cheerfully to sound genuine. "Three hundred and fifty of our closest friends all gathered to honor the great nation of Panama," she added.

He laughed. "Ralph wouldn't have it any other way."

Charlotte laughed, too. "Have a good week, Peter," she said.

"Thanks, Charlotte."

She hung up and felt lonelier than before. She wished she hadn't called at all. Confronting your husband as the stranger he had become was a lot more depressing than remembering a time when he wasn't a stranger at all.

She changed out of her clothes, now covered with dog hair, into an identical pair of black slacks and a black turtleneck. She slid into low heels and made her way downstairs. The three dogs walked a few steps ahead of her to where the twenty-car motorcade with flashing lights and men with automatic weapons hanging out of SUVs was waiting to escort her the two and a half miles to Roger and Stephanie's house.

CHAPTER FOUR

Melanie

Melanie passed the motorcade and waved at the agents as she pulled into the White House. Sunday night work sessions were Melanie's secret weapon. They allowed her to start Monday mornings on the offense, as they'd say during the campaigns. Late Sundays, she'd distribute what the staff called Melanie-grams.

To the White House press secretary, she sent an article from the Sunday paper about how calls seeking comment on Friday night went unanswered. Melanie circled the comment and wrote, "This is what interns and the night-duty officers are for!" To the domestic policy council, she sent an article from *Science Times* about organ transplants in cloned sheep, with a note asking them to schedule a policy time on medical ethics for the president. To the national security advisor, Melanie attached her own comments to Charlotte's notes from a classified memo on the increased use of women and children as suicide bombers in Afghanistan. And to Vice President Neal McMillan, Melanie sent a recipe from *Cooking Light* for a jerk spice rub for ribs, which the vice president was famous for making at his ranch in New Mexico.

She had a separate stack for Ralph, most of it responses to things he'd sent in her direction. His strategy was to bury her in paper, but she didn't have time to engage in the bureaucratic infighting Ralph had mastered in his fifteen years on the Hill. Ralph was a student of Lee Atwater, James Carville, and other great political gurus, and he saw in himself the same genius. All Melanie saw was his insecurity and overly partisan instincts. From Ralph's perspective, Melanie monopolized Charlotte's time and marginalized him. What Ralph didn't understand was that Melanie didn't need to monopolize the president's time. She had something Ralph would never have: naked time in the steam room with the president.

Charlotte wasn't a fan of the gym, but she loved the steam room. She said it helped her get out of her head and tap into her gut. It was there she told Melanie what she wanted done at the White House. The problem for Melanie, besides her aversion to nakedness and heat, was that it was impossible to take any notes in a steam room. Melanie was convinced that was why Charlotte gave her most important orders there.

Melanie glanced at her call log from the previous week. There were seventy-eight unreturned calls. She scanned the names. At least half of them were probably birthday calls, she thought.

One name stuck out and gave her a job in the pit of her stomach: Michael Robbins. He was an investigative reporter at one of the newsmagazines. She had become well acquainted with Michael during the Harlow administration. His specialty was breaking the news when a high-ranking government official was about to get indicted. Every press secretary in Washington, D.C., cringed when his name showed up in the inbox. The message for Melanie simply said, "Call ASAP."

Melanie looked at the Boston cell-phone number and recognized it as his personal number. She lifted the receiver of the phone on her desk and dialed. Her call went straight to voice-mail.

Of course. I called from a blocked number, she thought. Michael didn't pick up his phone on Sundays unless he knew who was on the other end.

She dug her personal cell phone out of the Dior bag and entered his number quickly.

"There you are," he answered on the first ring. "I knew you'd call."

"Michael, is everything OK?" Melanie asked.

"I need to see you. Your girl's in trouble, Melanie," he said.

CHAPTER FIVE

Dale

D ale always knew when Charlotte was on the phone.

It was the only time Peter ever looked as if he felt guilty.

Charlotte was lonely, and if she wasn't the president and he the first husband, they would have been the type of couple who would have divorced and remained friendly enough to meet for lunch once a month. But they were not a normal couple.

Dale jumped out of bed when she heard Peter speaking in the tones reserved for his wife. She pulled on a robe and started separating their tangled clothes from where they'd been flung hours earlier.

Dale and Peter never took stupid chances. They were careful not to tempt fate. She never traveled to Washington, Connecticut, when his kids planned to sleep at his rented house. She refused his pleas to stay with him at the residence when Charlotte was out of the country. He never went to her apartment or her hotel room. But they were both growing anxious. Charlotte hadn't set up a reelection campaign yet, and Dale sometimes wondered if she knew about their affair. Part of her would be relieved to have things out in the open. Peter could move out of the White House. They could have more than secret meetings and private moments. They could have a life together.

As she stepped into the shower, she heard him laughing at something Charlotte said about the state dinner the following week. Dale had been invited. In itself, that wasn't strange. The White House always invited one or two members of the press corps to each state dinner. But because of her aggressive reporting on several of Charlotte's Cabinet appointees and a general unease with her frequent scoops, Dale wasn't exactly high on their list of favorite reporters. She was invited to bring a guest, and she planned to invite Brian Watson, the new Pentagon reporter. Dale made a mental note to e-mail him first thing in the morning.

Just as she was starting to worry that Peter was still chatting with Charlotte, the shower door opened, and he joined her.

She smiled all the way back to the airport the next morning. She planned to spend her day off getting organized and shopping for a dress for the state dinner. Brian had replied immediately to her invitation and was thrilled about coming to the dinner.

She hoped he wouldn't get the wrong impression. For the most part, her friends had stopped trying to set her up after their efforts all ended without success. She often agreed to go on first dates—to dinners with other correspondents or producers on the White House beat or daytime dates to museums or baseball games. She felt she had to maintain some charade of life as a single girl, but she never accepted invitations to second dates. She had few female friends, so no one did much prying about her status. Her mother was the only person she'd confided in about her affair with Peter, and only because she'd begun to worry when she couldn't reach Dale over the weekends. Her mother was so concerned about what would happen to Dale if word of her affair ever became public that she didn't even share her daughter's secret with Dale's father.

On the night of the state dinner, Dale met Brian at the network's Washington bureau. He was known as the "male Dale" for being just as much of a workaholic as she was, but that didn't bother him.

Dale wore a long, sleeveless red silk dress with an open back—a little sexy for a night out in Washington, but everything else she'd seen at Neiman's was black or beige and looked like mother-of-the-bride garb. The dinner was to honor the president of Panama, but it fell on Valentine's Day, so Dale figured she could get away with wearing red.

Heads turned as Dale walked through the newsroom dressed for the formal affair. In a business suit or jeans and a T-shirt, Dale was a striking woman whose good looks rarely went unnoticed. With her hair swept off her face in a loose updo, her makeup expertly applied, and her elegant evening gown clinging to her petite curves, she was traffic-stopping gorgeous. She'd inherited the best of her mother's Greek genes and her father's Irish genes. She had olive skin, bright green eyes, and long, straight chestnut hair.

"You clean up pretty well," Brian said to her.

"Thanks. You, too." She laughed. "Ready?"

"Let's do it."

They entered the White House residence through the East Wing with the other dinner guests. As Dale and Brian passed through the entrance and walked toward the coat check, a military aide greeted them and directed them to the receiving line. Every guest was invited to have a picture taken with the president and Peter. Dale smiled at the members of Congress as they snapped pictures of the residence. Official White House functions had a way of turning even the most cynical Washingtonians into starry-eyed tourists. Dale spotted members of Charlotte's Cabinet, a few Hispanic celebrities, and members of the diplomatic corps jockeying for spots in the photo line.

"Let's get our picture taken," Brian suggested.

"I've done it a million times. Let's just get a drink and do some people watching," Dale said.

Brian looked crushed. "Come on, Dale. Who knows when I'll be invited back here? Come through the photo line with me," he pleaded.

"I'm going to pass, but you should go through by yourself. Tell the president about your last trip to Afghanistan—she'd be really interested."

"I can't go through alone," Brian whined.

"Sure you can." Dale laughed.

"Please? I need the White House insider to introduce me to the Kramers."

Dale reluctantly agreed to go through the receiving line with Brian. He looked like a little kid as he gazed at the well-known faces. As they neared the president and Peter, Dale grew anxious.

"When we get there, we should keep moving," she said to Brian. "They have to do this all night."

As soon as Peter turned to look at her, Dale realized her mistake. He stared at her with a mix of such blatant affection and possessiveness that Dale half expected Charlotte to smack him. She averted her eyes and said, "Good evening, Madam President, Mr. Kramer." Charlotte didn't look at her but instead took Brian warmly by the arm and stood between her cheating husband and Brian for a photo. Peter leaned in toward Dale before she could escape and said, "Meet me in the Family Theater in twenty minutes." She spun around to face him to see if he was joking, but he'd turned his gaze to the couple behind her.

Dale knew instantly that it was a terrible idea to meet Peter in the Family Theater. She also knew that she would be there in exactly twenty minutes. Brian was giddy with excitement about being at the state dinner. He was taking pictures with his cell phone and sampling every appetizer offered to him. Dale made her escape.

"I've got to make a quick call," she told him.

"No way. No work tonight. Not even you, Dale," he protested.

"It'll just be a second," she said, sliding her cell phone out to see the messages that she knew would be there from Peter.

"Where r u," he had texted.

She made her way down the stairs and walked quickly toward the theater. People were milling around outside the Library and the China Room, but the hall outside the Family Theater was empty. She nodded at Peter's agent and walked into the theater. Her eyes were still adjusting to the darkness when Peter came up from behind and started kissing her neck and bare back.

"Not here!" she said.

"Why? Are you on a date?" Peter teased.

"Yes, I am on a fake date, so that people will stop debating whether I'm a lesbian workaholic or just a workaholic who can't get laid." She pushed him away. "Seriously, Peter, not here. Your wife is up there, my colleague is up there, and your guests are touring the residence. People could walk in at any moment. We shouldn't even be in here."

He looked amused. "I told the agents to gun down anyone who tried to come in."

Dale shook her head. "You're crazy!"

He put his arms around her and traced circles on her bare back. "Relax," he said. She leaned her head against his chest and breathed in the smell of his shampoo and his deodorant and his toothpaste. She could smell that he'd been drinking. She looked up at him.

"I'm sorry," she said.

His hands were still on her bare back. And then they slid her dress off her shoulders, and he was kissing her, and she gave in and kissed him back.

"Stop," she said halfheartedly as they moved to the floor. "We really should not be doing this here," she tried one last time.

As was always the case with Peter, he got what he wanted with her. Afterward, Dale pulled her hair into a ponytail and smoothed her dress down.

"You are out of control," she said, "and you ruined my hair."

"Your hair looks better like that," he said, leaning over to kiss her while he tucked in his shirt with one hand and reached for his jacket with the other.

"That was the dumbest thing we have ever done," Dale told him. She was furious at herself for letting it happen.

She put her hand on the door to go out the way she'd come in, but just before she opened it, she heard voices in the hall outside the theater.

It sounded like Charlotte.

She couldn't tell whom she was talking to, but if Peter was in the Family Theater with her, it was a safe bet that Charlotte was no longer in the receiving line.

CHAPTER SIX

Charlotte

Charlotte cornered Roger in the hallway outside the Family Theater. Since the state dinner fell on Valentine's Day, the residence was covered with red roses. Charlotte hated red.

"Roger, I'm not asking you to come with me to Afghanistan, I'm telling you. I still have that authority, don't I?" she asked playfully.

"Yes, you do, Charlotte, and usually, I take my orders from you, but right now, I have a higher calling," Roger said.

"There's a higher calling than visiting the troops and being there for the election?" Charlotte asked.

"Yes. My wife. Stephanie found a lump in her breast, and we're waiting to find out if it's cancer."

"Oh, my God! I'm so sorry. Is that why she isn't here tonight? I feel awful. What can we do? Are you seeing the best doctors? Let's go call her!"

Charlotte felt like an idiot for being demanding. She relied on Roger for so much that she felt a flash of anxiety that the center of his universe would be somewhere other than the work they were doing together.

"God, Roger, what are you doing here? Go home to Stephanie. Please. I need to go find my husband, anyway. We are supposed to pretend that we enjoy each other's company on nights like tonight."

"Charlotte, don't," Roger said.

"Don't what?" Charlotte asked.

"Don't act like I've rejected you and you don't care. I have not re-jected you, and I can see on your face that I have disappointed you, and I hate it. There is nowhere I'd rather be than with those guys—and with you—and you know it. But I need to be there for her. She was there for me, and I need to be there for her now."

"Of course you do. I completely understand. I would do the same," Charlotte said, forcing a smile.

He reached to pull her into a bear hug. She hugged him back.

"And that's why I love you, Roger—you're so decent. You always do the right thing. Stephanie is lucky."

"So is Peter," Roger said, but even as he said it, he knew it wasn't a plausible statement.

Charlotte laughed. Roger just smiled at her and hugged her closer than he would have if anyone had been watching.

Charlotte took a deep breath and hugged him back for a few sec-onds before releasing him and pushing him away. "Go home. I insist. If I can't handle the Panamanians on my own, we've got a very serious problem on our hands," she said.

Roger laughed. "Are you sure you don't mind?"

"Yes. And I can't believe you didn't tell me right away. Please tell Stephanie that I'd like to come see her whenever she's in the mood for a visitor."

"Thanks, Charlotte. As soon as we get through this, you know I'll be back one thousand percent."

"I know."

Roger turned to go, and she stood in the hall watching him walk toward the West Wing. Charlotte noticed that her guests had all mi-grated to the floor above, so she hurried upstairs to take her seat at the head table for dinner. She had no idea what was on the menu or who would provide the evening's entertainment. Formal dinners were typically the responsibility of first ladies, but since she didn't have anyone to fill that role, the White House social secretary made all the decisions. As she entered the Cross Hall at the top of the stairs, Sam appeared and gently directed her to her seat.

"Roger had to leave early for a family emergency," Charlotte whispered to Sam.

"We're on it. We'll put Melanie next to the Panamanian defense minister and move Ralph into Melanie's seat," Sam said, turning her head to speak into her sleeve, where a two-way radio was hidden to allow her to communicate with the other staffers in charge of making sure the event came off smoothly.

"Thanks, Sam. Any other changes I should know about?" Charlotte asked.

"We can't seem to find Mr. Kramer," Sam said.

CHAPTER SEVEN

Melanie

M elanie walked into Washington's Union Station just after six-thirty A.M. and strode purposefully through the lobby. She'd never seen the train station so empty, but none of the regulars took the Saturday regional train to New York City. Only someone trying to avoid lobbyists and reporters would travel the regional, and that was exactly Melanie's hope. She purchased her ticket and made her way to the waiting area. She bought a large coffee and a bottle of water and unfolded the newspapers she had brought from home. The festive photos from the state dinner days earlier were long gone. She glanced at the headlines: "President's Approval Ratings at New Lows," "Women's Group Assails Kramer's Apathy on Abortion Debate," "Conservatives Plot Third-party Challenge to Kramer," "Economy Continues to Falter." Melanie sighed. She folded the papers back up and shoved them into her bag. She pulled out her personal BlackBerry and skimmed the e-mails that had come in since she went to bed the night before. She found one from Michael: "Forget Sarabeth's—meet me at diner on 9th and 58th. Better bacon and more privacy."

She hadn't seen Michael since the year before, when they'd run into each other at the Caucus Room in D.C. Michael didn't frequent the D.C. establishment restaurants. Most of his sources couldn't afford to be seen with him. He'd been out with his twenty-two-year-old daughter, Elizabeth, the night Melanie saw him. They were celebrating her graduation from Georgetown. Michael had mentioned that Elizabeth was trying to get an interview in the White House communications office. Melanie had arranged the interview and put in a good word for her. It had been enough. Elizabeth had just completed her first year as a junior press aide in the regional press office, and she sat in the same cramped office that Melanie had occupied when she started with President Harlow fifteen years earlier.

The seven A.M. train arrived, and Melanie stood with the small group of travelers to board. She settled in an empty seat in the quiet car and tried to remember the last time she'd been on the train. When she'd first started working at the White House, she took the train to New York every weekend she could. She'd stay with her older sister, Claire, and they'd wake up early to jog around the reservoir in Central Park. Afterward, they'd order steaming cups of coffee and pastries from one of the bakeries on Madison. If Claire didn't have to work, they'd visit the Met or the Guggenheim and shop at Bloomingdale's and Barneys. At night, Claire would take her to Craft or Pastis or one of her other favorite restaurants. Melanie loved those visits. She'd depart Union Station an underpaid and overworked government staffer and arrive at Penn Station ready to dive into her sister's glamorous New York life. As the head of antique furniture at Sotheby's auction house, her sister ran with a hip, artsy crowd that couldn't be more different from the buttoned-down political types who surrounded Melanie.

This was a very different kind of trip. Melanie had lied to Charlotte about needing to visit Claire to get out of going to Camp David. Charlotte's best friends from college, Brooke and Mark Pfiefer, would be there, Melanie reminded herself, pushing her guilt aside. She tilted her seat back as far as it would go and closed her eyes. Unlike the Acela, which sped to New York in less than two and a half hours, the regional train took more than three and a half hours. Plenty of time for a nap, Melanie thought, covering herself with her coat and turning the ringers down on all her phones and BlackBerrys.

She had known Michael since she first arrived in Washington. One of the last of the old-fashioned "source" reporters, he'd earned a special place in her heart early in the Martin administration when he waited for her outside the White House gate to tell her that he'd seen her husband making out with a twenty-four-year-old legislative aide the night before.

Melanie was one of Michael's best sources at the beginning of her career without even knowing it. He'd befriended her at the bar at the Hay-Adams, where Melanie and other press staffers used to convene after long days in the office. She'd drink big glasses of merlot and enjoy how quickly the alcohol would erase her insecurities. When she met Michael the first time, she'd just been noticed by President Harlow's senior staff for her attention to detail and sharp political antennae.

"Hi there. You look like someone important," he'd said to her the first night they spoke.

"You must have me confused with someone else," Melanie had said, turning back to her friends.

"You're Melanie Kingston, rising star in the White House press operation and the provider of Harlow's daily fix of Florida news."

His lines had been cheesy, but Melanie had desperately wanted his words to be true.

"Uh, I don't know where you get your information, Mr.—" Melanie started to say before he interrupted.

"Michael. Call me Michael," he'd said, taking a seat at the table next to Melanie, shoving a handful of wasabi peas into his mouth, and washing them down with a large gulp of his martini.

"Michael. Well, you have my name right. I'm Melanie."

"I know," he'd said.

"Why did everyone warn me about talking to you? You're not exactly subtle." She'd laughed.

"Maybe that's my secret."

"What are you working on?" she'd asked.

"You really want to know?"

"Sure."

"Doug Fischer is going to be indicted by the end of the week for perjury, and I'm trying to figure out if the special prosecutor has given the president a heads-up," he'd said.

Doug Fischer worked in the White House counsel's office, and he'd testified before a grand jury investigating an unauthorized leak that lead to an undercover FBI agent's cover being blown. The agent had been killed as a result.

"And you know this how?" Melanie had asked.

"My ex-wife is the public affairs officer for the special prosecutor's office, and when I went to pick up my daughter last night, I heard her on the phone. He was asking her to come back in, and the special prosecutors always fill in their press staff at the last minute—always the very last to know anything big, just like the White House, Kingston."

"Does that actually work for you? I mean, do people actually tell you things after you insult them like that?"

He'd laughed. "Believe it or not, they do."

He'd been right about the White House lawyer getting indicted. Melanie had been sitting at her desk in the OEOB when she saw the breaking news on CNN. The OEOB was across the driveway from the West Wing, but it might as well have been on another planet. Melanie had stayed glued to the television all day. President Harlow had given a statement in the East Room shortly after the news broke. Melanie remembered reading in the papers that his communications director, Barry Donaldson, had written the statement on a computer without a hard drive so it wouldn't show up in the White House records in case the White House staffer hadn't been indicted.

I want to have that role someday, Melanie had thought at the time. *I want to be the person the president turns to in the middle of a crisis.*

Melanie and Michael had started meeting periodically at Starbucks across the street from the White House. He'd ask her about the mood at the planning meetings she went to, the cliques at the White House, and rumors about tensions or affairs between various staffers. And there was no shortage of scurrilous gossip to pass along, off the record, of course. When hundreds of young political animals from all across the country spent fifteen-hour days together, seven days a week, working inside the confines of the eighteen acres that made up the White House complex, there was plenty of friction.

Melanie had loved how important she felt meeting Michael for these visits. She didn't realize at the time how valuable her rambling reports of life as a junior staffer were until she'd read an "analysis" piece Michael wrote about President Harlow a few weeks after the indictment.

"It's Business as Usual in President Harlow's White House," the headline had read. The story had gone on to say that "staffers attended meetings for the White House egg roll and planned for a bird flu outbreak just days after the resignation of one of the most powerful aides on the White House staff." Michael had quoted her as an "administration official" saying that "nothing's changed for those of us functioning at the nuts-and-bolts level." His article had concluded that the White House was "out of touch" and "out of line" for refusing to discuss the indictment openly with staff.

Melanie had been mortified when she read the piece and saw slivers of stories she'd shared over the previous weeks reflected and in many cases distorted to fit Michael's thesis that everyone at the White House was in denial. She'd phoned him and told him she needed to see him immediately. He'd laughed and said she was being childish. He'd assured her that he had many sources who told him similar things. Melanie had wanted to believe him, but she was fairly certain that he'd taken her stories and built his mood piece around her account.

"It's unethical," she'd said to him on the phone.

"Lesson number one, Kingston: getting a national security story or an indictment wrong is unethical. Mood stories are all bullshit. My editors wanted a mood story. I trust your judgment about the mood, so I wrote off what I understand to be true from our visits. Take it as a compliment. You're a credible source."

"And you're a piece of shit," she'd retorted.

She didn't talk to him for months. Then, one day, when she was dropping off President Harlow's Florida clips, she'd heard Barry Donaldson, the communications director, on the phone in the West Wing basement. He must have thought he was alone. It was just after six A.M., so it was a reasonable assumption.

"Listen, you need to protect my ass. Can't you ID me as a 'senior government official' instead of a 'senior White House official'? No, not White House official—it needs to be 'senior' so they know it's real. Listen, Harlow is going to dump her like a hot potato—he's just waiting for our friends on the Hill to start complaining in the press. Then he can say that it was a matter of party unity. No, he isn't going to throw her overboard until she embarrasses herself in front of Congress. I know, it's cruel, but life's a bitch. Welcome to the big leagues, Dottie. No, no, you can't quote me on that, no way. Listen, I've gotta go." He'd hung up and rounded the corner, where Melanie was standing in front of the West Wing security guards.

Melanie had kept her head down and tried to avoid making eye contact.

"Hey, Marnie," he'd said.

"Melanie," she'd corrected.

"Right, Melanie. Uh, how long have you been standing here?"

"I just walked in and was on my way to the staff secretary's office," she'd said.

"I've never seen you in the West Wing before."

"I deliver President Harlow's Florida clips each morning."

"You're here at this hour every day to satiate POTUS' obsession with his beloved Sunshine State?"

"Yes, sir," she'd answered. President Harlow had been governor of Florida for eight years before being elected president, and he loved keeping up on his hometown press.

"Cool. Hey, anything you hear over here is classified, right, Leonard?" he'd said, turning to the security guard.

"Whatever you say, sir," he'd said, winking at Melanie.

She'd smiled at the guard. "OK, well, I have to go."

"I'm serious, Melanie. Classified," Donaldson had emphasized.

Her hands had been shaking when she handed the clips over to the staff secretary. She'd felt her stomach tie into a knot and her palms begin to sweat. The president's communications director had been trashing the president's nominee for homeland security secretary. Dottie Flor was President Harlow's pick for the post, and her confirmation process was not going smoothly.

She couldn't go to her boss. Donaldson was her boss's boss. She couldn't go to the chief of staff. He played golf with Donaldson every Saturday. He'd never believe Melanie. She'd waited until ten A.M. and called Michael's number.

"Kingston, how the hell are you?" he'd asked on the first ring.

"I need to see you."

"Usual spot?" he'd asked.

"No, let's meet in Dupont Circle."

They'd met twenty minutes later at the Krispy Kreme on Dupont Circle.

"I think Barry Donaldson is trying to sabotage the president's nominee for secretary of homeland security," Melanie had blurted out as soon as they'd ordered their donuts and coffee.

"Slow down, Kingston. What did you hear?" he'd asked.

"Listen, you burned me once, so I need to do this off the record—like one hundred percent off the record. You can't tie me to this information in any way, shape, or form, or I'll get caught."

"Get caught doing what? Sticking up for the president's nominee? That doesn't sound so bad," he'd said.

"I'm serious."

"OK, OK, Kingston. You got it. Double secret off the record. Now tell me, again, what you heard."

Melanie had told him the whole story, and he was able to confirm it independently with sources on the Hill. The front page of the paper had carried a banner headline the day the story broke: "Top Aide Runs Coordinated Effort to Sink Dottie Flor."

Donaldson had been fired, and Flor had been confirmed. Melanie hadn't slept for a week. She'd kept waiting for the White House chief of staff to hunt her down in her office in the Old Executive Office Building or call her in the middle of the night to accuse her of leaking information. But no one had come after her, and after a while, no one spoke of Donaldson anymore.

Melanie and Michael had remained friends. During the eight years she'd served as press secretary, he often gave her a heads-up when a crisis was about to break. When she took the job as Charlotte's chief of staff, he'd sent her a dozen roses with a note: "I'm always happy when my friends keep their security clearances. Kramer is lucky to have you, Melanie. Fondly, Michael." In her three years as chief of staff, Melanie had hardly spoken to him. He'd been pursuing corrupt members of Congress in recent years, and with his daughter working in the White House, he'd laid off the executive branch, much to Melanie's relief.

Now, when Melanie opened her eyes, the train was forty minutes from New York's Penn Station. She walked back to the dining car for another cup of coffee, then tried to get through the newspapers but found her eyes skimming the words without taking in any of the stories. She kept starting over and ended up reading them out loud to herself to get through them.

She arrived in New York at around ten. She walked out of the train station and pulled her black wool coat tightly around her. She was always surprised by how much colder it was in New York than in D.C.

She got into a cab and gave the driver the address where she was to meet Michael. The cab stopped in front of the diner. Through the window, the crowd looked as if it was made up mostly of tourists. Melanie paid the cab driver and walked inside. She spotted Michael in a booth near the back—a cup of coffee and a copy of the *New York Times* were in front of him.

He smiled at her as she approached. "You look tired as shit," he said.

"Thanks. I feel like shit," Melanie said.

"I didn't say you looked like shit. I said you look tired as shit. There's a difference," he said, smiling again.

"I'm fine. Living the dream," she said.

He laughed and stayed quiet, waiting for her to say more.

"We've been pushing hard—totally off the record, like so off the record that even after it happens, you and I never had this conversation. Charlotte's going to Afghanistan again to be there for their elections, and it's been a bitch to get the trip together. There's still no functioning government, and the military is pissed at Roger over the budget, so they have refused to participate in any of the planning. It's just been a brutal couple weeks," Melanie said.

"How is Charlotte?" he asked.

"She's good."

"Really?"

"Yeah, why?"

"I don't know—she seems distracted when I see her on TV," he said.

"I mean, between the anemic recovery and two wars, she's been dealt a pretty crummy hand, and every time she opens her mouth to discuss any of those topics, her approval ratings go down, but you know Charlotte, she's good. I mean, she never complains, and she takes her lumps. Congress shits all over her, and she still treats them like they're her best friends in the world. I don't know who treats her worse—the Democrats or the Republicans—but she rolls with it. She works her ass off. I've done this for three of them now, and I've never seen anyone like her—she is a machine," Melanie said.

"Maybe that's her problem," Michael said. "With her poll numbers, she needs something big to change the dynamic, or she might get a third-party challenge from the right, and I'm not sure she'd survive that."

"Let me see if I understand this. Her problem is that she works too hard and doesn't pay enough attention to her poll numbers?" Melanie asked, sarcastically.

"No. But one of the problems voters have with her—and you know this as well as I do, Melanie—is that she seems superhuman, you know? She never stops—she doesn't show any emotion. People want to know that she gets pissed, that she gets sad, happy, angry, something."

Melanie looked at him and didn't say anything for nearly a minute. "I'm pretty sure you didn't summon me to New York to give me political advice, Michael," she finally said.

"No, I didn't."

"So, what is it? Peter Kramer is the leader of a polygamist family in Utah? The kids are growing pot at boarding school? What? What crazy conspiracy tale do you have for me?"

"I can see you've lost your sense of humor, Mel, so I'll cut to the chase. I've got a source who claims to have photos, taped conversations, and all sorts of other sordid evidence that Charlotte's marriage is a sham." He stopped to gauge Melanie's reaction.

Melanie laughed. "And in Washington, that makes her what? Part of the silent majority? You didn't drag me here to tell me that you have some loony source who heard rumors that Charlotte is gay or Peter is a swinger, did you? Because I can walk down to the briefing room and get that from any twenty-four-year-old blogger. Jesus, I can see clearly now why journalism is on its last legs. I'm embarrassed for you, Michael."

"Listen, save the pissed-off act for your underlings; I'm sure they love you for it. I came to you because we're friends and because I know it's been an undercurrent for a couple of years, but this feels like it's about to break, and I wanted to give you a chance to work with us and frame it yourself. People will have sympathy for her—I mean, assuming Peter is the one having the affair. If it's her . . ." He stopped.

"If it's her, what?" Melanie asked.

"Well, if it's her, that changes things. You know that."

She fumed silently. She and Charlotte talked about everything. But Charlotte and Peter's marriage was one topic Melanie never asked about. And Charlotte never volunteered any information outside of what was obvious.

Charlotte and Peter Kramer lived separate lives.

But so did every politician on Capitol Hill. Most senators and House members lived one life in Washington and another in their home states and districts. And Peter was the first man ever to fill the role of a first husband. There wasn't exactly a play book for him.

Had she let Charlotte down by not insisting that she appear more often with Peter and the family? Should she have dug deeper about why Peter stayed so far away from the White House most days of the week and every weekend?

"I know how close you and Charlotte are, and I thought you might know what was going on with her, but it's clear you don't," Michael said.

"How do you know I don't?" Melanie asked.

"I know you, Mel. I know you can't always tell me what you know, but I also know when you don't know something. And you don't know what's going on with her and Peter," he said.

He was right.

"If you have it, why haven't you written it yet? The *Dispatch* loves your big scoops," Melanie said.

"You know I hate personal tragedy stories, Melanie, but if I don't do it, someone else will. And if I do it, I'm going to get it right. I don't have the whole thing yet. But I will get it, and I think you know that, too."

"It's not her. I promise you. She'd be a lot less uptight if she was having an affair, but she isn't, Michael," Melanie said, racking her brain to try to solve the riddle.

Who would go to the press now? The list was endless: Republicans trying to get her to step aside so they could run a hard-core conservative; Democrats trying to weaken her so that a third-party candidate could get into the race and split the Republican and independent votes; the Democrats in Congress who wanted to further weaken her so they could run roughshod over her on the budget.

Melanie had long suspected Peter had entanglements, but if he did, he was always discreet. And Charlotte would never do anything. It wasn't even a possibility.

"So, what you can do for me—" Michael started to say before Melanie cut him off.

"What I can do for you? Are you kidding me? Do you think it's still my job to run around and chase down every lead you have, no matter where your crazy tips take me?" She was starting to lose her cool, and she hated how her voice sounded.

"Melanie, I can do this with or without you, as you well know."

"I know, I know. Damn, damn, damn. Let me think, Michael. Let me think," she said.

"You're burning the candle at both ends, and I know this is a lot to take in. Why don't we talk in a few days, and I'll let you know what I learn."

"You're really going after this story, huh?" Melanie asked.

"Of course I am. The country elects the whole package—the man or woman, the mother or father, the husband or wife. Isn't that what you always told me during the campaigns when you pushed me to write shit about Martin's political opponents? The fact that you are my friend doesn't change any of that, Melanie."

As she looked Michael in the eye for the first time that morning, she felt she was seeing him for the first time in her life. His dark brown hair was streaked with gray. The lines around his mouth and eyes had deepened since she'd first met him. He was handsome in the scruffy, badly dressed, cigarette-breath kind of way that only a reporter can be handsome. All she could do was look at him. And then exhaustion hit her like a wave. She was suddenly so tired she couldn't form a sentence or a thought. She just stared at him and tried to will herself to stand up and walk out. She felt as if she was in a nightmare where you want to run but your legs are stuck in concrete. So she stayed. He ordered pancakes, and she pointed at the picture of toast on the menu. She wasn't sure how long she sat there and nodded and smiled while he went on about how much Elizabeth was learning at the White House and about how Charlotte should dump her vice president.

Something was ringing.

"Are you going to get that? It looks like the Situation Room," Michael said, pointing at her phone.

Melanie stared at her phone. She knew it was Charlotte. She didn't want to talk to her in front of Michael, but she couldn't let it ring, because the Situation Room never gave up. They'd call all her cell-phone numbers, her sister, her mother, and then start over with her cell phones again. She picked up.

"This is Melanie," she said.

"Brooke and Mark tried to smoke a joint at Camp David," Charlotte said. She sounded as if she was laughing—something she didn't do much of, but she always lightened up when Brooke and Mark were around. Charlotte's college friends had caused Melanie plenty of headaches over the years. Brooke and Mark had no idea how they were supposed to act now that their best friend was the president. They threw Charlotte a huge party at their beach house in Coronado for her forty-fifth birthday, and a near-naked man jumped out of a cake. The White House press corps had a field day when they caught wind of it from one of the guests. As far as presidential pals went, they were hardly the worst Melanie had seen. President Martin's old buddies from business school used to bring young women back to the residence at all hours to party in the bowling alley and skinny-dip in the pool. Melanie sighed deeply.

"I'm going to have to call you back. My sister and I are at brunch, and it's pretty loud in here," Melanie said.

"OK, but hurry up. I had them flush it down the toilet, but I just want to be ready in case, you know, I mean, do you think that was a good idea? Oh, damn, here they come—call me back, Mel," Charlotte said.

Melanie pulled two twenty-dollar bills out of her wallet and tried to catch the attention of their waitress. She didn't want to leave with Michael thinking she was upset. That would make things worse.

"I appreciate that you came to me, really, I do, I just don't know what you expect me to do with this information," Melanie told him.

"There's nothing you can do. I just thought I owed it to you to tell you what I was working on. I won't publish anything without giving you a head-up."

"Thanks for that, at least," she said wryly.

"I've got breakfast. Why don't you get out of here? Get some rest, Melanie. Unfortunately, I think things are going to get tougher before they get easier."

"Sounds like it," she said, trying to sound airy.

CHAPTER EIGHT

Dale

"Hi, honey, I'm home," Dale announced as she entered Peter's rented colonial in Washington, Connecticut. She'd made the drive in less than an hour and a half. It was a new record.

He rushed to the entryway and helped her take her coat off with one hand and pulled her to him with the other. He kissed her. "How was your day, dear?" he asked.

It was one of their inside jokes, pretending they were a normal couple. She smiled and kissed him back. She was where she belonged, and her whole body melted into his embrace. She moved her hands to his face and held it to hers.

He pulled back and looked at her. "You hungry?" he asked.

She laughed. "I'm starving. What are you cooking?" She noticed the massive undertaking in the kitchen for the first time. Appliances lined the kitchen counter. A bread maker appeared to be heating up. The food processor was in use, and various blades and attachments littered the countertop. At least half a dozen pots and pans were spread from the stovetop to the butcher block.

"How long have you been in there?" Dale asked.

"It took me a while to get started. I dragged the agents back to the store three times for things I forgot. I'm making homemade pasta with peas and crab. Sound good?"

"Sounds wonderful," she said.

Dale slid in next to him in the kitchen, and they chopped and steamed and sautéed and boiled as effortlessly as they seemed to do everything else together. He handed her a glass of wine, and they cooked and drank in silence for a while.

"So, what's going on in that head of yours tonight?" he asked.

"I need to tell you something, and I know you're not going to be excited, but you need to be excited for me, because it's a really good thing," Dale said.

"You're leaving me for a man who can take you on a date in a restaurant?" he asked.

"Very funny," Dale said. She'd trade a million dates at fancy restaurants for one night with Peter. "I'm going to Afghanistan," she said, lifting her wine glass to her mouth and taking a large sip as soon as the words were out.

He lifted his glass and did the same. "I think you'll be very happy there, honey. I hear Kabul is beautiful in March," he said.

"I'm serious. I'm going with Charlotte for the elections. The White House is taking a very small press pool, and they asked me to go."

They hadn't exactly asked for her, but she was going. They'd invited the network, and Billy had insisted that they take Dale.

Peter stopped chopping and looked at her. He didn't move toward her or say anything; he just looked at her. Dale's heart was racing. She needed this trip. She was slipping away from the hard-news circles at her network. It was a trap she'd seen many women in the business fall into. She knew that if she did too many soft profiles and easy interviews, she'd be on a fast track to daytime cable. She wanted to anchor an evening newcast someday. She needed to keep herself in regular rotation for substitute anchor during the week. She needed to be seen in a war zone with the president. And she wanted Peter to be happy for her.

"I'll be with Charlotte the whole time, and nothing is ever going to happen to her. The military will make sure of it. I'll be fine. I promise," she said, smiling hopefully up at Peter.

"It's been really bad lately. There are no safe places in Afghanistan right now, so you can't promise me that you'll be fine," he said.

"You can't guarantee my safety when I drive the two hours here and back every weekend," Dale answered.

Peter winced. "You're right. I can't even protect you from a traffic accident. But I do know a lot about these places, Dale. Charlotte's been going over there for years. She takes risks I wish that the mother of my children wouldn't take, but I gave up my right to weigh in on the chances she takes with her life when—" He stopped and looked away from her.

"What? When you started cheating on her with me?" Dale said, sounding defensive.

"When I fell in love with you," Peter said quietly.

Dale moved toward him. He stiffened at first but then put his arms around her and pulled her toward him.

"Nothing is going to happen," she promised.

He sighed deeply.

"Do you have any idea how much I love you?" she asked as Peter stroked her hair and held her to him.

"Mmm," he said.

She stood on her toes to kiss him. He put his hands on both sides of her face and looked her in the eye.

"You are the only thing that propels me through my own strange existence, and I wish I could make you understand how frightened I am by the thought of you going over there without making you feel like I'm not supportive of your career."

"I do understand, but I am not making the choice that you think I'm making," Dale said.

Peter gave her a look she couldn't read. She tried to kiss him, but he pulled his face away from hers. She leaned into his chest, and they stood like that for a long moment. Then he sighed again and stepped back. He put his hand under her chin and looked into her eyes.

"You don't owe any explanation or apology to a man who can't walk down the street with you and hold your hand."

She stood on her toes and tried to kiss him again. She was desperate to show him what she couldn't tell him, that she would choose him, that she wouldn't make any other choice when he was hers. But right now, there was no excuse she could offer her colleagues at the network. She had no family and no personal life that she could claim, and until that changed, the holiday shifts and hazard assignments were hers for the taking.

"I'm sorry that I've put you in this situation. I can't help but wonder if you'd be risking your life on a trip like this if you were married to some nice guy who could give you the life you deserve instead of sneaking around with me," Peter said.

"The answer is yes. I'd still be taking a trip like this, because this is what I do. I cover the president of the United States, and she is going to Afghanistan, so that's where I have to go to cover her. And you are the nice guy who gives me more happiness than I deserve," Dale said, moving closer to him and planting kisses on his neck.

He was kissing her back now. He lifted her off the floor, and she wrapped her legs around his waist. He set her down on the kitchen counter and unbuttoned her blouse. She kissed him hungrily and pulled his body closer to hers with her legs. He buried his head in the space between her collar bone and her shoulder. She couldn't get close enough to him. She kept pulling him closer, and soon their bodies moved as one.

CHAPTER NINE

Charlotte

"H ere," Brooke said, handing Charlotte a cigarette.

"That's just a cigarette, right?" Charlotte quipped.

"Of course. Come on, I'm sorry about last night. I thought you could use a good laugh. I forgot it was, you know." Brooke stopped to take a sip of her wine.

"Illegal? You forgot it was illegal?" Charlotte said, laughing at how ridiculous her life was sometimes.

"It's medicinal. I get migraines."

"I think I made that illegal, too," Charlotte reminded her.

"That's why you're so unpopular in California now," Brooke said.

"Thank God you're here. You're a genius. I can fire my pollsters." Charlotte grinned. It felt good to be with people she'd known long before her life had become so limited. It also hurt like hell to be with people she couldn't fool about what her life had become.

Brooke and Mark were Charlotte's best friends from college. The three of them had been inseparable at Berkeley, and their friendship was one of the few things Charlotte could rely on never to change. Peter had joined the threesome when he and Charlotte started dating during their junior year. He'd been visiting Berkeley for the Cal-UCLA football game. He was injured that season, so he'd made the round of pregame parties. His first stop had been a party at Mark's fraternity. Mark and Peter were best friends from home, and when Charlotte and Peter fell in love, he'd rounded out their group perfectly. Peter had taken Southwest Airlines to the Bay Area almost every weekend to hang out with Charlotte and Brooke and Mark. After college graduation, he'd gone to law school at Hastings in San Francisco, and Charlotte had gone to business school at Stanford. Hastings was a good law school, but Stanford was one of the best business schools in the country. It was the first time Charlotte had outshone Peter, but they were young and happy and in love, and it hadn't come between them. They had shared a two-bedroom apartment in Pacific Heights with Brooke and Mark, and the four of them had been a single unit. They'd vacationed together, spent every night on the weekends together, drank Bloody Marys at tailgate parties before football games together, and shared the laidback life of successful twenty-somethings together.

Now that Charlotte was president, Brooke and Mark shared those moments, too. Charlotte looked over at her friend and thought back to her first night at the White House. Brooke and Mark had spent the night after Charlotte's inauguration. It was one for the history books. Brooke had read online about ghosts in the Lincoln Bedroom, so she'd refused to stay there. There was a second guest room on that floor called the Queen's Room, where she and Mark had stayed that night and on all subsequent visits. Brooke had run around the residence scantily clad in a nightgown until Charlotte went to her closet, where her clothes had miraculously been unpacked, pressed, and organized during the day's events, and pulled out a robe for Brooke to cover up with. Brooke had rummaged through the family kitchen looking for a blender and ingredients for frozen margaritas. She'd found margarita mix but no tequila.

"The Martins wiped you out, Char. They took everything. There isn't even any tonic water in here," Brooke had shouted from the small kitchen.

"He was a former alcoholic. They didn't keep anything here, I'm sure," Charlotte had shouted back, laughing to herself as she wondered what kind of impression she was making on the White House ushers during her first hours as its new resident.

Even Peter had seemed excited that night. It was one of the nights Charlotte let herself believe that her marriage could recover. Charlotte almost laughed out loud when she remembered that Brooke had settled for gin in her margarita mix that night, and they'd all sat up drinking Brooke's disgusting concoction in the Yellow Oval.

Brooke stamped her cigarette out on the deck with her two-thousand-dollar Hermès riding boots and lit another one, bringing Charlotte back to the present.

"It's a tie for best perk—Camp David and Air Force One. I love it here," she said. "I get to wear all my country clothes." She fingered her cashmere blazer.

"I'm so happy that the whole presidential retreat thing works for you," Charlotte said, laughing at her friend. Brooke wore her hair in a short blond bob. She had pale blue eyes and a splash of freckles across her nose, but her prim looks were misleading. She drank most men, including her husband, under the table and swore like a sailor. And she was born without the gene that prevented one from saying things that were impolite or inappropriate.

"How are you and Peter?" she asked.

"Same," Charlotte said, inhaling deeply on her cigarette. She made a mental note to quit smoking as soon as she got back from Afghanistan.

"I'm sorry, Charlotte," Brooke said.

"It's OK. I was just thinking back to the night after the inauguration. Can you believe that was three years ago? Peter seemed happy then, didn't he?" Charlotte asked.

"He did, but you know, maybe he was just hammered. I think we started drinking at four in the afternoon," Brooke said.

Charlotte laughed. "Maybe. I can't remember the happy stuff anymore. I know it happened, but I can't remember any of it."

"You guys were happy," Brooke said.

"How does Peter seem to you?" Charlotte asked.

"He seems good. You know, he's Peter—always acts positive and seems to love having the weekends with the kids. It has to be lonely, though, Char. He loved being half of Charlotte and Peter. He loved it more than you did," Brooke said.

"That's not true. I loved it, too. We just outgrew each other."

"You outgrew him, Charlotte. You were always one step ahead of him. I think it almost killed him to try to keep up with you. You were always overachieving and standing out in the crowd, and he was so proud of you, he couldn't stand it," she said.

"Mmm," Charlotte murmured.

"I remember when you won the governor's race, his head spun for about thirty days. He went to bed with a successful Internet executive and woke up with a governor. And then you were off, Char—no one could stop you. And now you're the goddamned president of the United States of America. Do you have that song? 'Hail to the Chief'? Can we play it at dinner?" Brooke giggled and poured herself more wine.

Charlotte sighed. "So it's my fault? I ran too fast, and I should have waited for him to catch up? I'm a selfish, ambitious bitch who put my career ahead of my marriage and ahead of my family?"

"No, Char. You've got incredible kids. You're my best friend, and you're the president. And for right now, that's gotta be enough for you. You'll have time after all this with Peter. He's not going anywhere," Brooke said.

Charlotte poured more wine into her glass and took a sip.

"Oh, Char, I shouldn't have said all that. What's wrong with me? Why do you put up with me?" Brooke asked.

Just then, Mark approached with a tray of martinis. "Cocktail hour, ladies—come, come," he said.

Charlotte laughed. "I thought that's what this was," she said, pointing to the empty bottle of wine between them.

"No, that was a gift from Napa Valley to remind you of your California roots. This is cocktail hour," he said, handing her a martini.

They sipped martinis, and Brooke and Mark filled Charlotte in on the gossip from their old college circle of friends. At around seven P.M., they moved into the dining room for dinner.

"You heading back to Afghanistan anytime, Char?" Mark asked.

"It's still top secret, so don't blab to anyone, but yeah, I am working on a trip. I want to be there for their elections," she said.

"I admire the hell out of you for going as often as you do," Mark said, "but I don't know what you think is going to change between trips. It took them hundreds of years to get into this mess—it's going to take longer than you have to fix it."

"Well, that doesn't mean that we can't make progress," Charlotte said.

"And I imagine it's a real morale boost for the troops, right, Char?" Brooke added.

"Exactly. It also provides comfort to the military families back here to see that the president hasn't forgotten about the wars their sons and daughters and husbands and wives are fighting."

"Come on, admit it, you feel like a total bad-ass riding in those humvees and checking out all that heavy artillery," Mark teased.

"You're a buffoon," Charlotte said, balling up her napkin and throwing it at him.

"I might be a buffoon, but I am a buffoon who has stocked your wine cellar downstairs with a tremendous supply of California wines for the summer. I can't wait till it warms up and we can barbecue out here," Mark said.

"Do you think we can just lurk around here all summer, honey? Charlotte is running for reelection this year. She's going to be on the campaign trail, not up here manning the barbecue with you, you fool," Brooke said, swatting her husband playfully.

"Ouch. You two are on your brooms tonight. I'm going to go smoke my cigar alone after dinner." Mark laughed.

They ate lamb chops and grilled asparagus and drank more of the wine that Brooke and Mark had brought from Napa Valley. After dinner, they returned to the deck, which Charlotte kept heated year-round. The dogs snuggled on top of their feet, and the three of them talked until after midnight about the stock market and the price of real estate in the San Francisco Bay Area, where Charlotte planned to return if she lost the election.

"What would you do, Char?" Brooke asked.

"She could do anything she wanted, honey," Mark said. Brooke shushed him.

"I don't know what I'd do, to be honest. Let me know if you come up with any ideas."

"Charlotte, it isn't going to happen. You're going to win. I know it," Mark said, stifling a yawn.

"You guys don't need to stay up—go get some rest," Charlotte urged.

Mark stood up and held his hand out for Brooke. "Are you ready for bed, my little drunk?"

"I resent that comment," Brooke said, standing up and swaying side-to-side.

"You coming inside, Char?" Mark asked.

"I'll be in soon. I'm going to sit here a little longer," she said, standing up to kiss them good night.

As she settled back down, she relished feeling normal. Other than Brooke and Mark, her parents, and her children, there wasn't any relationship that hadn't been dramatically altered by her ascension to the presidency.

After a few minutes, she went inside to make a pot of decaf. She sat watching it drip into the pot.

"Char, you sure you're okay?" Mark said.

She hadn't heard him enter the room, and she jumped when he spoke.

"I'm sorry. I didn't mean to startle you," Mark said. "You seemed a little lost in thought tonight. I wanted to make sure you're not down. Brooke told me that her Tourette's syndrome kicked in tonight before dinner."

"You're sweet to check on me. I'm fine. Want some coffee? It's decaf."

"Sure, I'll take a cup. Brooke passed out already."

Charlotte smiled.

"So, what's going on? Is it classified, or can you tell me?" Mark asked.

"No, it's nothing like that. Things aren't going very well, as you know. My approval numbers are in the high twenties and low thirties. There's no chance I'll be reelected, but I can't exactly acknowledge that, so we just go through the motions of a campaign, and I lose anyway. It's like fighting a battle that you know you can't win. It's tough to get fired up for it, you know?"

Mark nodded. "I do."

They watched the dogs readjust themselves on the sofas where they were sleeping.

"I've got something for you—it's not much, but it's something," he offered.

"What?" she asked.

"Will came home and told Brooke he wanted to enlist in the Marine Corps, but only if you are elected president again in November."

"You're joking," Charlotte said.

"I wish I were. Our only son wants to fight for his country. Brooke is beside herself, and I'm not thrilled about it, either, to be honest. But what's remarkable is that he is only going to go through with it if you win. He only wants to serve his country if you are its commander in chief."

Charlotte swallowed a lump in her throat. "Jesus, Mark, I don't know what to say. Why didn't Brooke say anything?"

"She refuses to believe that he'll go through with it, and she said it would be the only silver lining for any of us if you lose."

Charlotte put her hand on Mark's. They finished their coffee in silence. He took his cup to the sink and then walked over to where Charlotte was still sitting.

"Get some rest," he ordered, giving her a kiss on the cheek.

"Good night." She smiled.

CHAPTER TEN

Melanie

Melanie spent Saturday night at the Ritz on Central Park South. She ordered room service for dinner and watched pay-per-view movies in her room. She kept her cell phone on but shut off the BlackBerrys. She slept in on Sunday morning and got a massage before heading to the airport for a flight home to D.C.

She went straight to her office. She and Ralph were meeting to talk about the reelection campaign. Charlotte had stopped trying to get an answer from Melanie about running the campaign, but she wanted to see their plan before she left for Afghanistan.

Ralph was in her office when she walked in.

"Hi, Ralph. You're two hours early," Melanie said.

"Didn't you get my e-mails?" he asked.

"No. I had some personal business that I was dealing with this weekend."

"Oh, well, listen, all my polling models show that the president's numbers are in a free fall. She has to either dump the VP or pull out—she can't win on the current path. Her approval on domestic policy is twenty-eight percent; foreign policy is better but not reflected in her overall approval number. Forty-three percent approve of her job in foreign affairs, but only twenty-four percent think she's a strong leader, and only nineteen percent think she relates to people's problems," Ralph reported.

Melanie's head started to pound. She shoved three Excedrin Migraine pills into her mouth and washed them down with a swig of Diet Coke. She stared at Ralph's ruddy complexion and receding hairline. He was so unattractive Melanie almost felt sorry for him.

"What's the bottom line, Ralph?" she asked.

"The bottom line is that she needs a miracle."

"You mean, we need a miracle, don't you, Ralph? We're responsible for her numbers—we write her speeches and bring her the policies that people say they hate in that poll. We need a miracle, Ralph."

"Yeah, whatever, we need a miracle," he said.

"What's going on with the third-party movement?" Melanie asked.

"There are some rumblings that the social conservatives are going to run a candidate against her, but it won't be anyone real. The base is happy enough with her leadership in Iraq and Afghanistan and her tough stand on taxes, so they won't get behind a third-party challenger."

"I suppose that passes for good news," Melanie said.

"Uh, do you want me to talk to her?" Ralph asked.

"No, I don't want to bring it up until after her trip," Melanie told him. "Let's just tell her we are working on a strategy, and we'll go over it when she gets back."

Ralph shuffled out of her office to return to his windowless cave down the hall. Melanie had offered him a vast suite of offices on the second floor of the West Wing, but he'd insisted on being on the first floor where Melanie and the vice president and national security advisor had offices. Melanie rubbed her head and prayed for a little miracle of her own. If she could avoid talking to Charlotte about the campaign until after she returned from Afghanistan, she could figure out what to do. She could think about what Michael had told her for a few more days and come up with a better strategy for telling the president what she probably already knew: that she couldn't win reelection unless something drastic happened.

Annie appeared at her door with a worried look. "She wants you to meet her on the South Lawn," she said.

"Seriously? Right now?" Melanie asked, squeezing her eyes shut and opening them to try to get rid of the spots she was seeing in front of Annie's face.

"Yeah. Sam said she's playing fetch with the dogs and would love some company," Annie said.

"Wonderful. Can I borrow your coat?" Melanie asked.

She walked out to the South Lawn, where Charlotte was flinging a bright orange ball with a device called the Super Chuck-It. The two younger dogs ran like wild horses after the ball. Cammie sat next to Charlotte as if she was supervising.

"Go run, Cammie, go play with Emma and Mika. You need some exercise, peanut, go run," Charlotte urged. The dog just stared at her.

"How was the weekend?" Melanie asked.

"It was really nice. You were missed, but Brooke and Mark were in rare form."

"Did their kids come?" Melanie asked.

"No, it was just Brooke and Mark. I think they're going to miss Camp David more than I am if I lose." Charlotte laughed.

Melanie didn't have the energy to offer Charlotte the usual assurances about how she would not lose. She looked down at her Black-Berry.

"How's Claire?" Charlotte asked.

"Huh?"

"Your sister? Didn't you spend the weekend with Claire?" Charlotte asked.

"Yes, yes, she's fine. We had a nice dinner, and we did some shopping. It was good to see her. Are you all set for the trip?"

"Yes, and I can't wait to get out of here. We go to the stupid press dinner, and then the motorcade comes back to the White House, and we'll pretend that I'm going upstairs, and then I'll change, and we'll drive out to Andrews, right?"

"Exactly. We'll give the press a full lid. They'll find out the next day that you flew to Afghanistan overnight. The press that's going with you will be waiting on Air Force One for you."

"So they'll miss the dinner?"

"I guess so," Melanie said.

"That won't work." Charlotte frowned.

"Why not?" Melanie asked.

"Won't the press notice that some of their colleagues aren't at the dinner? Won't that set off alarms? They live for the idiotic dinners."

"It's a very small press pool. We're only taking the wire guys, one newsmag, and Dale Smith and her crew," Melanie said.

"We're taking Dale Smith to the front lines?" Charlotte asked, surprised.

"Yeah. I tried to get Billy to send their new Pentagon reporter, but he refused, and I couldn't pull them out of rotation again. We've skipped them twice."

Charlotte sighed loudly.

"What?" Melanie asked.

"Nothing. It's just that she's never seen combat, and I don't like to use these trips to break in new war correspondents for the networks."

"Do you want me to call Billy about it? He'd probably make a swap if I said it was a personal request from you," Melanie offered.

"No, no. Don't do that. It'll be fine. I'm more concerned about the press pool missing the dinner and arousing suspicion."

"Would you rather we let them go to the dinner and then to Andrews in a car that follows yours?" Melanie asked.

"Yeah, I think that's safer. I don't want anyone to suspect anything until we are on the ground in Afghanistan."

"I understand. It's no problem. I'll have the press office handle the logistics," Melanie said, rubbing her head as she sent Annie an e-mail asking her to call the press secretary in right away.

"You look terrible. Are you coming down with something? Go see Dr. Holden for some Ambien or something. You look like you could use a good night's sleep," Charlotte said.

"I'm fine. Just tired."

"Take care of yourself, Melanie. I need you in fighting form."

"It'll be good to catch up while you guys are gone. I'll spend some time with Ralph, and we'll get a plan together for the campaign," Melanie told her.

"Yeah, how's that going? I gave Ralph permission to poll on everything from my hair to my clothes to my children's after-school activities. Anything come out of the data that's encouraging?"

"Not sure. We didn't go over it in detail yet," Melanie said.

"Melanie, I'm not an idiot. I know that barring some act of God, I'm in deep shit. All we have to do is leave everything on the field. And we should be able to come up with some way to turn my political position into an asset, don't you think? We should run the 'nothing but the truth' campaign or something that conveys that we have nothing to lose, so we'll put it all out there and let voters decide."

"Put it all out there, huh?" Melanie asked.

"Sure, why not? Stand on our record, take questions from real people, do some interviews, and let the chips fall where they may," Charlotte urged.

"Madam President—" Melanie started to say.

"Uh-oh, I'm Madam President now. Something really is wrong."

"Is there anything going on that I should know about—anything on the personal side of the house?" Melanie asked.

"No. Why do you ask?"

"It's just, you know, I need to be read in on everything to do my job effectively, and if there's something out there that could have an impact on the administration, it's best if I can plan for it," Melanie said. "Whatever it is."

"I'm not sure what you're suggesting, but I think I resent the implication that I'm withholding information from you."

"That's not what I'm saying. It's just, if there's anything else I can do to help—to support you," Melanie said.

"You can start by agreeing to run the campaign and then coming up with some glimmer of hope for getting me reelected."

"Yes, ma'am," Melanie said.

Charlotte turned and flung the ball so far that the dogs lost its scent and started to whine for a new one.

"Emma, Emma, it's over there!" Charlotte shouted, pointing as though the dog could understand her wild gestures.

Melanie watched Charlotte try to cajole the dogs. She wasn't having much success, and after a few attempts to get them to run down the hill after the lost ball, she pulled another one out of her pocket and flung it toward the two younger dogs. Cammie remained seated by her side.

Melanie turned to Cammie and knelt down on the ground to scratch her head. The dog raised her lip to bare her teeth and growled.

"Jesus, was it something I said?" Melanie stepped away from the dog.

"Cammie, stop it," Charlotte said. "Ignore her. She's tense. She senses that I'm leaving again." Charlotte planted kisses on the dog's head.

Melanie sighed and turned to walk back to her West Wing office. "I'm going to go make these changes to the departure plan, Madam President."

"Thank you, Melanie," Charlotte said, swinging the Chuck-It back and forth and looking out toward the Washington Monument.

"Anything else I can do for you?" Melanie asked.

"Nothing I can think of," Charlotte murmured, her eyes not moving from the monument.

CHAPTER ELEVEN

Dale

D ale left Peter's place so late she almost missed the Sunday newscast. She didn't know exactly when they'd leave for Afghanistan, but she was pretty sure she wouldn't get to spend time with Peter again before she left. When he'd gotten up to make coffee, she'd followed him to the kitchen. They'd sat on the couch together under a blanket and held hands while they stared at the Sunday morning talk shows.

He'd walked her out to the car and held her to him before she left.

"I don't want to go now," Dale had said, clinging to him.

"I'll see you when you get back. You're going to be fine. It's going to be amazing. *You're* going to be amazing."

He'd kissed her on the forehead and opened the driver's-side door. Dale had climbed in, put on her seatbelt, and started the car. Tears had run down her face as she pulled out of the driveway. She wanted to race back inside and assure Peter that she would be fine—that they would be fine.

She made it to the newsroom in time to read through her scripts once while she had her hair and makeup done. She pulled an emerald-green jacket on over black slacks and a black silk tank. She raced into the anchor chair with bare feet twenty seconds before the show started.

"Good Sunday evening," she said with her dazzling smile. "Vio-

lence rocked Afghanistan again today. Our chief foreign-affairs correspondent has the story."

While Dale was on the air, the White House press secretary called
and left a message with details about the trip: "We'll leave from the
White House immediately following the correspondents' dinner
Wednesday night. You'll ride in the president's motorcade from the
dinner, and then we'll put you guys in a car that'll take you out to
Andrews. Bring whatever you need to the press office Wednesday
morning before five A.M. Call us back if you have any questions."

Dale rushed to the airport after the newscast to catch the last
shuttle to D.C. She called Peter on the way and was relieved to get his
voice-mail.

"We go Wednesday. I will call you tomorrow. Love you," she said.

Dale spent her two days off shopping and packing for the trip.

She stopped by the Patagonia store in Georgetown to look for a
thin fleece to fit under her flak jacket. Dale pulled three different sizes
and colors and was changing into them in front of a full-length mirror near the back of the store when she saw Stephanie Taylor, Roger's
wife, looking at men's fleece vests.

She caught her eye and waved.

"Hi, Mrs. Taylor," Dale said. "Dale Smith. I interviewed you about
a year ago about your work with injured vets."

"Of course, we watch you every night, or I watch you every night.
It's not like Roger's ever home at that hour," she said, smiling tightly.
"He's usually off saving the world with Charlotte."

"I'm so glad you watch. I imagine it's been a very busy time for
Secretary Taylor," Dale said.

"Yes, he keeps saying it will slow down, but I haven't seen any evidence of that," Stephanie said.

Dale smiled sympathetically. Everyone liked Stephanie Taylor.
She was the most politically active spouse of any defense secretary
in history. She served as an advocate for various veterans' groups
and had testified on Capitol Hill about the need to provide funds
for spouses and children of injured troops so they could afford to
stay in town while their loved ones recovered at the area's military
hospitals.

"Can I tell you something super-secret and ask you not to tell anyone, not even your husband?" Dale asked Stephanie.

"If I couldn't keep a secret, people like you would know it by now," Stephanie said.

"I'm going on the trip this week," Dale whispered. She'd been given strict instructions not to tell anyone, not even her family, but Roger always accompanied Charlotte to the war zones, so Dale assumed Stephanie knew.

"This week?" Stephanie asked.

"Yes, Wednesday night," Dale said.

Stephanie looked puzzled.

"I was told by the press office that Roger was a late addition but that he'd decided to come on the trip this week to be there for meetings with his counterpart. Did I get that wrong?" Dale asked.

"The White House press office or the Pentagon press office?" Stephanie asked.

"The White House," Dale said.

"Of course," Stephanie said.

Now Dale was confused. Maybe Stephanie was pretending not to know because it was forbidden to discuss the president's travel to the region.

"I'm sorry. I understand that you can't say anything. I shouldn't have mentioned it. I could get in a lot of trouble. Please don't tell Secretary Taylor," Dale begged. "If they think I broke the confidentiality agreement, they could cancel the entire trip because of me."

Stephanie regained her composure and put one arm around Dale's shoulder. "Don't worry. I won't say anything. Is this your first time?"

"Yes."

"Then you need some of these," Stephanie advised, walking Dale over to the heavy-duty hiking boots. "Your feet will bleed the first day, but after that, they'll fit like a glove."

"Thanks," Dale said, picking up a pair in her size.

"Be safe over there," Stephanie told her.

"Will do. And I'd love to interview you again about the work you do for veterans."

"I'll look forward to it." Stephanie smiled, waving over her shoulder as she left the store.

Dale paid for her boots and fleece. She was furious at herself for opening her big mouth. Stephanie's reaction had been so strange that she double-checked the coded message the White House press office had sent her the day before when she'd asked who was traveling to Afghanistan. It simply read: "In response to your q, POTUS, SEC DEF, dep. COS, NSA, MIL AIDES and Pool." Translated, the list meant that the president, the secretary of defense, the deputy chief of staff, the national security advisor, military aides, and the press pool were all making the trip.

When she got home, she packed and repacked her bag a dozen times and then lay in bed checking and rechecking the two alarms set for three A.M. She was too nervous to sleep. She was already in the shower when the alarms went off. She dressed carefully in a black Akris suit with a purple blouse underneath—the first of three outfit changes before taking off for Afghanistan that night. The black suit was for her live shots on the seven A.M. and the six-thirty P.M. newscasts. A bright pink strapless gown went into a garment bag for the correspondents' dinner, and a pair of jeans and a turtleneck sweater were folded and stowed in a tote bag for the flight to Afghanistan. She pulled a coat on over her suit and carried her bags down to the garage.

Dale drove the two miles to the White House and approached the security barricade on E Street where the press office had told her to enter. She rolled down her window, and a Secret Service agent in a black jumpsuit approached.

"Hi. I'm supposed to park on the driveway and drop some things off for transport to Andrews," she said.

"ID, please," he said.

She handed him her D.C. driver's license.

"Pull up to that spot there, and turn off the motor, please," he said.

Dale did as she was told and held her breath while a large German shepherd sniffed her car and examined the contents of her trunk. There was no reason to hold her breath, but the process was nerve-racking.

"Head up to the next gate, and show him your ID, Miss Smith," the agent said.

"Thank you," Dale said.

The large black pillars lowered into the ground, and she drove onto the closed street and toward the next security checkpoint. She was cleared for entry at the next gate and waited while a large iron fence swung open. She drove inside the White House complex and parked in an open spot. She pulled her bag out of her trunk and walked over to a white van, where she saw a couple of reporters she recognized doing the same thing.

"Good morning," she said to them.

"Morning," they replied.

Dale left her bag and walked to the spot on the front driveway of the White House where she'd give a report for that day's morning news show. She had plenty of time before her live shot, so she decided to walk across the street for coffee.

She checked her cell phone and saw a text from Peter: "I will see u at the dinner 2nite."

"Really? What happened?" Dale responded.

"Ralph must want to improve Charlotte's poll numbers among sports fans," Peter wrote back.

"I'll be the one in pink," Dale texted.

"I'm sure you'll be hard to miss," Peter wrote.

Dale smiled and put her phone back into her purse. She ordered a mocha and sipped it slowly as she walked back toward the front lawn of the White House. She laughed to herself as she thought about an alternative report for her morning live shot: "Today, the president will accompany her cheating husband to the White House corre-spondents' dinner, where she will pretend to enjoy the company of her disrespectful and annoying press corps. Immediately following the dinner, President Kramer will get into a motorcade, where the slut her husband is sleeping with will ride in a car behind her to Andrews Air Force Base. From there, President Kramer will sneak out of Washington en route to Afghanistan."

Dale laughed at her own dark humor and took another sip of cof-fee. The sugar and caffeine were hitting her system and warming her from the inside out. She couldn't remember the last time she'd eaten.

She bounced through her morning live shot and the rest of her day. The president's schedule included a meeting with her economic team to discuss the challenges facing small businesses, an event honoring Women's Heart Health Month, and a meeting with the British prime minister.

After her live report for the evening newscast, Dale went into the ladies' room in the West Wing of the White House and stepped into the floor-length pink gown. Layers of fabric skimmed her body. She slid into a pair of heels and stuffed her cell phone and BlackBerry into her evening bag. A few of the correspondents shared a car to the Washington Hilton. They arrived seconds before all roads were closed to accommodate the arrival of the president's motorcade.

The White House correspondents' dinner was jokingly referred to as Washington's "Prom Night." Reporters, not known for their devotion to fashion or style, donned formal attire one night a year, and many tried to pull off looks that didn't flatter their figures or the decade. The president, not known for her affection for the press that beat her up day in and day out, had to attend hours of cocktail receptions followed by a four-hour dinner in which her success would be determined by how hard she made them laugh. She'd also have to endure a comedy act by some B-list celebrity who would tell a new version of the same jokes they told every year about Charlotte wearing the pants in her marriage and scaring the crap out of everyone from her husband to her Cabinet.

No wonder Charlotte can't wait to get to the war zone, Dale thought to herself.

She passed through the metal detectors and made her way to her table. Billy was already there.

"You ready for tonight?" he whispered.

"I think so. Thanks for making them take me," Dale whispered back, hugging him warmly. He was her biggest champion at the network, and his close relationship with Melanie had come in handy more than once.

"They're lucky to get you. I told Melanie that if anything happens to you, I'll kill her," Billy said in a low voice.

Dale laughed nervously.

"You got a custom-fitted flak jacket, right?" Billy whispered in her ear.

Dale nodded.

"Take care of yourself over there, Dale. I need you in one piece." Billy hugged Dale again before turning to greet the secretary of the treasury, who was seated on his other side.

CHAPTER TWELVE

Charlotte

C harlotte had thirty minutes to kill before the motorcade would leave to take her to the press dinner.

I'd rather be water-boarded, she thought to herself.

She considered walking down the hall to say hello to Peter but didn't have the energy for the charade. She was furious that Ralph had called him and ordered him to come. Charlotte hated to subject him to the same stupid jokes year after year about being "Mr. Charlotte Kramer."

She thought about calling Roger, but he'd told her earlier in the day that Stephanie hadn't taken the news about the trip very well. Charlotte didn't want to complicate things any further for him.

She and Stephanie had been friends since Charlotte had arrived in Washington, but the relationship had cooled recently. Stephanie had turned down Charlotte's last few invitations to Camp David, and she'd canceled a dinner date at the last minute the week before.

Charlotte figured Stephanie was drained from the breast-cancer scare or frustrated by the demands on Roger's time, but she couldn't imagine that there was anything she had done to put Stephanie off. She'd given Roger time off, sent her personal physician with Stephanie to the oncologist, and sent flowers, fruit baskets, books, and movies to Stephanie while she waited for the test results.

And when Roger had, at first, refused to come on the trip, she hadn't pushed. But when he'd called her over the weekend with the news that he'd changed his mind, she'd been elated. He was the closest thing she had to a partner.

Charlotte looked out the window and saw the motorcade lining up on the driveway below. She stood and went into her dressing room to get ready. She'd had her makeup and hair done earlier. The dogs were out for a session with the trainer, and the house felt empty without them underfoot. She changed into the gown she'd had flown down from New York for the occasion and walked back toward the West Wing to discuss final details for the trip with Melanie before they left.

She stopped outside Peter's suite of rooms on her way out. She heard the evening news on inside and proceeded toward the staircase without knocking.

CHAPTER THIRTEEN

Melanie

Melanie stared at the simple black Vera Wang gown she'd pulled out of her closet that morning. She'd meant to grab a different one, but they all looked the same at four-thirty in the morning. She kept all of her black formal dresses in a separate closet in her apartment, and she tried to keep track of which one she wore which years, but the dresses and the dinners all blurred together. She put it on in her office and stepped into a new pair of Jimmy Choo's. She buzzed Annie's desk to ask her to come in and zip her dress, but Annie didn't answer. She struggled with the zipper herself but gave up after a muscle spasm ripped through the side of her neck.

"Damn," she said under her breath.

She opened her door and peered out to see if there were any suitable dress zippers in the waiting area. Brian, the new Pentagon reporter at ABC, was standing there smiling at her.

"I heard some banging around in there, but I didn't want to interrupt," he said, flashing a mouth full of teeth that were so white they looked as if they'd glow in the dark.

"Oh, hi. Do we have a meeting now?" Melanie asked.

"You're supposed to 'meet and greet' me for five minutes before tonight's dinner. If this is a bad time, I can call Annie and reschedule," he said.

"No, no, it's fine, come in. Just don't look at my back, I'm half-naked," Melanie said.

He smiled and took a seat in front of her desk. "I would offer to help, but that seems a little inappropriate," Brian said.

Melanie's eyes moved from his green eyes to his perfect haircut and down to his masculine jaw line. He looked like a Ken doll.

"Unless you'd like me to help," he added.

She couldn't decide if it was tacky or endearing that he was trying to flirt with her. He was at least five years younger and very attractive in a perfect, anchorman-in-the-making kind of way.

"That's probably a little much for a first meeting, but thank you for the offer. How long have you been on the beat?" Melanie asked, sitting back and trying to look as calm and professional as she could in an unzipped formal gown.

"About a month."

"Have you spent much time with Secretary Taylor yet?" Melanie asked.

"Not really. I saw him at the state dinner a couple of weeks ago, but he left before I had a chance to introduce myself."

"That's where we met. You came with Dale Smith, right?" Melanie asked.

"Yeah. She ditched me about forty-five minutes into the night, so, other than the two minutes I spent talking to you, I passed the evening talking to strangers and trying not to drink too much."

"I hate it when that happens." Melanie laughed.

"Judging by the crowd gathered around you that night, I have a hard time picturing you taking to strangers or drinking too much at a White House function," he said.

Melanie smiled. "So, are you and Dale . . . ?" She was suddenly very curious about his relationship status.

"Are Dale and I what? Dating?"

"Yes. Are you and Dale an item?" Melanie asked.

"Definitely not. No one knows what Dale does with herself. I'm convinced she sleeps in front of a live truck so she never misses a chance to be on television. Others think she must be sleeping with a married man."

"Interesting," Melanie said.

"She said that no one was closer to Roger than you. Said you were responsible for bringing him into the Cabinet three years ago."

"I've known Roger a long time. We worked together during the last administration, and I knew he and Charlotte would have a real mind-meld. I played Cupid in a way, I guess, but I didn't make the decision. That was all President Kramer. The president likes Roger's independence," Melanie said. "And the two of them have made more progress in three years than their predecessors did in two terms each."

Brian agreed with her assessment but felt that the original invasion had been so badly botched it would take a generation or two to repair the damage. Melanie always felt defensive when people suggested that the decision had been a mistake. She felt it was still part of her job to defend the legacies of the previous presidents she'd served. Maybe that was why she was so tired. Presidents Harlow and Martin spent their days golfing and giving speeches for one hundred thousand dollars a pop, and Melanie was still fighting with reporters about their presidencies. She glanced at her watch, and Brian took it as a sign that the meeting was over. She hadn't really intended to rush him out. Other than his critique of her former bosses, she was enjoying his stories about life as a war correspondent. He wasn't enamored with his own views on the wars, which was refreshing to Melanie. He didn't see himself as an expert but rather as the network's eyes and ears. It was too bad he'd rotated out, Melanie thought.

"I'd love to get on a trip to the region with the president and Secretary Taylor sometime," he said.

Melanie wasn't sure if he knew about the trip that was hours away. She couldn't risk it. "I'll keep that in mind next time we pull together a press pool," she promised.

"Thanks, and thanks for your time tonight. I know you've got a lot on your plate. I appreciate it."

"No problem. Come by anytime," she said. "I'd get up, but my dress still isn't zipped, and I'd rather not flash you."

He laughed.

"Can you send my assistant in here if you see her on your way out?" she said.

"Of course," he said, flashing his brilliant smile again.

Melanie watched him walk out. He was more interesting than she thought he'd be. A lot of the new correspondents were boring, predictable, and vain. When she'd first started at the White House, the television correspondents had been some of the most aggressive and well-connected reporters covering the beat. Now she couldn't remember the last time one of the White House correspondents had been in to speak to her off the record about Charlotte's agenda or the state of the party.

Melanie held her dress with one hand and peered into the reception area. Annie still wasn't at her desk. Melanie saw a copy of her call log on Annie's desk and walked out quickly to pick it up. There were half a dozen calls from members of Congress with various gripes, three messages from Ralph, a dozen messages from various staffers, and there, at the bottom, the call that Melanie had been dreading since her breakfast meeting in New York.

"Michael called. He needs to talk to you before the dinner. He said you have his number," the message read.

Melanie closed the door to her office and let her dress flop open in the back. She held her breath and dialed Michael from her personal cell.

"It's me," she said.

"Thanks for calling. Can you meet me tonight?" he asked.

"I really can't, Michael. I've got to go to this stupid dinner, and then I have to come back here and deal with something for Charlotte afterward. Can it wait until tomorrow? I'll have plenty of time tomorrow. I could meet you for breakfast somewhere."

"I'm not certain I will be able to sit on it for long. Can you excuse yourself at nine and meet me in front of the hotel? The agents will let you back in," he said.

"I know perfectly well what the agents will let me do, Michael. But I can't walk out of the dinner."

"Melanie, we need to talk. Tonight."

"Fine. Come to where the motorcade parks. I'll meet you there at nine."

"See you then," he said.

He had that voice. All reporters had the same thrill in their voices when they were about to break something big. Melanie had heard it so many times she recognized it in anyone. But she'd only heard it in Michael once before: the night she'd first met him and he was about to break the story about Harlow's lawyer getting indicted. She felt sick to her stomach.

"Need a hand with your dress?" Charlotte asked, strolling into Melanie's office in a white gown that rustled when she walked.

"Jesus, you look incredible," Melanie said.

And Charlotte did. The gown was made of layers of white silk that flowed to the floor. It was an Oscar de la Renta custom-made for her.

"Do you like it? I don't look like an over-the-hill bride or anything, do I?" Charlotte asked.

"No. You look regal. And yes, I would love a hand with my dress," Melanie said, standing to let Charlotte zip her in. "Did you get a chance to read through the speech?" she asked.

"Yeah, it's really funny. Thanks, Mel. I wish you were coming to Afghanistan tonight. You need to come with us one of these days. If I lose, there won't be many more opportunities."

"You're not going to lose. We'll figure this out. When you get back, we'll have a plan. Election Day is more than seven months away. That's an eternity," Melanie said.

"Thanks, Mel. At least I won't have to go to this dinner next year if I lose. Look, I'm not delusional, and you and I both know that the universe is pulling against us."

Melanie thought about Michael's call. "It certainly feels that way sometimes, doesn't it?" she agreed.

"It does." Charlotte nodded ruefully.

Annie knocked on the door. "Excuse me, I'm sorry, but the motor-cade is ready when you are, ma'am."

"Thanks, Annie," Melanie and Charlotte both said.

"Let's get this goat rodeo over with," Charlotte said. "Peter is meeting us in the limo."

"He's coming?" Melanie asked.

"Yeah. Ralph called him and told him it would be helpful if he were around more."

Melanie didn't say anything. They walked slowly out to the limo.

"I wish I could fast-forward the evening about five hours," Charlotte said.

"I know. Just try to look like you're having fun, at least." Melanie laughed.

They stood outside the limo for a moment. Melanie thought that Charlotte might tell her what was going on with Peter. She saw her open her mouth to say something, but then Peter appeared, and she got into the car and plastered a smile onto her face for the ten-minute ride to the Washington Hilton.

Once they arrived at the dinner, Charlotte and Peter put on one of the best shows Melanie had ever seen. They gazed adoringly at each other. They hugged and kissed the reporters. They remembered the names of every reporter's kid, where they went to school, and where they'd interned the summer before.

"Where is Jimmy going to intern this summer?" Charlotte was asking the host of *Meet the Press*.

"He would love to do something at Treasury."

"Have him call Melanie," Charlotte said.

Melanie made small talk with a few of the anchors and network executives and then went to find her table. She was sitting with Billy Moore at the network's head table. As she neared the table, Dale and Billy appeared to be having a serious conversation. He whispered something in her ear and hugged her. Melanie started to turn away, but Billy saw her before she could make a detour.

"Melanie, join us," Billy said. Melanie always thought he was too nice to work in the news business.

"Melanie, Dale, obviously you know each other," he said.

"Of course. How are you doing, Dale? All set?" Melanie asked quietly.

"Yes, thanks," Dale said.

"I met Brian today. He came to see me," Melanie told them.

"He's a good guy and a great reporter," Billy said. He spoke of his reporters with a parent's pride. "He spent the last six years in Iraq and Afghanistan, and he knows more people there than most of your generals, Melanie."

"I'll keep that in mind, Billy."

"And he speaks four languages," Dale added.

"Impressive," Melanie said.

The lights flashed twice, and the guests took their seats. Melanie looked around at the crowd. The first year of Charlotte's presidency, the dinner had been packed with celebrities. Movie stars, talk-show hosts, anchors, and television stars all lined up to kiss Charlotte's ass. Now, with Charlotte down in the polls, a few reality-television stars and the regular cast of on-air news anchors and journalists were the only ones who turned out.

Melanie checked her watch every five minutes. At ten minutes to nine, she excused herself. Charlotte hadn't begun her remarks yet. They were still handing out "excellence in journalism" awards to a group of reporters who had done a series attacking Charlotte for neglecting poor pregnant women.

"What an awful night this is," Melanie muttered to herself as she walked through the empty hotel lobby.

"First I catch you half-naked, and now I catch you talking to yourself," said Brian, stepping out from behind a pillar in the hotel lobby where he'd been reading his e-mail.

Melanie couldn't help but smile back. He looked even more handsome in a tuxedo. "I know. I'm officially one of those crazy women who talk to themselves and collect cats, right?"

"That appears to be the case, but I won't tell anyone. Hey, are you leaving? I'd love to get out of here myself. This has to be one of the worst Washington traditions I've experienced in my short time in this town."

"I would love to leave, but my boss hasn't delivered her brilliant remarks yet," she said.

"I meant that I'd love to get out of here as soon as her speech is over," he said.

Melanie laughed at his correction. "I'm actually just running out to make a call."

"Good. Then I'll see you back in there, cat lady," Brian said, smiling.

"Yes, I'll be right back." Melanie turned to leave.

"Melanie, are you making the round of postparties?" he asked.

"I usually don't stay up that late," she said over her shoulder. She could feel her phone vibrating in her evening bag.

"Too bad," Brian said with another smile.

Melanie didn't know what to make of that comment, but she enjoyed turning it around in her head as she walked away slowly.

When she was sure she was out of his view, she scooped her dress up with one hand and quickened her pace. She made her way to where the motorcade had dropped them off two hours earlier. Michael was leaning against one of the press vans, smoking a cigarette.

"Hey," he said when he saw her.

"Hey," she said back.

"You clean up pretty good," he said.

"That's better than my last greeting from you. I think it was something like 'You look like shit,'" she said.

"I'm an idiot. I'm sorry," he said.

"What have you got? I need to get back in there," Melanie said.

"I have a source who is acting as a middleman for a very close personal friend of the first family. The source says that he, he or she, is ready to go public with photos, phone logs, gifts, and eyewitness accounts that verify an affair."

"That's basically what you told me when we met in New York," Melanie pointed out.

Michael took a final drag on his cigarette and then stomped it out.

"Have you advanced the story at all, or are you still barking up trees?" Melanie asked.

"My middleman says his source is getting more and more comfortable with the idea of going public to make sure the real Charlotte is revealed. Once I get photos and the eyewitness account on the record, the magazine is going to print the story."

"So, you're not exactly on the cusp of breaking much of anything, Michael," Melanie accused. "All you have is a source who thinks he has a source who is willing to string together some clues that point to troubles in Charlotte's marriage. So what? I can knock that down in a round of cable interviews by accusing some Democrats of being on a partisan witch hunt against America's first female president. And I don't need to tell you that once we turn the story into one about sexism in the mainstream media, we'll have no problem changing the subject."

"The source is unimpeachable Mel. I wish I could tell you who it is. God, do I wish I could tell you, because you would know how serious this was if I did, but if I blow it, they take the story to the networks."

"Wait, you know who the source is?" Melanie asked.

"Yes. I demanded to know. I told them I wasn't putting my name on anything unless I knew."

"But you won't tell me?"

"I can't," Michael said.

"Then what am I doing out here?" Melanie complained.

"I thought you should know something about the story we're hearing from the source," Michael said.

"What?"

"It's not Peter," Michael said.

"What?"

"Peter's not the one having the affair," Michael said.

Melanie looked at him blankly.

"I'm sorry, Melanie."

She felt as if she was underwater again.

"Melanie, are you going to be able to talk to her tonight? If I can get my source to go on the record, I'm going with the story," he said.

Melanie's ears started to ring. "What do you want me to say to her?" she asked.

"I don't know," he said. "Isn't that why they pay you the big bucks?"

"Yeah, right. I need to get back in there. I'll call you later."

"Thanks for meeting me," he said.

Melanie turned to go back to the dinner and nearly tripped over Ralph. "What are you doing out here?" she practically screamed at him.

"I came out to get my things out of the motorcade to go to the afterparties," he said. "Is everything OK?"

"Yes, everything is fine, Ralph. You just scared the hell out of me."

She made her way back to her table just as Charlotte was taking the podium.

"I want to thank my husband for being here," she was saying. Melanie looked at Peter. He was staring right at her. He must have seen her ducking and weaving her way back to the table. She smiled and rolled her eyes. He hated these dinners even more than Charlotte did. But he kept staring. Melanie gave him a small wave, and he still just kept staring. Melanie looked behind her, and there, looking up at Charlotte and laughing at one of her jokes, was Dale Smith—directly in Peter Kramer's line of sight.

CHAPTER FOURTEEN

Dale

The ballroom shook with laughter as Charlotte took on every last stereotype and caricature of herself. Some of her harshest critics were wiping tears of laughter from their eyes. Dale laughed and clapped enthusiastically, even though all she could think about was the fact that Peter was sitting twenty feet away from her pretending to be in love with his wife. She hated that this was the last time she'd see him before leaving for Afghanistan.

She excused herself as soon as Charlotte's remarks ended and made her way to the motorcade while the comedian was making a crack about Charlotte and Roger ruling the world together. Dale slid into the van that would take them the twenty blocks to the White House as soon as the comedian was finished. She read and responded to the e-mails that had come in since she'd been at the dinner. She smiled as an e-mail from Peter appeared at the top of her messages: "Be safe, and enjoy the experience. I'll be waiting for you."

She exhaled deeply for the first time all night and wrote back immediately: "I promise to be safe and come home to you in one piece. I love and miss you, xxoo. Hey, BTW, Charlotte was hilarious tonight."

Dale looked up, and they were moving.

The motorcade sped back to the White House. Charlotte and Peter got out of the limo at the front of the motorcade and walked into the residence. Press aides came back and told the reporters in the van that they had a "full lid," meaning that the president was in for the night, and they were free to go. Dale was supposed to walk back into the briefing room and wait for the press secretary to retrieve her and put her and the wire reporters into an unmarked van for the secret ride to Andrews Air Force Base.

She sat in one of the theater chairs and took her shoes off. "G'night," she said to one of the other reporters who had taken the ride back with them.

"Wanna get a drink?" he asked Dale.

"No, I've got to file a script for my package for the morning show," she lied.

"Oh, shit, that sucks. I'll have a drink for you," he said.

"Thanks," Dale said.

She was alone in the briefing room. The other reporters traveling to Afghanistan had gone outside for a cigarette.

One of the agents stuck his head in and called her name. She jumped up from the seat and hurried toward him. "Wait here," he said. Dale stood in the cool night air alone and wondered if she should grab the others.

"The president asked us to put you in the car with her, Miss Smith," the agent said.

"Are all the reporters traveling with her?" she asked.

"No, ma'am. They'll be in the van back there." He pointed at a white van a few feet behind the SUV. The agent walked over to the black SUV and opened the passenger door. "You can sit on this side. The president will be down in a couple of minutes."

Dale struggled into the SUV in her evening gown. She was carrying a change of clothes, but the press staff had forbidden them from changing out of their formal attire. Dale sat in the car and waited. Her mind was racing. She wanted desperately to e-mail Peter, but she was suddenly paranoid that someone was watching her every move. She had a feeling that this was it, the moment that Charlotte would confront her for having an affair with her husband. She felt slightly nauseated but not as terrified as she thought she'd feel.

What can she do to me? Dale wondered.

She wished she'd talked to her parents earlier in the day. She didn't want to lie to them about the trip, so she had avoided her mother's call. *Better that they find out I went to Afghanistan after I'm back home safely,* she'd decided. Dale's mind was spinning from one anxious thought to the next. She tried to take deep breaths.

Suddenly, an announcement from the car's radio system jolted her back to the moment. "Wayfarer departing residence. Wayfarer arriving Diplomatic Room."

The agent started the car's engine.

"Here we go," he said to her.

CHAPTER FIFTEEN

Charlotte

T hanks for waiting for me to change. I wanted to thank you for coming tonight, Peter. I know how much you loathe press dinners, and I had no idea that Ralph had called you. I would have let you off the hook if I'd known," Charlotte said as they stood in the Diplomatic Room, where presidents usually greeted visiting dignitaries, not estranged husbands.

"It was my pleasure. By the way, you were hilarious tonight," Peter said.

"I had good material."

"You delivered it like a pro," he said.

"Thanks. Listen, I didn't tell the kids about the trip. Penelope worries so much, I usually call her when I'm on my way back, but please tell them this is the last time I'll sneak off without telling them where I'm going."

"Don't worry about the kids. I'll go see them tomorrow."

"They'll love that," Charlotte said.

"Take care of yourself over there, Charlotte. Don't let Roger drag you into any caves or anything," Peter warned.

"Of course not. He's on a short leash these days anyway. Stephanie almost didn't let him come."

"Well, I'm glad he's going to be there," Peter said.

Charlotte smiled and took a breath. "Dale Smith is coming with us for the first time," she said. She wasn't even sure why she said it.

"Is that right?" Peter said.

"I figured you knew already. You guys are friends, right?" Charlotte said. She hadn't planned to put her husband on the spot, but something about traveling in such an intimate group with Dale was more than she could take. She didn't think Dale was entitled to any special access. She had enough of that, Charlotte thought.

"Uh, yeah, you know, I, you know, met her years ago in Sacramento."

"I know," Charlotte said.

They stood there for a minute, neither one of them saying anything.

One of Charlotte's agents stuck his head in and cleared his throat loudly. "Excuse me, Madam President, but we're wheels up from Andrews in exactly forty minutes," he said.

"I'm coming. Is Miss Smith in the car?" Charlotte asked.

"Yes, ma'am," the agent replied.

"Thanks again for coming tonight. I hope you have a good week," she said to Peter before turning to walk out of the Diplomatic Room.

"You, too," he managed to say.

As she walked toward the SUV, looking sporty in jeans, a black fleece, and black running shoes, Charlotte tried to shake off the guilt she felt for reducing Peter to a flustered mess. She pulled her ponytail through the back of her black baseball cap and stuck her head into the drivers'-side window.

"Hey, guys, we'll get going in a minute. Good evening, Dale. I thought you might want to ride with me and Roger since this is your first trip."

"Yes, of course, thanks so much," Dale gushed.

"I just need to talk to Roger about something briefly, and then we'll be on our way," Charlotte told her with a smile.

"Great," Dale said.

Charlotte and Roger stood talking a few feet away from the car.

"Everything OK?" Roger asked.

"Yeah, everything is fine. How's Stephanie?"

"Pissed as hell that I'm going, but she'll get over it."

"Did you ever think that it would be like this?" Charlotte asked.

"Like what?"

"You know, that we'd fix the stuff over there and screw things up back here?" Charlotte said.

Roger smiled and put his arm around her. "We did more than fix stuff, Char," he said.

Charlotte smiled. It felt so good to talk to Roger. Just thinking about being out of Washington for four days lifted her spirits. The trips boosted Charlotte's morale by distilling her job down to its most essential elements. The commander-in-chief role had always been more comfortable for Charlotte than any other aspect of the presidency, which was ironic, since convincing Americans that a woman could serve as commander in chief had been her greatest hurdle in getting elected in the first place. Her strengths were well suited for the decisions she faced as a wartime leader. While her private deliberative process alienated and offended many in Congress and some of her Cabinet who preferred long, public debates about the future of health care or education, Charlotte's ability to seek advice on the wars and reach a conclusion without any public hand wringing or hedging earned her great respect up and down the military's chain of command.

It helped that during Charlotte's presidency, support for the wars and the men and women who were fighting them rose to their highest levels since the months after September 11, 2001. Charlotte had honed her message to one that perfectly calibrated the public's need to hear the difficult truths, on the one hand, and its need for leaders who displayed confidence about the prospects for victory, on the other.

Charlotte looked back at the residence to see Melanie crossing the lawn in the black gown she'd worn to the dinner.

"Hey, Mel," she said.

"Madam President, I need to speak to you."

"What is it?" Charlotte said.

"Alone, please."

"I can't imagine why that's necessary."

"Please," Melanie insisted.

"Fine," Charlotte said, leaving Roger on the South Lawn and walking into the Rose Garden with Melanie.

"I need to ask you about something before you leave," Melanie said.

"What is it, Melanie?" Charlotte said.

"I need to ask you one more time. Is there something going on that I should know about?"

Charlotte looked at her. Melanie's hair had come out of the updo she'd worn for the dinner, and her makeup was smudged. She was breathing heavily from her speed walk from the West Wing to where the mini-motorcade was parked.

"No," she said calmly.

"This is the point where I can do something to help you, Charlotte. After this, after tonight, if you walk away and don't tell me what's going on, I'm not sure I can."

"I don't know what you're talking about or what kind of rumor you're chasing down for one of your buddies in the press corps, but there's nothing going on," Charlotte said.

Her comment about "buddies" just about ruptured Melanie's forced composure. She was pissed enough at Charlotte to ruin her trip by telling her exactly what Michael had told her. The only reason she didn't mention the affair rumor was to preserve Charlotte's focus on the high-stakes trip she was about to make to the front lines. Melanie took a breath and blew it out slowly before turning to face Charlotte again.

"Madam President, I have been here for fifteen years. I have never had my neck out as far as it's out now. If there are things that have happened or things that are happening that could be used against you by your political opponents, I need to know about them so I can help you. That's all. I would not be standing out here in a strapless gown in forty-degree weather at midnight for my buddies in the press corps. Besides, most of them hate me these days." She forced out a smile and a nod in Roger's direction and then turned to leave. She didn't know what else to do. Charlotte was either playing dumb or in complete denial.

Charlotte followed her and put her hand on Melanie's shoulder. "Can we talk about this when I get back?" Charlotte asked.

"Sure," Melanie said. "Have a good trip." She turned and walked back toward the West Wing.

Charlotte stood watching Melanie.

"Charlotte?" Roger asked.

"I'm coming. Everything is fine," Charlotte said. "Let's go." She climbed inside the SUV and sat next to Dale.

Roger sat in the backseat and leaned forward between Charlotte and Dale. "So, Dale, this is your first trip, right?" he asked.

"Yes. I'm really excited. Thanks so much for allowing me to come with you," Dale said.

"It's a serious place," Charlotte warned.

"Yes, ma'am," Dale replied.

"A lot of brave people think they can handle what they see there, and then they get over there, and they choke. You know, they think about their families and their loved ones, and they can't put one foot in front of the other. I need to make sure that you're not going to freeze, Dale, and put the whole group in danger. I usually don't take anyone who hasn't done at least one solo trip," Charlotte said.

"I know, and I really appreciate it, Madam President and Mr. Secretary. I assure you that I am prepared for the trip," Dale said.

"How can you say that?"

"Excuse me?" Dale said.

"How can you say that you are prepared if you have no idea what you're about to see?" Charlotte asked.

Dale wasn't sure what the right answer was to her question. It didn't matter.

Charlotte continued, "You can't imagine what it looked like three years ago when Roger and I first visited, right, Roger?"

She talked all the way to the airport and seemed to lose herself in the details of the countries she'd tried so hard to put back together. Dale was surprised by how transported Charlotte was when she talked about what she and Roger had done in Afghanistan and Iraq.

When they arrived at the airport, Charlotte didn't stop talking until her agents interrupted her. "Why don't you board from the back, Madam President?" one suggested.

Charlotte got out of the car and walked toward the plane, talking to Dale the entire time about the generals who had been in charge and the debriefings she'd done when she became president.

"I hope you'll come back here and help us tell the story, Dale. It's important that the public understand how much has been accomplished," she said as they climbed the stairs to Air Force One.

Dale smiled and nodded.

"I hope you'll come back as changed as I have been by every one of my trips," Charlotte said.

She greeted the other reporters in the press cabin, and then disappeared to the front of the plane with Roger.

CHAPTER SIXTEEN

Melanie

Melanie waited until she was back in her office with the door closed and locked. She wanted to hurl her phone against the wall and watch it smash into tiny pieces. She wanted to scream at the top of her lungs. She wanted to throw her chair through the window. But she couldn't do any of those things. She wasn't sure precisely what had set her off. She felt as though she'd been broken by the proverbial straw on the camel's back. As she paced back and forth in front of the fireplace, she tried to determine if it was her fear of another looming crisis on top of everything else she had to manage or the fact that she felt trapped in her job by her own demented sense of loyalty and duty that had her feeling so enraged. Whatever it was, it had pushed her over the edge in the Rose Garden. She had never lost her cool with any of the presidents she'd served. Everyone always said that she'd know when it was time to go. Others who had held her position told her that the trick was leaving before the job altered your personality and turned you into someone you neither recognized nor liked. She was certain that moment had arrived. After her breathing returned to normal, she sat at her desk, booted up her computer, and did something she'd fantasized about a great deal in recent weeks. She started drafting her resignation letter.

A few minutes later, Annie knocked softly on her door. "Mel, it's me. Do you need anything?"

"No, Annie, I'm fine. You should be at one of the afterparties. Why don't you get out of here? I'll manage," Melanie said.

"Are you sure?" Annie asked.

"Yes, positive. I'll see you in the morning."

"Good night, Melanie. Call me if you need anything," Annie said.

Melanie heard the door close behind her. Less than a minute later, the phone rang. She wanted to ignore it. She looked to see who was calling. It was the White House operator. Charlotte would have called through the Situation Room switchboard.

"Hello, Melanie Kingston's office," Melanie said, trying to disguise her voice by sounding extra-polite like Annie.

"Uh, hello, is Melanie there?" asked a vaguely familiar voice.

"It's after midnight," Melanie said.

"I know. I just thought maybe she'd be there, since the motorcade went back to the White House," he said.

"Who is this?" Melanie asked in her normal voice.

"Oh, hi, Melanie, this is Brian. I was calling to see if your night got any better. You were talking to yourself last time I saw you," he joked.

"Actually, it got worse. Much worse."

"I'm sorry to hear that," Brian sympathized.

"Why aren't you at the afterparty?" she asked.

"I was there. It was awful. This town might kill my soul. How do you live here?"

"Good question," she said.

"What are you doing now?" Brian asked.

"Right now?" she said, glancing at the letter she'd started typing on her screen.

"Yes, right now."

Melanie was silent for a moment, and then she sighed and held down the delete button until the screen was blank.

"Nothing," Melanie said.

"Do you want to get a drink?" he asked.

"Actually, I would love a drink, but I don't think there are many places still serving in the District of Columbia at this hour."

"I've got that under control. Where should I pick you up?" he said.

"I've got a built-in ride, you know, one of the few perks of the job," Melanie said.

"Of course. Well, that ruins my element of surprise," he said.

"Surprise?" she asked.

"Yeah, OK, forget about the surprise. Can you meet me at the Jefferson Monument in ten minutes?"

"The Jefferson Memorial?" she corrected.

"Yes, sorry, the Jefferson Memorial."

"Seriously?" she asked.

"Seriously. Don't stand me up, or I will develop a complex and have to leave D.C."

Melanie glanced at herself in the mirror. Her makeup had smudged a bit, but she didn't completely hate her reflection.

"One drink," she said.

"All I ask," he said.

Melanie hung up and went down the hall to the bathroom to brush her teeth and splash some water on her face. She grabbed Annie's coat from the coat rack in her office and walked out to West Exec.

"We're making a stop, guys," she said to Walter and Sherry.

They pulled up in front of the Jefferson Memorial, and at first Melanie didn't see anyone.

"It would be just my luck to get stood up tonight on top of everything else," she muttered under her breath. She got out of the car and walked up the steps toward the rotunda. All of the monuments were illuminated after dark, but the Jefferson Memorial shone brighter than the others and had always been Melanie's favorite.

Brian was standing in front of the statue of Jefferson.

"You came," he said.

"I came," Melanie said. He was holding a six-pack of Heinekens and two heavy blankets. They sat on the bench inside the rotunda in front of Jefferson's statue. Brian opened a beer for her and one for himself.

"I love this place," he said.

"Me, too," Melanie said. She shivered a little bit, and he moved closer to her and wrapped the blanket around her legs.

Melanie drank her beer and looked up at the quotations she had memorized. Her favorite was the one about the need for institutions to change. Every time she read it, she felt as if Jefferson had been talking about Charlotte's presidency.

"Now I get it!" Brian exclaimed.

"What?" she asked.

"Why people live here. I mean, this is cool. Where else can you share a beer with Jefferson?"

Melanie laughed. "Exactly. And you get free political advice," she said, standing up to read one of the inscriptions carved in the massive marble walls of the rotunda.

"Jefferson was ahead of his time," Brian said, gazing up at another one of the quotes.

"This one is my favorite," Melanie said. She wrapped a blanket around her shoulders and walked to the far side of the rotunda. Brian followed her. She read the last couple of lines out loud:

"'Institutions must advance to keep pace with the times. We might as well require a man to wear still the coat which fitted him when a boy as civilized society to remain ever under regimen of their barbarous ancestors.'"

"I can see why you'd like that one," he said, putting his hands on her shoulders and rubbing them up and down to warm her. Melanie wasn't sure if it was a romantic gesture or a friendly one. After a few seconds, he dropped his hands from her shoulders and shoved them into his pockets.

"You're not going to like Washington very much," she predicted.

He looked surprised. "No?" he asked.

"I've seen lots of reporters leave the foreign desk to come to Washington. You guys think you're moving up, because you've left the region to come cover the decision makers, but most policy makers would kill to know what you know about how their decisions affect the region. Be careful not to stay in this town too long, or you'll forget what you loved about your job in the first place."

"Sounds like you had more than a bad day. Sounds like you've had a bad year. There must be some things you still enjoy about the job. You've been there longer than anyone else in White House history," he said.

Melanie groaned. "God, you make me feel one hundred years old."

"Surely you could have left between Harlow and Martin, or between Martin and Kramer, or after the midterm elections last year. I mean, that's what most people do, right?" he asked.

"Yes, and I'm beginning to understand their wisdom." Melanie sighed.

"No, it's very cool that you've stayed. It says something about you. You stayed and put all these people—Kramer, Martin, Harlow—you put them ahead of yourself. It's very impressive."

"I don't know about that," she said gloomily.

"I see it's true what they say about you, then," he teased.

"What are you talking about?"

"I was told by people at my network and others around town that you are loyal to a fault and completely unaware of your stature," he said, taking a swig of his beer.

"That's not true!"

"Melanie, it's a compliment. Your loyalty to these people is obvious. Why else would you still be there? And you're one of the most powerful people in the federal government, but you act as if you're a twenty-five-year-old staffer."

His comments didn't feel like a compliment, but Melanie was too tired to argue. She mulled over Brian's description of her. It wasn't how she saw herself, but she hadn't spent much time worrying about her reputation lately. She looked across the Tidal Basin toward the Washington Monument. Her thoughts returned to the conversation she'd been trying to have with Charlotte since Sunday. She sighed. She had tried to force Charlotte to come clean before she was ready. It was a miscalculation, Melanie now realized. Charlotte would come to her. She'd tell her what was going on when she got back from Afghanistan. Melanie took another sip of beer and tried to shut out the flood of potential political nightmares heading her way. Just when she'd pushed her tense discussion with Charlotte out of her mind, she remembered her conversation with Michael. And once she pushed the day's worries aside, her thoughts turned to the unpleasant assignments awaiting her the following morning. She had a breakfast meeting scheduled with the president's domestic policy advisor in the

White House Mess. The domestic policy advisor thought they were meeting to discuss education reform, but Melanie had scheduled the breakfast so she could break the news to him that he could not work at the White House while he was under investigation for shoplifting. That meeting would be followed by all the other crises and snafus that would land on her desk by sunrise.

She'd nearly forgotten about Brian. When she looked over at him, he was smiling at her.

"What were you thinking about?" he asked.

"I was thinking about how I'd give anything to be a twenty-five-year-old staffer again," she said. "I was so happy to be there in those days, and now each day feels like a punishment for sins I must have committed in a past life."

"What did you love about it when you were twenty-five?" Brian asked, sitting down next to her.

Melanie smiled. "Everything. Walking up to the gate and watching the tourists' faces light up a bit when I flashed my badge and passed through security, ordering lunch from the Mess, having the OEOB to myself early in the morning when I came in to prepare President Harlow's clips, walking over to the West Wing to drop off the clips and seeing the staff vacuum the already spotless carpets. I loved everything about it. I used to give all the tours for the senior staffers' families and friends. Some junior staffers hated doing it, but I loved it. I couldn't believe they'd let me roam the entire White House complex. I used to wait for someone to say, 'Sorry, ma'am, you can't go in there,' but they never did." Melanie smiled at the memory. I gave one mean tour. I wouldn't let anyone talk or take calls during my tours, and there was a quiz at the end to make sure everyone was paying attention."

"When was the last time you gave a tour?" Brian asked.

"I haven't given one in years," she admitted.

"Let's go do one now," he said.

"A White House tour?" Melanie asked.

"Yeah. You've got all the badges and stuff. Let's go do a West Wing tour."

"It's almost one in the morning," she objected.

"Perfect—no crowds."

Melanie smiled. She knew more about the furniture and the art and the history of the West Wing than anyone.

They finished their beers and got into Melanie's car.

"Back to West Exec, please, guys," she said.

"Yes, ma'am," Walter said.

Sherry turned around and gave her a thumbs-up while Brian was looking out the window.

They got out on West Exec and walked back into the West Wing.

"This is the West Wing basement," Melanie said.

It was lined with photos of presidential events from recent days. Brian stopped to look at a photo of Charlotte reading to a class of first-graders.

"This was yesterday, right?" he asked.

"Yep. Quick turnaround. Sometimes they're up by the end of the day they're shot," she said.

Melanie would have walked him into the Situation Room to point out the high-tech systems that allowed Charlotte to monitor the world's hot spots and stay in touch with foreign leaders, but she was afraid he'd see something that would reveal Charlotte's location as en route to Afghanistan.

They walked up the stairs toward the Oval Office. Melanie felt funny walking into the Oval when Charlotte wasn't there, so they stood in the doorway, and she described everything to Brian in excruciating detail. With the exception of a small handful of them, every U.S. president had used the desk Charlotte had chosen. It was made from the wood of the HMS *Resolute,* and it was a gift from the British. She had designed her own rug, a presidential tradition, in shades of cream, beige, and yellow. Alongside photos of the twins, she had a picture of the Ellison family framed on her desk. Charlotte had met Mr. and Mrs. Ellison during her campaign for the White House. They had four sons serving in Iraq, and they had asked her to promise that they'd all come home. She'd taken an interest in the family, and she'd met all four of the boys on her trips to Iraq and Afghanistan. Charlotte spoke to Mrs. Ellison every Sunday.

Next, Melanie showed Brian the Roosevelt Room, with its portrait of Teddy Roosevelt hanging above the fireplace. Republican presidents always placed Teddy's portrait above the fireplace, and Democratic presidents placed FDR's portrait there. It had been a long time since Democrats had decorated the West Wing, and Melanie felt a familiar wave of anxiety at the thought of turning the place over to the Democrats in November. If she couldn't figure out how to turn things around, that would be the likely outcome. They walked into the Cabinet Room, which Melanie knew well. She'd sat in on hundreds of Cabinet meetings over the years. She'd seen the nameplate on the back of each chair changed for half a dozen different Cabinet secretaries for each agency. Every retiring Cabinet secretary got to keep the chair with his or her name engraved on the back. She showed Brian Charlotte's chair, which stood slightly higher than those of the Cabinet members. They left the West Wing and walked past the Rose Garden toward the East Wing.

"Is the president sleeping?" Brian whispered.

She didn't want to lie to him about the trip to Afghanistan, but she couldn't risk a leak. She couldn't figure out if he knew or not. "I don't know," she said.

He didn't push it.

Melanie showed him the East Room, the Red Room, the Green Room, and the Blue Room. She lost herself in her memories and stories from each of the presidents she'd worked for.

"Remember when the British prime minister got food poisoning?" she asked.

"Yes. He threw up on Mrs. Martin," Brian said.

"Exactly. They were sitting right here." Melanie pointed to a settee in the Red Room.

"Fascinating," he said, smiling at her.

They made their way back to the West Wing and ended up outside Melanie's office. It was after two A.M.

"Thanks for the tour," Brian said.

"You're welcome. Thanks for making me do it."

"You probably have to be back here in about three hours, right?"

"Something like that." She leaned toward him, and he seemed to lean toward her.

"I'd better let you go," he said.

"Yeah, that's probably a good idea," Melanie agreed, stepping back and feeling embarrassed that she'd thought he might try to kiss her.

"I'm going to grab a cab," he told her.

"Are you sure you don't want a ride? I can ask Walter to drop you off."

"Nah, I'm fine. They should get you straight home."

"I'll walk out with you," she said.

They walked down the stairs and out to West Exec. Brian gave her a peck on the cheek and turned to walk toward the gate on Lafayette Park. Melanie climbed into her car with Walter and Sherry.

Walter kept eyeing her in the rearview mirror.

"Stop giving me that look, Walter," Melanie said.

"I didn't say anything," Walter said, smiling at her.

They drove in silence the rest of the way. Melanie said good night and went upstairs to her apartment. Her alarm would go off in less than two hours.

CHAPTER SEVENTEEN

Dale

D ale considered texting Peter one last time, but the ride to the airport had been too strange to summarize in a text message. She had a strange feeling that the animosity toward her that the White House staff had long expressed as coming "from the top" had been an exaggeration. Sure, her reporting had helped usher in the end of Charlotte's honeymoon in the early days of the administration, but the White House beat brought that out in everyone. And Dale had more to prove than her colleagues. She'd been dubbed a "pageant correspondent" by the *Washington Post*'s media critic. The term was a reference to the growing number of attractive, inexperienced on-air reporters being assigned beats long reserved for more seasoned journalists.

As the military aide made his way down the aisle to collect everyone's BlackBerrys and cell phones so that there wouldn't be any temptation on the part of the reporters to inform their bosses or families of their whereabouts, Dale quickly typed "love you" to Peter's personal cell number. The aide arrived in her row and asked her to turn the phone off before the message could transmit.

She tried to shake off the anxiety Peter had created with his concern for her safety and focus on the opportunity the trip presented. She'd been on a meteoric rise, and at thirty-two, she sometimes wondered how much longer she could keep up the pace. As much as she fantasized about a life with Peter, she also coveted a spot at the top of her field. The year before had seen the third woman ascend to the anchor spot, and Dale was hoping to make a good enough impression on her superiors to be in the running for the weeknight anchor post when the job opened up in another couple of years. She had the talent and the confidence to pull it off. As the only child of a doctor and a schoolteacher, she'd been surrounded with so much love and praise that she never experienced self-doubt until she found herself shooting her own stories and filming her own stand-ups as a television reporter in Redding, California, one of the smallest media markets in the country. The reporter she'd replaced as the Redding bureau chief had gone on to anchor a newscast at ESPN, and she had taken the job hoping for a similar leap from local to national news. When the opportunity had failed to materialize after nine months, she'd almost given up on reporting. She was in New York visiting a friend from college when she decided to drop in on an agent who'd spoken at her journalism school years before. She was surprised that he'd agreed to see her and even more surprised when he'd agreed to represent her. She'd been quickly promoted to a job as a reporter and anchor in Cleveland, Ohio. From there, she'd done a short stint in Miami at a network affiliate before being promoted to the overnight shift at ABC in New York. She'd been noticed by the morning anchor, who'd championed her for a spot as a special correspondent for the morning show. She'd started doing stories about Charlotte Kramer when she was the California governor, and her connections and history of covering Kramer had landed her the spot as the network's "girl on the bus" with the Kramer campaign.

Now, Dale was one of six reporters following the American president to the battlefield. She selected a movie from the Air Force One entertainment system and adjusted the volume on her headset. Dale had just kicked off her shoes and tucked her legs under her when the press secretary entered their cabin. Even he looked excited.

"How's everyone doing?" he said cheerily.

He went over travel times and information about when and where they'd be able to file their reports. Dale was promised a ten-minute interview with the president that she'd "pool" for all of the networks—essentially sharing her content with all of the broadcast outlets.

After the movie, she read a set of news clips and talked with the reporters who had been on previous trips to the region.

"When we land, it's like a scene in a movie," one of the wire reporters told her.

"We land in a corkscrew to avoid sniper fire," another added.

Dale was getting excited. The other reporters took Ambien and slept, but Dale didn't want to be groggy, so she reclined her seat and plugged in her iPod. She reviewed the questions she'd prepared for her one-on-one interview with Charlotte. She'd tracked down the family members of an entire unit serving in Afghanistan and planned to ask Charlotte questions they had proposed. Her eyes started to grow heavy, and her thoughts turned to Peter as she finally drifted off to sleep.

When one of the flight attendants came through with coffee and breakfast, Dale felt as if she'd only just shut her eyes, but she'd actually slept for four hours. She sipped her coffee and picked at a blueberry muffin.

Before they began their descent, they were told to put on their bulletproof jackets so they could get off the plane and onto their assigned helicopters quickly. Air Force One would be moved to another location after they deplaned so that insurgents couldn't find it. They landed just as the other reporters had said they would—in a fast, dark corkscrew.

Afghanistan was more mountainous than she'd envisioned, and as the first glints of sunrise started to brighten the dark hills around them, Dale thought about how strange it was that she and Charlotte were in this faraway place together and Peter was thousands of miles away. She couldn't wait to get on the ground. Dale felt a thrill she hadn't experienced since her early reporting days.

This is just what I needed, Dale thought as she hurried off Air Force One and toward her assigned helicopter.

CHAPTER EIGHTEEN

Charlotte

As Air Force One sped toward the front lines of the war in Afghanistan without any lights or radio communication, Charlotte felt peaceful for the first time in weeks. She was glad she'd asked Dale to ride to Andrews Air Force Base with her and Roger. What was it they always said about acceptance? Awareness is the first step to forgiveness? Or forgiveness is the first step to acceptance?

Facing the truth about Peter and Dale was on her long and growing list of things to deal with. Most of the time, she didn't have the time or the energy to contemplate what it would mean for her and the twins, not to mention the impact it would have on her political future. And she knew Peter wouldn't push it.

She had known about Peter and Dale for a while. She had detected a change in Peter as soon as he'd returned from a trip to Africa during her first year in office. The trip was designed to draw attention to the plight of young women living with AIDS, and Peter was accompanied by several of his star athletes and a handful of celebrities. Dale Smith was part of a press contingency that was assembled to travel to Africa with Peter to report on the group's efforts. Her coverage of the young African women had been so powerful that she'd won an Emmy for her reporting. After the Emmy was awarded, the network rebroadcast Dale's one-hour special. Charlotte had been on her elliptical machine in the residence when it came on. As she'd watched the images of her husband and Dale walking through the clinics and hospitals fill the television screen, the chemistry between them was obvious. The way they'd looked at each other during the sit-down interview was so intimate that Charlotte was surprised she'd been the only one who noticed.

Charlotte's suspicious had been confirmed by subtle but marked changes in Peter after the trip. He didn't sulk or complain anymore about relocating to the East Coast, and he'd stopped trying to engage Charlotte on any topic other than the kids. In some ways, it had been a relief. Her inability to give him any of the things he needed was no longer something she had to feel guilty about. But the reality of having a husband who was in love with another woman was something she never discussed with anyone. She knew Peter well enough to know that she was correct, but she didn't feel the need to share her knowledge with anyone else. She didn't tell Roger, Melanie, Brooke, or Mark, and she convinced herself that she simply disliked the tone of Dale's coverage of her administration, when the truth was that Dale's was hardly the toughest coverage the White House received.

One of Charlotte's gifts was the art of extreme compartmentalization. After the ride from the White House to Andrews that night, she'd contemplated Dale Smith from an objective perspective and decided that she was a good fit for Peter. Charlotte could see how he'd have been attracted to her. She wasn't self-important like so many of the other White House reporters, and she seemed smart.

Charlotte stretched her arms above her head and looked around her cabin on Air Force One. She'd logged a lot of hours on the plane, and it was one of the only places where she felt protected from the mounting threats to her political and personal well-being.

Charlotte appreciated that Dale had done her homework on Afghanistan. She knew about the setbacks the Afghans had experienced over the years in taking on the Taliban and dealing with Pakistan. In another part of her mind, Charlotte hated Dale for having the energy and the time to give her husband the things he needed and obviously wanted, but she pushed those feelings aside. Melanie had arranged for Charlotte to do a sit-down interview with Dale to be shared with all of the television networks. Charlotte had made a mental list of the points she wanted to make to help the generals get the funding they needed from Congress for more training and equipment.

She'd just kicked off her shoes and stretched out on the couch when Roger entered her cabin—without knocking, as usual.

"What will you do the day you barge in here and I'm half-naked?" she scolded.

"Do I have to answer that, or can I take the Fifth?" he said, grinning.

She made a place for him on the couch and handed him the plate of cookies that her personal steward had placed in her cabin. He took two.

"I know it didn't go over well at home, but I wouldn't have wanted to do this trip without you," Charlotte said.

"And I wouldn't have wanted to miss it," he said, brushing cookie crumbs from his sweater. "What was Melanie so worked up about before we left?"

"I'm not sure. I bet she's getting heat from some of her press contacts. I feel bad for her—for all of them, really. They think that if they come up with the right message or policy or line of attack, they can turn things around and get my numbers up. But it's not that easy. Sometimes circumstances dictate an outcome that you can't escape, you know?"

"If the voters are stupid enough to vote for Fat Frankie, then fuck them. Let them have her. She'd fuck things up so royally she'd be impeached in six months. Stupid cow," he said, shaking his head in disgust.

Frankie was Senator Fran Frankel, Charlotte's likely opponent in the November election. She was a former Miss Texas who, at fifty-two, was more than twice the size she'd been in her beauty pageant days. Roger and Melanie had given her the nickname "Fat Frankie" to make Charlotte smile. It worked.

"Can you imagine her over here?" Charlotte smirked.

"No, and neither will the voters once they sit down and think about it. Just be patient," Roger said.

"I've got nothing but time," Charlotte said, smiling and stretching out her legs so her feet touched Roger.

Roger took her feet into his lap and leaned back. "We should get some rest," he said.

Charlotte closed her eyes and fell asleep.

The crew woke her up an hour before landing for a final briefing in the conference room on Air Force One.

"Madam President, there's a lot of fighting around the U.S. bases and the polling stations we were planning to visit, so we're going to cut two or three of the stops from the itinerary," said Albert Dawson, her deputy national security advisor.

"Doesn't that send the wrong signal? If the polling station is too dangerous for me to visit, how do we make the case that the Afghan people should feel safe to exercise their right to vote?" Charlotte asked.

"The truth is that in parts of the country, it actually *isn't* safe, Madam President," said the intelligence briefer who traveled with her.

"You guys really think we need to scrap that much of the trip?" Charlotte complained. "I hate to do that."

"It's the only way to be in the country without taking unnecessary risks," Albert said.

"Bullshit," Roger said, looking up from the intelligence report. "The fighting is unchanged from two days ago, two weeks ago, and two months ago, and if the president was going to fly to Afghanistan to spend her whole time in heavily fortified bases, I would have told her not to waste her time. This trip is about being on the ground for their first real election—the first one that isn't tainted by corruption or intimidation. She needs to be seen moving all around the country if the people are ever going to trust us."

"Roger, we understand the objectives for the trip, and we did the advance work for all of the stops you specified, but we're getting intelligence that suggests a real uptick in chatter and activity since we left Washington," warned the CIA briefer.

"Can I see some of the actual intelligence reporting?" Charlotte asked.

"Of course, Madam President," he said, handing her photos of insurgents running up to the perimeter of a U.S. base near Kandahar.

"All of the insurgents were taken out, but two U.S. soldiers were hit in this attack. One died last night in surgery."

"Roger, this is pretty daunting. They don't even pretend to be afraid of us anymore," Charlotte said.

"And they never will be if we land in the country and never see any of it," Roger said, pounding his fist on the desk for effect.

Charlotte was quiet.

"Madam President, the final decision is yours. Your national security team is divided on this, obviously, and the Secret Service agrees with me that the risks outweigh the benefits, but the final decision is yours," Albert said.

"Thank you, gentlemen," Charlotte said. "I'll let you know what I decide."

"Yes, ma'am." They filed out of the conference room.

"Roger, it seems like a silly risk to take. Why don't we visit the troops and make one other stop to rub shoulders with some locals and then get out so we don't give the rest of the team a heart attack?" Charlotte suggested.

"Because, Charlotte, this is exactly what the enemy wants. They want to create a climate that is so unstable, unpredictable, and inhospitable that nothing ever really changes," Roger argued.

"But the rest of the national security team understands our objectives. They want the same things. And we've been here half a dozen times. I've never seen our guys this rattled, Roger." Charlotte frowned.

"Charlotte, you have to go with your gut, but mine says that we execute the itinerary as we planned it. You're protected by the best military in the world. Nothing is going to happen to you."

Charlotte looked at the photos of the attack from the day before. She made a note to call the families and then looked up. Roger was watching her.

"Send the guys back in here, will you?" she asked.

They landed quickly in the usual corkscrew. Charlotte liked to watch the landing from the cockpit. They got off Air Force One minutes before sunrise. Charlotte looked around and was amazed, as always, by how green everything was. In the early morning light, it looked almost beautiful.

She proceeded to Marine One to make her first stop at a polling station. The stop was designed to congratulate the Afghans on their first truly free and fair elections. It had taken years to rid the country of its corrupt leaders, but Charlotte was confident that either one of the two leading candidates for president would be the best partner America had had to work with since the original invasion years earlier.

The next stop was a meeting with local leaders, which went better than expected. Charlotte was feeling good. She was glad she hadn't abbreviated the schedule. She had involved herself in planning every meeting on her schedule, and these interactions informed her thinking on the overall strategy. Achieving stability in Afghanistan was proving far more difficult than their work in Iraq had been. She relied on her trips to the region to fill out the pictures painted by her various military and diplomatic advisors, as well as the allies that were still working alongside U.S. troops in the region.

From the meeting with local leaders, they traveled to the first of two bases they'd visit to thank U.S. and coalition troops. She gave a rousing speech to the troops and moved to a separate part of the base for her sit-down interview with Dale. She was feeling so good she allowed Dale's ten-minute interview to go long. She knew that Dale had been affected by what she'd seen so far that day. Charlotte had seen enough reporters make their maiden voyages to the front lines. They either loved it or were too scared to really see it. She could tell that Dale loved it. She'd seen her face when she interviewed the troops, she'd seen her nodding when they spoke about staying until the job was complete, and she could tell that Dale was touched by the soldiers who spoke movingly about their fallen comrades and their loved ones at home. After the interview, Charlotte posed for pictures with Dale's crew. She was heading to where Roger was huddled with officials from the base when she heard the first shots. Suddenly, her Secret Service agents were at her side.

"Let's go, Madam President," they said, surrounding her and half running, half dragging her toward Marine One. They shoved her onto the Blackhawk helicopter like a sack of potatoes.

The agents were still climbing in when Roger started shouting at the pilot to get the helicopter into the air. But Marine One didn't go anywhere at first.

The propeller was struggling to rotate in the dust that surrounded them. Two of Charlotte's agents were on top of her to protect her.

"What the fuck is happening?" Roger shouted.

"We had some dust in the prop, but it's clear now. We're on our way, sir," the pilot said as Marine One lifted into the air.

Everyone breathed a sigh of relief.

After about ten seconds, Roger started screaming at the pilot again. "Put it down! Put the helicopter down on the ground now!"

"I can't do that, sir," the pilot said, climbing higher.

"Land this fucking helicopter now!" Roger shouted. "That is an order."

"The helicopter is fine, sir. It was just dust in the prop," the pilot protested.

"I said land it!" Roger roared.

"Yes, sir," the pilot said.

The helicopter returned to the ground. Roger stood up and jumped out of Marine One.

"Roger, what are you doing?" Charlotte screamed.

"Marine One isn't working properly, Charlotte," Roger said.

"Put the president on the other helicopter!" Roger barked at the agents.

They hoisted Charlotte off Marine One and started running toward the next helicopter.

"Who rode over in this helicopter?" Charlotte yelled as they got closer. "How will they get out of here?"

The agents didn't say anything. Charlotte stopped and grabbed Roger's arm.

"I am not leaving anyone here. Who rode in this one? How are they getting out of here?" she asked.

"They'll get Marine One off the ground, Charlotte. Just get on this one. Everything will be fine," he said.

Roger pushed her into the Chinook and climbed in after her. They lifted off the ground before all of her agents were even onboard. Two of her agents climbed in as the aircraft swerved violently from side to side to avoid sniper fire.

"They are trying to get the fuel tank," she heard one of them say.

"Go, go, go!" she heard Roger yell.

She couldn't see anything.

She could barely breathe.

She freed her hands and wiped her hair from her mouth.

"Madam President, take these, please," the White House medic said to her, shoving three white pills in front of her face.

"What are they?" she asked.

"It's Cipro—in case of a bio attack, it might help a little bit. Just take them," he said, smiling sympathetically.

He handed her a bottle of water, and she swallowed the pills. She looked over the medic's shoulder and saw Marine One. It was still on the ground. She was relieved when a minute later, she saw it lift off the ground and begin to rise into the air behind them. She saw people running toward Marine One. She thought they were going to help, but seconds later, she saw one of them load something onto his shoulder and take aim. She tried to scream, but when she opened her mouth, nothing came out. Everything slid into slow motion.

She kept trying to scream at the pilot to go down and help whoever was on Marine One, but she couldn't scream. She could only watch.

"Get her the fuck out of the area, now!" Roger yelled at the pilot.

"All cars, all stations, Wayfarer depart," Charlotte heard over the radio system.

She turned her gaze to Marine One and saw smoke coming out of it. Seconds later, there was an explosion, and it struggled to stay airborne.

"Go help them!" she screamed at the pilot. "We need to go help them. They're going to crash!"

"Charlotte, we need to get back to Bagram right away," Roger said. He got on the radio and started barking orders.

"Please go help them!" she pleaded. But they were speeding away in the opposite direction. No one was talking to her. She had never felt more helpless in her life.

She watched everyone aboard the helicopter as they worked quietly and efficiently. After a couple of minutes, one of the military officers came and sat next to her.

"Ma'am, our guys took out the enemy, and a recovery mission is under way," he said.

She nodded. "Who was on Marine One when it went down?" she asked.

"It was the news crew, Madam President," he said.

Charlotte felt as if she might pass out. "And it went down from the missile, right?" Charlotte asked.

"Yes, ma'am."

"Were there mechanical problems with Marine One?" she asked.

"Not that registered in the logs, Madam President, but we need to do a full AAR," he said.

She looked at him blankly.

"After-action report, Madam President. Standard procedure for an incident like this," he said.

"Of course. And the crew?" she asked.

"We'll take care of them, ma'am," the officer said.

"Are they—I mean, did they survive?" she asked.

"We don't know their status yet, ma'am, but we'll get an update as soon as we get back to the base."

"Thanks," Charlotte said, wrapping her arms around herself and praying as she'd never prayed before.

CHAPTER NINETEEN

Melanie

Melanie dug around in her lingerie drawer for the lacy black bra-and-panty set her sister had sent her for her thirty-fifth birthday. It had never been worn, and while she didn't plan to go to bed with Brian on their first date, she figured it didn't hurt to be prepared. He'd e-mailed her the morning after their White House tour to say that he'd forgive her for not telling him about Charlotte's secret trip if she'd meet him for coffee. At the Starbucks across the street from the White House, he'd insisted that she promise him that the next time Charlotte ventured to Iraq or Afghanistan, they'd both be on the trip. "Deal," she'd committed.

And tonight they were going on their first real date. He was taking her to Bistro Lepic, a tiny French restaurant on Wisconsin Avenue in Georgetown. It was Melanie's last night of freedom before Charlotte returned from Afghanistan. Having Charlotte out of the country had allowed Melanie's anxiety to ebb a bit. In the days since her confrontation with Charlotte in the Rose Garden, she'd come to see Michael's affair rumor as less catastrophic than it had initially felt. If Charlotte was having an affair, which Melanie doubted she was, they would deal with it, she decided. She'd convinced herself that the rumor would prove false and that she and Charlotte would laugh about it when they finally discussed the topic again. She also had come to terms with the fact that it was time to step off the treadmill and get out of politics. Her sister had urged her to come live in New York, and Melanie was considering it. As much as she didn't want to admit it after knowing him for only a week, she wanted to see if there was any potential for something real with Brian.

Melanie had struggled with the wardrobe decision. She didn't want to wear a suit, but it was a graver sin to overdress than to underdress in Washington. She'd settled on a black wrap dress that flattered her small waist and gave her a little bit of cleavage. Brian wore dark slacks and a button-down shirt. Melanie thought he looked even younger and more attractive in his casual attire than he had in a texedo. They were seated in the corner, and they shared a laugh about the brusque French service. They drank two bottles of wine with their entrees and shared a chocolate mousse for dessert. The conversation between them was easy and comfortable, and Melanie found herself wanting the night to go on longer than she knew it would. D.C. had no nightlife to speak of for adults over twenty-eight years old.

When they were done with dinner, Brian paid the bill, and Melanie thanked him.

"I have a live shot in the morning, and I know you have to be at the office at the crack of dawn, so I should probably let you go home and get some sleep," Brian said.

Melanie was disappointed, but she smiled. "Sounds like a plan," she said.

She stood up and felt the effects of the wine. She put her hand on the chair to steady herself, and Brian put his arm around her waist. They walked to the car like that.

"Can we give you a ride?" Melanie said.

"That would be great," Brian said. She debated asking him to come back to her apartment for a drink. She didn't want to misread his signs. He had ended the date, but he'd been the one pursuing her all week. She glanced down at her BlackBerry. He did the same.

"Anything good on yours?" he asked her, skimming his messages.

"Nothing," she said, smiling at him, "How about yours? Anything good?"

"Nothing," he answered.

As they rode the short distance to Melanie's building, Walter and Sherry were doing their best imitation of invisible people. Brian glanced toward the front seat, but neither of them looked up. He moved closer to Melanie and leaned in to kiss her. She kissed him back.

They stopped at the last traffic light before Melanie's building. *What the hell*, Melanie thought.

"I was wondering if you'd like to come up for a drink," she said quietly.

"I would like that," he said, smiling and kissing her again.

Walter and Sherry were silent when they pulled up to Melanie's building, but Melanie could swear she saw Walter wink at Brian when he got out. She cringed.

"Good night, guys," she said to them. "See you tomorrow."

They waved. "G'night," they said in unison.

Melanie felt some butterflies in her stomach on the elevator ride up. Once inside, he pulled her toward him and kissed her again. It was a long, flirty kiss that felt like the beginning of exactly what Melanie had been preparing for when she'd pulled out her lacy underwear.

He untied her wrap dress, and it fell open as they stood in her entryway kissing. It was so natural, but she needed to slow things down a bit. She pulled away from him slightly.

"Why don't you open the bottle of wine on the counter, and I'll just be one second?" she said to him.

"I can handle that," he said.

She went into her bedroom and sat down on her bed. She slipped out of her dress and sat on the bed in her underwear. It had been so long since she'd had a man in her apartment. Charlotte would have gotten a kick out of the fact that Melanie had lured a younger man back to her place.

Thinking of Charlotte made her look at her BlackBerry. She saw an urgent message to call the Situation Room at the same time her cell phone and home phone rang. She heard another phone ringing that didn't sound familiar to her. It was Brian's cell phone. She heard him answer before she could get to her own phones. She opened the door to her bedroom and saw his face turn white before he hung up his phone.

"Marine One crashed in Afghanistan," he said. "I need to confirm that the president is still alive." He looked at Melanie as she stood in the doorway between her bedroom and the living room, suddenly feeling foolish in just her black bra and panties.

CHAPTER TWENTY

Dale

D ale heard voices, but she couldn't make them out. She thought, at times, that they were talking to her, but she couldn't be sure. She knew someone had been hurt. Something had crashed.

Was I in a crash? she wondered. She wasn't sure. *No, I'm fine,* she decided.

But then she tried to open her eyes, and she couldn't. She'd start to try to talk, but there were tubes in her mouth. She'd try to move her hands, but they were tied down. She felt panic growing in her chest and legs. Where was she?

But then the woman with the cool hands and familiar voice would put her hand on her arm or her face and talk in low, soothing tones. The woman would call for someone else, and that person would come into the room and put something into the bag hanging above her arm, and she'd sleep again.

Dale kept trying to make out her face. She recognized the voice but couldn't place it yet. At first, she thought it was her mother, but it wasn't her mother's voice.

And her mother's hands were always warm. Besides, her mother wouldn't be this calm if someone had crashed.

Dale could hear the woman breathing in the chair next to her bed. The woman didn't talk, and when she left the room, it was never for long.

She always came back and sat in the chair next to her bed.

Dale was tired again.

She'd figure it out the next time she woke up.

CHAPTER TWENTY-ONE

Charlotte

H ow is she?" she asked the doctor for the hundredth time.
"We don't know, Madam President. We won't know until
she wakes up," she said.

What she did not and would not say was that they didn't know for
sure *if* she would wake up.

Charlotte didn't know how long she'd been sitting there. It felt like
days, but there wasn't a chance that she'd be left alone that long, especially after what had transpired. She'd stood in the operating room
while they worked on Dale. It wasn't like scenes of operating rooms
in the movies or on television shows. It was quiet and calm. No one
talked. The doctors just worked on her for what felt like twelve hours
but was probably more like five or six. She had shrapnel in her lower
abdomen. It had hit her just where her flak jacket stopped and had
gone almost all the way through her body, from just below her belly
button all the way through to her back. At first, they were concerned
that she'd be paralyzed, but her spinal column had been spared. They
worked to repair her stomach and intestines for hours, and just as
they repaired one organ, they found bleeding in another. The doctors
asked Charlotte to leave a few times, but she made it clear that she
wasn't planning on going anywhere.

Charlotte hadn't been more than twenty feet away from Dale since they'd brought her in from the crash site. When they moved her to the ICU, where she'd stay until her condition was stable enough to travel to the military hospital in Germany, Charlotte sat in a chair in her room.

A military aide knocked on the door. "Madam President, Secretary Taylor would like to see you," he said.

"Please tell him to stay away from this room."

"Yes, ma'am."

"What time does Melanie Kingston land?" she asked.

"She left Andrews at one A.M., Madam President."

"I don't have any idea what time it is here, or in Washington. Please just tell me how much longer until she lands," Charlotte snapped.

"About an hour and a half."

"Please send her straight here," Charlotte ordered.

"Yes, ma'am."

Charlotte looked at Dale. She was breathing through a ventilator, and various other machines and monitors surrounded her. Even with a sheet and a blanket covering her wounds, Charlotte could tell that her body was swollen and mangled. Charlotte stood up and walked to the table where they had set up a secure phone for her to use. She picked it up and asked the military operator to connect her to Melanie on the military transport plane that was rushing her to Afghanistan.

"I have Ms. Kingston on the line, Madam President," the operator said.

"Melanie, can you hear me?" Charlotte asked.

"Yes, Madam President, I can hear you. How are you?" Melanie asked.

"I'm fine. Come see me as soon as you land. We need to do a statement soon."

"I've been working on a statement on the plane. I spoke to Roger, and—"

"You spoke to Roger?" Charlotte asked.

"Yes. He went over the fact pattern for me. We're going to need to brief the press on the entire operation. The military will brief after you, and—"

"Operational briefing? Melanie, do you have any idea what happened?" Charlotte said, her voice rising.

"I think so. There was sniper fire on the airstrip, so Roger put you in the closest helicopter to get you out of there, and then the helicopter with the press pool on it was hit. Dale is in critical condition, but the others are OK. She'll be moved to the military hospital in Germany as soon as she's stable enough to travel," Melanie recited.

"God, Melanie, no. No, that is not what happened," Charlotte moaned.

"I'm sorry. What am I missing? I have been on secure video conferences for the last seven hours. What did I get wrong?"

"That is not what happened. They told us to cut the trip short. They told me on Air Force One, and I didn't listen," Charlotte said. "Melanie, are you there?"

"I'm here, Madam President. I'm listening."

"We left the interview location, and we were heading back to the helicopters. I got on Marine One, but something was wrong—or that's what I thought, but now I don't know. Roger grabbed me, literally pulled me out of Marine One before the agents could even get to me. There was sniper fire. Did they tell you that?"

"Yes, that's what I said, Madam President. Listen, you might be in shock. Have you been checked out by the doctors?"

"Stop talking to me like I'm a fucking idiot. Listen to me," Charlotte insisted.

"I'm listening," Melanie said.

"Melanie, we knew it was too dangerous. The intelligence suggested that there was an uptick in violence, and Albert suggested we cut the trip short, but Roger said it would be OK. And then, as we were taking off, they just came out of nowhere and started firing. The base was under attack. I was on Marine One, but Roger made them land, and then he pulled me out and put me on the other helicopter. He told them the mechanics didn't sound right, but I was told that Marine One was fine. I didn't know, Melanie. And it all happened so fast. I didn't know what was happening until we lifted off the ground on the press chopper, and I saw them. I saw them running toward Marine One. They must have fired a shoulder-launched grenade. I saw it go up in flames and crash. They thought they had killed me and they were celebrating. But Roger left Marine One on the ground as a decoy. Do you understand what I'm saying, Melanie? Roger left Marine One there as a target. He used Dale and her crew so I could escape on another helicopter. He left them on Marine One to die." Charlotte's voice started to strain with emotion, but she steadied herself. "Melanie, are you there?" she asked.

"I'm here."

"Melanie, I need you to ask Roger for his resignation as soon as you get here."

"Charlotte, you need to do the statement as soon as I land. The public hasn't seen or heard from you in nearly twenty hours. All they know is that Marine One went down, and word is getting out that Dale was hurt. There are rumors that she's dead. We need to get in front of this before it's too late."

"Melanie, for once, this isn't about getting ahead of the press. If that girl dies, our administration has blood on its hands. Roger nearly killed her. We need to announce his resignation," Charlotte insisted.

"We'll talk when I get there. He thinks he saved your life, Charlotte. He thinks he deserves your gratitude, and he can't figure out why you won't see him."

"What he did was not brave. He traded one life for another. That's not heroic—it's criminal."

Melanie sighed. "I'll be there in about an hour. Don't do anything until I get there, Charlotte, OK?"

"Yeah. OK. See you soon," Charlotte said.

She hung up the phone and asked to be connected to Peter's cell phone. A military aide had called Peter and her parents immediately following the crash. They were told that there had been an unanticipated security breach and that Charlotte was safe and being taken to an undisclosed location from which she would call as soon as she could.

"Charlotte, are you all right?" he asked on the first ring.

"Yes, I'm fine. Are you with the kids?"

"Yes, we're all here. They want to talk to you. Let me put them on."

"No, not yet. I need to tell you something, Peter."

"What? Were you hurt? Are you OK, Char?" he asked.

"Yes, yes, I'm fine. It's Dale," she said.

She heard him take a breath.

"She was in a helicopter, and it was hit by a shoulder-launched grenade. They went down, and she was brought to the hospital here, in Afghanistan. She was in surgery for, I don't know how long, a long time. I was in there the whole time, Peter. I was in there, and they took really good care of her. She's in the ICU now. She hasn't woken up yet." Charlotte's voice cracked. She couldn't cry. She wouldn't cry. She took another breath. "Peter, a plane is waiting for you at Andrews. It will take you to the military hospital in Landstuhl, Germany. They're going to move her there as soon as they can," she said. "Peter, listen to me. She's tough, and she's going to be fine." Peter still hadn't said anything.

"I'm in her room now. She's resting, and she looks really peaceful. I am going to call her parents next and have them meet you at Andrews." She could hear him breathing. "Peter, say something," Charlotte said.

"Why are you in her room?" he asked.

"What?" Charlotte was stunned by the hostility in his voice.

"Why are you with her? You don't sit at the kids' bedsides when they're sick," he said.

His words were like body blows. Peter's resentment had been building up for so long that even he seemed surprised by its ferocity.

Charlotte took a breath and spoke calmly. "You're right. I've missed a lot of colds and flu bugs over the years. But we both know that's not what this is about, don't we?"

He was silent.

"You think I put her in danger. You think that I am so petty that I put your girlfriend in harm's way, what, to punish you? Give me a fucking break, Peter. For once, give me a break."

"I wish I could," he said.

CHAPTER TWENTY-TWO

Melanie

The president has been in the room the whole time," the military aide said. "She hasn't left to eat, and she didn't go to bed last night. Just slept sitting in a chair by the bed."

"Really? The president has been in there the whole time?" Melanie asked as they walked down the hospital corridor. She doubted that the president had done any sleeping.

"Yes, ma'am," he said, pleased to be briefing the White House chief of staff on the president's actions.

They came to a stop. "Thanks for your help," Melanie said.

"My pleasure," he said.

She gently pushed the door open.

Charlotte was sitting next to Dale's bed with her head in her hands. Her clothes were uncharacteristically disheveled, her face was ashen, and her hair was pulled back in a messy ponytail.

Charlotte gave Melanie a weary smile when she saw her. "Hi, Mel," Charlotte whispered. "Let's talk in the hall," she said, pointing at Dale. She stood up and walked into the hallway.

"Madam President?" Melanie asked.

"I'm fine, Melanie. Thanks for coming."

They went into a room that had been set up as an office for Charlotte. Secure video-conference equipment lined the wall, and secure phone lines had been installed. A computer and printer had been set up on a desk against one wall, and a small sofa had been pushed against the opposite wall.

They walked slowly over to the sofa and sat down.

Charlotte looked at her hands and cleared her throat.

Melanie braced herself.

Charlotte didn't say anything, so Melanie spoke first. "Madam President, we really need to get you in front of the press. It's important that the American people see you take charge of the situation, especially right now."

Charlotte stared off into space. Melanie was starting to worry that she wouldn't be able to pull off the press statement.

"Melanie, I need to tell you something."

"What is it?" Melanie asked.

"I don't think I want to do this anymore," Charlotte stated.

Melanie didn't know if it was the tension created by their extraordinary circumstances or the simple truth Charlotte had spoken, but she started to laugh. She couldn't help it.

"I'm sorry, Madam President. I just, you just, you took the words right out of my mouth," Melanie said.

Charlotte looked at her for a few seconds, and then she laughed a little bit, too.

Melanie was relieved.

Charlotte was back.

With the tension broken, they leaned toward each other, and Charlotte told Melanie what had happened. Melanie took notes so she could turn Charlotte's words into the framework of the press statement. Charlotte was calmer than she'd been when they'd spoken by phone, and her account was clear about one thing: Roger had dramatically altered the chain of events on the landing strip by ordering the pilot of Marine One to land the helicopter after it had taken off. What was unclear was whether Roger had actually believed there was something wrong with Marine One and whether he knew for sure that the Black Hawk they were using to transport Charlotte was the target. According to Charlotte's account, the pilot's log showed no mechanical defects with Marine One. If Roger did, in fact, land Marine One as a decoy so Charlotte could escape, then Charlotte was correct—he'd been willing to trade the lives of the news crew for Charlotte's.

"Melanie, we don't save anyone—not even the president—by sacrificing another life," she said.

"I understand how you feel about this, Charlotte," Melanie started to say.

"How I feel? This isn't about my emotional reaction. This is clear-cut to me, and I think it will be to most of the American people. Do you disagree? Are you taking Roger's side, Melanie?" Charlotte stood up.

"No, of course not," Melanie soothed.

"Good," Charlotte said.

"I'm just saying that it's a big deal to force Roger's resignation less than twenty-four hours after something like this. And not that this figures into your decision making, but the political reality of forcing Roger to resign before any investigation is done is devastating. The press will say you threw him under the bus, and Republicans will probably attack the hell out of you for letting him take the fall. I know it's sexist, but some of them think he's the only reason you've been successful here and in Iraq."

Charlotte stood and walked across the small room. "I meant it when I said that I don't want to do this anymore," Charlotte said.

"Yes, ma'am," Melanie said.

"I want to put it all out there, Melanie," Charlotte said. "All of it."

She pulled a chair in front of the computer and motioned for Melanie to sit next to her. Charlotte talked, and Melanie typed, stopping to read sections out loud and then making revisions as they went. The words came much easier for both of them than they had in a long time, and when Charlotte was finally done talking, Melanie asked for some time alone to fine-tune the remarks.

The light on her BlackBerry that flashed when it was receiving a message had been blinking nonstop. Reporters, White House aides, members of Congress, and Cabinet members were all looking for advance notice of what Charlotte would say. She hadn't responded to a single message.

It'll be worth the wait, ladies and gentlemen, Melanie thought as she printed out a copy of the speech for Charlotte's final review.

CHAPTER TWENTY-THREE

Dale

D ale stared at the ceiling and tried to figure out how long she'd been there. She knew she was in a hospital, but she didn't know where, and she didn't know why.

She tried to speak to the nurse who was changing the IV in her arm. After a couple of failed attempts, she managed to make a sound. She tried to cough, but there was something in her throat. Her hands flew to her mouth, and she started to panic when she felt the tubes there.

"Easy, girl, easy does it. I'll get that out. Just settle down. Take a breath and exhale, now," the nurse said, pulling out the breathing tube.

Hers was definitely not the voice Dale had heard while she slept.

Dale felt as if her throat was on fire.

"How you feeling?" the nurse asked.

"Everything hurts," Dale whispered.

"I know, I know. Everyone's gonna be so happy that you're awake," the nurse said.

Dale was in a daze. She tried to nod at the nurse, but she couldn't focus on what she was saying.

"Let me get the doctor, and there's someone else who wanted us to get her as soon as you woke up."

When she returned, she was followed by a woman in scrubs.

"Hi, Miss Smith, how are you doing?" the woman in scrubs asked. "I operated on you when you came in. How's your pain level on a scale from one to ten?"

"Eight," Dale lied. It was more like twenty-five.

"We'll get you some Percocet, and if it's really bad, we'll give you morphine, but I want to start getting you off that."

Dale closed her eyes briefly. It was clear now that she was the one who had been in a crash.

"My crew?" Dale said.

"They're OK," the doctor said.

Dale tried to smile. The nurse was saying something to the doctor, but Dale couldn't make out their conversation.

"Go get her" was all she heard.

"I'm going to do an exam. I want to check the incisions," the doctor said.

She pulled the sheet down and exposed Dale's midsection. It was tightly wrapped with bandages that went all the way around her body. The doctor peeked through some of the gauze.

"You had a good deal of internal bleeding. We couldn't figure out where you were bleeding from, so we had to open you up," she explained. "You were really lucky," the doctor added.

Lucky wasn't the word that came to Dale's mind.

"Thank you for taking care of me," Dale said, closing her eyes again. She could feel someone enter the room.

"Madam President, she's been up for about five minutes," the doctor said.

Dale's eyes flew open.

"Hi, Dale," Charlotte said.

"Hi," Dale said, struggling to try to sit up.

"No, don't move, please, Dale," Charlotte said. "I'm sorry. I should let you rest."

"It's all right," Dale said, forcing a smile.

"Do you remember what happened?" Charlotte asked.

Dale shook her head.

"What's the last thing you remember?"

"Her memory is likely to be foggy from the anesthesia," the doctor said.

"You interviewed me. Do you remember that?" Charlotte said.

Dale nodded.

"We went long," Charlotte said, smiling at Dale.

Dale nodded again.

"And then we were heading back to the helicopters, and there was sniper fire. Do you remember that?" Charlotte asked.

Dale racked her brain, but she couldn't remember anything after the interview.

"Don't worry. I'm sure it will all come back," Charlotte said.

Dale tried to smile.

"We were heading back, and the base came under attack," Charlotte said.

Dale stared at her.

"We were boarding when the sniper fire got closer, and Roger and the agents realized at some point that we were under attack," Charlotte continued.

Dale's eyes widened.

"And I was about to board the Black Hawk that we were using as Marine One. I did board, but Roger decided to switch me to another helicopter at the last minute. So, they, the agents, pulled you off your helicopter and sent you to Marine One."

Dale just stared back at her.

"While you were boarding Marine One, we took off on the press helicopter. And once we were in the air and on our way, we saw that insurgents had fired at Marine One. It went down, and you were hurt and brought here."

Dale stared, unblinking, at Charlotte.

"Do you understand? Roger put you on Marine One so I could escape," Charlotte said.

Dale squeezed her eyes shut and opened them again.

"Dale, your mom and dad are on their way to Andrews. They're going to meet you at the hospital in Germany," Charlotte said.

Dale tried to nod.

"And Peter is going to meet you there as well," Charlotte said.

Dale's eyes widened.

"It's OK," Charlotte said.

Dale's breathing quickened, and her eyes moved around the room.

"Please, do not worry about anything except getting better," Charlotte said, touching Dale's arm lightly.

In that instant, Dale realized that it had been Charlotte's voice she'd heard and her cool hands that had touched her face.

It had been Charlotte sitting by her bed while she slept.

Her head was spinning. She was suddenly exhausted again, and the pain was too much. The last thing she heard before she fell asleep was Charlotte asking the doctor to give Dale something for the pain.

CHAPTER TWENTY-FOUR

Charlotte

The morphine made its way into Dale's system quickly. Charlotte sat watching her sleep as the monitors beeped and flashed with comforting regularity.

"She's gonna be just fine, Madam President," the nurse said, turning to Charlotte.

"I hope so," Charlotte said.

She leaned back in the chair where she'd spent most of the last twenty-four hours. She contemplated calling Peter again to tell him Dale had woken up, but he'd been so icy before. She'd told him again that it was her fault Dale had been hit. She'd insisted that he catch the flight to Germany and told him she was sorry she hadn't let him out of their marriage sooner.

He'd remained silent. She knew him well enough to know that his silence was a protective measure. He was angry at Charlotte for ignoring him for nearly a decade, but he was also scared that Dale might die.

Charlotte pressed her temples and took a deep breath. She only had a few minutes until she'd have to give the statement to the press. She dialed Sam back at the White House and asked to be put through to her parents.

"Hi, it's me," she said.

"How are you doing, sweetheart?" her mother asked.

"I'm about to do a statement, but I need to ask you and Daddy to do me a favor."

"Of course, honey, what is it?" her mother asked.

"I need you to head up to Connecticut and stay close to the kids for a little while. I don't know when Peter is going to be able to get back up there," Charlotte said. She didn't feel like explaining the whole thing, and her mother didn't ask any questions.

"We're on our way, honey. Don't worry about anything."

"Thanks, Mom. I'll call when I can and fill you in. I'm going to call the kids next and tell them you're coming up for a visit."

"Stay safe, honey."

"I will. Tell Daddy I'll talk to him when I call you back in a couple of hours."

Charlotte hung up and asked the Situation Room to call the kids on their cell phones. She hated that she couldn't speak to them in person, but her parents would be there soon.

"Hi, sweetie," she said when Penelope picked up.

"Hi, Mom. Aren't you about to give a speech?" Penelope said.

"I have a few minutes, and I wanted to talk to you first. Are you with Harry?" Charlotte asked.

"Yes, he's right here."

"Do you want to put the phone on speaker?" Charlotte asked.

"Yep. Hang on."

"Hi, Mom," Harry said.

"Hi, sweetheart. Listen, guys, I wish I could talk to you in person, and I promise that when I get home, we're going to go to Camp David and talk about all of this stuff, but I need to talk about our family a little bit when I give this statement tonight."

The kids didn't say anything.

"Do you know where Dad went?" Charlotte asked.

"We know, Mom. He went to see his friend who was hurt in the helicopter crash," Penelope said.

"Yes. That's right. His friend Dale is very important to him, and he's going to spend time with her while she gets better, and that's OK with me, and I want it to be OK with you guys, too."

"It's OK," Harry said.

"Don't worry, Mom," Penelope added.

"Thanks, guys. Gammy and Gramps will be there tonight, and they'd going to take you to dinner, and I'll be back in Washington tomorrow. I'm going to call you from the plane on my way home. I love you guys," she said.

"Love you, too," they said in unison.

Melanie had entered the room while she was talking to the twins.

"How's she doing?" Melanie asked, looking at the monitors surrounding Dale.

"They just gave her morphine, so she's out for a little bit."

"A shot of morphine sounds pretty good right about now," Melanie joked.

Charlotte smiled wearily. "She woke up, which is a good sign," Charlotte said. "After surgery like that, they don't know exactly how the body is going to rebound from all the blood loss and trauma."

"I'm glad she's safe," Melanie said.

"She's not out of the woods yet," Charlotte warned.

"I brought you a copy of the statement. If you want to make changes, we need them in the next ten minutes so we can load them into the teleprompter," Melanie said.

Charlotte read the statement through twice. "It's perfect. No one else could have written this."

"Thank you. Listen, it's time for you to get ready," Melanie said.

"I know. Let me read it through one more time."

"I thought it was perfect," Melanie teased.

"Not for edits, just for practice. I'll be out in five minutes. I'll meet you back in the hold room."

"And you'll be out of this scary outfit, and your hair will be combed?" Melanie prodded.

"Yes, and I'll even put on makeup."

When Melanie had left the room, Charlotte turned her chair to face Dale and read the statement all the way through. When she finished, she looked up.

"Dale, you probably just slept through the first scoop I've ever given you," Charlotte said softly.

Dale didn't stir.

Back in her quarters, Charlotte showered and changed. She was nibbling on a chocolate-chip cookie when Melanie burst into the room.

"We have a situation," Melanie said.

"What?"

"I think you need to let Roger resign in person. He's not onboard with the plan yet, and if you refuse to see him, I think he's going to be very combative about the whole thing. His career and reputation are on the line."

"There's nothing to say," Charlotte retorted.

"I know, but I think you need to listen to him and let him make his case. He's been your closest advisor for three years, Charlotte, and one of your closest friends. You owe him ten minutes," Melanie pleaded.

"Fine. Send him in," Charlotte said.

Roger walked in and came toward her. He looked as if he'd been up all night, too.

"Can we talk alone?" he asked.

Melanie started to go.

"Melanie, please stay," Charlotte said.

Roger took another step toward Charlotte. "Charlotte, don't do this—don't prove everyone right," he said.

Charlotte glared at him. "Roger, I need to get out there. I don't have time for this."

"I have to say one thing to you, Charlotte, before you walk out there and ruin both our careers. It matters over here. Things like this matter. If the enemy sees that he can take down the closest person to you in the entire U.S. government with stunts like this, what do you think he'll do next time? Take a hostage from a presidential entourage? Or, worse, torture a hostage from your travel party for the world to see on the Internet? What about all our conversations about not giving the enemies what they want most? This flies in the face of all of that."

Charlotte didn't say anything.

"Why do you think I did what I did? Do you think I was trying to hurt that girl? I was not. I was trying to save you. Do you have any idea what kind of world Harry and Penelope would grow up in if the

American president—not to mention their mother—had died here yesterday?"

Charlotte looked away.

"And I have to say, finally, that it is clear that I'm being punished because of our special relationship. Since the day I met you, you have come first, Charlotte. You come before Stephanie, before the kids, before everything and anyone else. And you had all of me. I gave you one hundred and fifty percent, seven days a week, twenty-five hours a day. But that wasn't enough. It is never enough with you."

She turned and looked at him.

"Sooner or later, everyone disappoints you," Roger said.

She had thought she might find it difficult to reject an apology if he had blamed his actions on the fog of war, but he hadn't shown any remorse about leaving Marine One on the ground as a target. Charlotte felt an ache deep in her gut. She missed him already.

"There has to be a line, Roger, a line that separates us from them. What you did made you more like them than us, in my book. That's why this is happening. Not because you tried to protect me, not because you didn't give me enough of yourself, and not because of our special relationship."

"You're going to regret this, Charlotte," Roger said.

"I already do, but this isn't about me. I took an oath, and I'm duty-bound to protect this country and everyone in it. I'm pretty sure sacrificing one of their lives for mine is a violation of everything that oath is supposed to mean, Roger." She turned to leave.

"I took an oath, too, Charlotte," Roger said. "It was to serve and protect the commander in chief."

"You took an oath to protect this country, Roger, not to throw half a dozen lives into the air to be shot down like clay pigeons," Charlotte said, her voice rising.

"I'm sorry you see it that way, Charlotte," Roger said.

"Unfortunately, for all of us, it isn't my perspective—it's a fact. And not everyone disappoints me, Roger," she said, walking toward where Melanie was standing on the other side of the room.

CHAPTER TWENTY-FIVE

Melanie

T he teleprompters are on the sides, at about two o'clock and ten o'clock," Melanie said as they walked toward the press briefing room.

"I've got it," Charlotte said.

"Once I give them the final heads-up, everyone will take the shot live, so just walk out and find the prompters, and gather yourself and go as soon as you're ready," Melanie said.

"Melanie, this is hardly my first live address. Stop worrying. I've got it from here."

"I know. I'm sorry," Melanie said.

"Relax. Everything is going to sort itself out," Charlotte promised.

"I know," Melanie said, trying to sound convinced.

Charlotte disappeared behind the blue drape and walked toward the podium. Melanie made her way down the side of the room and stood with the small gaggle of senior military and White House aides. She watched Charlotte place her remarks on the podium and look up to find the teleprompter screens. Charlotte cleared her throat and looked directly into the sea of cameras and reporters assembled for her remarks.

Melanie plastered a confident smile on her face in case the press was filming her. They loved to use shots of worried aides to add color to their reports.

"Good evening," Charlotte said. "To the press joining me here tonight in Afghanistan, thanks for staying up so late. And to those of you joining me from the States, welcome.

"I want to use this opportunity to inform you about the events of the last twenty-four hours. As many of you know, we were visiting a base outside Kabul yesterday. After our visit, your colleague, Dale Smith, conducted an interview with me. As soon as that interview was complete, we started to board our helicopters. After I boarded Marine One, U.S. government officials made a decision to transfer me to another helicopter, based on an assessment about the threats we faced from an imminent attack on the base. I was put inside the helicopter that had been transporting the traveling press pool. The press was then put in Marine One. My helicopter took off, and thanks to the brave and skilled work of our pilot, we made it back to the base safely. Marine One took off moments later. Just as it was lifting off the ground, the helicopter was hit by a shoulder-launched grenade that we believe was fired by local Taliban members. The U.S. military will do a briefing after I'm done here on their response to the attack, but let me say that it was swift and decisive.

"Marine One crashed, and Dale Smith and her crew were brought here to the hospital on the base. Her crew members and the helicopter's pilot and crew suffered minor injuries. They were released from the hospital and are doing well. In fact, I see some of them here tonight. Dale Smith's injuries were critical. She was brought to the hospital's trauma center, where Dr. Margaret Sladen, who is also here tonight, headed the surgical team that worked for about six hours on Ms. Smith. Ms. Smith is recovering faster than her doctors predicted. She is breathing on her own, and it is their judgment that she will make a complete recovery. However, we won't say anything else about her medical condition from here today, and we defer to Ms. Smith's family and the military hospital system for any further updates.

"One member of my team, who has served this country with honor and distinction for nearly three decades, informed me just before I walked out here that he would be placing himself on administrative leave pending a joint Pentagon-CIA investigation of the sequence of events leading up to the decision to move me from one helicopter to the other. This individual is Secretary Roger Taylor. Since his judgment has served me so well in my three years as president, I find myself in the difficult position of having to accept his determination that a leave of absence is necessary in this instance. It is Secretary Taylor's judgment that this measure is vital if we are to have a full and complete airing of the facts leading up to yesterday's attack. In the interim, I have asked my national security advisor, Tim Hansen, to serve as both my national security advisor and the acting defense secretary while Secretary Taylor is on leave.

"For those of you returning to Washington with me tonight, we have a busy several days ahead. I'll be heading to Capitol Hill to brief the House and Senate Foreign Relations Committees, the Armed Services Committees, and the Intelligence Committees on the events of the last twenty-four hours. We will work in a bipartisan fashion to understand how an attack on the presidential traveling party could happen and how to make sure it never happens again.

"As I mentioned before, Ms. Smith is fighting hard to join all of you back in those chairs. She will be moved to Germany first thing in the morning, where she will be met by her family and her loved ones."

Charlotte paused, and Melanie held her breath.

"Those loved ones include Peter Kramer, my husband," Charlotte said.

Melanie thought the press would gasp, but they did not. She thought perhaps they'd missed it. She and Charlotte had discussed this possibility.

"My husband, Peter Kramer, and Dale Smith are involved in a close personal relationship. I make the following request for their benefit, not mine. I ask that you respect their privacy during Dale's recovery.

"As an elected official, I owe you and the American people an explanation, and I promise you all that there will be a time and a place for us to have a discussion about my personal life if the American people so choose.

"I want to say something tonight about families. We all do the best we can, and our failures are ours alone. As I said, there will be a time and a place for you to probe about my marriage, and I understand why it's of interest to you and to the voters. I will be as candid as possible, at the appropriate time.

"Now, I want to speak directly to the American people. When you elected me a little more than three years ago, you trusted me to protect you from threats to our security and threats to our economy. We had moved on from nine-eleven, but we'd healed in a way that left us more broken, in many ways, than before. I have worked every day in office to create economic opportunity for all Americans and to reward and welcome innovation and entrepreneurship. I have collaborated with members of both parties to strengthen the safety nets in this country for those who rely on them for the basic services that create a life of dignity. I have fought every day in office to make sure that the threat of terrorism never again touches our shores. I've worked every day to protect your families, and sometimes that's been at the expense of my family.

"I am often asked about the impact of a life in politics on a family. And a lot of politicians offer half-truths about what that impact really is. I am guilty of this. There is a stigma associated with having to admit that you've made sacrifices or tradeoffs, that you don't really have it all. As a result, many of us in public life cobble together the image of ourselves that we think you demand of us. We hold up our perfect marriages and our perfect families, and we hope you believe those images. In many cases, the images match the reality.

"Not mine. I have a wonderful husband, but he did not choose this public life. We have great kids, and you have all been very generous about granting them their privacy. I ask for your continued generosity toward my family during this difficult time. I am sorry for not being completely honest with all of you about my family, and I hope that you and your families will forgive me for that.

"Finally, I want to say something about the people who keep me safe. They include some of the finest agents the United States Secret Service has ever produced. I owe them my life, on a normal day. This week, they went well above and beyond the call of duty, and to all of them, and their families, I am grateful. To the men and women of our military, we add to your burdens by coming here, but your performance yesterday was heroic. Thank you. To the doctors and nurses who work to heal our national treasures when they are injured, you have the gratitude of a nation. And to my entire White House staff and Cabinet, thank you for supporting me.

"Before we leave here, I want to thank all of you for the risks you take every day to bring news about this important place to the American people and to people around the world.

"Thank you for listening. God bless all the men and women who fight to keep us safe from harm. Good night."

The press was so stunned by Charlotte's remarks that some of them joined the military personnel from the base who stood and applauded when Charlotte was done. Most of them caught themselves and sat back down to pound away furiously at their laptops. The television correspondents were breathless in their live reports, each outdoing the other to describe the speech as a "bombshell" or a "jaw dropper." The troops who'd gathered to listen to Charlotte's remarks lined up to take their pictures with the president. Melanie waded through the press scrum to find Charlotte.

"How long have Peter and Dale been together?" one reporter asked her.

"Was Roger fired?" shouted another.

"Is she still running for reelection?" yelled another, while his cameraman panned to Melanie.

Melanie politely brushed them all off. "The president gave all of you a great deal of information. We'll take questions on the way home. Don't miss the flight. We're wheels up in twenty minutes," she told them.

She made her way to the holding room, where Charlotte was shaking hands and saying good-bye to the generals.

"Let us know if you need anything from Washington," she was saying to one of them when she saw Melanie. "Melanie, how's it playing?" Charlotte asked.

"I got an e-mail from Ralph, who said that the speaker and the Senate majority leader were both on the phone before the speech was over to say that they are thrilled that you're coming up tomorrow to debrief them. And he thought the Roger language was artful enough to buy us a couple of days with Republicans, so I'd say it's going over pretty well," Melanie said.

"And the news about Peter?" Charlotte asked.

"I haven't been able to watch any of the coverage from here, but I'm sure that's all the chattering class is talking about," she said.

"I tell them about a crash that almost killed one of their colleagues and the resignation of the secretary of defense, and all they care about is who my husband is sleeping with?" Charlotte said.

"Yep," Melanie said.

An aide came back to the hold room and told Charlotte and Melanie that it was time to board Air Force One.

Once onboard, Charlotte and Melanie settled into the conference room to discuss their next steps. It was getting late in Washington, so they made a few brief calls to key senators.

"Yes, yes, I look forward to speaking to you about it when I come up tomorrow," Charlotte was saying to the head of the Senate Foreign Relations Committee. "Yes, thank you. Honesty is certainly the best policy, that's right. Thanks for your kind words. Yes, my kids are fine, thanks so much. See you tomorrow," Charlotte said, rolling her eyes.

She covered the mouthpiece and leaned toward Melanie while the Air Force One operator connected another call.

"Do these guys ever stop talking?" she asked.

"Nope, that's why we never send you up there," Melanie said.

"Are we going to bring the press up to talk off the record?" Charlotte asked.

"Yes, I think it would be a good thing to do. Let them see that you're not rattled, that we put everything out there, and we're going to deal with this thing head-on."

"Whatever you say," Charlotte said to Melanie, just as her call was connected to another senator. "Hi, Senator, how are you? Charlotte Kramer here. Yes, thank you. I thought honesty was the best policy. Yes, we'll be on the Hill tomorrow. We'll get to the bottom of it. I thank you for your support. I look forward to seeing you, too. Thanks, Senator. See you soon."

Charlotte hung up and sighed loudly.

"Am I done yet?" Charlotte asked Melanie.

"We should make a few more calls to the Hill before we bring the press up."

"How many is a few?"

Melanie ignored that. "I'll let the press call in their stories from Air Force One so we can manage the news cycle," she said.

Charlotte stood up. "I'm going try to reach Peter to see if he's landed in Germany yet, and I want to check in with the kids," she said.

"I'll be right here," Melanie told her.

Charlotte turned to leave the conference room for her private cabin. "Melanie, I'm sorry about not telling you about Peter and Dale."

Melanie didn't look up. "Don't worry about it," Melanie said. "I should have figured it out."

"I'm just curious. Is that what the press was badgering you about before the trip?" Charlotte asked. "Is that what you were trying to ask me in the Rose Garden?"

"Actually, no," Melanie said, looking at Charlotte. "It was not."

Charlotte sat back down. "Then what *were* they asking about?" Charlotte said.

Melanie stood up and closed the door to the conference room. "I guess this is as good a time as any to talk about it. Michael from the *Dispatch* has a source who claims to have photos and other information proving that you are having an affair."

"Me? With whom am I having this alleged affair? Let me know so I can enjoy it." Charlotte laughed.

"I don't know. I couldn't get it out of him, but he has a source who is almost ready to go on the record."

"That's ridiculous. I've made a mess out of my marriage, but I'm not having an affair," Charlotte protested.

"Do you have any idea who would suggest that you are?" Melanie asked.

"No, and I can't believe Michael won't just shut this down when you tell him it isn't true."

"I know. That's how it usually works."

Charlotte gave her a curious look. "Usually? Does this happen often?"

"Not this specifically, but I get all sorts of crazy questions from serious reporters. You wouldn't believe half the crap their editors make them run down. Or at least that's what they say."

"Like what?" Charlotte asked.

"Oh, let's see, I get questions about whether you're gay about once a month," Melanie said, smiling as Charlotte gasped.

"You're kidding."

"And let's see, I get questions about you and Roger sometimes," Melanie continued.

"Really?" Charlotte looked away.

"Yeah, those are easy. I tell them that you and Stephanie are as close as can be and that you've always been friends with both Taylors, blah, blah, blah."

"Melanie," Charlotte said, grabbing her arm.

"What's wrong?" Melanie said.

"That could be Michael's source."

"Who?" Melanie asked.

"Stephanie."

"Why would she do that?" Melanie asked.

"She's been annoyed for months about all the travel Roger and I do together. She didn't come to Camp David the last couple of times I invited them, and when I was there for dinner a few weeks ago, she was really distant. Roger didn't think he'd be able to come on this trip because she didn't want him coming over here again."

"So she's pissed off, but that doesn't mean she called Michael and made up a story about an affair."

"Maybe she doesn't think she's making it up," Charlotte said, leaning back in the chair and looking out the window.

"What are you talking about?" Melanie said.

"I heard Roger on the phone recently. I heard him say, 'You're being paranoid and ridiculous.' It had to be Stephanie. And then he pulled out of the trip when we were planning it last month because she found a lump in her breast, but when I asked about it the next time I saw him, he said that it had been a false alarm and that Stephanie was trying to get his attention. And the night before we left, I heard him on the phone with her. He hadn't told her he was coming to Afghanistan this week. She found out from Dale."

"Dale wasn't supposed to tell anyone," Melanie said, indignant.

"Considering the fact that we almost killed her, I don't think she should get into any trouble for saying something to Stephanie. She assumed Stephanie knew."

"Do you think Roger knows what Stephanie is up to?" Melanie asked.

"No way," Charlotte said.

Melanie sighed.

"And he has enough problems," Charlotte added.

"Let me see if I can get Michael to kill the story. I'll see if I can call his bluff on Stephanie."

"He should do that, don't you think? Doesn't his daughter work for you?" Charlotte said.

"That won't help us here. Listen, I need to ask you something. The photos and recordings—is there anything that could paint an unflattering picture?" Melanie asked.

"I don't know. I talk to Roger all the time. If she recorded our calls, she could splice it all together to paint a picture that raises questions. And photos—I mean, I've spent a lot of time with Roger. I swear to you, Melanie, I never slept with Roger, but we are, or were, close," Charlotte said.

"The worst-case scenario is that Stephanie alleges an affair, you and Roger deny it, and then, with her back up against the wall, she releases recordings of you guys and photos that depict an unprofessional relationship but no evidence of a sexual relationship, right?" Melanie said.

"Yes. I suppose that's about it. And if Roger wants to screw me over for the leave-of-absence trap I set for him at the press avail, he can join forces with his wife and really do a number on me," Charlotte said, pressing her fingers into her temples.

"That's a risk, but for that to happen, Stephanie would have to confide in Roger, and there's no indication that he's in on this," Melanie said.

"True, but who knows what will happen now? Spouses have a way of banding together when the world turns against them," Charlotte said.

"I'm going to bring Michael in when we get back to Washington. I'll get him to confirm Stephanie as his source, and then maybe you can come in and ask to speak to him alone about the Roger dynamic. Give him reason to suspect that Roger and Stephanie are trying to sabotage you. The best-case scenario is that this all dies a quiet death."

"Right. Roger is going to be raked over the coals by Congress. We don't need to expose his wife's *Fatal Attraction* streak. Let's do whatever we need to do to kill the story," Charlotte said.

"I'll call Michael first thing," Melanie promised.

"I'm sorry this hasn't exactly turned out to be a dream job. I'm sure your time in the Martin administration was much more civilized," Charlotte apologized.

"Nah, there was always a crisis to be managed then, too," she lied. "Don't worry about it."

"I couldn't do it without you," Charlotte said.

"No, you could not," Melanie said, smiling and writing down items on her to do list for when they landed in Washington.

CHAPTER TWENTY-SIX

Dale

D ale woke up on the seventh day of her stay in Germany the same way she had the previous mornings. She started by reminding herself where she was. Then she ticked through the various injuries she had suffered. Finally, she took an inventory of the things that had changed in the days since she'd left Washington, D.C., for Afghanistan.

First, the president of the United States liked her. Even before the crash, they had bonded. She was sure of it. Second, she had been sent up on Marine One so that the president could escape safely. Third, her relationship with Peter was out in the open.

What she couldn't figure out was why Peter was so furious at Charlotte, and it was a topic Peter wasn't interested in discussing.

She looked at him as he slept fitfully on a hospital bed they'd moved into her room for him. She knew the last few days had been hard on him. He worried about the kids and hated that he wasn't with them. He worried about Charlotte's political fate. And he worried about her. She reached out and smoothed his hair. He opened his eyes.

"Was I sleeping?" he asked.

"Yes. Go back to sleep." She smiled.

"No chance," he said, yawning and rubbing the arm he'd been sleeping on.

"Come up here with me. It's more comfortable," she offered, scooting to the side of her hospital bed.

"That won't be comfortable for you."

"It would be the highlight of my week," she said.

He sat gingerly on the edge of the bed in the space Dale created for him. "Am I hurting you?" he asked.

"Not a bit," she said.

He lay back cautiously, then settled into the space she'd left him. He closed his eyes and was asleep in minutes.

Dale ran her fingers across his arm while he slept. He put one hand over hers and sighed deeply. She closed her eyes and tried to rest before the doctors came through on their morning rounds. Every time she closed her eyes, Charlotte's press statement replayed in her mind: "Peter and Dale are involved in a close personal relationship; Peter and Dale are involved in a close personal relationship; Peter and Dale are involved in a close personal relationship."

Thank God her father had been on the flight when Charlotte delivered her speech. Her parents were staying at a dorm near the hospital for families of wounded soldiers, but when they were all in her room together, the mood was tense. The news about Dale's relationship with Peter had shaken her father. And he wasn't alone. Charlotte's personal approval numbers had plunged to the teens.

Dale hadn't read the thousands of e-mail messages she'd received since the crash, but she was following the news as closely as she could. Members of both political parties and several editorial pages had called for Charlotte's resignation. Others called for investigations into the crash and urged Charlotte to announce that she would not seek reelection. The nastiest and most personal criticism came from Charlotte's nemesis on the *Washington Post* editorial page. She'd written every day since the crash, and the latest was titled "Impeach the Ice Queen." It accused Charlotte of neglecting the American people to "hopscotch" around war zones in humvees and helicopters, said she deserved to have her "hunky" husband leave her, and urged the Senate to begin impeachment hearings to remove Charlotte from office because of her "reckless and willful endangerment" of the news crew traveling with her in Afghanistan.

The harsh newspaper coverage paled in comparison with the death watch under way on television.

Since arriving in Germany, where there was satellite television, Dale's days consisted of sleeping, watching cable news, and trying to reassure her parents, Peter, and the doctors that she wasn't in pain. Mostly, she wanted them to leave her alone so she could watch the coverage of the crash and the political fallout. Each time a correspondent or anchor began a news report about Charlotte or the investigation into the crash, CNN blasted ominous music and filled the screen with a giant graphic that read, "A President in Crisis." MSNBC simply ran "Is Kramer Finished?" under every newscast or interview it broadcast, and Fox News was obsessed with the fate of Roger Taylor. All of the cable channels were running an endless loop of exclusive interviews with marriage counselors, child psychologists, pollsters, feminists, security experts, pundits, reporters, politicians, and former politicians. The networks were doing daily polls on everything from Charlotte's chances of being impeached to the perils of dating in office. The news anchors began each evening newscast joined by experts and historians who described Charlotte's presidency as "squandered," "swallowed by scandal," and "finished."

Dale turned up the volume when one of the stations teased a segment called "Dale Smith: The Other Woman." She hoped it would air before Peter woke up again.

Dale knew she was lucky to be alive, and she was thankful that Peter was there with her. And of course, her parents provided some comfort. But she was frustrated about being on the sidelines for one of the biggest stories of the century, not to mention the biggest political crisis since Watergate. And the fact that she was a key figure in the very presidential crisis she yearned to cover made her begin to wonder if her career would recover. She tried to imagine herself in front of the White House, reporting on the calls for impeachment. She couldn't make out exactly what she'd say to carve herself out of the story, but surely her producers would help her finesse her scripts.

Her head started to ache, and she reached for the painkillers the nurse had left on her last visit.

Peter stirred in his sleep, and Dale quickly muted the television.

He didn't approve of her cable news addiction. "You shouldn't watch the coverage. It upsets your parents," he'd said the night before. She'd changed the channel, but she knew that what upset her parents was their new reality, to the extent that they understood it. Dale's mom had been bombarded with e-mails from her friends. "That's not your Dale that President Kramer nearly killed, is it?" they'd asked. "Is she having an affair with Peter Kramer? Is she in trouble?" their friends wondered. Her father still hadn't looked Peter in the eye or spoken to him about anything other than Dale's condition.

The phone rang, and Dale reached over and picked it up on the first ring so it wouldn't wake Peter.

"This is the White House operator. I have the president for Ms. Smith," a friendly voice said.

"Thank you," Dale said quietly. She looked over at Peter. He didn't stir.

"Hi, Dale. Are they taking good care of you?" Charlotte asked.

"Yes, ma'am," Dale said.

"That's good to hear. Please call me Charlotte."

"Thanks for calling. I know how busy things are for you. I've been trying to follow it from here."

"It's a full-fledged media circus."

"The press loves a crisis," Dale said.

"That's for sure."

"Do you want to talk to Peter?" Dale asked, realizing that she might have called for him in the first place.

"No, just tell him we'll be at Camp David this weekend if he wants to say hi to the kids," Charlotte said.

"No problem."

"Any idea when they'll send you to Bethesda?" Charlotte asked.

"They're moving me early next week."

"I heard you had a second operation a couple of days ago."

"Yes, they went back in to make sure nothing was bleeding."

"And everything looked good?" Charlotte asked.

"Yes, they took care of everything."

"Good," Charlotte said.

Dale wanted to ask Charlotte how she was coping. She wanted to know if she was feeling the strain of the media frenzy and the political pressure. She wanted to tell her that the *Washington Post* editorial page was full of jerks. She wanted to tell her to hang in there.

"Thank you again for calling," Dale said.

"You're welcome. Let us know if you need anything," Charlotte offered.

"I will. Thank you, Madam President," Dale said.

Charlotte hung up. Peter stirred again.

Dale's back felt stiff, and her hips were starting to ache from spending so much time in bed. She wiggled her arms and legs to get her blood moving.

Peter yawned and stretched his arms above his head. "Who was that?" he asked.

"Charlotte. She called to see how we were doing."

He turned on his side to face her. "I'm going to rent a place for us in D.C. so we can be near the hospital."

"Charlotte sounded good—unfazed, if that's possible," Dale told him.

"It's possible. She thrives in disasters. What do you think about Georgetown?" he asked.

"Why don't we just stay up in Connecticut so you can be close to the kids?"

"Because the only doctors in that part of Connecticut are for the horses, and I want you near first-rate trauma centers."

"I'm not going to need ongoing trauma care," she said.

"I don't care," he said. "I want you near the best doctors, just in case."

"Whatever you say," she agreed.

It felt good to have someone else make the decisions, and at least they were finally making plans together.

CHAPTER TWENTY-SEVEN

Charlotte

C harlotte thought her chest might burst when she caught her first glimpse of her kids. She rushed to them as soon as she stepped off Marine One at Camp David.

"Hi, guys," she said.

"Hi, Mom," Harry said.

Charlotte pulled Penelope and Harry into a hug.

The dogs raced toward her, and she looked up to see her parents, Brooke, and Mark standing a few feet away. She smiled at them. Cammie jumped into her lap and licked her entire face. Emma and Mika wriggled next to her. Charlotte laughed.

"How about a hug for your dad before you get covered in dog slobber?" her father teased.

"I'm coming," she said. She embraced her parents and her friends and then pulled the kids aside.

"Let's take a walk," she said to Penelope and Harry. "I want to talk to you."

She told them that Congress was investigating her administration, that Roger had made a decision that she didn't support about putting the reporters on Marine One, and that it was unlikely she'd be reelected. She left out the topic that was of greatest interest to them.

"Are you and Dad getting divorced?" Penelope asked when Charlotte finished.

"I don't know, honey," Charlotte said. She knew the answer was yes, but she didn't think it was fair to confirm this to the kids before she and Peter could speak. Besides, she couldn't give the kids one more thing to worry about. They were too young to worry about their parents as much as they did.

Harry looked concerned. Penelope was trying to act mature, but Charlotte saw worry flash across her face.

"I would be fine. I want Dad to be happy. Just like he wants me to be happy," she said.

The kids looked skeptical.

"Daddy's friend is a nice lady," Charlotte said. "And things with Dad and me are complicated, but we both want the best for each other." Harry and Penelope were looking at her as if she was full of it. "Is anyone hungry? I'm starving. Let's get some food," she said.

They made their way back toward the main house. Charlotte was aware of her daughter's eyes on her. She couldn't explain the intensely contradictory things she was feeling to a teenager. She could not make her children understand that, while it was painful, setting Peter free made her feel generous for the first time in a very long time. As difficult as it was to tell them that their father loved someone else, Charlotte was certain that this was a blow she'd survive. She took a deep breath and tried to smile.

Penelope had a very serious look on her face.

"Penny, what's wrong?" Charlotte asked.

"I don't want you to be alone, Mom," she said.

"I'm not alone, honey, and you don't have to worry about me. I promise," she said. "I could never be alone with Brooke and Mark following me everywhere I go. You know, we are going to give them their own seats on Air Force One for Christmas if we win."

Penelope didn't look convinced.

"Maybe we could go to school in D.C.," Harry said. "Then you wouldn't be at the White House by yourself."

Penelope looked panicked.

"Is that what you want?" Charlotte asked Harry.

"Sure," Harry said.

"I've got one rule. One thing you need to promise me you'll do for me. Will you promise me you'll do this one thing every day?" Charlotte asked.

"What?" Penelope asked.

"You need to swear you'll do it," Charlotte said.

"What is it?" Penelope said.

"I swear," Harry said.

Charlotte looked at them and wondered how she had given birth to such decent children.

"I need you to promise me you'll tell the truth—to me, to each other, to Dad, to your friends, to Gammy and Gramps."

"I don't want to go to school in D.C.," Penelope said.

"I know, sweetie." Charlotte laughed, putting her arm around Penelope.

They finished the loop, and Harry went inside to work on homework while Charlotte and Penelope shared a pot of tea and some chocolate-chip cookies.

"You sure you're OK with all this?" Charlotte asked Penelope.

"Mom, it's not like we didn't know."

"Right," Charlotte said, wondering what exactly Penelope was referring to. She was afraid to ask.

Charlotte wondered if the topic of her troubled marriage was something Penelope would want to discuss in detail. While Charlotte was practicing answers to questions such as "Do you still love Dad?" Penelope received a text from a friend and excused herself.

Charlotte pushed away her tea and looked around for an open bottle of wine. With Brooke and Mark in residence, one couldn't be far away.

"Am I disturbing you?" Mark asked, appearing in the doorway.

"No, no, come in," Charlotte said. "Thanks for being here this weekend."

"Where else were we going to be, Char?"

Charlotte smiled.

"How are you holding up?" Mark asked.

"My strategy is to keep plowing forward," she said.

"That makes sense, for now," Mark agreed.

"I'm curious. Did you guys know?" Charlotte asked.

"About Dale?"

"About Peter. Did you know?" she asked.

Mark looked at her for a few seconds before he spoke. "I figured it out," he said. "But I didn't know who, and he never said anything to us. I swear."

"Then how did you know?" Charlotte asked.

"During the campaign, he'd call every night and ask us how you were doing. He'd complain about leaving you out on the trail by yourself to be home with the twins, but when he was on the trail with you, he'd torture himself about leaving the twins home alone. At some point, during that first year, he stopped asking us how you were doing. It was as if he'd given up or run out of energy or something."

Charlotte felt her chest tighten a bit, and she nodded. "Oh, well. Everything is out in the open now," she said, forcing a smile.

"Charlotte, I'm so sorry. What can we do?"

"You're already doing it," she said, standing. "I'm going to lie down for a few minutes before dinner. Don't let my dad drink too many cocktails."

Mark gave her a hug before she left the room.

Charlotte went into her bedroom and closed the door. She sat on the bed and willed herself not to do the one thing she'd wanted to do more than anything else for the past several days. She'd thought of a dozen different ways to start the conversation: *Roger, what you did was inexcusable, but we have to find a way through it,* or *Roger, I need to ask you to resign permanently from DOD, but I want to find a way to keep you as my friend,* or *Roger, what the hell were you thinking? You ruined everything.* She put her head in her hands and forced herself not to pick up the phone and ask the operator to connect her to Roger, as she had done hundreds of times before. Losing Roger made her feel more alone than losing Peter to Dale.

After a dinner of salad, crab cakes, and baked potatoes, Charlotte asked everyone to move into the family room. As they arranged themselves on the comfortable sofas and chairs, she tapped her wine glass and cleared her throat.

"I want to thank all of you for being here this weekend," Charlotte said. "Obviously, it's been a difficult week, and not one day went by that I didn't draw on all of you for strength. I'd like to raise a glass to my wonderful children, Penelope and Harry, to Mom and Dad, and to the ever-present Auntie Brooke and Uncle Mark."

"Here's to the bravest woman in America," Mark added, raising his wine glass.

"That's one word for it," Charlotte's father said.

They all laughed and drank and talked with the dogs sprawled across their laps. Charlotte stood to refill the plate of cookies, and Brooke followed her into the kitchen. When the door closed behind them, Brooke turned to her friend.

"In the end, Peter was too weak for you, Char. Too needy."

"I suppose," Charlotte said.

"You're better off. I swear to God, you'll be fine. It's the public aspect of it that has you off your game," Brooke said.

Charlotte nodded. "I know. I'm worried about the kids, but I know it's better this way with Peter," she said.

"Did you and Peter talk?" Brooke asked.

"We didn't exactly have time for a heart-to-heart. And I'm fairly certain that this is not how he'd have wanted to go public with his affair, but I didn't see any other way for them to be together, and obviously, they should be together right now."

"I don't know at what point you'll cross into martyrdom, Char, but it is remarkable that you're always fretting about everyone else."

"We both know that's not true. It's my fault that my family is in this situation. I didn't even try to make Peter a part of any of this."

"It's not as if you had a lot of people to turn to for tips on how to make it work," Brooke scoffed.

"And now I get to add 'first president to be divorced in office' to my bio. Not the kind of history I wanted to make."

Brooke looked at her without a scrap of judgment on her face. "He took the easy way out, Char," Brooke said. "It's not your fault."

"I should be mortified, but I can't even get to it yet. I feel sick about Roger and sad for my children and angry at myself for letting my marriage disintegrate before my eyes. I should be humiliated, but I don't have the bandwidth."

Brooke put her arm around Charlotte's shoulder. "We can both boss Mark around for now, and you have to know that you'll find someone else. You're forty-seven years old and hotter than you were in college. We'll find you some dot-com gazillionaire or something when this is all over."

"I thought they all went broke," Charlotte said, smiling at her friend.

"We'll find one who stuffed money in his mattress during the roaring nineties."

"I don't know what I'd do without you guys," Charlotte said.

"I don't think you'll ever find out. Mark is ready to move to D.C. to head the morale committee. He e-mailed Melanie to find out if he can travel on all the campaign trips."

"Oh, God, the campaign," Charlotte said, her face falling.

"What's wrong?" Brooke asked.

"Nothing. Do me a favor, and tell the kids and my folks I'll be back in five minutes. I need to call Melanie about something." Charlotte slipped out of the kitchen and into her study.

CHAPTER TWENTY-EIGHT

Melanie

Nothing solidifies Washington's status as the center of the universe like a presidential crisis. The restaurants on Pennsylvania Avenue buzzed with lobbyists, lawmakers, and reporters swapping the latest gossip about what would happen to Charlotte Kramer in the aftermath of her Bagram Blockbuster. In admitting that her husband was sleeping with a White House reporter and accepting the temporary resignation of her defense secretary, Charlotte was in uncharted waters.

On top of that, Melanie was unable to convince the editors of the *Dispatch* to kill their story about an alleged affair between Charlotte and Roger. She'd exploited their reservations about the source, which everyone knew was Stephanie Taylor, but no one would acknowledge it publicly because of the long-held Washington tradition of protecting an anonymous source above all other considerations. And Melanie managed to poke enough holes in the veracity of Stephanie's account by acknowledging that Charlotte and Roger were extremely close but never intimate. Three weeks after Charlotte returned from Afghanistan, a series of grainy photos of her and Roger hiking at Camp David accompanied a one-page story about "rumors of romance" buried deep inside the magazine. Bloggers and some of the seedier cable news programs devoured the sordid details, but most people in Washington were on scandal overload by that point. Besides, the affair between Charlotte's handsome husband and the rising star at one of the networks made for far better television.

Everyone in D.C. was glued to their BlackBerrys and cable news channels, and even the cab drivers were apprised of each new development in the crash investigation. Melanie was photographed and followed each time she ventured outside the gates of the White House complex. She started referring to the frenzy as the new normal and warned everyone on the White House staff to keep their heads down and mouths shut. She enacted a zero-tolerance policy on leaks and blackballed reporters from the White House briefing room who cobbled together hit pieces with unnamed sources. Melanie was determined to keep the White House complex a placid place, even in the midst of Charlotte's political Armageddon.

Some senior staffers chafed at Melanie's strict new rules, but in the wake of the accident, Melanie was invigorated by a new sense of purpose. She was the only one on the White House staff who spoke with Charlotte's full authority, and that made her more indispensable than usual. Lines of authority that had become blurred by three years of familiarity were sharpened by the shrinking of Charlotte's inner circle. With Roger out of the picture, Charlotte turned to Melanie for everything.

Charlotte and Melanie were spending so many extra hours together during the week that Melanie turned down Charlotte's invitation to travel to Camp David for Easter weekend. Brooke and Mark would be there again, so Charlotte would be entertained and distracted, which meant that Melanie could get some work done.

She was catching up on paperwork when she saw Brian's number flash on the caller ID for her main line. She let Annie pick it up. They'd swapped e-mails and voice-mails a few times since she'd been back from Afghanistan, but he hadn't asked her on another date.

"Brian's on the line," Annie said, sticking her head in and smiling.

Melanie reached for the phone.

"No, don't pick up!" Annie practically shouted.

"Why?"

"Wait a couple of minutes. You don't want to appear too eager," Annie said.

Annie was well versed in all of the books about dating rules, and the results spoke for themselves. Annie usually juggled several suitors on the weekends, and there was always a different clean-cut male staffer loitering in Melanie's lobby to talk to Annie.

"Count to sixty," Annie ordered.

Melanie waited a full sixty seconds and then picked up. "Hi there," she said.

Annie smiled and left her office, closing Melanie's door on her way out.

"How's it going?" he asked.

"Good. I mean, considering," she said, looking around her desk at the stacks of speeches, documents, and policy briefs awaiting her review.

"Considering the world has gone to hell in a handbasket since I last saw you?"

"Yes, that's about right," Melanie said, standing up to pace slowly in the space behind her desk, her eyes wandering among the framed pictures of herself with the various presidents she'd worked for.

"How have you been?" Brian asked.

Melanie contemplated saying something about how he would know if he had tried harder to find out, but she was the one who had ignored his last two e-mails. "I've been fine. Busy but good. How about you?" she said, smacking her head with her fist for her unpithy response.

"Everything is good. Listen, I'm sure you're working all weekend, but I wanted to see if I could buy you a drink tonight. I have to do the Sunday show tomorrow, and I have some work to do tonight, but I thought maybe around eight or nine, we could meet somewhere. What do you think?"

Melanie contemplated blowing him off for not calling sooner, but she wanted to see him. She examined the upholstery on the sofa and matching armchairs in her office and noticed some fraying at the bottom.

She heard Brian clear his throat.

"That sounds good," Melanie said, smiling and sitting back down behind her desk.

"Should I pick you up at the White House? Or will you have made it home by then?"

"I should be home by then. If for some reason I'm still here, I'll shoot you an e-mail."

"How romantic," he joked.

"Would you rather I texted?"

"How about an instant message? It just feels more intimate, don't you think?" he said.

Melanie laughed. "If you're not careful, I'll have Walter and Sherry retrieve you. There's no telling what they'd do to you to verify that your intentions are pure," she said, e-mailing Annie as she talked.

"Meeting B tonight," she wrote. "When does my NSC meeting end?"

"YAY!" Annie wrote back. "NSC meeting goes for hours. I told them you could only stay until six."

"I like the idea of being fetched by your security detail," Brian said.

"Really?" she asked.

"Oh, yeah," he said.

She laughed again. "I'll meet you at my place at eight o'clock," she said.

"Good. I hope we can pick up where we left off."

Melanie blushed and was glad he couldn't see her. "Uh, yes, we do have some catching up to do."

"You're funny when you're flustered," he said, laughing.

"I'm not flustered," she protested.

"Yes, you are," Brian said.

"I'm not flustered. I'm busy."

"Flustered is more sexy than busy," he said.

She blushed again. "I will see you tonight," she said.

"I'm looking forward to it."

She hung up before he could make her make her blush again. She looked at her watch and calculated how much time she had between the National Security Council meeting that she was now five minutes late for and Brian's arrival for some personal maintenance. She picked up the phone and made an appointment to get her legs waxed.

She hung up with the salon and tried to wipe the smile off her face before she grabbed her binder off Annie's desk and ran down the flight of stairs to the Situation Room.

All of the national security players in the Cabinet were meeting to discuss the parameters of the internal investigation Charlotte had called for in her address to Congress the week before. The strategy was for Charlotte to get ahead of the congressional investigations into the crash. Even though Charlotte had spent hours with the committee chairmen from the House and the Senate in the immediate aftermath of the crash, the investigations were unavoidable in a politically charged election year.

Charlotte had insisted on announcing her own investigation so she could present herself to the voters as standing on the same side as her political opponents in wanting to know exactly what had happened in the hours and minutes before Marine One was attacked. So far, Charlotte's political survival skills had kept her one step ahead of the Democrats, but her charm offensive had its limits. She'd invited the different committee chairmen and their families to Camp David in the weeks since she'd been home, and she'd been filling Air Force One to capacity with members of Congress every time she left D.C. While these things smoothed her relations with Congress and made governing easier, it was clear that the Democrats who hoped to take her job in the November election smelled blood in the water. If they could lay blame for the helicopter switch at Charlotte's feet, they could dismantle her advantage on national security issues and beat her in November.

While a policy advisor from DOD droned on, Melanie looked over a stack of polling data Ralph had churned out the night before. Charlotte's poll numbers on questions about her ability to relate to the problems of everyday Americans had leaped twelve points since her return from Afghanistan. Melanie thought it was a typo. Charlotte never polled well in that category. Women found her aloof, and men couldn't get comfortable with the idea of a woman in charge of two wars.

She e-mailed Ralph to get the verbatim responses, the detailed answers that respondents offered to the questions asked in the polls.

He wrote back right away: "I came by earlier to point that out to you, but Annie said you were on the phone. There's some puzzling stuff buried in the data. Her numbers are still bad, but there are bright spots. Seems the public feels sorry for her over the whole Peter and Dale thing, and others are rallying around her at a moment of crisis. Do you want to meet tonight to discuss?"

"I can't meet tonight. How's tomorrow morning?" she typed, despite the fact that BlackBerrys were banned in the Sit Room.

"I have church in the morning. How about one P.M.?"

"See you then," she responded.

The poll numbers could be a fluke, and it wasn't enough to change the dynamics of a national election, but it was the first piece of evidence she'd seen that the public was open to changing its mind about Charlotte.

"Melanie, do you agree with the proposal DOD laid out?" asked the national security advisor.

Melanie hadn't been paying attention to the back-and-forth in the meeting in the Situation Room for at least fifteen minutes.

"Uh, yeah, I think so. Do you mind recapping it? I was dealing with something for Charlotte," she said.

"We're all dealing with things for Charlotte," snapped the secretary of state.

The national security advisor shushed her.

"Sure. We decided to allow the Dems in Congress to appoint four members to the bipartisan commission. Then we'd allow the Republicans in Congress to do the same, and we would appoint the final four members. How does that sound, Melanie?"

"Bold," Melanie said sarcastically. "Why would the public give Charlotte political courage points if she stacked the commission with members of her own party?"

"You'll lose total control if you do it any other way," the secretary of state said.

"I'm sorry. Did you say we'd lose control?" Melanie said.

"Yes. And you know that, Melanie, so I'm not sure why you're resisting the consensus decision," the secretary of state said, crossing her arms in front of her chest.

"In case you haven't noticed, Madam Secretary, we have already lost control. Split the commission in half. The president wants this to be real. Half Democrats, half Republicans—two cochairs, one Dem and one R—and we'll let the Congress pick all of its members," Melanie said, pushing her chair back from the table.

"Melanie, this is very constructive feedback," the national security advisor said. "What time can you reconvene tomorrow to finalize this?"

"I have to do the Sunday shows, and then I have a one P.M. and a four P.M., but I could do something after those meetings wrap up," Melanie said.

The secretary of state sighed loudly. Melanie ignored her and hurried from the Situation Room. She took the stairs to her office two at a time, grabbed her purse, and ran out to West Exec to where Walter and Sherry were waiting for her.

"Can you drop me off at the Four Seasons?" she asked.

"We'll wait for you," he said.

"Thanks, Walter," she said, pulling out her BlackBerry and scanning the messages.

She made it home at seven-thirty and took a long, hot shower. Melanie dressed carefully in skinny black Calvin Klein pants that only fit after a few days of not eating and a fitted white blouse, and left more buttons unbuttoned than she would have if she'd planned to leave her apartment. She was barefoot, and her hair was still wet, when the doorbell rang at ten minutes before eight.

"You're early," she said when she opened the door.

"I know. And the sad truth is that I've been walking around M Street for the last twenty minutes, killing time before I came up here," Brian said, smiling at her.

"Really? You were just walking up and down the street?"

"Yeah. Walter and Sherry drove by twice, which was when I decided to come up. I was afraid they'd pick me up for suspicious behavior or something."

She laughed.

"So, how have you been? It feels like a lifetime ago when I was here last," he said, smiling again, this time a little shyly.

"I'm doing fine. There's a certain order that sets in when things go this far off the rails, you know?"

"Actually, I do. In a lot of ways, a crisis is easier to manage than sustained chaos, because you get everyone's attention," he said.

"Exactly," she said, remembering how easy he was to talk to and how much she enjoyed telling him things about her job.

"How is Dale doing?" he asked.

"I think she's OK. Charlotte checks in with her doctors all the time," she said.

"Really?"

He looked surprised, and Melanie reminded herself that he was a reporter tasked with breaking news about the White House. He was covering for Dale while the network figured out what to do.

"What was the reaction at the network to the news about Peter and Dale?" Melanie asked.

"There were a lot of 'aha' moments for people who suspected that something was going on with her but could never quite figure out what. She was always one step ahead of the competition on any story about the White House, and she didn't seem to have any rapport with Charlotte, so it makes sense now. I think people might have figured it out if they hadn't been so blinded by her looks and big-time scoops."

"What's going to happen while she's out?" Melanie asked.

"There's a mad dash to get her gig. Everyone in the Washington bureau is lining up for the White House job, and everyone in New York is lining up for her weekend anchor gig. It's unseemly. It's not like she died," he said, shaking his head.

"And you?" Melanie asked.

"As you know, I'm helping out on the White House beat a few days a week and still figuring out the Pentagon beat. With the Taylor drama there, I'm not sure it isn't as good a place as any."

"That makes sense," she said.

"I'm not going to push, but if there's anything you feel comfortable talking about on the Roger and Charlotte front, I'm all ears. I'd love to understand what the hell happened."

"You know, I wasn't there, so I don't know exactly what happened."

"Everyone knows the administrative-leave thing was a trap—a very good trap but a trap all the same," he said.

Melanie smiled at him.

"And the rumor over at the Pentagon is that Stephanie Taylor was behind the *Dispatch* story about the affair between Roger and Charlotte. Apparently, once Roger found out the story came from his wife, he moved out with his dogs," Brian said.

"It sounds like you've got perfectly good sources already," she said.

"Not really. I just don't want you to think I'm trading sex for scoop."

"Who said anything about scoop?" she said.

He laughed.

"Can I get you a drink?" Melanie asked.

"That would be great. I brought some wine," he said, handing her two bottles. She went into the kitchen to open one of them.

They sat on her balcony and talked until the bottle was empty. She stood up to bring out the second bottle. He hadn't made any attempts to get her into bed, and Melanie was beginning to wonder if she'd missed her opportunity to be more than a well-placed source to him.

When she came back to the balcony, he was standing and looking out toward the Potomac River. He walked toward her, took the bottle from her hands, and put it on the table. He took both of her hands in his and pulled her toward him. He wasn't as tall as he looked on television, and her mouth was barely an inch from his. She felt herself melting into him, but she didn't want to kiss him first.

"Melanie," he said in a very low, soft voice.

"What?" she said.

"I have wanted to kiss you since the first time we talked, but you were sitting in your fancy West Wing office with your dress unzipped," he said, smiling at her.

She couldn't remember the last time she wanted someone to kiss her as much as she wanted him to kiss her.

"And then, the last time I made it up here, the presidential helicopter crashed," he said. He was kissing her neck now, and she was trying to keep her breathing even. "Melanie," he said in a low whisper.

"Yes," she said.

"Do you think it's possible that no one will need you for a few hours?" he asked.

"I hope so," she said.

CHAPTER TWENTY-NINE

Dale

"Billy, it's a simple yes-or-no question. Do I still have a job or not?" Dale asked.

"Dale, you have been through so much. Why don't you focus on getting well, and we'll figure out the work piece down the road—when you're ready to come back?"

"Billy, please don't bullshit me. I'm going to be well enough to start working again in a month or so. I want to know if I have a job at the network," Dale insisted.

"I don't know exactly where, but yes, you will always have a job here."

"You don't know where? What in the world does that mean?" Dale practically shrieked.

Peter stood up and walked toward her.

"Dale, let's talk when you're released. I'd like to come see you next week, either at Bethesda or at home."

"Fine. That's fine. I'll see you next week," Dale said, placing the phone in its cradle.

"What did he say?" Peter asked.

"Nothing. He said nothing. How did this happen? I left here with an exclusive interview with the president, and somehow I've returned without a job," she said bitterly.

Peter put his hands over hers, which were still gripping the phone. "You're forgetting something," he said.

"What?" she asked.

"You're stuck with me now, too," he said, smiling.

She tried to smile back at him, but having their relationship out in the open was turning out to be more difficult than she'd imagined.

He sat on the edge of her bed. "I'm sorry for all of this," he said.

"It's not your fault."

"Of course it is. You're getting hate mail from all the right-wing nuts, and your face has been plastered all over the tabloids. And your big crime is being with me. I'm so sorry for all the ways this is going to change your life."

"What do you mean?" she asked.

"You can't blame Billy for not wanting to put you back at the White House. Charlotte is going to be dealing with the fallout from the crash every day until the election, and it's not like you can cover that story with a reporter's objectivity, Dale."

She didn't say anything.

"And from Billy's perspective, there's the fact that you've been engaged in a secret affair with the president's husband," Peter said. "I'm sure there are viewers who want to see you get fired."

Dale remained silent. Slowly, it was sinking in. Her career as a network correspondent and anchor was probably over. Of course, they couldn't stand her in front of the White House and ask her to report on the president's day or sit her at the anchor desk and expect the viewers to take her seriously. She was the first husband's secret mistress, and she'd played a role in a helicopter crash in Afghanistan that could result in the president being impeached. Tears slid from the corners of her eyes down to her pillowcase. Peter pushed her hair away from her eyes and sat with her while she cried. The tears kept coming. She cried for what she'd lost, but she also cried tears of shame. If she'd been given a choice between being with Peter and never working again as a correspondent and giving up Peter to keep her job, she wasn't sure what she'd choose. And fueling her tears was the fact that she hadn't been given a choice at all.

While Peter seemed to fall naturally into the new public phase of their relationship, Dale cringed every time someone described her as Peter's girlfriend. She was starting to remember things from the day of the crash. One of the thoughts she'd had that day was to request a rotation in the Mideast bureau to hone her skills as a foreign correspondent. She remembered thinking, as she flew low over the Afghan mountains, that it just might give her the upper hand in the competition for weeknight anchor. None of that mattered now. She was on the outside looking in at the world she'd worked so hard to penetrate.

CHAPTER THIRTY

Charlotte

Charlotte woke up before her alarm and looked out the window of her hotel room. New York wasn't an early city like Washington D.C., and at four-thirty A.M., there wasn't much activity on the street below. She looked at the tables and chairs set up on the sidewalk outside the restaurant next to the hotel and thought about how soon the kids would be out of school for summer break. The last time she'd been in New York, it had snowed.

She climbed out of bed and grabbed her briefing book off the desk. She'd tape interviews with two of the morning shows at six A.M. and six-thirty A.M., and then she would do the third network morning show live at seven A.M. From there, she'd go straight to two of the daytime talk shows for sit-down interviews. It was all part of what Ralph had coined the "Sympathy Tour." He was convinced that she had an opening to show voters a different side of her personality. She thought it was unseemly that voters should have to endure the details of her failed marriage, but Ralph and Melanie rarely agreed on anything, and they both thought she had an opportunity to come across as more human in the wake of the crash.

She sighed and glanced at the briefing paper that the press office had prepared for her: "Topics will include: the breakup of your marriage, how a separation might affect the twins, and whether it's all worth it. They might get to the crash, too, but just say it is still under investigation."

She put the briefing paper back in the binder and pulled out the draft of the speech she planned to give when she got back to Washington. The speech was too sensitive to circulate among the entire senior staff and Cabinet. Charlotte's said "One of five" on the top. Melanie, Ralph, the vice president, and the chief speechwriter held the only other copies. Charlotte's pulse quickened a bit when she read it. No one would her accuse her of not thinking outside the box once they heard this speech.

Charlotte made notes on her copy. She glanced at the clock. It was five A.M. She asked the Situation Room to dial Melanie's home number.

"Hi, Melanie. Am I getting you at a bad time?" Charlotte asked.

"I'm about to head into the office. What's wrong?"

"Nothing. I just went over the first draft of the speech, and I wanted to talk through the final section, but we can do it later today if this is a bad time."

"Did you read the briefing papers for the morning shows?" Melanie asked.

"Yes, I read them," Charlotte said.

"Don't be afraid to open up. Ignore the anchors. You're talking to people like my mom. Voters are pulling for you for the first time in your career. You have to let them."

"I know, I know. Talk about my feelings, blah, blah, blah. I've got it," she said.

"Do you need me to take down your edits on the speech now?"

"No, I can tell you're trying to get ready. I'll call you after my emotional colonoscopy is over," Charlotte said.

"Come on, it won't be that bad." Melanie laughed.

Charlotte sighed loudly. "It will all be over in a few months anyway."

"Don't say that! You're not going to lose," Melanie insisted.

"Oh, I didn't mean it like that. I just meant that after this November, I will never run for anything ever again."

"Amen," Melanie said. "How'd your other meetings go last night?"

"Good. Billy came to see me. He's struggling to try to figure out how they cover the whole crash investigation without making the network part of the story. Billy isn't going to put Dale back at the White House, and he said he doesn't think he can use her on the air at all right now."

"I know," Melanie said.

"Is there anything we can do?" Charlotte asked.

"Other than hire her, no."

"I feel sorry for her," Charlotte said.

"Excuse my bluntness here, Madam President, but she did end up with your husband," Melanie said. "You shouldn't feel too sorry for her."

Charlotte made a sound that was half chortle and half gasp.

"Moving on," Melanie said.

"Yes. I'll be back there around one P.M., and we can go over the speech. I want it to be short and to the point. We do an update on the parameters of the investigation in one short paragraph. Then we make it crystal-clear: there will be no campaign. We'll do the basics: the debates, the convention, the Web site and the volunteers, but no rallies, no political ads, no attacks on my opponent. The country has been through enough, and they have more than enough information about me. I don't need to have a five-month cat fight with Fran to prove a point."

"I've got it. Ralph is reviewing the language now. He wants to make sure we don't inadvertently ignite a third-party movement. The new speech language will be loaded in the teleprompter in the Family Theater for our practice session when you get back," Melanie said.

"Good. I'm so happy my demise has finally brought you and Ralph together. If either of you needs me, I'll be drumming up support from scorned women across America all morning."

"No sarcasm. Voters hate sarcasm," Melanie reminded her.

"I know, I know, and voters hate when I wear black, and they hate when I wear white, so I'll be the one in powder blue today."

"The indignities of ruling the world!" Melanie exclaimed.

Charlotte laughed and hung up. She knew she was taking a risk by calling off the campaign. It was a risk she was willing to take if it meant that her family would be spared additional scrutiny and her White House could remain focused on the nation's business. What she couldn't predict was how the voters would feel about it, but she pushed aside those concerns and rushed into the bathroom to get ready.

CHAPTER THIRTY-ONE

Melanie

$\mathbf{M}$elanie strode into the Oval with her copy of the *New York Times* opened to the editorial page. She read out loud from the page while she walked toward Charlotte, who was seated behind her desk reading the overnight intelligence reports.

"The decision to suspend her campaign cements Charlotte Kramer's place in American political life as above the fray. She has proven herself as a leader cut out for the complex times we face," Melanie said, beaming at Charlotte. A glowing review from the *New York Times* was rare, and as much as they loved to insult the paper, its praise rarely went unnoticed.

"It was a very smart move, Madam President, very smart. I wasn't sure at first, but you were right," Melanie said.

"It can't be helpful with the base to have the *New York Times* fawn all over me," Charlotte said.

"No, but they weren't very excited about your reelection before the speech. And the *Times* won't stay impressed with you for long, we can be sure. At least now you have a shot at changing the press narrative. I know it's not everything, but it's better than four months of stories about how your defeat is imminent."

"True," Charlotte said. "Is Ralph out there, or did he get hauled off to the medical unit when he saw the *Times*?"

"He was having his second breakfast in the Mess when I last saw him," Melanie said.

"Do you want to have dinner tonight?" Charlotte asked.

"I can't. I have a date," she said, blushing.

"I'd suggest that you bring Brian, but it feels too much like meeting the parents, doesn't it?" Charlotte said.

"A little bit. Maybe with a larger group. When are Brooke and Mark coming back to town?" Melanie asked.

"Soon, I'm sure," Charlotte said.

"Did you read the draft statement on the commission findings?"

"I did not, but I will look at it this morning," Charlotte said, pulling a thin white folder from the small, neat stack of papers on her desk.

"Obviously, we don't know exactly what they're going to say, but we can assume that they will find Roger's actions to have violated his authority as secretary of defense," Melanie said.

"Will they recommend any criminal charges?" Charlotte asked.

"I don't think Congress can do that, but they can certainly indict him in the court of public opinion."

"Hasn't that already happened?" Charlotte asked.

"Basically, but if the commission finds him guilty of negligence, it will carry more weight. No one will want to touch him."

"He didn't help himself by taking the Fifth every time the commission asked him a question," Charlotte said.

"I don't think he had an explanation for why he ordered Marine One to be put down except to leave the crew on the ground and let you escape. He can't offer any explanation for leaving them to die, because he doesn't regret it. And I know him well enough to know that he'll never see it differently," Melanie said.

Charlotte sighed deeply and looked pained as she walked back and forth behind her desk.

"Madam President?" Melanie asked.

"Call me if it starts to leak. I don't want Roger blowing in the wind. As soon as we get the report, we go before the cameras and deliver the statement, even if it's the middle of the night."

"Yes, ma'am. That's the plan."

"Have fun on your date tonight," Charlotte said.

"Thanks, and I'll see you at the economic policy meetings this afternoon," Melanie said.

Melanie delivered a speech to the incoming batch of interns in the Old Executive Office Building, had lunch with the secretary of transportation to discuss the Highway Bill, invited a handful of reporters into her office to provide some of the atmospherics surrounding Charlotte's decision not to campaign for reelection, and then sat through three and a half hours of policy briefings on economic and monetary policy. At around six forty-five, Brian e-mailed.

"I just finished my live shot. Do you still want to have dinner tonight?"

"YES!" she wrote back.

They dined at Hook in Georgetown and walked back to Melanie's place afterward.

"Thanks for your help today on the tick-tock. Billy was thrilled that I had the color from your internal process," Brian said.

"That's what I'm here for," Melanie said. "Who says there are no benefits to dating a tired, cranky government official?"

"Not me," Brian said, kissing her.

They fell asleep before the local news came on and woke three hours later to Melanie's cell phone.

"Hello?" she mumbled.

"Melanie, it's Annie."

"What's wrong?" Melanie asked.

"The report is out. I just e-mailed it to your White House account."

"Thanks for calling, Annie. Try to go back to sleep."

"You're not going to get up and read it now, are you?" Brian asked groggily.

"I have to," Melanie said, rubbing her eyes.

"You already know what's in it. Everyone knows what's in it," he said, his voice muffled by the pillow he was holding over his face to block the light.

"I know, but I should read it again to make sure it's the same as the version that leaked, don't you agree?"

"Fine, go read the report, already. You'll feel better," he groused.

"Sorry," she said.

Melanie left the bedroom and turned on the computer on her dining-room table. She added paper to her printer and waited for the two-hundred-page report. She went into the kitchen to turn on the coffee maker. With a steaming mug of coffee in hand, she sat down and started reading the pages off the printer.

The final report found Roger guilty of gross negligence and behavior unbecoming of a senior government official. The report also found that Roger had acted well beyond his constitutional authority by ordering the landing of Marine One. They were unable to prove that Roger had knowledge that the crew would be attacked by a Taliban missile or that he intended to see them attacked, so the report stopped just short of recommending criminal prosecution. But it did ban Roger from further government service for life. Melanie cringed. He would go crazy.

She rubbed her forehead and tried to brace herself for the inevitable. Roger would retaliate out of sheer desperation, and there wasn't much they could do about it. He'd go on Fox News and make his case for the constitutionality of protecting the commander in chief above all others. Charlotte would have to endure watching Roger reduced to pandering to the zealots on the far right, who had always distrusted and disliked her. Melanie was frustrated that she couldn't do more to help. With the affair rumors published by the *Dispatch*, Peter carrying on with Dale, and all of the various congressional committees and subcommittees focused on further investigations into the crash, there was ample suspicion among the press and Congress that Charlotte's White House was in complete meltdown.

That's why it had been so surprising when Charlotte's poll numbers had started inching upward. Apparently, voters admired a president who could endure adversity. Something else was at play in Charlotte's steadily improving poll numbers. In revealing Peter and Dale's relationship, Charlotte had admitted that she wasn't perfect, that she was prone to the same sorts of heartbreaks and humiliations as any other married woman. Her approval numbers among married women doubled. And in the twenty-four hours since Charlotte had announced that she would not campaign for reelection, her approval ratings surged ten more points.

Melanie pulled up the statement she'd written for Charlotte the day before. Charlotte wanted to take the high road. In the statement, she praised Roger and Stephanie for their service to the country and said she would take the report's recommendations seriously.

At around four-thirty, she heard Brian get up and turn on the shower. She reviewed Charlotte's statement and printed out a copy for him. Once Charlotte delivered the press statement in response to the report, Melanie had to figure out how to get Charlotte reelected in the absence of a campaign.

Brian came into the dining room in a towel. "Anything in there that I need to know?" he asked.

"No, it's the same version I got yesterday. I printed out a copy of Charlotte's statement for you to take—embargoed—with you this morning."

"You're just trying to get yourself out of the dog house," he said with a smile while walking into the kitchen and pouring a cup of coffee.

"I am not. I am a good and generous girlfriend looking out for her boyfriend," she retorted.

He walked over and gave her a kiss. "Nice try, but you're still in the dog house," he said as he walked back into the bedroom to get dressed.

CHAPTER THIRTY-TWO

Dale

D ale walked down the cereal aisle at Whole Foods in a daze. She'd been out of the hospital for two weeks, and the house they'd rented in Georgetown already felt like a prison.

The doctors had told her to walk as much as possible, but every time she traveled farther than the house next door, she ended up doubled over in pain. Peter hated seeing her in so much agony and discouraged her daily walks. He showered her with affection, attention, and sympathy. And he didn't mind that, most of the time, she wanted to sit alone on the couch and stare out at the garden in the back of their house.

"Do you want to sit outside?" he'd asked the first couple of times he'd seen her staring toward the backyard.

"I'm fine right here," she'd said.

He didn't seem to take her moods personally, but she knew he worried. She'd heard him on the phone with one of his clients a couple of days after she came home from the hospital.

"I can't come out there. No. I can't leave her for that long. Why don't you come to D.C.? I'll take you to dinner, and we can talk it through," he'd said to one of the athletes he represented.

Before he'd hung up, she'd dragged herself off the couch and into the shower. She'd shampooed her hair for the first time in several days. After the shower, she was winded, but she'd blow-dried her hair and applied makeup. She'd pulled on jeans and buttoned them gingerly over the incisions on her stomach. It was still tender. She'd put on a white long-sleeved T-shirt and slid into ballet flats.

She'd walked to the doorway of the room Peter was using as his office. He was sitting in front of his computer. She had watched him for a minute. He hadn't shaved in a couple of days, but instead of looking bedraggled, she'd thought he looked more handsome. He was wearing jeans and a snowboarding T-shirt the kids had given him. He was tan from sitting on the sidelines at the kids' water polo matches the week before. She'd still been in the hospital at Bethesda, but she'd insisted that he go. It was the only time he'd left her side. She'd noticed for the first time that he looked thinner than she'd ever seen him.

Dale had tried to observe Peter the way she would have had he not been her lover. She had tried to envision how she'd react to him if they met on the street. She had tried to imagine how she'd feel about him had he not been bequeathed to her by the leader of the free world.

He was lovely, she'd decided. She had what she'd wanted for so long. He was hers. Why was she so miserable? She'd walked toward him and put her hands on his shoulders.

He'd turned around, and she'd leaned down and kissed him.

"How are you feeling?" he'd asked.

"I'm feeling better," she'd said, smiling weakly. "Little by little, right?"

"That's what the doctors said."

She'd come around and stood between him and the computer. He'd pulled her carefully into his lap.

She'd winced as she settled in and looked at the screen in front of him. He had been looking at the *Washington Journal* Web site.

"You look more like yourself today," he'd said.

"I feel more like myself. And you should take that trip I heard you cancel earlier."

"No. I don't want to leave you here. You really shouldn't drive yet, and if something happens, it would kill me to be on the other side of the country."

"Nothing is going to happen, and if it does, I am conveniently located within one mile of four major hospitals. I will be fine. I promise."

So he'd gone. And her first big adventure out of the house was to Whole Foods.

She got to the end of the cereal aisle and realized that she hadn't picked up any cereal. She carefully turned the cart around, breathing in sharply and bracing herself for impact when someone passed too close to her cart.

She turned back around and put a can of steel-cut oats in the cart. She'd never made oatmeal in her life, but it seemed like the kind of thing she should be eating in her recovery. She wandered up and down each aisle, putting one random item in her cart every few minutes. When she found herself back in the produce aisle for the third time, she looked at her cart's contents: a bottle of wine, a carton of half-and-half, a large chunk of cheddar cheese, a bag of lemons, and the container of steel-cut oats. She sighed. She had failed to hang on to her job, and she had failed to put anything in her cart that would make up a healthy or complete meal—not exactly a difficult task at Whole Foods. She left the cart in front of the summer fruit display and left the store without any of the items. She was suddenly exhausted and couldn't wait to get back to the house she'd wanted to escape from an hour earlier.

CHAPTER THIRTY-THREE

Charlotte

"S am, can you let the dogs in, please?" Charlotte yelled from her desk in the Oval Office. "Sam!" she yelled again, standing to let the dogs in herself.

When she stood, she saw the vice president in the waiting area outside by her assistant's desk. Neal McMillan was not the partner that the previous vice president had been to her predecessor, but he was exactly what Charlotte needed. He was someone she trusted, someone who did not crave the spotlight, and someone who had her back and never asked for any recognition or credit for doing so. He was in his seventies, and he had a life outside Washington politics, which grounded him in real-world sensibilities.

"Neal, come in. You don't have to wait for a formal invitation. Where is Sam?" Charlotte asked.

"Here I am, Madam President. I'm sorry. I ran over to the residence to get the bully sticks you asked us to keep here for the dogs," Sam said, out of breath. She gave each dog a bone, and they settled down in front of her desk to chew.

"Neal, come sit down," Charlotte said. "Can I get you some coffee?"

"That would be lovely, Madam President," he said.

"Charlotte. How many times will we have this conversation? You have got to call me Charlotte," she said.

"Yes, Charlotte. I'm pretty sure we'll only have this particular conversation once," he said with a glint in his eye.

She leaned forward. "What's going on, Neal? Is Mary all right?"

"Yes, Mary and I are fine. We're worried about you. You are going to lose unless something dramatic happens. We both know that."

"Shhh. Melanie says it's very demoralizing to the young people if they hear us talk like that. But yes, I can read a poll. I was my own pollster the first time I ran for governor. We couldn't afford a consultant, so Peter averaged all of the polls that the newspapers and televisions stations in California ran. He had a formula for adjusting for their oversampling of Democrats. It was the most accurate system I've ever had in any of my campaigns."

Neal looked at her warmly. "It makes you nostalgic, doesn't it?" he asked.

"What? No, are you kidding? I'm not nostalgic. I just want to hang on to whatever vestige of self-respect I can salvage and get Iraq and Afghanistan to a good place. I get sick when I think about turning the country over to Fran and her left-wing loonies, but we couldn't campaign, Neal. Not in this climate."

"I remember a time when it wasn't like this. You were making your millions in Silicon Valley, or maybe you were still in college, but there was a time when we all came down here and smoked cigars on the balcony. The fights and the big debates were just for the cameras. Now the cigars and the civility are for the cameras, and what's real is the fighting."

The vice president stood, wandered over to the window, and looked out. The Rose Garden was in full bloom.

"Charlotte. I've got an idea, and I want you to listen and then promise me you will not say anything today. I want to come back here in twenty-four hours, and we'll finish this conversation. Is that a deal?" he asked.

"Why? What is going on, Neal?" Charlotte asked.

"I need you to agree to the ground rules," he said.

"I agree," she said.

"Good. Let's take a walk, Charlotte," he said, opening the door onto the colonnade and stepping into the muggy, fragrant summer air.

CHAPTER THIRTY-FOUR

Melanie

Melanie looked up from her computer when she heard the White House generators kick in. They were installed decades before to protect the president from service interruptions caused by weather or attack, but more often than not, they powered the air conditioners that cooled the West Wing and the residence during Washington's summer heat waves. The rest of the District of Columbia was experiencing rolling brown-outs.

Annie opened her door and stepped inside, wearing a pink and white halter dress that bordered on inappropriate but that she had wisely covered with a demure pink cardigan.

"Melanie, it's the third time he's called. What do you want me to tell him?" Annie asked.

"Tell him I'm in a meeting," Melanie said, pulling her black suit jacket around her shoulders. "Is it me, or is it freezing in here?"

"It's freezing in here, but apparently, it's about eighty degrees in the Sit Room, so they turned the AC up in the entire West Wing to cool it."

"Tell them we're going to undo all our progress toward ending global warming if we keep running the AC at fifty-eight degrees," Melanie said.

"So you'll pick up and talk to him?" Annie pleaded.

"No. Tell him I'm still in that meeting."

"I did. He said you loved nothing more than getting pulled out of meetings."

"Tell him I'm in the Oval."

"He said you'd say that, and he said he knows you're not, because Charlotte is at the Pentagon for a reenlistment reception."

"Tell him I don't have time to talk to him today, and I'll call him back when I have time," Melanie snapped.

Roger had called her three times in the last three days and twice the week before. He'd called a dozen times since the report came out. She didn't want to blow him off, but she did not have the energy to deal with his bruised ego on top of everything else she was juggling.

Some of the Pentagon reporters she knew confirmed what Brian had mentioned about Roger moving out of his house in Wesley Heights and into an apartment in Pentagon City. They'd seen him sitting outside Starbucks with his dogs and a stack of newspapers. She'd heard from the same reporters that he was having a hard time finding consulting work and seats on corporate boards—the kind of offers that traditionally follow decades of government service.

Annie reappeared in her doorway. "He wants to know when," Annie said.

"Who?" Melanie asked, exasperated.

"Roger," Annie said nervously.

"Why are you still on the phone with Roger?" Melanie shouted.

"I can't just hang up on Secretary Taylor," Annie said.

"Yes, you can, and you must, or I will pick up the phone, and that will end very, very badly for everyone," Melanie said through clenched teeth. She felt as if her head was going to explode.

Annie scurried back to her desk.

Melanie couldn't hear what Annie was saying. She poured four Aleves and six Zantacs into her palm and swallowed the pills with a swig of Diet Coke.

"I hate my life," she said to herself.

Annie stuck her head in again. "I heard that. Don't yell at me. I thought you'd want this one. Brian. Line two," she said.

Melanie picked up. "Is the first night of the Republican convention a big enough story to crowd out news of my demise?" she asked Brian.

"Probably not. It would end up inside the paper next to some story about the budget deficit," he said.

"Damn," Melanie said. "You just ruined my plans for drinking myself to death tonight."

"Bad day?" he asked.

"Very." She sighed.

"I'm sorry. I just wanted to say hello. I'm flying to Michigan to do that battleground story I told you about last night, so I'll see you at the convention later this week."

"Sounds good. I'll call you tonight. Where will you be?" she asked.

"Michigan. I'm going to Michigan. I just said that. You're busy. I'll talk to you later."

"No, I'm sorry. I'm being rude, I know. You're going to Michigan for the network's battleground series. Would it screw things up if I told you Michigan is no longer a battleground state?" she asked.

"Very funny. Just because you never win it doesn't mean your party doesn't spend millions of dollars trying."

"You've got me there. Have a safe flight. I'll see you in Philly."

As soon as she hung up, Annie was in her doorway again.

"What?" Melanie barked.

"Thank God for Brian. He's the only person who makes you smile like that," Annie said.

"Where are the goddamned speechwriters? Did you check the staff table at the Mess? They never miss a meal," she said.

"They are standing next to me," Annie whispered.

"Oh. My bad. Send them in."

They filed into Melanie's office with their notebooks and sat in the chairs scattered around Melanie's desk.

"Hi, guys. How's everyone doing?" Melanie asked.

Melanie loved to tease the speechwriters. More than any other White House office, they hung together like a pack. She adored this particular team of speechwriters. They were the unsung heroes of any White House, but this group was exceptional.

"BlackBerrys, cell phones, and pagers, ladies and gentlemen," Melanie said, holding out her inbox. The box went around the room, and they dropped their electronics into it.

"I have a secret mission for all of you. Should you decide to take it, you will not be going home tonight," she said.

Their eyes glistened with anticipation. They were in.

CHAPTER THIRTY-FIVE

Dale

D ale wiped her forehead with the back of her hand as she stood waiting in the East Wing lobby. She had no idea what she'd been summoned for. A military aide met her and walked her down the red carpet past the Family Theater and the stairs to the East Room. He held the door to the president's private elevator open for her and pressed three when he joined her inside. She stepped out, and he pointed in the direction of a bright, sunny room overlooking the South Lawn of the White House. Dale's eyes were still adjusting to the bright light when she heard Charlotte's voice.

"Thanks for coming by on such short notice," Charlotte said, rising from a sofa in the room Dale recognized from photos as the Yellow Oval, so called because it was shaped just like the Oval Office and decorated in bright shades of yellow. One of the dogs sat on the sofa next to Charlotte, and the other two were lying near the air-conditioner vents in the floor.

"It's my pleasure," Dale said, crossing the room to where Charlotte was standing. The dog sitting on the couch lifted her head, looked at Dale, and then put her head down in Charlotte's lap as soon as she sat down.

"Please sit. Can I get you something? Coffee? Tea? Iced tea?" Charlotte asked.

"No, I'm fine," Dale said.

"Does Peter know you're here?" Charlotte asked.

"No. He's flying back from San Francisco tonight, and I didn't mention that you'd called."

"That's probably a good idea," Charlotte said.

Dale didn't say anything. She just nodded.

"I promise I didn't invite you over here to talk about Peter. I have an idea about something, and I wanted to see if it was of interest."

"I appreciate that," Dale said.

"What's your take on where the election stands today?" Charlotte said.

"You have a couple of months left to get your numbers up five to six points depending on which poll you're looking at. Your internals probably show it about a three-to-five-point race, but the trend is more troubling than the gap. People who are just tuning in are more likely to support your opponent, if for no other reason than the fact that she's asking for their support. Fair or not, people who just figured out there's an election looming have forgotten that you announced that you wouldn't campaign because you didn't want to politicize the crash and everything else. Undecided voters think you aren't even trying."

Charlotte stood up and walked across the room to look out at the grounds workers tending to the South Lawn below.

"I wish they wouldn't work in this heat," she said.

Dale nodded in agreement.

"You're exactly right about the election," Charlotte said, turning and facing Dale. "And Ralph and Melanie warned me that the decision that felt right in the spring would feel awful at this point in the campaign season, so I can't say I wasn't warned. I don't regret it, though. I didn't see how I could have launched a national campaign and turned on a major fundraising operation while the entire Congress and half a dozen bipartisan commissions were investigating what happened in Afghanistan."

Dale nodded. "It was the right thing to do. You treated the voters as if they're smart enough to understand that there are some things more important than the next campaign."

"Right. But that was then. Now I need a game changer," Charlotte said.

"That's what everyone seems to believe," Dale agreed.

Charlotte put down her coffee cup and pushed her hair behind her ears. "The vice president offered to resign. He's a very good man, and I would not have won four years ago without him. He supported my decision not to campaign for reelection, and he's eager to see how much further we can push the envelope. He offered to step off the ticket if I agreed to replace him with a Democrat so we could run a true unity ticket, something that has always appealed to his sense of nostalgia for the way things used to be in this town."

Dale's eyes widened. "Who would you pick?"

"What do you think about the New York attorney general, Tara Meyers?" Charlotte asked.

"Wow. That really *is* a game changer!" Dale exclaimed.

"As you said, we are about four to six points back in our internals. We need to change things up or resign ourselves to a certain outcome, and the only thing I could think of to get the right wing to stop sticking knives in my back is to put a Democrat a heartbeat away from the Oval Office. That way, I'll be more use to them alive," Charlotte said, beaming with excitement.

Dale smiled back at her. "She's your game changer in more ways than one."

"If you're interested, I thought you could do the first, and only, interview with the outgoing VP and his wife and Tara and her family, assuming that the vetting doesn't turn up anything troubling. And me, of course. We'd have to tape tomorrow night. What do you think?" Charlotte asked.

"Madam President, that is very generous. Thank you," Dale said.

"No ground rules. No time limit. You can ask us anything. If you say yes, Melanie will work it out with Billy."

"This is incredible. Yes, of course I'll do it. Thank you again!" Dale exclaimed.

"Good. I'm so pleased," Charlotte said.

"I'll be in touch with Melanie, then. And I'll let you get back to work," Dale said, rising to leave.

"Dale, do you want to know why Peter started hating me?" Charlotte said.

"I'm sorry?" Dale said.

"Do you understand what Peter does for a living?"

"Of course," Dale said.

"But do you understand why he's so good at it?"

"I think so. He's brilliant and easygoing and everyone trusts him."

"Yes, he's all those things. But the reason he's the best in the business is that he knows how to chart a path for his clients, and he does it with such a gentle touch they don't even know they're being handled. He is better at it than anyone I have ever known. At some point, I shut him out. I stopped letting him help me chart my path. I thought that the problems I had were too difficult for him to solve. I turned to the experts," Charlotte said quietly, the regret visible on her face. "Let him help you, Dale."

Dale smiled at her. She'd never thought of Peter that way. Charlotte had just given her some very good advice. "Thank you," Dale said. "For everything."

Charlotte's face became veiled again. "So, we're all set. I will see you tomorrow night," she said, standing.

They shook hands, and Dale walked out of the residence and toward her car parked outside the East Wing. She couldn't believe that the president was the one person willing to throw her a lifeline. It had been nearly three months since Billy had sentenced her to network-news purgatory. He had given her the title "national correspondent," but so far, there had not been a single assignment for her. She hadn't appeared on the air since her return from Afghanistan. To make matters worse, they'd refused to let her out of her contract because of the investment they'd made in grooming her for the anchor chair.

Dale cranked the air conditioner in her car and started thinking through the script she'd write. Candidates had floated the idea of a unity ticket before, but no one had ever had the guts to try it. Charlotte's announcement would either dismantle what was left of her political coalition or get voters to give her a second look. Dale was eager to tell Peter the news. She dialed his number, and the call went straight to voice-mail. She went home to their house in Georgetown.

She called his cell phone two more times, and he didn't answer. She pulled a black skirt and a turquoise blouse out of her closet for the interview and then sat in front of the computer and started drafting questions for the president, the vice president, and the new nominee.

"Hey, honey, you in here?" she heard Peter call from the front entryway.

"Hi. Where have you been? I've been calling you," she said.

"We took off late because of fog, and I forgot to turn the phone off during the flight, so the battery was dead when I landed. Is everything OK?"

"Everything is better than OK. Charlotte called me this morning."

Peter stood very still and said nothing.

"I went over to the residence, and she told me that the veep is stepping down and she's putting a Democrat on the ticket. She offered me the exclusive interview with the VP and the new nominee and her family," she said proudly.

Peter exhaled. "That's great, Dale. That's really great, honey," he said with a smile Dale recognized as forced.

"Don't you want to know who she picked?" Dale asked.

"Of course," he said.

"Tara Meyers, the New York AG. Ballsy move, don't you think?" Dale said.

"Very," he said.

"What's wrong?" she asked.

"Nothing. If this is something you want to do, I'm behind you one hundred percent," he said.

"What do you mean?" she asked. "Why can't you just be excited for me?"

"I am excited for you. You're the best person to do the interview. And Charlotte was smart to pick you. She has good intentions, but she also knows that you'll give the story the time it deserves and that Billy will run the whole thing because he's basically run you off the air."

"But I can tell you don't think it's a good idea," she said.

"That's not it. I am just protective of you," he said.

"Why do you have to do that?" Dale complained.

"Do what? Be protective?" he asked.

"No. Why do you have to knock the one good thing that's happened to me since this whole stupid thing blew up in my face and ruined my career?" she said, fighting back tears of frustration.

Peter appeared to swallow whatever his first thought was. When he spoke, he did so in a low voice. "I don't want you to get disappointed again. One interview doesn't change anything," he said. "They aren't going to suddenly remember how talented you are and give you your job back. They'll air the interview, thank you for your good work, and go back to ignoring you because they don't know how to deal with you."

"How do you know it won't change anything?" Dale asked.

"I don't. Tell me I'm wrong. I'd love to be wrong," he said.

She stared out toward the garden. She was too frustrated to speak without saying something she knew she'd regret later.

"Dale, don't make a decision right now. Think about it for a couple of hours. I'm behind you whatever you do."

"It doesn't change anything," she said, her eyes glued to the window.

"And it makes you part of the story again," Peter said.

Dale looked at the outfit she'd pulled out of her closet and felt foolish for thinking that one interview could erase the revelation of her three-year affair with the president's husband and return her to broadcast-news prominence. She still had an urge to yell at Peter or throw something at him, but she knew he was right.

And she remembered Charlotte's words. She stewed silently for a few more minutes. When she turned to look at Peter, he was staring at her intently.

"The president and her new nominee are expecting me at the residence for the interview tomorrow night," she said. "What do you suggest I do?"

CHAPTER THIRTY-SIX

Charlotte

"D ale was supposed to be here at eight," Charlotte said, glancing at the clock in the Map Room.

"I'll go check East Exec to see if she's arrived yet," Melanie suggested.

"I'll come with you," Charlotte said, rising to walk out of the room where Neal and his wife, Mary, were sitting across from Tara and her husband on yellow loveseats. "Maybe you can talk to Tara about her look," Charlotte said to Melanie as they walked toward the east entrance of the White House. Tara was wearing a bright white suit that was made of some sort of stretchy material that hugged her thighs when she walked. The outlines of her undergarments were visible, and she wore an orange tank top and matching high heels.

Melanie groaned inwardly. "Sure," she said.

They walked out to the driveway just as Peter's car was pulling in.

"Here she is," Charlotte said.

The car came to a stop, and the back door opened. Brian stepped out.

"What are you doing here?" Melanie asked him, astonished. She'd thought he was in Michigan.

"I don't know. Dale said it was an emergency. She and Peter picked me up at the airport about twenty minutes ago and told me they'd explain when we got here," he said.

Dale stepped out of the passenger side and walked toward Melanie and Charlotte. "Madam President, I appreciate what you tried to do for me. It's more than anyone has done for me in a long time," Dale began.

Charlotte folded her arms in front of her chest and shook her head ever so slightly. "Melanie, why don't you bring Brian to the Map Room and explain what's happening tomorrow? We'll get started in a few minutes," Charlotte said.

Brian looked puzzled. Melanie's face turned white. She hadn't revealed Charlotte's news about Tara when they spoke by phone that morning, and she thought she had twelve more hours to figure out how to explain why she couldn't tell him, even off the record. Their arrangement regarding off-the-record information had worked out smoothly so far. Melanie told him things—never pertaining to national security, but everything else—on an off-the-record basis and insisted that he seek out independent sources if he pursued any of the topics she shared with him. It was how dozens of reporter and source couples survived life in Washington.

She and Brian turned and headed back toward the residence.

"Dale, I didn't ask you to do the interview because I felt sorry for you. I asked you to do the interview because you're the only person who would wrap the announcement into the larger sweep of history and not cover it as a political maneuver," Charlotte said.

"I appreciate that," Dale said.

"It's true," Charlotte said.

"It doesn't seem to matter to anyone in New York," Dale said wistfully.

Charlotte shook her head again and sighed. "Do you know what I was thinking about when I sat next to you in the hospital?"

"I'm afraid to ask," Dale said.

"I kept thinking, how long until she realizes that we did more than nearly kill her? In some ways, I felt worse about taking away your very bright career."

"You realized I was finished at the network before I did," Dale said.

"What are you going to do now?" Charlotte asked.

"I mailed my resignation letter on the way over here. Billy will get it in the morning. We're going to spend some time in San Francisco. Peter will see the kids on the weekends, of course, still. Maybe I'll freelance or produce or take time off. I don't know."

"I'm sorry," Charlotte said.

"Thank you. And good luck tomorrow with all of this." Dale motioned toward the residence.

"You'll watch the speech from San Francisco?" Charlotte asked.

"Yes, of course. Peter talked to the twins on the way over, and they're very excited about being in Philly with you this week."

Charlotte smiled. "I'd better get back inside."

"Brian will do a good job with the interview," Dale said, turning back toward the car.

Peter was standing a few feet away.

"Good night, Peter," Charlotte said, nodding in his direction.

He nodded back and put an arm around Dale.

Charlotte stood and watched Peter help Dale into the car. She waited until they'd driven past the iron gates, and then she walked down the stairs to stand in the driveway. She'd never noticed how many gates there were protecting her from the outside world. It was a steamy night, and the humid air felt good. She took a deep breath and wondered if rolling the dice on Tara Meyers would pay off.

Meyers was a law-and-order Democrat. She'd been the U.S. attorney for the southern district of New York and had prosecuted terrorist cases during the Martin administration—a nonpartisan post. When she'd run for attorney general as a Democrat, New York Republicans were disappointed. She'd won her first statewide race with sixty-four percent of the vote. She had an excellent reputation in law-enforcement circles, and when she'd landed in the national spotlight for prosecuting one of the big investment banks, she'd gained additional admirers. Meyers had a six-year-old daughter, and her husband was an FBI agent. They seemed perfectly suited for a life in politics. Charlotte sighed as she turned to walk back toward the Map Room for the interview. Life took such strange turns, she mused. She never thought she'd be bidding her husband and his girlfriend a goodnight while she prepared to upend the political world order by tapping a Democrat as her VP. She shivered as the air conditioned air blasted her warm skin. Charlotte rubbed her arms and steeled herself for the political attacks that were sure to come from Democrats and Republicans.

Brian conducted a short interview with the outgoing vice president. He honed in on questions about what McMillan wanted his political legacy to be. Then he interviewed Charlotte and Tara together about serving as a team after meeting for the first time only days earlier. Finally, he interviewed Tara about her record as attorney general and her political views on a host of social and foreign-policy issues.

When they finished, Brian thanked everyone and turned to leave.

Melanie followed him into the hallway. "I'm sorry for not telling you about this," Charlotte heard Melanie say to Brian.

He didn't say anything. Charlotte watched as he kept walking toward the North Lawn of the White House. Melanie stood in the middle of the hallway, watching him walk away.

"Did you see the way he looked at me?" Melanie said to Charlotte when she noticed her standing behind her.

"Yes. His ego is bruised because you didn't spill the beans about Tara. He'll get over it."

"I don't know," Melanie said.

"If he doesn't, you were going to get in trouble at some point anyway," Charlotte said.

Melanie stared in the direction in which he'd walked away.

"Don't worry about it tonight, Melanie. Try to get some rest. Tomorrow is going to be a long day." Charlotte stood there for another moment before turning to head up the stairs toward the residence.

Once upstairs, she read through her convention speech and reviewed the stage directions so she'd know where to stand for the vice president's speech and where to turn when Tara came onto the stage. The press would go nuts over the announcement. As much as they loved the unexpected, they hated to be surprised; it made them look bad.

Charlotte wandered around her bedroom, straightening items that didn't need straightening and triple-checking her luggage for the next day. She looked at the dogs sleeping in a heap of cinnamon-colored fur in the center of her bed. She smiled and climbed in beside them.

She wasn't tired yet, and she wanted to share the news about Tara with someone. She dialed Brooke and Mark's number. They were flying to Philadelphia in the morning to be there for her speech. Brooke picked up on the first ring.

"Hi," she said. "It's Charlotte."

"I know, silly," Brooke answered.

"Were you sleeping?" she asked.

"It's only ten P.M. here. What's up?"

"I might have done something crazy tonight," Charlotte said.

"You didn't fire Ralph, did you?" Brooke asked.

"No, I didn't fire Ralph, for Christ's sake. I picked a Democrat for vice president."

"Holy shit," Brooke said.

"It's a secret, but the vice president is going to introduce me tomorrow at the convention and announce that he's stepping aside. Then I'm going to come out and announce a new running mate."

"Can I tell Mark?" Brooke asked.

"Of course. Just tell him not to talk about it at the airport or on his cell phone."

"Oh, wait, I forgot to ask. Who is it?" Brooke asked.

"New York attorney general Tara Meyers," Charlotte said.

"Wow. You might be stuck with this gig for four more years after all," Brooke said.

"It should not be possible that I can win, should it?" she asked.

"Probably not. But voters like the way you've handled yourself, Char. You've been tough and graceful. I'm proud of you," Brooke said.

"Don't screw it up by telling your neighbors. This is top, top secret," Charlotte warned.

"I got it. I've got to go talk to the nanny about the kids' schedules. We'll see you tomorrow night, Char. Love you."

"You, too. Give the kids a hug from me," Charlotte said.

CHAPTER THIRTY-SEVEN

Melanie

Melanie ignored Charlotte's advice and followed Brian to the North Lawn of the White House, where he was taping a stand-up.

"Brian, please, can we talk about this?" she asked while he rehearsed.

He didn't look away from the camera.

"Are you even going to look at me?" she asked.

He stopped and turned to face her. "What the hell are we doing, Melanie? Do you think it's funny that I sleep in your bed at night and listen to hours and hours of your complaints about your horrible job, and then when something this big is happening, I don't get any sort of signal or warning that something major is coming? It takes Dale Smith calling me and telling me she's been handed a big scoop by the White House and she wants to hand it off to me. The funniest thing is that Dale assumed I already knew. That's why she asked me." He wasn't yelling, but his voice had an edge to it that she'd never heard before.

"I didn't have a choice about Dale," Melanie said.

"I believe you. And I'm not mad that Dale got the scoop and the interview, but I have never compromised the things you've told me, and I've never violated our agreement about what stays off the record and what I shouldn't even hear in the first place. I would rather be the last person on a story than betray your trust," he said.

"I know," Melanie said. "I'm sorry."

"It never crossed your mind that you could have shared this, that you could have trusted someone else. You're a one-woman band. You and Charlotte against the world, so help you God."

"That's not fair," she said.

"No? Do you think I would keep it from you if I heard that Fran was dumping her running mate?" he demanded.

"I don't know," Melanie said.

"You don't know? Well, that's great. I would *not* keep it from you. I might tell you not to tell Charlotte, but I would not keep it from you."

"I should have told you," she said.

"Yes, you should have told me."

"I'm sorry," she said again.

"You're sorry that I'm angry," he answered.

Melanie was silent.

"See, that's why this isn't going to work," he said sadly.

She looked at him. "What are you saying?"

"I'm not saying anything at one in the morning. I'm going to sleep at home tonight. I need to be up at the crack of dawn," he said.

"Me, too. Can't we just go home and sleep on it and figure things out later?" she asked.

"I can't deal with this right now, Melanie," he said.

She watched him pack up his things and walk away from her. She stood there until she heard the northwest gate close behind him. She saw Walter and Sherry sitting in the front seat of the SUV parked on the other side of the driveway. She walked over to the car and climbed into the backseat. Walter and Sherry were quiet.

"Hi, guys," she said.

"Good evening, Melanie," Walter said, smiling at her sympathetically.

She sent an e-mail to Charlotte's stylist, asking her to bring a dozen suits to the convention for Tara. The stylist wrote back: "Desired look?" Melanie replied: "Less Erin Brockovich, more Jackie Kennedy."

She e-mailed Annie to make sure she was traveling to the convention in the morning, and she typed out a lengthy note of congratulations to the speechwriting team. Charlotte's convention speech was a masterpiece, and they'd written a fiery address for Tara as well. Melanie leaned back and closed her eyes.

"It's almost over," Walter said from the front.

"Yep," Melanie said. "Sure is."

CHAPTER THIRTY-EIGHT

Dale

Y ou sure you want to watch it?" Peter asked.

"Yeah. I mean, it's not like I'm going to have a breakdown or anything. I know the interview could have been mine, but like you said, it wouldn't have changed anything," Dale said, reaching for the remote.

Peter sat down next to her, and they turned on the network Dale had spent the better part of five years working for.

"We have some breaking news to share with our viewers," the anchor said.

"He is so pissed about this," Dale said, leaning forward and staring intently at the screen.

"How can you tell?" Peter asked.

"He is trying so hard to smile that his face muscles are in spasm. See?" Dale pointed to the bottom left side of the screen.

"What do you know, you're right," Peter said, laughing. "Do you really think Billy and Brian kept the Tara announcement a secret from the anchor?"

"I wouldn't have guessed that they would have, but it's obvious from his face that he had no idea," Dale said, laughing and relaxing for the first time since they'd returned the night before from Washington.

238 * Nicolle Wallace

"This is going to be fun," she said, reaching for the can of Coke Peter had brought in for her.

The anchor tossed to Brian.

"At around eight P.M. last night, Alan, we were invited deep inside the White House residence, where the president of the United States shared a secret announcement only with us. We'll have that secret here, exclusively, on the other side of the break," Brian said, tossing back to the anchor.

Peter looked at Dale to gauge her mood. "How are you doing?"

"I'm fine," she said.

"All right. I'll stop fretting," he said.

"Here we go," she said.

"If you're just joining us, we have some breaking news. Our very own Brian Watson is reporting on a dramatic development from President Charlotte Kramer—a decision that could make this week's Republican convention very, very interesting. We're going to go to Brian now. Brian, what can you tell us?" the anchor said.

"Thanks, Alan. We were invited to the White House residence last night—the part of the White House rarely seen by the public because it's where the first family actually lives. But we were invited there last night for an exclusive interview with President Kramer, Vice President Neal McMillan, and Tara Meyers. Some of our viewers might recognize that name. Tara Meyers is the New York State attorney general. She is a Democrat, and after tonight, she will be the vice-presidential nominee for the Republican ticket. The vice president will step down at the end of his term, and President Kramer has replaced him as her running mate with Tara Meyers, a Democrat and the current attorney general for the state of New York," Brian said.

"Brian, what do we know about how this came to be?" the anchor asked.

"In my exclusive interview with all of the parties involved, I asked the vice president why he was stepping down, and he told me, quote, 'It is time to see how far we can push the process,' end quote, a reference, Alan, to what he described as the very nasty and partisan nature of the last several presidential campaigns."

"Interesting, Brian. And what do we know about Tara Meyers?

She is a woman, obviously, and that makes the Kramer-Meyers ticket historic in more ways than one."

"That's right, Alan. Obviously, Charlotte Kramer is sending all sorts of messages here. First, she's picked a Democrat, and she joked with us last night that the right wing of her party, which has given her all sorts of grief over the last four years, might appreciate her a little more now that there's a Democrat who could be standing, as they say, a heartbeat away from the Oval Office," Brian said.

"Fascinating. Historic. And only here. Stay with us for continuing coverage of this breaking news. We'll be right back with Brian's interview with President Kramer, Vice President McMillan, and the Republican Party's new vice-presidential nominee, Democrat Tara Meyers," the anchor said.

Dale clicked the television off and took a deep breath, blowing it out through her lips with a loud shushing sound. She had overestimated her ability simply to observe the world that she had been a part of for so long. "Honey, I think I'm going to go for a walk," she said.

"Want some company?" Peter asked.

"No. I think I need a head-clearing walk along the water."

"I understand. Will you bring your cell phone in case you want a ride back?"

"Sure," she said. She was wearing black yoga pants and running shoes, and she put on a fleece jacket over her long-sleeved T-shirt. San Francisco was freezing in August.

"I'll see you in a little bit," Peter said.

Dale hurried out the front door.

Once outside Peter's Pacific Heights Victorian, she crossed Divisadero and walked into the Presidio. The old military base made her feel as if she was stepping back in time. She made her way through the Presidio and down to the waterfront. She walked along the dirt path toward the Golden Gate Bridge and tried to breathe deeply. She had spiraled into a funk that she could no longer figure out how to pull herself out of. It wasn't just that she'd lost her job. She'd lost everything that went with it.

She knew she was lucky to be alive. She also knew she was lucky Charlotte had created a circumstance that allowed her to be with

Peter. Charlotte had paid a hefty political price for doing so, one that might cost her the election. But Dale had not asked Charlotte to give up Peter for her. She wasn't sure she knew how to be with him in the real world, and there was no one to turn to for advice. She didn't have any friends or hobbies. Work had always crowded out everything else. Without it, she had no idea who she was.

More than anything, she hated that she was so cold to the one person who was truly there for her. Peter spent every waking moment trying to make her happy, and she knew she was wearing him down with her sulking. She had tried to recapture the excitement she used to feel with him during their secret meetings and brief encounters, but she didn't know how to be excited about anything anymore.

She stopped to watch the fishermen pulling in their lines. The fog had come in, and a cool mist was blowing into her face. She closed her eyes and threw her head back. *Get a grip*, she said to herself over and over.

Watching Brian do the interview that she had been promised wasn't torture, but it didn't feel like her life anymore. She knew what she had to do. She had to reclaim something for herself. She needed a job. She'd call her agent again when she got home. There had to be someone in local news in San Francisco who would value her experience enough to put her on the air.

CHAPTER THIRTY-NINE

Charlotte

M elanie, these aren't right, are they? I'm only down two points among likely voters? That can't be, can it?" Charlotte asked as they jostled along the highway on a bulletproof, state-of-the-art bus somewhere in the middle of Ohio.

Since Charlotte had promised not to campaign, they'd embarked on a four-week "Conversation with America," and even though it wasn't a campaign trip, they'd decided to travel by bus. Her staff hated the bus, but Charlotte enjoyed seeing more than the airports and runways of the cities she visited.

In the weeks since the convention, Charlotte's poll numbers had inched to within striking distance of her opponent. The crowds that came out to see Charlotte and Tara were huge. Donations poured in through her campaign Web site. Most of the contributions were returned because of Charlotte's no-campaign pledge, but without the expense of television advertisements, they didn't need the money, anyway. Besides, Charlotte and Tara were a media sensation.

Tara's speech had electrified the Republican convention. Instead of walking out and refusing to nominate Charlotte for picking a Democrat, as some in the media had predicted when the news broke, the party faithful had been delighted by Tara's tough line on terrorism and her sharp attacks on Charlotte's opponent. While Charlotte's speaking style was elegant and nuanced, Tara went for the jugular with blunt language and crowd-pleasing applause lines.

The network and cable news shows couldn't get enough of the Charlotte and Tara Show. They ran packages on their clothes, their hairstyles, the significance of the first-ever all-woman ticket, and the impact on women and girls in America and around the world.

None of the staff on the bus paid any attention to the feel-good aspect of their all-female ticket. It was crunch time, and Melanie and Ralph were laser-focused on moving Charlotte's numbers among the voters who'd delivered her original victory four years earlier. Those were the easiest votes to recapture, and with the choice coming down to two women, Charlotte or Fran Frankel, the "women's story" had less impact on undecided voters than the idea of a bipartisan "unity ticket" running the federal bureaucracies.

Reporters and media outlets polled voters across the battleground states about their views on Charlotte's selection of Tara as a running mate. Most of the reviews were positive, but voters remained skeptical that their leaders could do much of anything to change Washington. Charlotte didn't blame them.

She looked around at the gaggle of staff, secret service agents, and political consultants traveling on her bus and concluded that she was either insane or brilliant for tapping Tara. She watched Tara as she listened intently to something her husband was saying. He was obviously her closest political advisor. Charlotte felt a flash of envy for what was clearly a seamless relationship between their personal and professional lives. Charlotte had experienced her happily married years, and they were followed by her professionally successful years, but she and Peter had never figured out how to be happily married and professionally satisfied at the same time.

"Look, look!" Tara shouted as one of the cable channels aired the newest cover of *Time* magazine.

"Look, Madam President—that picture was taken last night at the event," Tara exclaimed.

It was a shot of Charlotte and Tara doing a "fist bump" on stage with thousands of supporters cheering in the background. Under the shot, in huge letters, it read: "Kramer's Kryptonite."

Charlotte smiled back at Tara. She had succeeded in changing the conversation.

CHAPTER FORTY

Melanie

M elanie, can you or Ralph go through the polls with us?"
Charlotte called.

"Coming," Melanie answered from the front of the bus, where she was going over the data with Ralph and trying to read the bill from the stylist who'd helped Tara with her look for her convention address. After throwing a tantrum about how frumpy the elegant suits looked on her, she had stuffed all of the clothes into duffel bags and squirreled them away somewhere. Two weeks later, she was back to wearing cheap, tight skirts and blouses that looked as if they'd been purchased in the young teens section. Melanie put the statement into her bag and made her way toward the back of the bus.

"What are you two doing up there?" Charlotte asked. She was sitting at the head of the small table in the back. Tara and her husband sat next to her, and two of Tara's aides from the AG's office were on the other side.

"We're trying to figure out where to steer this jalopy next," Melanie said, growing dizzy from facing backward. "Hang on," she said, looking down at her phone. "It's Brian."

Charlotte raised an eyebrow.

Then Melanie's other cell phone rang. She looked at the number quickly. It was Michael from the *Dispatch*. She picked up Michael's call. "I need to call you right back," she said to him.

"Don't hang up," he told her.

Melanie was afraid she wouldn't get Brian's call in time. He was barely talking to her. "Brian, hang on one second," she said, holding one phone on each ear.

"Roger shot himself," Michael and Brian said in unison.

"What?" She didn't know which one of them she was talking to, but she dropped one phone when the bus lurched suddenly to one side.

"The cleaning lady found him this morning in his apartment in Pentagon City," Michael said. She'd hung up on Brian. "He'd been dead for hours, so it must have happened last night."

"Jesus Christ," Melanie said. Charlotte was eyeing her suspiciously.

"He left a note," Michael said.

Melanie was silent. She was using all of her mental energy to command her body not to throw up the moon pie she'd eaten for lunch.

"For Charlotte," he said.

"I'm going to need to call you back," Melanie said.

"Hurry."

Melanie stood in the doorway that separated the back section of the bus from the front. She looked around on the ground for her other phone. She didn't see it. She took two deep breaths and turned around to face Charlotte. "Can I talk to you?" she said.

"What, what is it?" Charlotte asked.

"Why don't you give us a minute?" Melanie said to Tara, her husband, and her two aides.

"They can stay," Charlotte said.

"Fine." Melanie's mouth was watering, and her ears were ringing. "Roger killed himself," Melanie said, turning and throwing up on the floor of the bus as soon as the words were out of her mouth.

Melanie apologized to the military aides who swarmed the area with 409, paper towels, and Lysol. She stepped over her mess to sit down next to Charlotte. Ralph followed, careful not to step in Melanie's vomit.

"She needs to get back to the White House as quickly as possible to do a statement from the East Room. If we do it tonight upon arrival, it will air on tomorrow's network morning shows," Melanie said. "It needs to be somber—something along the lines of 'My thoughts and prayers are with his family, he was a dedicated public servant,' and so on," she said, typing the same thought in an e-mail to the speechwriters that she was sharing with Ralph, Charlotte, and Tara on the bus.

A nurse from the White House medical unit handed Melanie a ginger ale with a straw in it. "Melanie, drink this, and we'll get more fluids in you once you keep it down," the nurse said.

Melanie looked up briefly and mouthed "Thank you." She put the soda down on the table without taking a sip.

"Do we cancel the next event, or do we do the event and go to Washington afterward?" Ralph asked as the bus continued down the interstate toward a five P.M. "Conversation with Ohio."

Melanie looked down at her BlackBerry and noticed that her hands were shaking. She moved them under the table and tried to focus on what Ralph was saying. "I'm sorry, what was the question?" she asked.

"The next event—keep it or cancel it?" Ralph asked.

"I'm not one-hundred-percent sure we should cancel it, but if we go forward with an event, how does she handle a question about the suicide? I'm worried that she gets a question, answers it, and then the tape that they run in a continuous loop about the suicide is from a campaign-style event. That would be bad," Melanie said, frowning at her BlackBerry. It wasn't getting a signal and had not transmitted her e-mail to the speechwriters. She held it above her head at various angles until it transmitted.

"If we pull the plug on the event, the local Republican committee will go crazy," Ralph said.

"So you suggest we go to Washington after the event?" Melanie said.

It wasn't like Melanie to solicit Ralph's opinion. He looked at her to determine whether she was patronizing him. "If we cancel," Ralph said, "we would need to promise that this is the next event we do when we return to the 'Conversation with America' tour. The tickets were gone in fifteen minutes, and the crowd has been waiting for four hours."

"My gut says cancel it, but I could be convinced that canceling would be interpreted by the press as an overreaction. I don't know. It's a close call," Melanie said with uncharacteristic indecision.

"Why can't she just stand alone outside Air Force One and read a statement in front of the cameras?" Tara asked. "That way, it would look presidential, and it would separate her from the day's campaign activity, but we could stick to the schedule."

Melanie shot Tara a look that said, *Stay out of this,* and sighed loudly before she spoke. "Because she can't. Roger was her secretary of defense, and they went through a lot together. This morning, he shot himself. He has a wife. He has kids. And he left a suicide note—not for his wife or his kids but for Charlotte. That's why she can't just walk out of a campaign rally with hay in her hair from some state fair and say, 'I sure am going to miss old Roger.' This is a presidential moment, Madam Attorney General," Melanie said.

"I see," Tara said.

Melanie was sure she'd back down. But she didn't.

This time, Tara faced Ralph when she spoke. "Isn't this also a moment when we risk turning the discussion back toward the past and everything they didn't like about Charlotte's first term? And aren't we moving up in the polls and succeeding in making the election about the future?" Tara asked.

Melanie was furious that Tara assumed she had a seat at the table for presidential decision making. So what if Charlotte's numbers had surged since Tara had joined the ticket? It didn't give her the right to weigh in on the things Charlotte did in her capacity as incumbent president. That was squarely Melanie's domain.

Melanie pasted a smile on her face and cleared her throat. "Madam Attorney General, with all due respect, the voters expect a leader to stand by her friends when the situation is this dire," she informed her.

"It's a little late for that, isn't it?" Charlotte said.

She'd been sitting at the table staring out the window, and it wasn't clear to Melanie whether she'd been listening to the exchange. If she had been listening, Melanie was irritated that she hadn't chimed in sooner to take her side.

"I mean, if I were inclined to stand by him when things were dire, I wouldn't have forced his resignation or agreed to all the recommendations from the panel," Charlotte said. "If I were inclined to stand by him, I would have called him when the report came out to see if he was doing OK. I would have called Stephanie. She was my friend at one time, too." Charlotte spoke in a voice that was so soft Melanie had a hard time hearing her. "I don't know why I drew such a bright line. I don't know why I hardened so completely against him," she practically whispered.

"Madam President, this isn't your fault," Melanie said quietly.

And she meant it. Roger's suicide wasn't Charlotte's fault. It was hers. He had called her nearly a dozen times.

Melanie still hadn't found her other cell phone. How was she supposed to manage the situation without her phone? She looked under the table, but every time her eyes moved to the floor of the bus, she felt as if she would vomit again. She shifted her gaze to the window and saw Tara whispering quietly to her husband. They looked as if they were conspiring.

"Madam President," Tara said, "I don't know if this is of any help, but I could pick up the 'Conversations with America' for a while if you want to go back to Washington to make a statement like Melanie suggests."

"Thanks, Tara. I appreciate that," Charlotte said. "Let's see what Melanie and Ralph decide. And I really do appreciate your offer."

"It's the least I can do," Tara said.

Charlotte returned her gaze to the view outside her window, and Melanie caught the look that Tara gave her husband. Tara looked satisfied that she'd infiltrated the inner circle, and her husband appeared to nod slightly, as though things had gone exactly as they'd planned. Melanie was tempted to say something to put her in her place, but she had too many other things to handle.

She moved slowly over to where the president was sitting. "Madam President, I'm going to have the speechwriters start working on a statement about Roger," she said.

Charlotte nodded.

"Is there anything else I can do for you?"

Charlotte was silent, but she moved her hand to her head and started rubbing her temples.

"Madam President?" Melanie said.

"I didn't have any idea that he was taking things this hard, or maybe I just didn't want to know," Charlotte said.

Melanie couldn't meet Charlotte's eye. "We should call Stephanie. Do you want me to see if I can get her on the line?" Melanie asked.

"I don't know if she'd take my call, but yes, we need to try."

They rolled along for twenty more minutes before the bus pulled up alongside Air Force One at the airport in Columbus, Ohio. Ralph convinced Melanie that Tara could handle the president's scheduled appearances while Charlotte was in Washington. Charlotte barely looked at Ralph and Melanie when they made the recommendation.

Before she boarded the plane, Charlotte moved over to where Tara and her husband were sitting and did her best to look cheerful. "Tara, I really appreciate your willingness to step in and handle the 'Conversations.' They're nothing more than town-hall meetings, but since I promised no campaign, they're all we've got."

"Madam President, it is my honor," Tara said.

"I'll give you a call in the morning to check in," Melanie told her.

"Great. You know where to find us," Tara said.

"Ralph is going to stay behind to staff you. We'll send written remarks to the bus overnight. Everything will be fine. Don't worry."

"I'm not worried. And don't you worry about us. We'll be fine." Tara gestured at the staff staying behind to work for the vice-presidential nominee's first solo trip.

"You'll be great," Charlotte added before she walked off the bus.

Melanie watched Charlotte walk up the steps of Air Force One. She didn't turn and wave to the cameras as she normally did. As soon as she disappeared into the front cabin, Melanie hurried up the front stairs and walked straight to the senior staff cabin to call the speechwriters back at the White House.

"Hey, guys, can you meet me when we land?" she asked.

"Yeah. We started something already based on your e-mail. We'll have a first draft for you to review. Couple questions, Mel. Where and when are we doing this?" one of the writers asked.

"I think we want to do it tonight. I need to talk to the president again. And I don't have a speech venue yet, but it will be somewhere on the eighteen acres. If you guys have suggestions, let me know. At first, I thought East Room, but that doesn't feel right. I was toying with Rose Garden, but I could be persuaded to move it indoors, maybe to the Briefing Room. I don't know. I'll call you back. If you have something you can fax to the plane before we land, we'll start reviewing it here."

"Melanie, one more question. Does she want to mention what happened in Afghanistan or just keep it broad? Lifetime of service, that sort of stuff?" the writer asked.

"I don't know. Let me call you back."

She hung up and asked the Air Force One operator to place a call to Brian's cell phone. His voice-mail picked up. Melanie was getting ready to leave a message when Charlotte appeared in the doorway to the senior staff cabin.

"I need to talk to you," Charlotte said. She turned and walked straight back to her cabin. Melanie stood and followed her, shutting the door behind her.

Charlotte was standing in front of her desk, leaning against it with her arms crossed. As soon as Melanie closed the door behind her, Charlotte motioned for her to come closer.

"He tried to see me," Charlotte said. "He called Sam, and he asked her for ten minutes to come see me, and we didn't give it to him. How would you feel? I should have shown him more compassion. He was my friend."

"He called me, too," Melanie said. "On multiple occasions. If anyone is to blame, it's me. I should have seen him. It's my job."

Charlotte didn't say anything.

"Madam President, even if we were unkind for not returning his calls, I do not believe we are responsible for what Roger did."

"Do you really believe that, Melanie? That we're not responsible? That we didn't hold the power to absolve him?" Charlotte said.

Melanie stared at the ground.

"Because I think we screwed this one up. Big time. We let Roger get destroyed because we saw this the way we see everything—black and white. There was no room to forgive, because we don't have a box for that in November. We cut him out like a cancer because he traded one life for another, right?" Charlotte said.

Melanie looked up. "Yes. You said at the time that doing so made him just like the enemy," Melanie reminded her, not sure where Charlotte was going.

"I remember. But didn't we just do exactly the same thing?" Charlotte said. "Didn't we trade Roger's life for Dale's?"

Melanie felt goose bumps rise on her bare arm. "No, no, it's not the same," she said, shaking her head.

"Melanie, if you are capable of that kind of denial, you are much better suited for this job than I am," Charlotte said.

Neither of them said anything else, and after a few moments, Charlotte sat down at her desk and pretended to read pages from a briefing book.

Melanie turned to leave. "Let me know if you need anything," she said.

Charlotte didn't look up.

CHAPTER FORTY-ONE

Dale

Dale stood stretching at the beginning of the path and told herself over and over that she could turn around if she got tired. Since the accident, her body felt foreign to her—fragile and untrustworthy. To regain her strength, and because she didn't have anything else to do, she'd started walking along the trail under the Golden Gate Bridge each afternoon. It was the only part of her day she looked forward to. The night before, she'd decided to advance to jogging. The thought terrified and excited her. She checked her shoelaces, turned up the volume on her iPod, and waited for a group of women in their sixties to pass before she jogged slowly onto the trail.

After only a couple of minutes, her breathing steadied. Her insides felt fine. She turned and looked back and figured she'd already gone about half a mile. With each step, she felt stronger. She felt her body moving beneath her without faltering or breaking. She felt her lungs taking in more air and pushing more air out than they had in ages. She jogged along in silence for about twenty minutes and stopped just under the Golden Gate Bridge.

A group of moms pushing strollers ran by while she stood stretching her hamstrings. She was breathing heavily, and her legs were burning, but she felt invigorated. She felt her cell phone vibrating in her pocket and pulled it out to check the caller ID. It was her agent.

"Hey, Arnie," she said.

"You sound like you're having a heart attack," he said.

"I'm running," she said.

"Why?" he asked.

"That's what people do out here. They run, hike, wind-surf, kayak, spin, yoga—all that crap."

"Sounds like your spirits are up. Maybe that's what you needed," he said.

"Any luck with the last round of calls?" she asked.

"Yes and no. You want the good news or the bad news first?"

"I should probably get the bad news over with while my endorphins are up," she said.

"The cables aren't hiring before the election. They all love you—said they hated what happened to you, and they'd love to talk to you after the election but can't hire you for the final stretch."

"How is that possible?" Dale asked, feeling her runner's calm evaporate.

"Hold on. I do not come to you empty-handed. The ABC affiliate in San Francisco is a great station, and they'd love to have you cover the vice-presidential campaign for them for the final weeks. They'd pay you a freelancer's day rate."

"I'm not even going to say out loud what I'm thinking, but tell me you're thinking it, too," she said.

"You can say it. How the hell did we get here? Next in line for evening anchor and now our best option is working freelance in local?"

"Exactly."

"Want my advice?" he asked.

"Not really," she said.

"You should buy a sailboat, have a kid, take up tennis, and relax for a year. Someone else will stumble by then, and you can make your comeback. You're trying to force something that just isn't there right now."

"Thanks, Arnie. You always know just what to say. How long do I have to decide on the San Francisco station?"

"I told them I didn't think you'd be interested, but they said if you were, you should go see them tomorrow."

"What time?" she asked.

"Dale, are you sure you want to do this?" he asked.

"What time?"

Her legs were aching as she walked back along the route she'd jogged minutes earlier. She rehearsed what she'd say to Peter as she made her way back up the hill to Pacific Heights.

He was in the den watching the news. She walked in and sat next to him.

"Hi, honey. How was your walk?" he asked.

"Good," she said, rubbing her quads.

She stood up to get some Advil just as the evening news was starting.

"You want anything?" she asked Peter, just as the anchor announced that with weeks to go before Election Day, Charlotte had abruptly left the campaign trail to attend Roger's funeral and had no immediate plans to return.

Dale sat back down to watch Brian's package and was surprised to see that Tara had taken over the role of chief campaigner for Charlotte.

"I can't believe Ralph and Melanie left Charlotte's reelection in Tara's hands," she said.

"I'm not sure they had a choice," Peter said.

"What do you mean?"

"I spoke to some old friends today whom I hadn't heard from in a while. They said Charlotte is taking the news about Roger very hard. She feels responsible. He left a note for her."

Dale was quiet. Since learning about Roger's suicide days earlier, she hadn't been able to begin to process the fact that he'd taken his own life. She took a deep breath and blew it out. "It will never end, will it?" she asked.

"What?" Peter asked.

"This story. The crash. The accident. Charlotte's speech. Getting outed for having an affair with you. Getting fired. I will always be the reporter who was sent up in Marine One, the one who was sleeping with the president's husband."

Peter didn't say anything.

"I know that you think I'm pathetic for feeling sorry for myself.

You never complain about anything, so you can't fathom why I can't get past this, but you don't understand. You can't imagine what it's like to have decisions made for you—decisions that you never would have made but you have to live with all the same," she said.

He looked at her.

She knew she was wrong. Of course, he knew what it was like to have decisions made for him—decisions that affected his life. Isn't that what Charlotte had done to him throughout their marriage? But Dale wanted to get a reaction from him. She wanted him to scream at her, to drag her out of the puddle of self-pity she was drowning in.

"You're right," he said. "I never went through what you've gone through—what you're still going through. And no, it will never go away completely. You will be part of the history of Charlotte's presidency forever. But you do get to decide one thing."

"What's that?" she asked.

"How long you stay pissed at the world. You get to decide when to stop being angry and start living again."

She looked at him. There was no bitterness on his face. She could detect only concern and the same weariness she'd first noticed when they were staying in Georgetown.

Peter stood up and went to his office. She sat in the television room and stared out at the fog below the window. She could barely make out the top of the Golden Gate Bridge. She pulled her BlackBerry out of her purse and sent an e-mail to the news director at the station that was interested in hiring her.

"I look forward to speaking with you tomorrow at noon. I'm confident we can work something out," she wrote.

CHAPTER FORTY-TWO

Charlotte

Brooke wasn't even quiet when she was whispering. Charlotte heard her on the phone talking to Mark about how Charlotte seemed paralyzed.

She had no idea.

In the days since Roger's suicide, she had simply put one foot in front of the other. But her paralysis, as Brooke described it, was protecting her from something far worse. By forcing him out and allowing him to take the fall, she'd killed Roger as plainly as if she had pulled the trigger herself.

Charlotte had delivered a statement in the East Room on the night they'd returned to Washington. She'd spoken to Stephanie and their children and offered her condolences. Stephanie had been polite and gracious. She'd invited Charlotte to speak at the funeral. Charlotte had attended the funeral and delivered a eulogy that Melanie and the speechwriters had stayed up all night writing. It struck the perfect tone of tribute and absolution.

Charlotte never would have acted on it, but Stephanie hadn't been crazy to worry about Charlotte's relationship with her husband. Charlotte had felt as possessive of Roger as if he'd been hers, and his death had extinguished her last reserves of emotional resilience. She could not muster the strength to push aside the sadness and regret that consumed her. Roger had been more of a companion to her than her own husband. They'd shared a passion for the nitty-gritty details of the military campaign and intelligence reports they received from Iraq and Afghanistan. They'd spent hours talking about what Iraq would be like in another generation. They'd shared tears when they learned that soldiers they'd met on their trips had been killed or wounded, and they'd made special trips together to Walter Reed and other military hospitals to visit the wounded soldiers.

Charlotte knew that too many days had passed since she'd left Tara on the campaign trail alone with Ralph to pick up the "Conversations with America." But she could not have a conversation with America when the only thing going through her mind was *I killed my friend and the only man I've loved since I've had this godforsaken job. I killed him by failing to show compassion or forgiveness.*

It was better to have Tara make the case on behalf of the campaign. Tara was bubbly and enthusiastic. Her public life seemed to have strengthened all of her relationships. Her husband was a doting and involved partner. Their daughter thrived on the campaign trail.

Charlotte sighed and lay back against the pillows. Sensing her troubles, the dogs stayed close. Cammie lay on top of her, trying to absorb her grief.

Charlotte knew Melanie was struggling as well. She wanted to tell her that she wasn't to blame. She wanted to be there for Melanie, but she couldn't. Not yet.

She needed to get through the debate. She had four days to prepare for the first of three debates with Fran. She'd walked out of debate prep earlier in the day. The staff had tried to get her to practice, but she couldn't concentrate. Melanie had broken up the session and told her to get some rest. She knew they were all starting to worry about her.

That's why Brooke was there. Melanie had called her the day before and asked her to come out for a few days. Brooke's company was a distraction but not a comfort. Brooke poured wine and lit cigarettes and made tea and sat with her.

Every time Charlotte tried to get herself to a place where she could imagine returning to the campaign trail with the kind of energy and focus she knew it demanded at this stage in the game, she'd come up with another excuse to delay it. The debate would be her official reentry point, and she knew she had work to do.

She opened one of the thick black briefing books and stared at a page of notes on health-care reform. She couldn't focus on the policy paper. Her thoughts careened from vivid memories of her most intimate moments with Roger, to memories of being a young, happily married mother working her way up to senior management at a Silicon Valley tech company, to memories of the way she and Peter had served as their own strategists during her long-shot run for governor.

She kept replaying all of the decisions she'd made along the way: the decision to stay at work late each night while Peter was home with the babies, the choices she'd made about leaving the parenting to Peter while she focused on her career, and the little ways in which she'd isolated herself as president. Just when she thought the memories had run their course, they would begin anew, and the debilitating feelings of regret would start all over again.

She heard a knock at her door. She rose and opened it.

"Hey," Brooke said. "Can I come in?"

"Of course. I just took an Ambien, so I'm not sure how long I'll be awake," she said.

"That's OK," Brooke said. "Mark and I have some of our best conversations on Ambien."

Charlotte tried to smile.

Brooke wandered over to Charlotte's desk and fingered the photo albums stacked on top. "Did Sam put these together for you?" she asked.

"No, the photo office does it. Those are from our surprise trip to Iraq over Christmas," Charlotte said.

"Of course. I have fond memories of taking part in your elaborate ruse to sneak out of Camp David on Christmas Day without the press noticing," Brooke said.

Charlotte laughed. "That's right. We sent you to Christmas services with the kids while Roger and I made our escape."

"Didn't you guys leave in the middle of an ice storm?" Brooke asked.

"Yes. The secret service didn't want us on the roads, but Roger insisted," Charlotte said. She smiled at the memory.

"Char, you're going to get through this. You know that, right?" Brooke said.

"I don't know. Maybe it's time to take all these things as signs that the universe has had enough of me," Charlotte said.

"Are we going to head down this road? The universe has not had nearly enough of you, and that's not why you're curled in a fetal position crying your eyes out. You miss him. You miss him so much that it hurts to breathe. I know how much he meant to you, and I saw how much he adored you, Char."

Charlotte's face crumpled. "I wasn't having an affair with him," she said before her voice cracked.

"It didn't matter. You guys were in your own world together. Anyone could see it," Brooke said, patting Charlotte's hand. "It's OK to miss him. It's OK."

Charlotte cried softly, and after a few minutes, she went into the bathroom to wash her face. She came back out of the bathroom and sat down on the bed. "I can't go back out there and ask people to vote for me," she said.

"Why? Because your marriage fell apart? Because your husband is shacked up with a reporter? Or because you're tired? Because those aren't good enough excuses. You go down fighting, Char, not like this."

"I hate you," Charlotte said.

"I know. I hate you for inspiring my son to risk his life, but we're stuck with each other."

"I'm sorry about that. Do you want me to talk to him?" Charlotte asked.

"No. I want you to get out of bed and go claim what is yours—a second term," Brooke urged.

"All right," Charlotte said.

"Atta girl."

"Tomorrow. Tonight I need to sleep," Charlotte said.

While Charlotte drifted off to sleep, Brooke e-mailed Sam and Melanie two words: "Mission accomplished."

CHAPTER FORTY-THREE

Melanie

Melanie was fuming. Tara was supposed to read the speech exactly as she'd approved it the night before. When Melanie turned on the television to catch Tara's "Conversation with Miami," the vice-presidential nominee was defiantly off-script.

"President Kramer is a great leader and a better woman than me. If Fran Frankel said the sorts of things about me that she says about Charlotte Kramer, I'd feel compelled to respond," Tara said.

The crowd applauded.

"And since President Kramer isn't here today, and since I know I can trust all of you to keep this little chat just between us"—Tara slowed down when she said "just between us," and the crowd hooted and clapped louder than before—"let me take on some of the lies our opponent is so fond of repeating about one of this country's great presidents.

"It might not be the ladylike thing to do, but we're voting for a president in four weeks, ladies and gentlemen, not a prom queen. We don't have time to be nice. It's time to get real," Tara said, crumpling the speech on the podium in front of her into a ball and tossing it into the crowd. The crowd was on its feet instantly, cheering so loudly that Tara had to quiet them down before she could go on.

Voters loved a good fight, and so far, Charlotte had refused to give them one.

"Annie, get Ralph on the phone!" Melanie shouted.

Annie appeared in her doorway seconds later. "Line two," she said.

"Ralph, what the hell is she doing?" Melanie asked.

"She's playing to the crowd," Ralph said, laughing.

"I can see that, but it isn't funny," Melanie said.

"Come on, our numbers pop in every market she visits. I know it wasn't the plan, but what she's doing is working. People love her," Ralph said.

Melanie sighed. "Then why do we bother with prepared remarks, Ralph? And how do we protect Charlotte from being called a liar? She promised there'd be no campaign, and every day this week, Tara has lit the other side up Lee Atwater–style."

"I know, I know. But Tara didn't make any promises."

"Ralph, she's her goddamned running mate. No more freelancing. No shooting from the hip. No audibles called from the road!" Melanie barked.

"Aye, aye, Captain," Ralph said.

"I'm serious, Ralph."

"I'll talk to her," he promised.

"Thank you," Melanie said, calming down a bit as she saw Tara make the transition from her fiery introduction to the approved stump speech that had been loaded into the teleprompter.

"How's the president?" Ralph asked.

"She'll be fine. She's just tired. We gave her the night off. If any of the traveling press asks, tell them she's cramming for the debate."

"Will do," Ralph said.

"How are the crowds?" Melanie asked.

"Huge. We registered ten thousand new supporters in Ohio during the three-day bus tour, and the Florida events have all been moved to larger venues to accommodate the requests for tickets."

"That's great, Ralph. Really great. Charlotte will be thrilled. I can't wait to tell her."

"She called Tara this morning after the morning shows. I think Tara told her about the crowds already."

Melanie wasn't aware that Charlotte and Tara had spoken. "Oh, that's good. I mean, they should be in frequent contact. Maybe we should set up a daily call between the two of them," she said.

"I think they've been speaking pretty regularly, but we could put it on the schedule if you want," Ralph said.

It wasn't often that Ralph told her what was going on.

"Maybe when Charlotte is back on the road and they assume separate schedules, we can add a call to the schedule," she said.

"Sounds good," Ralph said.

"All right, then. Keep Tara on script, or at least give us a heads-up when she's planning on playing chief campaign strategist, so I can get the president on message," Melanie said.

Ralph chuckled. "The president doesn't seem to mind her independence," he said.

"Charlotte doesn't have time to worry about her running mate's disdain for message discipline," Melanie said.

Inexplicably, he laughed again. "Good luck with debate prep," he said.

"We'll see you out there in a couple of days," Melanie said.

She hung up and returned her attention to the mountain of paperwork awaiting her review. At six-thirty, she turned the volume up on her televisions. The remote was supposed to control one set at a time, but it never worked properly. Suddenly, all of her televisions were blaring.

Annie rushed in and muted all of them except Brian's network. "Mind if I watch the news in here?" Annie asked.

"Of course not," Melanie said.

It was one of their little rituals. Annie came in at six-thirty, and they watched the evening newscasts together. During the commercials, Annie gave Melanie all of the West Wing gossip. It was remarkable to Melanie that the people who ran the country had no ability to communicate efficiently with one another, while all of the personal assistants to the people who ran the country swapped intelligence and information effortlessly. Melanie always took her young assistants under her wing, promoting them to better jobs as rewards for their service. She didn't have any choice but to trust her personal assistants with the most sensitive and vital information imaginable. Melanie was re-warded with their fierce loyalty, around-the-clock service, and a daily download of gossip culled from the other assistants in the West Wing.

"So, what's really happening on the road?" Melanie asked.

"Ralph has been buying drinks every night for the staff," Annie said.

"Really?" Melanie was surprised. He always seemed so uptight.

"Yep. And there's something else," Annie said.

"What?" Melanie asked.

"Promise you won't get mad?"

"Yes," Melanie said.

"They've started calling you Mean Mommy," Annie told her.

"Who has?" Melanie said.

"The traveling staff."

"That's ridiculous. I'm not mean, am I?" Melanie asked.

"No. I don't think so," Annie said. Annie was so devoted she wouldn't tell Melanie she was mean even if she thought she was an ogre.

"Why do they think I'm mean?"

"They say you're always reining them in," Annie said.

"Reining them in? Excuse me. How about trying to elect Charlotte to a second term so they all have jobs?" Melanie said.

"I know. As if they could handle your responsibilities," Annie said, shaking her head.

Melanie let out a "hmft" and stared at the unread e-mail messages on her computer screen. She was tempted to have IT change her e-mail address to meanmommy@eop.who.gov. She would show them who had a better sense of humor.

"Mean Mommy," she said to herself, shaking her head.

"Want me to get you a frozen yogurt?" Annie asked.

"Not yet. Maybe after dinner," Melanie said, leaning back to watch the news.

They watched Brian first. He was standing in the back of the Miami event. His live reports were the closest Melanie got to him these days. Not calling him back after he'd called with the news about Roger's suicide had been the last straw. She'd e-mailed him to apologize, and he'd never answered.

She'd thought about typing him a note after watching his report on Tara's natural talents on the campaign trail, but she was afraid that he would tell her that he never wanted to speak to her again. That was what she'd said to her ex-husband, Matthew, the last time they'd spoken, and it was the kind of thing you only said when things were so far gone you didn't care if the person fell off a cliff.

She rarely allowed herself to think about Matthew, but every time she went through a breakup, she pulled the memories of her failed marriage off the shelf and reminded herself she was damaged goods. Her eighteen-month marriage was the kind of surreal detail of her life that she saw in her Wikipedia entry and had to think about for a minute before she was certain it was true.

She'd met Matthew in typical Washington fashion—in a green room. Theirs was a cross-party romance. He'd been the chief spokesman for the Democratic leader in the Senate, and she was President Martin's newly appointed press secretary. They'd flirted over bad coffee and bottled water while the producers connected their microphones and earpieces. The sparks had flown when they took their seats on the set of CNN's *Situation Room* for a debate on health care.

At the time, they'd been two spokespeople at the top of their games. They would become one of Washington's favorite power couples. The problem with power couples, Melanie soon learned, was that things only worked out when the balance of power was unchanged. If one half of a power couple moved ahead of the other, the whole thing fell apart. As White House press secretary, Melanie's star had been rising faster than his.

Melanie had known he was cheating before she actually caught him in the act, because Michael had told her, but she hadn't figured out what to do about it. Fortunately, the relationship unraveled before she had to do anything. Melanie had come home early from an overseas trip with the president to find her husband's deputy in her bed watching the Sunday shows. Her husband hadn't even tried to explain.

Now, Annie cleared her throat and stood up when the newscast was over. Melanie refocused on her e-mail inbox.

"Want me to place a dinner order from the Mess?" Annie asked.

"Sure. The usual," Melanie said.

As soon as Annie stepped out of her office, Melanie reached for the remote and replayed Brian's report. He looked as if he was enjoying himself. His network released a poll as part of its newscast that showed Charlotte two points behind her opponent among women and tied among men. *If those numbers hold, Charlotte might win,* Melanie thought. She couldn't believe how backward everything seemed. Roger was dead, Charlotte and Peter were separated, the president was upstairs having a breakdown, and her running mate—an eccentric Democrat from New York who said "y'all" ten times a day, even though she'd never lived or worked in the South—had hijacked the campaign.

Melanie disliked everything about Tara. She was loud, tacky, and rude. She seemed to calculate the least presidential approach to every situation and pursue it with vigor.

Melanie nibbled on a veggie burger and reviewed the debate-prep book—four hundred pages of policy papers on every topic from global warming to assisted suicide. At around nine P.M., she stood to stretch her legs.

She wandered down to the Sit Room one floor below and chatted with the smokers who inhaled cigarettes two at a time and e-mailed furiously outside the West Wing basement door.

"Melanie, the president is on the phone for you," a breathless Annie said, appearing suddenly.

"OK, take it easy. I'll take it in the Sit Room," Melanie said. She stepped into the Situation Room and picked up the phone. "Madam President?"

"Melanie, I want to get back out there," Charlotte said. Her voice was groggy, but she sounded determined.

"I'm already working on it," Melanie said, grateful for Brooke's e-mail. "I think I can get you to the evening rally tomorrow," she said.

"I want to be at the first event tomorrow," Charlotte said through a yawn.

Melanie looked at her watch. The event was in twelve hours. "Yes, ma'am," she said.

CHAPTER FORTY-FOUR

Dale

D ale had friends who planned date nights with their husbands
after they had kids, but she didn't think she and Peter would
turn to such an artificial device so soon in their newly outed relationship. He'd suggested it, though, so she went along.

Dale rehearsed what she'd say to Peter at dinner. She was nervous.
She knew she bore most of the responsibility for the strain between
them, but it still bothered her that on top of everything else, she had
to worry about his feelings all the time.

She dressed for dinner in black pants and a gray sweater. Something about the layer of fog that always hung over San Francisco in the
evenings made her colorful television clothes feel all wrong. When
she walked into the entryway to greet Peter, he looked surprised that
she'd dressed with such care.

"We really are having a date night tonight," he said.

She examined his face for sarcasm but didn't see anything but affection and a bit of boyish excitement. *What is wrong with me?* she
thought for the thousandth time.

She smiled and tried to look equally excited. "I'm really looking
forward to trying this place," she said.

Peter came to her and kissed her cheek. "You look beautiful," he
said.

She smiled and tried to relax.

They were seated at a table in the corner. She knew she needed to tell him about the job she'd accepted, or it would hang between them all night.

"Charlotte is feeling pretty good about things," Peter said.

"Did you talk to her again today?" Dale asked. She knew how it sounded, and she didn't intend for it to come out like an accusation.

"The election is a month away. The kids are on the road with her, and I checked in. It's pretty exciting to think that she might actually win."

Dale drained her wine glass and looked up for the waiter to order another glass. "I met with one of the local stations this week," she said.

"That's great. I mean, if you think you want to do some freelancing, it's probably good to have relationships at the affiliates out here, right?" He was smiling at her and trying to sound supportive, but she could tell he was annoyed that she had surprised him again.

"I interviewed for a job covering the last month of the campaign for the ABC affiliate out here, and they offered it to me on the spot," she said.

"Of course they did. You are a network anchor."

"Was a network anchor," she corrected him.

He finished his glass of wine.

"They want me to start Monday."

"You're not considering it, are you?" he asked.

"I don't know. I never would have before, but it's not like there are any networks knocking down my door," she said.

"Is this what you want?" he asked.

"Is freelancing for a local San Francisco television station what I want? Yes, it's a dream come true. Of course, it isn't what I want. What I want is my old job back, but that isn't in the cards for me."

"It sounds like you made a bum trade, Dale," he said.

"No, that isn't what I mean. I love that we're together. I just don't know how you can love me when I'm like this."

"Some days are easier than others," he admitted.

"I'm serious. I have nothing to give to you because I feel as though I don't have anything for myself anymore. I need to do this. I need you to understand and support me."

He looked at her with an expression she couldn't discern. She thought he looked indifferent—a look she'd never seen cross his face since they'd first met. "I always support you, but that's not what you're asking me to do," he said.

"Yes, that's exactly what I'm asking you to do, and if this is you supporting me, then I'm afraid for the day I make a choice you don't support or understand."

"You've already made a choice?" he asked.

"I'm trying to do that here, with you," she said, exasperated.

"What you're asking me to do is to let you go," he said.

"That's not true, Peter." But his words had sucked all the air out of her lungs. She breathed shallowly and didn't look up.

"You might not be ready to admit it, but that's what you want. I have known that for a while, and I think you have, too," he told her.

"I don't agree with you," she said in a very small voice.

Their food arrived, and they made mostly small talk for the rest of the night. They didn't touch their meals. Dale asked questions about the campaign, and he asked what kind of stories she had in mind for her first week.

When they got home, Dale changed into pajamas and crawled into bed. Peter kissed her good night and went into his office to do some work. She was still awake when he came to bed an hour later. He didn't move toward her, and she debated whether to move closer to him. She inched toward him and slid her body into its usual spot behind his. She put an arm around him, and he took her hand in his. They lay there awake until sunrise and then he got out of bed without so much as looking at her. He took a shower, dressed, and kissed her on the cheek.

"I'll see you in a few weeks," she said. "I'll be back the day after the election ends."

"Have fun," he said to her before turning to leave.

CHAPTER FORTY-FIVE

Charlotte

It's the best high in the world, Charlotte thought to herself as a screaming crowd of more than twenty-five thousand supporters in Milwaukee chanted "Four more years" and the advance crew blasted a Shania Twain song so loudly Charlotte could feel the ground shaking beneath her.

Since she'd rejoined the "Conversation with America" tour, the rallies had grown larger and the crowds more enthusiastic by the day. Charlotte's return had been kept a surprise until an hour before Air Force One touched down in Pensacola, Florida, five days earlier. When news had broken that she was en route from Washington, the crowd grew so fast the advance team had to build a second stage in an overflow arena.

Charlotte believed that politicians either loved the trail or hated it. She'd always loved it. Peter thought she loved it too much, but she knew voters responded to candidates who left everything they had on the campaign trail.

As she looked out at their faces—mothers standing with their daughters, couples holding hands, a group of men from a local construction site standing together with their hard hats on—she saw something different from what she'd seen four years ago. They were taking her measure, and their intensity crowded out the doubt that had crippled her since Roger died.

When the crowd refused her repeated attempts to quiet them down, she laughed and called Tara down from the bleachers behind her. They waved and pointed to signs from the mostly female supporters in the front rows that said "Women Do It Better" and "Kramer-Meyers on Nov. 4."

Picking Tara as her vice-presidential nominee was a decision that Charlotte never revisited. Once she was on the ticket, Tara was a natural fit. Charlotte and Tara occupied the same dangerous swath of their respective parties: the center. As a result, they both had more enemies in their own parties than from across the aisle. They'd both been celebrated and vilified by the media, and they knew how to use the press without mistaking them for friends or allies. And they saw eye-to-eye on the issues Charlotte was most passionate about.

When the crowd finally quieted down, Tara returned to her seat.

"Let me tell you a little bit about the woman I picked to serve as my vice president," Charlotte said to cheers from the crowd. "If we are fortunate enough to win on Election Day and to serve as your president and vice president for the next four years, we will do our best to protect you from harm. We will assemble the best business minds from across this land—not from places like Wall Street and Washington but from places like Reno, Nevada; Miami, Florida; and Milwaukee, Wisconsin."

The crowd roared again.

"Tara Meyers has a record of taking down and locking up those who threaten this great country," Charlotte said. "Tara Meyers has a record of working across the aisle with members of both parties and of cracking heads when that's what's necessary to get things done on behalf of her constituents," she said to even louder cheers. "And Tara Meyers has a record of putting the people she serves ahead of personal interests, political interests, and polite interests." The crowd was on its feet.

Charlotte was wise enough not to make any attempts to emulate Tara's toughness, but she did enjoy pumping up the crowd by talking up her running mate.

When they were back on the bus, Charlotte still felt the adrenaline in her blood.

"Sam, do you mind getting me some tea? Chamomile, if they have it," she requested. "Melanie, what did you think? The crowd was really fired up." Charlotte beamed.

"It was a good event," Melanie said.

"If that's good, honey, I can't wait to see what you call great," Tara said, plopping down onto the bench seat next to Charlotte.

Charlotte saw Melanie give her an annoyed look, but Tara didn't appear to notice.

"You were awesome, Madam President," Tara gushed.

"Please call me Charlotte, in here and out there," Charlotte said, patting her knee warmly.

"You kicked some serious ass up there, Charlotte, am I allowed to say that?" Tara giggled.

Melanie glared at her and watched as Charlotte put her arm on Tara's.

"Yes. It's been a while since anyone has said that to me, but thank you, I think. That's a compliment, right, Ralph?" Charlotte asked as Ralph joined the group, taking a seat next to Tara.

"Yes, Madam President. I just got the overnight poll numbers, and you are both kicking some serious what she said," Ralph said, gesturing toward Tara.

Charlotte saw Melanie roll her eyes again.

"The overnights are unreliable, though, aren't they, Ralph?" Melanie said. "I thought the only numbers that really tell us anything are the three night rolls."

"Technically, that's correct," Ralph said, looking at Tara as he spoke. "But the overnights show our numbers moving among all categories of voters, and that's a good trend even without the other two nights. Now, of course, Melanie's right, and we won't know for two more days whether this is a durable surge or just our numbers popping because of the debate last night or because of something in the news, but it's still a good sign."

"Beats an overnight dip in the numbers, right?" Tara said.

Melanie sighed loudly and started to make her way toward the front of the bus.

"Where are you going, Mel?" Charlotte asked.

"I'll be right back. I just need to make a couple of calls."

"Hurry back. We need to discuss the pros and cons of amending the no-campaign pledge here in the final weeks."

Charlotte could see Melanie's face tighten as she shot a nasty look at Ralph and Tara. Charlotte knew that Melanie felt threatened by her growing reliance on Ralph's political judgment, but he had a better sense of what was going on outside Washington than Melanie did. What took Charlotte by surprise was the hostility she sensed that Melanie felt toward Tara.

"I wasn't aware that we were seriously considering a reversal, but I'm happy to discuss it when I get back," Melanie said before turning and walking toward the front of the bus.

Melanie and Ralph had bickered like siblings for the past three and a half years. Charlotte knew how to make both of them feel essential. But Melanie's resentment toward Tara was something Charlotte hoped would dissipate.

Melanie was dead set against reversing course on the no-campaign pledge, but Charlotte had had a decent political radar of her own at one time, and every instinct told her that the voters would forgive her. She sensed that her supporters desperately wanted her to spend the final days blasting her opponent for smearing her record and attacking her personally. Now that she was out of Washington, she understood what Tara described in her nightly calls to Charlotte. The voters needed Charlotte to prove that she still had the stomach for the fights that would surely come if she was reelected.

As they'd made their way through Wisconsin, Michigan, Ohio, Colorado, and Nevada, the crowds continued to swell in size and intensity. And after some late-night number crunching from Ralph and some calls to Tara's remaining political allies, they planned a surprise Northeast swing to make a play for New Jersey, New Hampshire, Maine, Connecticut, and New York. Ralph acknowledged that it was a long shot but thought it was worthwhile.

Two weeks on the campaign trail had sped by in a blur of bus trips, town halls, television interviews, radio shows, rallies, and debates. As Charlotte sipped her coffee and flipped through the front pages of the papers that the press office had assembled for her, she let herself reflect back on the turmoil of the previous six months. She thought about Peter out in San Francisco. He checked in with the twins frequently and passed along astute advice. Brooke and Mark had flown in the night before to join them for the final week on the road. She smiled at the thought of the twins and Brooke and Mark sitting behind her at all of the remaining events. If anyone could keep the mood light in the final days of a presidential campaign, they could. And her parents were planning to join them for the final weekend.

She'd be surrounded by people who would love her no matter what happened on Election Day. Increasingly, it looked as if she'd have her job for four more years.

Am I really up for doing this again? she thought to herself. She smiled. She knew the answer.

CHAPTER FORTY-SIX

Melanie

Y ou don't look like someone about to win your fourth straight presidential campaign," Michael said, surprising Melanie by pulling up a stool next to her at the hotel bar where Charlotte and Tara and their respective entourages were staying.

"What are you doing out here?" Melanie asked. She was happy to see Michael, but she figured she'd have the bar to herself while Charlotte and Tara were at the rally.

"Whoa, easy, you're going to fall off that stool," Michael said when Melanie nearly tipped over as she reached out to give him a hug.

"I'm so happy you're here, but seriously, what are you doing on the road? I thought you'd be back at the bureau trying to dig up some dirt on Charlotte or Tara in the final days," Melanie said, slurring her words slightly.

"I wanted to see your dynamic little duo with my own eyes."

Melanie rolled her eyes. "What are you *really* working on?"

"Unless you have been under a rock—which, come to think of it, you look like you *have* been under a rock. What's wrong?" he asked.

"Nothing. I'm fine," she reassured him, taking the last sip of her martini.

"Well, the country is in full swoon mode over Charlotte and Tara. I came out to write about Charlotte Kramer's final week as a candidate. Ever," he added.

"I'll have you know that my day started with a very awkward conversation with Tara about wearing undergarments that offer a little more support and coverage," Melanie said, while waving her hand to get the bartender's attention.

"Her wardrobe choices are probably worth a couple of points with male voters, Mel," he said.

Melanie put her head in her hands. "Two martinis over here, please!" Melanie shouted, her head still resting on the bar.

The bartender nodded at them. "I've got it," he said.

"Thanks," Michael said to him.

"When did you arrive?" Melanie asked.

"About an hour ago. Too late to get to the event, or I would have gone. I didn't expect to find you here. Thought you'd be at the rally."

"Why? Haven't you read the papers?" she said.

"So, the shit Ralph is putting out is getting to you?" Michael asked. "That's not like you."

"What shit, specifically, are you referring to?" Melanie asked.

"Ralph's floating rumors that you're being eased out, that you're burned out and losing your touch with Charlotte."

"Ah, those rumors," Melanie said as the bartender placed another martini in front of her.

"Listen, don't take this the wrong way, but you look a little strung-out," Michael said.

"I've been living on a goddamn bus with Tara, Ralph, and Charlotte. Can you blame me?" she said.

"No. But as your friend, I think you need to nip these stories in the bud. You're about half a news cycle away from a feeding frenzy. There's a lot of rumbling out there about how you can't get along with Tara," Michael warned her.

"You're joking, right?" Melanie said. But she knew he wasn't. Ralph and his toadies were pushing all sorts of nasty rumors to the blogs. They were dying to see Melanie fail and Ralph replace her as chief of staff as a reward for winning the election.

"It's not even worth responding to," Melanie said.

"Why not?" Michael asked.

"Because I'm done. I've been run out of the place by Ralph and Tara."

"You're so melodramatic," Michael said, taking a sip of his drink.

"Perhaps, but even you can't deny it. It's over," she said.

"So you're not staying, assuming Charlotte wins in a week?"

"No way," Melanie said.

"Well, I'll toast to that," he said, clinking his glass against hers. "And no one will blame you. Sixteen years is a record. Believe me when I tell you that leaving will do wonders for your personal life," he added.

Melanie snorted. "What personal life?"

"Weren't you seeing that correspondent? Brian something?" he asked.

"Yes, but I screwed that up royally. Maybe I'll sign up for eHarmony when this is over. The Secret Service doesn't even let me have a Facebook page, but when I'm retired, I can join one of those online dating services. That sounds like fun," she said, laughing into her glass.

Michael didn't laugh. He shot the bartender a look that he hoped would convey that it was time to cut Melanie off.

"Listen, Melanie, why don't you let me walk you to your room? You look exhausted," he offered.

"I'm going to have one more." She waved at the bartender. He ignored her.

"Come on, Mel. You'll regret that in the morning," Michael warned.

"I will add it to the list," she said.

"Don't be like this. The motorcade will be back here in ten minutes. You don't want the junior staffers to see you."

"Why the hell not? Shouldn't they see what sixteen fucking years of loyalty gets you?" she said, a little too loudly.

"Come on. You're the White House chief of staff, for Christ's sake. Let's get out of here. Let's go have a cigarette, OK? Will you come have a cigarette with me?"

"I don't smoke," she said.

"Yes, you do. You and Charlotte order Marlboro Lights by the carton."

Melanie giggled. "How do you know everything?" she asked as she slid off her bar stool.

Michael put the bar tab on his room and steered Melanie out to the front of the hotel. They sat on a bench, and he pulled out a pack of cigarettes.

"Stay here while I go get matches," he said sternly.

"Yes, sir," she said.

As she sat on the bench, the presidential motorcade pulled up. The SUV carrying Charlotte and Tara pulled into a covered area, and they exited without seeing Melanie, but the press van came to a stop directly in front of where she was sitting.

Brian was the first one out. "Meet you guys in the bar in ten minutes," she heard him say to the rest of the press.

She watched him pull a tape out of his cameraman's bag and write something on it. Then she saw him check his BlackBerry. Finally, he looked up and saw her. She smiled and waved.

He walked up to the bench and sat down. "How's it going?" he asked.

"Living the dream," Melanie said.

"Looks like you've had a long night already," he said, smelling the martinis on her breath. At least she hadn't started smoking yet. He hated the smell of cigarettes.

"I'm fine," she said.

"I thought about calling when I saw the papers this morning," Brian said.

"What are you referring to?" Melanie asked.

"Come on. I know you saw it. Everyone saw it," Brian said.

The *Washington Journal* had run a front-page story on Ralph's rising prominence in Charlotte's inner circle, particularly with Tara. The headline read "Mind Meld" and the photo they ran showed Ralph whispering in Tara's ear just before she went onstage. The story made it clear that Ralph's success was likely to bring about Melanie's demise.

"I couldn't be happier for Ralph. He'll make a great chief of staff," Melanie said.

Just then, Michael walked out and approached the bench. Brian stood up.

"Hey, man," Brian said, reaching his hand out to shake Michael's hand.

"How's it going?" Michael asked.

"Good. Just back from the event," Brian said.

"How was it?"

"Good crowd, the standard stump speech, no news."

Michael smiled. "At least I didn't miss anything."

"Definitely not. Uh, OK, then, I'll leave you guys alone," Brian said, turning to leave.

"Actually, Brian, I need to file something for the Web site tonight. Would you mind walking Melanie up to her room? I think she's a little wiped out."

Melanie felt pathetic.

"Of course. Melanie, do you have your key?" Brian asked.

Now they were talking to her as if she was eight years old. She pulled out the envelope carrying her keys and held it in front of her face.

"You ready?" Brian asked.

"Sure," she said, embarrassed that Michael had dumped her on Brian but incapable, in her current state, of doing much about it.

She stood and tried to stop the spinning. She must have swayed, because Brian's arms were suddenly around her.

"Are you sure you're all right?" he asked.

"Can we sit here for a minute?" she asked.

"Sure," he said.

They sat back down.

"You don't have to stay here with me," Melanie said. "You can go meet your friends at the bar. I'll get up to my room just fine."

"I'm not going to leave you out here," he said.

"There's not a lot of crime in . . . where are we, again? I can't remember."

He laughed. "I can't remember most of the time myself."

Melanie leaned back against the bench and looked up at the sky. "Have you noticed that there are more stars in the red states?" she said. "Blue states have all the culture, but red states have all the stars."

He leaned back and looked up. "You might be right about that," he said.

She loved sitting next to him. "I miss you," she said without looking at him.

He didn't say anything.

"I know I screwed up, and I know you think I'm saying this now because I'm drunk, but I really miss you. And I'm sorry," she said.

He looked at her. "I know," he said.

Melanie wasn't sure if he meant that he knew she was sorry or that he knew she missed him.

"I understand why you were frustrated when we were together," she said.

He sat there looking at the stars and then turned to face her. "Don't worry about it, Melanie," he said.

She didn't know how else to say she was sorry, and she was too scared to come out and ask him for a second chance. Before she could say anything else, he stood up.

"Come on. Let's get you into bed."

He held out his hand, and she took it. They walked inside hand-in-hand and passed the bar area. A couple of the reporters looked up at them, but most were too busy swapping gossip and planning their postcampaign trips. Of course, if Charlotte won, they'd be positioned to get jobs covering the White House. Some of them would skip vacations to claim their spots in the White House briefing room.

Melanie didn't even look over at the bar. She was focusing on putting one foot in front of the other without falling on her face. "Have you ever seen such a nice carpet?" she asked Brian without looking up.

Brian looked down and laughed. "It is pretty nice," he agreed.

Melanie concentrated on walking normally.

When they arrived at her room, she handed him her key and leaned against the wall while he opened her door. Once inside, he sat her down on the bed and sat in a chair across from her.

"Thank you for taking care of me," Melanie said.

"You're welcome," he said. "Do you want to brush your teeth and wash your face, or do you want to get into bed?"

"I'll go wash up," she said.

She went into the bathroom and brushed her teeth. When she came out, Brian was still sitting in the chair. He was reading his BlackBerry.

"You can go down to the bar. I'll be fine." Melanie said.

"Where are your pajamas?" Brian asked. Melanie pointed at her suitcase. He opened it and pulled out a white tank top and some white cotton pajama bottoms. "These?" he asked.

She nodded. He handed them to her and smiled.

"Put them on. I won't look."

She wished he would. She changed and slid into bed.

Brian had laid two Aleves on her nightstand with a large bottle of water. "Take these," he urged.

She swallowed them and drank a third of the bottle of water.

"Get some rest, Melanie," he said.

She didn't want to fall asleep, because she knew that when she got up, he'd be gone, but she couldn't fight it for long. When she got up to use the bathroom, she was alone. She looked at the clock. It was three forty-five. She contemplated a trip to the gym, but her head was pounding, so she climbed back into bed. She couldn't fall asleep. She got up at around four-thirty and packed for the five A.M. bag call. Her news clips were dropped off at five-fifteen, and as her eyes glazed over the stories about how the election was now Charlotte's to lose, she knew she was finished.

She wasn't even angry at Ralph or Tara anymore. Ralph was succeeding in squeezing her out because he wanted it more than she did, and Tara's only crime was her ambition.

At six A.M., she went next door to Charlotte's room for the daily briefing. She sat quietly in the corner while Ralph went over the overnight polls and the press secretary did a readout of the daily papers. She listened as the speechwriters went over the message for the day. The plan was for Charlotte to go after Fran's record of voting against troops in the field, and Tara would take a swipe at her for voting for higher taxes. Melanie had lost the debate over whether to go after Fran in the final days. They were locked in a death match against their opponent, and it seemed to be working. When they finished prepping

Charlotte for the day's events, Melanie lingered after the rest of the staff had filed out.

"I'm sorry I missed the event last night," Melanie said.

"You earned a night off. I heard you had a few cocktails," Charlotte said, raising an eyebrow.

"Yes, a few too many," Melanie said, rubbing her head.

"Want some Aleve?" Charlotte asked.

"I've taken five since I woke up."

"Good. Have some coffee. Somehow, the advance guys got Starbucks to open early for us," Charlotte said.

Melanie was always amazed by Charlotte's wonder at occurrences like this. She refilled her cup.

"Is everything OK?" Charlotte asked.

"Yes. Why?" Melanie asked.

"You seem a little too calm. It's not like you," Charlotte said.

"I got an update from Tara's personal assistant, and apparently your running mate's skirt comes within inches of her knees and her bra isn't showing, so I feel good today. Let's go do this," Melanie said, grinning at Charlotte. Charlotte stifled a laugh and nodded at her Secret Service agent, who also appeared to be stifling a snicker as he opened the door.

Tara was waiting for them in the hallway outside Charlotte's suite. "Good morning," Tara chirped.

If she'd heard Melanie's crack about her outfit, she didn't let on. She was wearing a bright pink suit that was at best a half-size too small for her, but at least it was longer than the skirts she usually wore. The blouse underneath was straining at her chest, but it was buttoned up over her cleavage, and her bra wasn't showing. Melanie winked at Tara's personal assistant, who smiled nervously and shrugged her shoulders.

"Good morning, Tara. You look lovely today. What are you hearing?" Charlotte asked.

Tara gave Charlotte a rambling report about all the people she'd heard from since Charlotte last saw her seven hours earlier. Tara's friend in Denver had e-mailed to say she liked Charlotte's speech about national service. Tara's hairdresser in Albany had suggested that Charlotte wear her hair down more often. Her former pollster had seen some promising poll numbers in New Jersey and New York, and her deputy in the attorney general's office had a suggestion about a political ad Charlotte and Tara could run about crime.

"Isn't this great information, Melanie?" Charlotte said, smiling at Melanie.

"Fantastic. It's like a real-world focus group," Melanie said with a laugh.

They piled into the limo, and Tara and Ralph kept interrupting each other to share their latest ideas for the final days of the campaign. Melanie could see that Charlotte was getting dizzy trying to follow the conversation. Melanie caught Charlotte's eye and smiled. She raised her eyebrows and looked out the window. Charlotte laughed a little, and soon Melanie was laughing, too. By the time Tara and Ralph noticed that Charlotte wasn't paying attention to them anymore, it was too late. Charlotte and Melanie were laughing so uncontrollably they were crying. Melanie took a sip of water, and before she could swallow it, she was hit by a giggling fit that caused the water to fly out of her nose. At this, Charlotte came undone and started taking deep breaths and wiping tears from her face.

"Ignore us. I think we're a little punch-drunk," Charlotte said to a mystified Ralph and Tara.

"Actually, I might still be technically drunk-drunk," Melanie said, causing Charlotte to laugh even harder.

The two of them had barely recovered when the limo pulled up to the next event. They stepped out of the car and stood by the limo together.

"Do you believe it's over in less than a week?" Charlotte said to Melanie.

"Thank God," Melanie said.

"I'm with you. I don't even remember when I was that excited to be out here," Charlotte said, watching Tara as she signed autographs and took photos with the supporters who'd gathered backstage.

"I don't think you were ever quite that excited," Melanie said. "I mean, that is not normal, but it *is* impressive."

"You're right," Charlotte said, squeezing her arm. "We're going to be able to relax in a second term, Mel, you'll see. It will be so much better. No pressure, no drama."

Melanie nodded and smiled at her, but at that moment, they both knew that it wouldn't happen. Their relationship had come full circle. They stood there, next to the limo, not as a president and her chief of staff but as two friends who'd been to hell and back.

"Go on, we'll talk after the event," Melanie said.

Charlotte was too intuitive to miss the significance of the moment. "Melanie, we'll find a place where you can be your own boss. No Ralph, no seven-thirty senior staff meetings. We'll find something cushy and wonderful," Charlotte whispered.

Melanie's eyes were starting to tear up, and she didn't want Charlotte to get emotional before the rally. "We'll figure it out. I'm not going anywhere," she said, smiling.

The advance woman led Charlotte to the place backstage where she'd hold until she was announced. With the music blaring and the crowd roaring, Charlotte took the stage. Melanie stood off to the side watching. Tears streamed down her face when the crowd erupted in a five-minute standing ovation for Charlotte after she ticked off her administration's accomplishments in fighting terrorism. Charlotte caught Melanie's eye a couple of times and smiled. Melanie kept clapping and tried to wipe her tears when Charlotte wasn't looking.

Toward the end of the speech, Melanie looked down at her Black-Berry. Brian had e-mailed. "How are you feeling this morning?" he wrote.

She looked for him on the press platform at the back of the room. He was looking right at her and waved when she spotted him.

She wrote back: "I owe you for last night. Please let me take you to dinner to make up for it."

"No way," he replied.

"Am I that unforgivable, or is a meal insufficient penance?" she wrote.

"If you're serious, meet me at DCA at nine A.M. the morning after the election," he wrote.

She didn't write back right away.

"P.S. Bring a passport and a bathing suit," he wrote.

She smiled. "Deal," she wrote.

CHAPTER FORTY-SEVEN

Dale

It wasn't glamorous, but Dale found comfort in the rigors of her new routine. She woke before sunrise for her morning live shots and compiled reports for the noon, five, and six P.M. newscasts. She stayed up—no matter the time zone—for a live shot for the station's eleven P.M. newscast. Her forced exile from network news had renewed her appreciation for the basics. She took pleasure in the writing, reporting, and tracking of her packages and pushed out of her mind the indignity of doing it for a local station again. The bleakness of doing nothing while the campaign neared its dramatic end would have been more than she could take.

But covering the campaign for a San Francisco station was like stepping back in time. Instead of covering the alleged infighting between the president's chief of staff and her top political advisor, Dale was assigned a feature story on the campaign's bag handler. He grew up in Marin County and graduated from UC Berkeley with a degree in political science. After the convention, he drove to Washington, D.C., and waited outside the White House until a staffer came out to talk to him about volunteering for the campaign. He'd been awarded a full-time position traveling on Tara Meyers's plane and delivering the senior staff's luggage to their rooms when they arrived in each new city. The differences between working for a local affiliate and working for the network didn't stop with the stories she was assigned to cover. While the national press corps enjoyed hot breakfasts at the hotels where the president and Tara spent the night, the locals were "prepositioned" for the day's major speech the night before. Many nights, Dale didn't even sleep in the same city as the candidate.

Dale was relieved to travel separately from her former colleagues. Most of them still felt awkward around her. Brian was the one exception, and the two of them met for dinner when they were in the same city. Dale and Peter had barely spoken since she'd left San Francisco the week before. He sent flowers to her hotel room a couple of times and left her supportive voice-mails and texts, but they'd mostly avoided each other. She hated herself for hurting him, but she was also angry at him for making her feel there was something wrong with her for wanting to work so badly.

As usual, she found her professional responsibilities easier to master than her personal ones. The station was thrilled with her and had already asked to speak to her about being a full-time correspondent after the election.

Dale was so absorbed in updating her script for the next newscast that she hadn't noticed that the vice-presidential nominee and her entire entourage had arrived. She looked up from her laptop and watched the aides place Tara's remarks on the podium and check the sound system. The usual lineup of local elected officials stood in formation at the side of the stage for the "pre-program."

"This seat taken?" she heard. Ralph had plopped down in the folding chair next to her.

"Hi, Ralph. How's it going? Are you slumming, or is the national press being mean to you?" she teased.

She'd always had a decent rapport with Ralph. He was always helpful when she went through phases of being shut out by Melanie, and even when he couldn't speak freely, he was good about waving her away from bad information.

"Dale, Dale, Dale. Do you know what day it is?" he asked, leaning back and revealing a large, round belly that was straining the button on his pants.

Dale looked away from his midsection. "No, but I'm guessing

you're about to tell me," she said, her eyes following the action on the stage.

"The White House wants to soften Tara's image a little bit. They think she's too feisty up there on the stump. The criticism is bullshit. I'm sure it comes from Melanie, who would hate anything Tara did up there because she can't stand her. I mean, can you believe that it took a Democrat to fire up our base?"

"You want me to help you soften Tara Meyers?" she asked.

"No. I want you to interview her. I can't pick from the sharks over there—they'll go crazy if I pick one network over the other. I know you were supposed to get the first interview the night before she was announced, and I respect you for letting your new White House guy do it, but I think you and Tara would hit it off," he said. "She likes you," he added. "She admires the hell out of you for getting back out here."

"What's the hitch?" Dale asked.

"No hitch. No ground rules. I've only got twenty minutes, but you can ask her whatever you want."

"I need thirty minutes," Dale bargained.

"Twenty-five."

"Twenty five plus a walk-and-talk," she insisted.

"Done," he said. "I'll have one of the press advance folks call you with the time and place. We'll do it later today or first thing tomorrow."

"Thanks, Ralph," she said.

"Welcome back." He smiled.

The press staff arranged for Dale to interview Tara that night in Albuquerque. Dale worked up a list of questions and sent them to her news director. He added questions about gay marriage and global warming. Minutes before she was supposed to begin the interview, Peter called.

"Hey there," she said.

"How are you?" he asked. He sounded far away.

"Good—about to interview Tara Meyers," she boasted.

"Nice," he said.

"So, how are you?" she asked.

"Good. Everything here is good."

"I miss you," she said.

"I miss you, too."

She felt regret wash over her when she heard the sadness in his voice. "Can I call you after the interview?" she asked.

"Sure. I'll talk to you later," he said.

Dale hung up just as Tara entered the room.

"Good evening," Tara said. She wore tight jeans and Uggs paired with a tight black jacket with a yellow silk tank top underneath. "We're just filming from the waist up, right?" she asked, winking at the cameramen.

"Sure, no problem," Dale said.

Throughout the interview, Tara gave crisp, rehearsed answers and refused Dale's invitations to make news. Dale decided to try a new tactic.

"Let me switch topics, Madam Attorney General, and ask you what you think of Charlotte Kramer personally. In what ways are you similar, and in what ways are you different, from a style perspective and a substantive one?" Dale asked.

"That's a great question, Dale, and one no one has asked me yet. Let's see. I think the fact that we're both juggling a lot of different roles has made us both aware of how our decisions affect different groups of people. And I think that we've both taken a more pragmatic approach to things. We care more about how things work than we do about politics or ideology," she said, smiling at the camera and then looking back at Dale.

"And how are you different?" Dale asked, looking down at her notepad.

"I don't know just yet, but I'd say that one difference is our focus. She has been governing on a national stage, and I've been working on issues affecting the great state of New York," Tara said.

"There's a lot of grumbling about the White House trying to rein you in and being overcontrolling. To what extent do you feel controlled by the White House?" Dale asked.

Tara shifted uncomfortably in her seat. "I don't feel controlled at all. And I'll tell you this much, I'm the one who stands before tens of thousands of screaming fans and gets them fired up for Charlotte Kramer. I'm the one they tune in to see, and I'm the one who turned the conversation toward the future."

Dale didn't look up from her notebook, a tactic she'd learned during a brief stint covering Congress. Members of Congress wanted to be liked so desperately that if you didn't look at them, they would continue talking until you offered some visual cue of approval like a smile or a nod. Dale kept staring at the questions she'd scribbled on her notepad.

"And I know that the president's team has been in Washington a long time, but all the wisdom in America does not reside in Washington, D.C. If there's a meaningful way that we're different, it's that I get my advice from ordinary folks, and she turns to Washington insiders," Tara said.

Dale looked up. "Thank you for your time today, Madam Attorney General," she said, trying not to betray her excitement about evoking such a frank rebuke of Melanie from Tara. Maybe Ms. Meyers wasn't as ready as she thought she was for the national spotlight.

"Why, thank *you*, Dale." Tara beamed.

After holding her final smiling pose for a few seconds, Tara pulled the microphone off her jacket and stood to leave.

"That was OK, don't you think?" she asked everyone in the room.

Ralph nodded, and the crew busied themselves with the breakdown of their equipment.

"It was real nice to meet you. I always enjoyed watching you on the air, and I thought that what happened to you after the crash was bullshit," Tara said.

Dale looked at her, unsure how to respond. People she'd known for ten years didn't have the courage to raise the accident, and Tara Meyers had done so after meeting her for the first time.

"Would you ever consider a job on the inside?" Tara asked.

"What do you mean?"

"In the White House. Would you consider coming in?"

Dale stared at her for a second, not sure if she was joking or not.

"I don't know. I've never thought about it," Dale said.

"Keep it in mind. I'll be in touch, and good for you for getting back to work. I couldn't do it," Tara said, flashing a pop-star smile and taking a sip from her frozen coffee drink.

Everything about Tara was intriguing to Dale. Fear and hesitation did not seem to enter the equation. Dale had never met anyone so sure of herself on the stump. Maybe Tara knew exactly what she was doing when she slammed Washington insiders. Perhaps she fully intended to use Dale to send Melanie a warning shot. Tara was unlike anyone Dale had ever covered in politics.

Dale sent her news director a note about teasing the bites about Washington and the president's team after the newscast so that the morning shows would pick them up as "new" news. She went back to the filing center to write her scripts for the station's late newscast. The regret she'd felt before the interview about leaving Peter for the campaign had evaporated.

Tara's question about working at the White House was one that she couldn't get out of her mind over the next few days. She thought about telling Peter, but she knew what he'd say. She considered confiding in Brian, but he was involved with Melanie, and she couldn't afford for anyone to know. Besides, the race was still close enough that anything could happen in the last week.

CHAPTER FORTY-EIGHT

Charlotte

I s anyone going to be sitting in my line of sight?" Charlotte asked, smoothing her skirt.

"Yes, the twins will be there," Melanie said.

"Where are you sitting?" she asked.

"Next to Brooke and Mark," Melanie told her.

"All right, I think I'm ready," she said. "I hate debates. I should have prepared more. I wish we'd had one more practice session last night. Why did you let me go to bed?"

"Because you are ready. Go out there and finish her off," Melanie said.

They walked out of the holding room and toward the backstage area. Charlotte nodded toward her opponent and looked back at Melanie. Melanie smiled and gave her a thumbs-up sign, then turned to take her seat in the audience.

Charlotte took her place behind the podium and tried to adjust to the bright lights onstage.

"President Kramer, do you understand the rules for the debate?" the moderator asked.

Charlotte was trying to find the twins in the audience. She couldn't see them. She put her hand over her eyes to shield them from the light and scanned the audience.

"Madam President, do you understand the ground rules?" the announcer asked a second time.

Charlotte spotted the twins and Brooke and Mark.

"I do," Charlotte said, smiling. "And let me take this opportunity to thank you, and everyone here, and most important, my opponent, Fran Frankel, for being here tonight. I know Fran had other places to be, but since we don't have a campaign machine like she does, we are relying on formats like this to get our message out to the American people," Charlotte said, stealing a glance at Fran, who was seething.

Charlotte smiled at the moderator and settled in for a ninety-minute ass kicking of her Democratic opponent. Fran was so frustrated that she yielded her response time to Charlotte on two separate occasions. Charlotte saw Melanie get up a few minutes before the debate ended to head into Spin Alley. After she left the stage, Charlotte moved into the hold room to watch the postdebate analysis. One screen showed the activity in Spin Alley on a closed-circuit television. Melanie was surrounded by reporters.

"Melanie, who won tonight's debate?" a reporter asked.

"The American people will be the judge of that, but clearly, there was one politician on the stage and one leader. We live in serious times, and most voters are looking for leadership, not politics. Charlotte Kramer stood before the voters tonight as a humble and competent public servant, and she created quite a contrast with her ideological and petty opponent, who was swinging below the belt," Melanie said.

"That's right," Charlotte declared, still fired up from the debate.

"Melanie, any comment on Tara Meyers's attack on the president's insiders?" one of the reporters shouted.

Charlotte leaned in to listen to Melanie's response.

"We just won the third and final debate, and we are going to stay focused on the things that Americans care about—fixing the economy and keeping America safe," Melanie said, looking the reporter in the eye.

Charlotte sighed and came back down to earth. She'd have to deal with the mounting tensions between Tara and Melanie now that the debates were over. She changed the channel to one of the cable outlets and watched with satisfaction as the analysts struggled to be even-handed in evaluating their performances.

"Any way you look at it, tonight was a win for the Kramer ticket," one of the hosts was saying.

"I agree. The fact that Fran Frankel let President Kramer frame the entire evening as one of politics verses public service was a mistake she never recovered from," the other pundit replied.

Charlotte muted the televisions and moved to where Brooke and Mark were pouring champagne and entertaining the twins and a handful of other friends and supporters. Mark handed her a glass.

"To President Charlotte Kramer—three for three in the debates and one step closer to victory on Tuesday," Mark toasted, raising his glass.

Charlotte put her arm around Harry and raised her glass. "I'll drink to that," she said.

CHAPTER FORTY-NINE

Melanie

The election is tomorrow. I am not dignifying that with an answer, Michael!" Melanie shouted into her cell phone. "Yes that's a denial!" she yelled. "Of course I'm sure. If you print that piece-of-shit rumor, I will bankrupt you with a libel suit that you will regret every morning that you wake up in the homeless shelter you'll be forced to live in," she said.

Tara and Charlotte looked on with wide eyes. They were sitting in Charlotte's front cabin on Air Force One, waiting for Melanie to get off the phone before they took off. The pilot was standing outside the door waiting for the OK.

"Fine, call me back, but don't print a single goddamned word until we talk again," she threatened. Melanie hung up and thanked the pilots for holding the plane. "I appreciate it, guys—let's get wheels up," she said. She sat down next to Charlotte.

"Did you ever consider trying to woo the press over to our side instead of scaring them into submission?" Tara asked.

Melanie shot her a look that silenced her. "What else do I need to know, Tara? There is no information that we can't handle. The only thing we cannot endure at this point is a surprise. I'm going to ask you one more time to go through the facts with me," Melanie said.

"Really, Tara, the public forgives just about everything except a bad inaugural gown," Charlotte said, smiling warmly at her running mate.

The press had been buzzing for two days about an anonymous report on one of the political blogs of Tara doing a stint in rehab the year after she graduated from law school. The news had finally gone mainstream, and the reporters were all waiting for a response from the White House.

Melanie looked at her BlackBerry. "Shit," she said.

"What?" Tara asked.

"CNN has a woman who says she was in rehab with you for the morning show tomorrow. I don't need to tell you how dramatically this can affect our turnout on Election Day," Melanie said.

"I swear to you, it is not true," Tara insisted, looking at Charlotte.

"I believe you. Will you give us a minute, Tara?" Charlotte asked.

"Of course," she said.

When she had left the cabin, Charlotte turned to Melanie. "You don't believe her, do you?" she asked.

"No, and neither do you," Melanie pointed out.

"What do we do?" Charlotte asked.

"Fight it. Call it a lie, attack the media, try to pin it on Fran, and if none of that works, we pray," Melanie said.

"Do what you have to do," Charlotte told her.

"Yes, ma'am," Melanie said.

She walked to the press cabin on Air Force One with the press secretary and a stenographer in tow.

The press secretary laid out the ground rules. "This is on background as a senior administration official. We'll let you use the phones on the plane to file as soon as we're done here," he said.

"Melanie, can you address the news report that Tara Meyers spent a period of time in rehab after completing law school? Doesn't that make her technically and figuratively unfit for office?" asked the AP reporter.

"The news reports that you refer to are part of an ugly and desperate attempt by Fran Frankel to smear the character of a decent and hardworking woman. Tara Meyers put herself through college and law school by working two jobs and studying all night. She and her husband have served their country and their state for many years," Melanie said.

"Come on, Melanie, what proof do you have that the report was leaked by Frankel's campaign?" the Reuters reporter asked.

"There's a record of swinging below the belt from the other side. The American people will have their chance to weigh in on who has handled themselves with more dignity over the course of the last several months, and I'm confident Charlotte Kramer will be reelected and Tara Meyers will be the next vice president," Melanie said.

"What if the reports turn out to be true? Would you dump her?" a network reporter asked.

"I'm confident that the information I've been given by Ms. Meyers is accurate and that the report is false," Melanie said.

"That's a nonanswer if I ever heard one," groused the *Washington Journal* reporter.

Melanie looked at the press secretary with impatience.

"Last question!" he shouted.

"Melanie, do you think Tara was referring to you when she said Charlotte Kramer relies on Washington insiders?" another network reporter asked.

Melanie flashed a smile at the gaggle of reporters she'd known for years. "The vice president's transition office will field those questions after tomorrow," she said.

They turned to walk back to the conference room where Tara and Charlotte were waiting.

"How'd it go?" Charlotte asked.

"Fine," Melanie said.

"She was great," the press secretary said.

"Thank you, Melanie," Tara said.

"You're welcome," Melanie said, turning to go to the senior staff cabin to check her e-mail.

Charlotte folowed her. "Thanks for doing that for her. I know you guys haven't exactly hit it off," Charlotte said.

"I didn't do it for her, Madam President. I did it for you," Melanie said.

CHAPTER FIFTY

Dale

Election Day was the strangest news day of all. Nothing happened until late in the evening, but there was still an entire day's worth of airtime to fill. Dale woke up early to tape a package on the impact of the weather on voter turnout. She fed it to her station before she boarded the plane with the rest of the local reporters for the final day of rallies. She had the stump speech memorized. Only the states in which the polling was too close to call warranted a visit on Election Day. Dale flipped through the schedule for the day. It was about an inch thick. She tried to figure out when she'd be able to do live shots.

Her phone was ringing.

"Hello," she answered.

"You're back," roared a familiar voice.

"Arnie, what are you hearing? I'm in a bubble out here. No cell service, and we are miles from a cable television set."

"No one knows shit about the election, I'm talking about you," he said.

"What's up?" she asked.

"My phone's been ringing off the hook since your interview with Tara Meyers aired. Jesus, Dale—you were heartless—she didn't even notice as you sucked all the blood out of her body. She looked like she enjoyed it."

"She knew exactly what she was doing," Dale said.

"In fact, it's entirely possible that the whole thing was a set up, but you know what? The beauty of being in local news is that it doesn't matter *why* the vice-presidential nominee wants to talk to me—I'm happy to have the interview these days." Dale reflected.

"Bullshit," Arnie said.

"You were in control the whole time. And, as a result of your hustling, Dale, I've got every one of the cables dying to sit down with you next week and the other nets want to take you to lunch and begin a conversation," Arnie said.

"That's great news," she said.

"Why don't you sound more excited?" he asked.

"I am. I promise. Let's set them up. Thanks for not giving up on me," she said.

The rest of the day sped by in a blur of takeoffs and landings, introductions and stump speeches, and roaring crowds at events filled to capacity. Dale tried to conduct interviews with supporters at the rallies, but by the time the press set up at one event, the campaign staff was rushing them back to the plane for the next one. She gave up after a while and tried to soak in the day. Her work would begin once the polls started closing. No one was predicting a blowout, but Charlotte had a four-point lead over her opponent. Dale flipped through the exit poll data her station e-mailed midday and thought back to the recount that had delayed any outcome for more than a month. She'd learned her lesson then, having to buy clothes at the Gap and toiletries and make up at CVS because she'd traveled with her cell phone and purse and nothing else. This time, she was packed for two more weeks on the road, just in case.

CHAPTER FIFTY-ONE

Charlotte

"What is taking so long?" Tara moaned, pacing back and forth across the Roosevelt Room, where the political affairs staff had set up computers to monitor the election returns.

"I'm sure Fran is checking all the numbers one last time and making sure none of the states from the last round of calls is close enough to demand a recount, right, Melanie?" Charlotte said.

"I guess so, but the networks called the election twenty minutes ago, so I'm not sure what Fran is seeing that no one else is," Melanie said, scanning the returns from Ohio while Ralph pored over the returns from Florida and Nevada.

Michael had called half an hour earlier to say that Fran was calling within the hour to concede. Melanie's phone finally rang.

"Hello," she said, with a hundred pairs of eyes on her. "Yes, the president is right here. Thank you. Yes, you, too." She handed Charlotte the phone and mouthed "Fran."

"Fran?" Charlotte said. "Thanks so much for calling. Yes, you are kind to say that. It was a very spirited debate, indeed. Yes, of course. Tara and I look forward to working with you as well. God bless you and your family."

She hung up, and the room erupted in cheers. Charlotte pulled the twins toward her. Tara and her husband hopped up and down in a celebratory embrace.

"We did it," Charlotte said to Melanie. "I could not have done it without you."

Melanie wiped tears from her eyes and hugged Charlotte and then the twins and Brooke and Mark.

"You did it, baby cakes," Mark said to Charlotte. "Four more years in this place." He popped open a bottle of champagne.

Penelope handed Charlotte her cell phone. "It's Dad," she said.

"Peter, Peter, hi," Charlotte said, plugging her other ear so she could hear over the noise in the room. "Yes, it's official. Fran just called. Thank you, Peter. You, too. Give my best to Dale."

She handed the phone back to Penelope to take a call from the British prime minister on the secretary of state's cell phone.

The congratulatory calls continued for thirty minutes.

"Madam President, it's time for the speech to our supporters," Ralph said. "Tara, why don't you ad-lib an intro for the president and then, Madam President, you should thank supporters and praise Fran and talk a little bit about the next four years."

"Actually, Melanie wrote something already," Charlotte said, looking around the room for Melanie. "Where did Melanie go?" Charlotte asked Annie.

Annie's eyes were red, and Charlotte knew the answer.

"She said she had to meet someone. She said to tell you she'll be watching," Annie said.

Charlotte nodded knowingly.

"Penelope, Harry, Brooke, Mark, Tara, I want all of you standing with me," Charlotte said. "Let's go."

She clutched the speech Melanie had drafted earlier in the day as she walked out to the South Lawn to make her first remarks as the newly reelected president.

CHAPTER FIFTY-TWO

Melanie

She was having a hard time seeing the road through her tears, but she made her way to Reagan National and parked in the hourly lot. She had about eight hours before she was supposed to meet Brian, but she didn't want to screw things up this time.

She turned up the radio when she heard the announcer introduce Charlotte. "And now, live from the South Lawn of the White House, we bring you President Charlotte Kramer and Vice President-elect Tara Meyers."

Melanie sat in the car and listened to the speech she'd written for Charlotte. She'd gone to her office that morning to write her resignation letter, but there were no words to capture what she felt about leaving her position as Charlotte's chief of staff. It had been so much more than a job. But now, it was time for Melanie to get a life. She patted her Dior bag to make sure her passport was inside. She'd grabbed it days earlier and zipped it into her purse's side pocket. She'd picked up a bathing suit at the hotel gift shop in Sarasota the weekend before the election, and she figured she could buy everything else there, wherever there was.

She pulled out her personal cell phone and wondered if anyone was looking for her. Most people called or e-mailed her on her White House numbers—the numbers she'd had for years now. She'd left all of her official equipment with Annie.

Melanie thought about taking a short nap in the car, but she was afraid she'd oversleep, so she got out of the car and headed inside to wait for Brian.

She must have fallen asleep at the gate area, because at around seven A.M., he was standing above her. "I've been calling you for hours," he said.

"I'm sorry. I turned in my phones and BlackBerrys." She rubbed her eyes.

"I thought you'd changed your mind," he said.

"No. I've been here."

"Since last night?" he asked, taking in her suit and smudged makeup.

"Yeah," she said, feeling embarrassed about not going home to freshen up.

Brian laughed.

"I need to go brush my teeth," she said, covering her mouth.

"Melanie, you are going to pay for all sorts of things on this trip. Starting with your elaborate ploy to get me up to your room and ending with hiding here all night while I searched all over northwest Washington, D.C., for you," Brian warned.

"I hope you don't harbor any hidden desire to get me to spill the beans on Charlotte's transition plans," Melanie said.

"Are you kidding? You are the worst source I have ever had anywhere, at any point in my entire career."

Melanie laughed. "Then you won't mind that I'm unemployed," she said.

Brian looked stunned. "You quit?" he asked.

"Yes. I quit," Melanie said. "Do you think I'm crazy?"

"Not at all. If this is what you want, I'm proud of you," he said, taking her hand and leading her toward the line of passengers waiting to board the flight.

"This is what I want," she said, more to herself than to Brian, but she saw him smile.

CHAPTER FIFTY-THREE

Dale

Dale leaned her head against the window and stared at the San Francisco skyline as it became visible through the fog. She'd left Peter a message telling him when she'd be back, but she hadn't left the flight number or the airline because she didn't want him to think that she expected to be picked up.

The flight attendant handed Dale her coat as the plane touched down, and Dale watched everyone around her turn on their phones and BlackBerrys. She left hers off. She pulled her garment bag out of the overhead compartment and walked off the plane. She saw Peter before he saw her. Her body took over, as it always did when he was in proximity, and she rushed toward him. He took her in his arms, and they embraced.

"What are you doing here?" she asked.

"Did you really think I wouldn't come?" he asked.

"I didn't know, you know, where we were with everything, so I figured I'd meet you at the house, but I'm glad you're here," she said, leaning into his familiar body and resting her head against his chest. She inhaled his good smell and closed her eyes.

"I thought we'd go up to Napa. I made a dinner reservation at French Laundry, but we can go somewhere else if you want to do something more low-key."

"That sounds perfect," she said.

"Do you have luggage downstairs?" he asked.

"No, I left some of my bags in D.C."

"Oh, OK," he said.

They walked to Peter's Range Rover holding hands and climbed in. Both were working hard at directing the conversation away from the topic that hung between them: what Dale would do next and where it left their relationship. He put a hand on her knee, and she placed her hand on top of his while they sped to the resort in Napa where they'd once hidden out for a long weekend before their relationship was public.

They checked into a private house at Auberge du Soleil. Dale didn't have to work hard to remember everything she loved about Peter. They gravitated toward each other like magnets as soon as the doting hotel staff finished pouring each of them a flight of wine and unpacking their bags. She pulled him closer and pressed her body against his with an urgency that took them both by surprise. They couldn't get enough of each other. When Peter looked at the clock in the room, he laughed.

"I hope you weren't looking forward to dinner at French Laundry. We missed our reservation by an hour and a half," he said.

"I wasn't that hungry," she said.

"We can drive to Mustards and eat at the bar," he said.

"Or order in," she said.

"Or order in," he repeated, smiling at her.

They didn't leave their room for the next two days. They slept, ate, made love, and sat out on the deck staring at the lush vineyards below. They kept the television off, but they were both keenly aware of what was happening outside their cocoon in Napa Valley.

On Sunday afternoon, they dressed for a walk around the property. Dale was sitting on the bed trying to script the whole thing out in her head.

"What's wrong?" Peter asked.

"Tara Meyers called me before I left Washington," she told him.

"Oh, yeah? I didn't know you knew her," he said.

"I got to know her a little bit on the road."

He stared straight ahead, as though he knew what was coming. Maybe he did. Dale would wonder after.

"She asked me if I'd think about coming to work for her," she said.

"Oh, yeah? Doing what?" he asked.

"As her communications director," she said.

Peter was silent.

Dale knew he wouldn't speak first, so she broke the news to him. "I accepted the job."

Charlotte

Hi, Mel, it's Charlotte. I don't know how often you're checking this, but please give me a call when you get a chance. I have a, uh, situation that I could use your help with. I'm sorry to bother you on your extended vacation, but it's not something Ralph can handle."

Charlotte put the phone down and walked into Sam's workspace outside the Oval Office.

"Did you leave another message?" Sam asked.

"Yes. Did we try her at her sister's?" Charlotte asked.

"Yes, ma'am," Sam said.

"And we sent an e-mail to her personal account?" Charlotte asked.

"Yes, ma'am," Sam said.

"Should we try her mom?"

"If you'd like me to call her again, I will, Madam President, but we just spoke to her a couple of hours ago, and she hadn't heard from Melanie in three days," Sam said.

"She'll call here before she calls her mother," Charlotte said, striding back into the Oval. She was wearing a black suit with black high heels. Her messy ponytail was the only clue that she wasn't planning on being seen by the public. It was her last day in the office before her inaugural address, and Melanie hadn't called her back about the speech. She hadn't delivered a speech to so much as a Rotary Club that hadn't been written by Melanie, rewritten by Melanie, edited by Melanie, or approved by Melanie in four years. "How can she abandon me before the most important speech of my life?" Charlotte said to Sam for the fifth time that morning.

"We'll track her down, Madam President," Sam said.

"I don't know. Maybe she got hurt. Keep Googling her to see if any police reports come up. I'm serious," Charlotte said.

Sam smiled. "Yes, ma'am," she said. "Can I send Ralph down? He's been waiting to see you."

"What are my other options?" Charlotte asked.

"Tara would like to speak to you about her inaugural activities," Sam said.

"Send Ralph down," Charlotte said.

Sam turned to call Ralph's assistant and saw Melanie's reflection in the window behind her desk. She hung up before Ralph's assistant picked up. "Where have you been? She's been trying to reach you for a week," Sam said.

"I've been on vacation, Sam. I told her I'd be back for the big speech," Melanie said, smiling.

"Sam, can you bring me some coffee? With cream!" the president yelled from her desk in the Oval.

"Go in," Sam said. "She is going to die."

Melanie pushed open the door and stood in the doorway until Charlotte looked up.

Charlotte's face melted into a huge grin when she saw Melanie standing in the Oval Office in flip-flops, white linen pants, and a turquoise cashmere cardigan. "You bitch," Charlotte said. "You look amazing. What have you been doing? Don't tell me. Not here, at least. I want to hear all about it, but I need your help on the speech. It's a mess."

"I told you I'd be here in time to help you," Melanie said.

"You sure cut it close," Charlotte said, looking at her wrist. She didn't wear a watch, so Melanie knew it was for effect.

"I'm sorry if I made you nervous. I didn't mean to," she said, walking over to the couch and sitting down.

"I saw that they named Brian the full-time White House correspondent," Charlotte said.

"Yes. I'm really excited for him," Melanie said.

"What does this mean for you?" Charlotte said.

"We're going to make a go at a real relationship. I mean, as real as it can be when you're dating someone who covers the White House."

"I think that's great. I'm happy for you, really," Charlotte said, her face barely masking her disappointment that Melanie hadn't missed the White House as much as it—and she—had missed Melanie. She wasn't really all that happy for her at all. Why did Melanie have to launch her search for balance now?

"I am really happy, and I appreciate that you didn't try to lure me back with some offer I wouldn't be able to turn down," Melanie said.

"You mean like Supreme Court justice?" Charlotte said.

"Exactly."

Charlotte buzzed Sam and asked her to bring in a copy of the inaugural address for Melanie's review.

"Maybe you can huddle with the speechwriters and polish this up a bit," Charlotte suggested.

"Sure. Has Ralph been involved with the speech?" Melanie asked.

"What do you think?"

Melanie laughed. "Right. I forgot. The miscast message man. I bet he's driving the speechwriters crazy." She flipped through the pages Sam had handed her. "Draft number sixty-seven?" she asked.

"We had a hard time getting started," Charlotte said. "I'm curious to know what you think of it."

"I'll find a place to work, and I won't leave until it's a speech you are proud of, Madam President. I brought my toothbrush," Melanie said.

"Thanks, Melanie. You can work up in the residence if you want," Charlotte offered.

"Actually, I'd rather be close to the speechwriters so we can talk it through."

"I understand," Charlotte said.

Melanie stood to leave. "I'll buzz Sam when we have another draft, and then we'll go to the Family Theater for a run with the prompters."

"Sounds great. Melanie, I need to ask you something."

"Sure," Melanie said.

"I know that you said there was nothing that would tempt you, but I have one spot I've had a very, very difficult time filling. I've looked at a few other people, and no one strikes me as having the spine to handle this post with all of its recent controversy and drama."

Melanie sucked in her breath.

"I want you to serve as my secretary of defense," Charlotte said.

Melanie was shocked. She had thought Charlotte would ask her to come back to the White House as a senior advisor or maybe head over to DOD as an undersecretary, but she'd never considered that Charlotte would ask her to serve as the secretary of defense.

"I don't have to tell you how important it is to have competent leadership at DOD right now, because you know better than I do how that place works, which is why I'm asking you to say yes," Charlotte said.

Melanie was afraid of what would come out if she opened her mouth, so she held her hand over her lips and tried to process the offer.

"Take a walk, Mel. Talk to Brian. Have some lunch. And then come back down here before speech prep and say yes," Charlotte said, turning to walk back to her desk. "Sam, tell Ralph he can come down now, and please make sure Melanie has a place to work."

Melanie walked out of the Oval Office and into the hallway, where she was instantly surrounded by West Wing staffers and old friends.

"We miss you," one of the policy advisors said.

"Ralph doesn't even get in until seven A.M.," said one of the lawyers.

"You look incredible, Mel. Post–White House life agrees with you," said the press secretary.

Melanie lingered for a few more minutes, then wandered over to the East Wing. She smiled at the Secret Service agent posted in the hallway and stepped into the Map Room for privacy. She dialed Brian's cell, and he picked up on the first ring.

"How's the speech?" he asked.

"It's fine. She's high-strung today, so I've been doing some hand holding, but the speech was in pretty good shape."

"That's good. So, you'll make it home tonight?"

"She asked me to be the Sec Def," Melanie said.

"Jesus. She really doesn't want you to leave!" Brian exclaimed.

"What do you think?" Melanie asked.

"What do *you* think?" Brian said.

"I can't believe it," she said.

"Why not?"

"I don't have to tell you how far out on a limb she'd be going to put me there."

"About as far as you've been hanging on that limb for the last four years for her," Brian said.

"What should I do?"

"You know what to do," he told her.

"Yeah, I do," she said. "But this is going to be complicated."

"I love complicated."

"Complicated loves you," Melanie said.

"See you tonight," he said.

Melanie hung up and put the phone into her pocket. She decided to make Charlotte sweat it out until dinner, so she walked over to the Old Executive Office Building, where the speechwriters were holed up. The room smelled like socks, chicken fingers, and air freshener. The head speechwriter pulled up a chair in front of the computer and handed Melanie the keyboard.

"We need some fresh eyes," one of the writers said.

"You want something from the Mess?" the head speechwriter asked.

"Never again," she said. "I think I've eaten my last meal in captivity."

Melanie took the keyboard and started tinkering. She struck a chunk of the middle of the address, where it got bogged down in a lengthy section about America's role in the world. She shared her idea for the end of the speech with the speechwriting team, and they talked through how to make it work.

They worked this way for about an hour and a half. When everyone was pleased with the revisions, Melanie called Sam to tell her they were bringing Charlotte a new draft to read before the prompter session.

"Mel, she wants to see you alone," Sam said.

"After speech prep," Melanie said.

"She won't like that," Sam said.

"I know," Melanie said.

They went through the inaugural address three times; Charlotte had most of the speech committed to memory.

Even Ralph admitted that the new material was better. "Thanks for saving the day, as usual," he said.

Melanie looked at his face for hints of sarcasm, but all she saw in his eyes was terror. "I didn't save the day, Ralph. The speech was really good. I hardly changed it. Charlotte knows that you guys did a great job without me. She just likes for all of us to feel needed," Melanie said.

"In your case, it's true. I don't know how you did this job for four years. I'm ready to kill myself," he admitted.

"You're going to do a great job," she said.

"What are you two talking about?" Charlotte asked.

"Sending you and Tara back out on another 'Conversation with America' tour," Melanie said, smiling mischievously.

"I'll have you killed before I'll do that again. Melanie, do you have a few minutes, or are you late for personal training or a hair appointment or something?" Charlotte asked testily.

"Someone is a little nervous about her big speech tomorrow," Melanie teased.

"Walk with me, Melanie," Charlotte said as she headed down the long red-carpeted hallway between the East Wing and the West Wing. She was walking faster than normal, and Melanie was walking slower than normal. Finally, Charlotte stopped and glared at Melanie. "I don't know what else to do. I offered you something that I thought would mean something to you, and you've been playing it cool all day long," Charlotte said.

"I'm sorry," Melanie said. "I would be honored to serve as your secretary of defense."

Relief washed over Charlotte's face, and she smiled at Melanie. "Thank God," she said.

Melanie smiled back at her. "Thank you for the opportunity," she said.

"Things are going to be different," Charlotte told her.

"I know," Melanie said.

The dogs bounded down the stairs and jumped up on Charlotte's black suit, leaving paw prints all over her. "Want to come outside with us?" she asked.

"Sure," Melanie said.

Charlotte slipped into a coat and handed a parka to Melanie. They walked out to the South Lawn.

"Why is it always so damn cold for inaugurals?" Charlotte asked.

Melanie rubbed her arms to keep warm. "Tradition," she said.

"I thought you might want to read this," Charlotte said, handing her a worn piece of stationery that Melanie recognized immediately as Roger's.

She took the letter from Charlotte and felt her throat tighten. She held it in both her hands.

"Hang on to it, and read it when you feel like it," Charlotte said.

Melanie smiled and nodded. She slid the letter into her purse and watched the dogs play in the snow.

"Do you and Brian have plans tonight?" Charlotte asked.

"No, but you have your folks and the twins in town, don't you?"

"Yes, but I thought we'd celebrate your new position. Roberta made your favorite chocolate cake," Charlotte said.

"I never say no to chocolate cake," Melanie said.

"Is that a yes?" Charlotte asked.

"Yes," Melanie said, laughing at Charlotte's persistence.

"Great," Charlotte said.

Melanie started back toward the Oval Office to gather her things. She stopped in the lanai and watched Charlotte on the South Lawn with the dogs for a minute. She saw Charlotte pat the coat pocket where the letter from Roger had been. Melanie put her hand in her purse to make sure the letter was where she'd put it. As Melanie watched Charlotte toss the ball to the dogs, she tried to see Charlotte as the most powerful head of state in the world. She watched the elegant woman in the beige belted winter coat wrestle with her three dogs and tried to imagine Charlotte the way others saw her.

Melanie knocked on the glass, and Charlotte's head spun around.

She motioned for Melanie to come back outside. Melanie shook her head, and Charlotte made her way toward the lanai with the dogs trailing close behind.

"You're still here," she said.

"How did you know I'd say yes?" Melanie demanded.

"What do you mean?" Charlotte asked.

"You made a chocolate cake. How did you know I'd say yes?" Melanie said.

Charlotte was scratching the dogs' backs. "You think you were the one handling me all these years, but I picked up a few things from you about the art of manipulation," Charlotte said, smiling slyly.

"I never manipulated you," Melanie protested.

"I don't mean it in a bad way—I needed to be manipulated most days, or I would have stayed in bed until noon," Charlotte said.

For once, Melanie didn't know what to say.

"Besides, I knew you wouldn't want to miss the show," Charlotte said.

"What show?" Melanie said.

"The Tara show," Charlotte said, fighting the urge to smile.

Melanie laughed. "She's going to be fine. I was too hard on her."

"Yes, you were."

"Sorry," Melanie said.

"No, no. You were right. She's a pain in the ass, but we wouldn't have won without her."

Melanie sighed. "I know. So, what now?"

"Well, tonight we celebrate your new job, and tomorrow we get up and start all over again," Charlotte said.

Acknowledgments

There were four miracles that made this book possible. The first was my husband's blind faith in my ability to write a novel. He is the reason I sat down at the computer and started typing. The second miracle was getting to know Wendy Button when I did. She is one of the most gifted writers I've ever known, and her approval and encouragement inspired me to keep going.

The third miracle was meeting Sloan Harris, the kind of agent people dream of having in their corner. His guidance, direction, and belief in this effort changed *everything*. The fourth and final miracle was the opportunity to work with Emily Bestler. I still get chills when I see all the amazing writers she edits. I'm grateful for her wisdom and kindness.

Thanks to my mom and sister who read pages as I wrote them and made them better, and to Aimee Violette and her mom who did the same. Thank you to the friends and family who cheered me on and lifted me up: Joe and Natalie Comartin, who inspired the story of friendship in these pages, Mark and Annie McKinnon, Matt and Liz Clark, Steve and Angela Schmidt, Ken Mehlman, Matt and Mercy Schlapp, Geoff and Ann Morrell, Dana Bash and John King, Michael Glantz, Barbara Fedida, Terry and Marci Nelson, and Pat and Milt Wallace. Thanks to Katie Couric who was one of the first people to encourage me to make lemonade out of lemons. Thank you to Tina Brown for offering me my first job as a writer, and to my colleagues at

The Daily Beast, Edward Felsenthal, Tom Watson, Bryan Curtis, and Andrew Kirk, for making sure I never fell down on the job. Thank you to Henley MacIntyre Old for keeping me honest, on time, and organized (a monumental undertaking).

Thank you to all the people who allowed me to witness history in the making. It was an unforgettable experience.

To Molly Rosenbaum, Michelle Humphrey, Kristyn Keene, and John DeLaney at ICM, thank you for your patience and support. To Paul Olsewski, Lisa Sciambra, and Mellony Torres at Atria, thank you for letting me be part of your team. To Jeanne Lee, Kate Cetrulo, and Rachel Bostic at Atria, thank you for sharing your talents with me. To Judith Curr and Carolyn Reidy, thank you for taking a chance on me.

Finally, thanks to Courtney, Ashley, Zack, and my parents, Ronnie and Clive Devenish, for always being there.

About the Author

Nicolle Wallace is a political commentator who appears regularly on news programs such as ABC's *Good Morning America, The Sean Hannity Show* on Fox News, and *Morning Joe* on MSNBC. She is also a contributor to *The Daily Beast.*

Wallace, who served as communications chief for George W. Bush's White House and reelection campaign, was credited with "injecting a tremendous amount of realism" into White House deliberations. According to the *Washington Post,* she served as "a voice for more openness with reporters" (*Washington Post,* June 28, 2006). The *New York Times* story announcing her presidential appointment carried the headline: *"New Aide Aims to Defrost the Press Room"* (January 10, 2005). Wallace was described by former colleagues as "very persuasive in the halls of the West Wing."

Wallace also served as senior advisor for the McCain-Palin campaign in 2008. She appeared frequently on network and cable news programs as the campaign's top spokesman and defender.

Wallace is a California native and graduate of the University of California, Berkeley and Northwestern University's Medill School of Journalism. She lives in New York City and Connecticut with her husband, Mark, a former ambassador to the United Nations, and their vizsla, Lilly. This is her first novel.

EIGHTEEN ACRES

Nicolle Wallace

A Readers Club Guide

INTRODUCTION

Eighteen Acres follows three powerful women in Washington, D.C.: Charlotte Kramer, the first female president of the United States; Melanie Kingston, the White House chief of staff; and Dale Smith, a White House correspondent for one of the top national networks. All three women struggle to balance their high-powered careers with their personal lives and relationships, to varying degrees of success. Charlotte and her staff must combat dangerous threats from abroad as well as from her very own cabinet, and even her husband. Melanie questions whether completely devoting her life to her job is really what she wants. And when Dale becomes the biggest news story of the campaign, she's suddenly on the other side of the news media.

QUESTIONS AND TOPICS FOR DISCUSSION

1. With all the risks Dale and Peter take for their relationship, even when they're trying to keep their affair a secret, it is still fairly obvious to those close to them what is going on. Do they almost want to get caught? Why doesn't Charlotte confront Peter until she does? If not for Dale's accident, do you think their relationship would have ever surfaced publicly? If so, by whom?

2. Why is Charlotte committed to fighting what everyone believes is a losing battle for her campaign? Does she make the right choice to continue? What do you think ultimately got her the win? Could they have won without Tara?

3. It's mentioned in passing that Charlotte is a Democrat, but although the story is set against a political backdrop, politics are hardly ever discussed. How did this impact the novel? Does it matter what political party the characters belong to?

4. Discuss Roger's role in the story. Did he do the right thing by switching the helicopters? What motivated his actions? Did Charlotte do the right thing, as his employer? As his friend?

5. Charlotte seems to have less emotion than the other characters. She is very stoic and always makes selfless, rational decisions. Discuss her

resigned acceptance of her husband's affair. Do you think this trait was what made her a good president?

6. Brooke and Mark seem to have the only happy, balanced marriage in the book. Why is this? Do you think it's possible for couples in the spotlight to maintain a healthy relationship?

7. Why do you think Peter is consistently drawn to powerful, career-driven women? Will his relationship with Dale deteriorate as her career strengthens, as it did with Charlotte, or do you think it will be different this time?

8. Compare and contrast the romantic relationships in the book and main character's views on love. Think about Charlotte and Peter, Dale and Peter, Melanie and Brian. Who is happiest? How does success impact their relationships?

9. Discuss how each character balances their priorities. What is most important to each woman? How do their personal and professional lives compete? Talk about the sacrifices they make for their careers and their relationships. Would you make the same choices?

10. Whose perspective did you enjoy reading from most? Which woman did you relate to? Who did you sympathize with?

11. Why does Melanie take the job as Charlotte's secretary of defense? She seemed ready to resign her post and excited to lead a less high-powered life—is she simply obligated to obey the wishes of her president and friend? Do you think she will be happy and fulfilled with this change in position, or do you think work will continue to suck the life out of her?

12. What do you think Roger's last note says?

13. The novel ends on an almost bittersweet note, with Charlotte saying "Well, tonight we celebrate your new job, and tomorrow we get up and start all over again." (p. 320) Were you happy with how the story ended for each character? Would you have wanted anything to turn out differently? What do you imagine happens to Charlotte, Melanie, and Dale next?

ENHANCE YOUR BOOK CLUB

1. If you live nearby, take a trip to Washington D.C. and tour the area where Charlotte, Melanie, and Dale live and work. Eat at the Caucus

Room, a "D.C. establishment restaurant" Melanie and Michael frequent, or Bistro Lepic, where Melanie and Brian have their first date. Take a tour of the White House, and visit Melanie's favorite D.C. landmark, the Jefferson Memorial. Or take a virtual tour of the White House online—visit http://www.whitehouse.gov/about/white-house-101.

2. Discuss Charlotte's leadership capabilities as the first female president of the United States. Do you see the U.S. having a female president in the near future? What obstacles do you think women in politics still have to overcome? Do you think the gender of the president matters, or just their ideas?

A CONVERSATION WITH NICOLE WALLACE

You're the former communications director for the White House and currently a political media strategist. How much of *Eighteen Acres* is based on your real life and the lives of those around you in Washington? Which of your three protagonists are you most like?

The story is about three women who are entirely fictional, but they work in a place I know very well. I can relate quite well to the extent that their jobs force them to make difficult trade-offs between their personal lives and their professional responsibilities, as can most women I knew in politics. Melanie's life as a "staffer" is the most similar to my experience in the White House, but she stayed much longer than I did and accomplished more—rising to the post of White House chief of staff.

What inspired you to write a novel, and this one in particular? Have you always been a writer at heart?

I first thought about writing a novel about the White House after I'd worked there long enough to realize that people had no idea what life is really like for those who live and work there. I never met anyone who wasn't fascinated by the place, regardless of their personal political views. Writing about the first woman president was an idea that came to me after the 2008 campaign. Everywhere I went, people wanted to talk about Hillary Clinton and Sarah Palin. It struck me that while their candidacies were unsuccessful, they had touched off a conversation about women in politics that was long overdue.

In a high powered job such as yours, or the women in *Eighteen Acres*, it seems difficult to maintain a balance with a personal life. How do you manage to do so?

It's one of the most difficult things about life in the White House for everyone who works there—men and women. I was very fortunate in that my husband also worked in high-level positions in the Bush administration and on the Bush and McCain campaigns, so we shared most of our professional experiences.

You largely leave politics out of the story, though it's set against an intense political backdrop. Why did you decide to write a relatively bipartisan story?

I wanted to write a story about the distance that Charlotte, Melanie, and Dale traveled personally and professionally, and I didn't want the reader to care about which political party they belonged to. It makes me happy when people say to me "I couldn't figure out for the longest time if Charlotte was a Democrat or a Republican."

The White House in *Eighteen Acres* is run by women. Do you think there will be a female U.S. president in the near future? Why do you think there hasn't been one yet?

I believe that the first female president is alive today. Women are coming into their own politically all over the country, in senate races and gubernatorial races. The sorts of intractable problems we face as a country are well suited for the intuitive diplomacy and learned patience of many women leaders.

Charlotte ultimately wins the election because she chooses a running mate from the opposing party. Is that a strategy you would advocate for politicians? Do you think such an arrangement would work?

People hold conventional politics in such low regard that it would seem to me that anything "outside the box" would be worth a try.

Tara seems to have a lot in common with Sarah Palin—they're both fiery stump speakers with an everyman appeal who aren't afraid to be blunt. Was this intentional?

I spent enough time in Washington to understand that Washington politicians have a limited appeal to voters. For the campaign section of the story, it was important that the story reflect the public's hunger for candidates who are plainspoken, direct, and relatable. Tara and Sarah Palin share those traits, but they are two very different women with different stories.

You were a spokesperson for John McCain's 2008 campaign and served as a campaign advisor to Sarah Palin. What role do you see yourself playing in the next election?

I traveled the country with two candidates for president—George W. Bush in 2003 and 2004 and John McCain in 2008. I treasure both experiences and the opportunity I had to visit every corner of this country and meet people from nearly every state, but it's a grueling job best left to people who are as eager now as I was then.

What writers and novels have had an impact on you? What are you reading now?

Run and *The Patron Saint of Liars* by Ann Patchett, *The Lovely Bones* by Alice Sebold, and *The Help* by Kathryn Stockett have stayed with me like few other novels I've read in recent years. *The Devil Wears Prada* by Lauren Weisberger inspired me to tell a story that was as much about the place, and its limitations and allure, as it was about the characters. *Prep* by Curtis Sittenfeld was the book I gave to everyone I knew for a couple years because I loved it so much. *The Great Gatsby* by F. Scott Fitzgerald and *The Catcher in the Rye* by J.D. Salinger were the first books that changed how I felt about the world. Right now, I'm reading *The Postmistress* by Sarah Blake, *Persuasion* by Jane Austen, and I have been planning to start the Stieg Larsson trilogy for months, but my deadlines keep getting in the way.

Do you see yourself writing another book? You have a very interesting life yourself, would you ever write nonfiction?

I'm working on the sequel to *Eighteen Acres* now. In it, Tara has her own voice, and we get to take the ride from the New York attorney general's office to the vice presidency with her. Dale, Charlotte, and Melanie also return. We get to know them better by spending more time with them. I'm enjoying their stories so much, I can't imagine doing anything else.